OFF
TOM
NEVERS

David Story Allen

WEST ESSEX PRESS - INTERLOCHEN, MICHIGAN

For information contact:
West Essex Press
9900 Diamond Park Rd.
Interlochen, Michigan 49643

Createspace Edition ISBN – 13:   978-154658184-0
Createspace Edition ISBN – 10:   154658184-7

First Edition: May 2017

10 9 8 7 6 5 4 3 2 1

For Harutaro
Nobody enjoyed Tom Nevers more.

It is all one to me if a man comes from Sing Sing Prison or Harvard. We hire a man, not his history.

- Malcom Forbes

August 31

"IF THE ONLY TOOL you have is a hammer, everything looks like a nail." Christ. Is there a book that all headmasters get somewhere that offers such uninspiring crumbs from the end of some tea bag? I sat there trying to make no gesture that would convey weariness at this sad excuse for sage advice. Barclay cupped a fist in his other palm and gazed across the picnic tables cluttered with plates and Soho cups. "I know...that each and every one of you has a lot more than just a hammer in your tool box." No faculty dinner in the failing days of summer would be complete without some Ed School pabulum. "Our students aren't nails. We need to remind ourselves of that every day." Perhaps, but one thing I do not need is refrigerator magnet wisdom courtesy of Columbia Teachers College.

A new year always brings a theme or direction from the top which is declared a tonic for all that might come a school's way in the nine months ahead, and is meant to be the mantra to guide decisions in and out of the classroom. Panacea by catchphrase. It's not that I know better than Barclay Crowninshield Sears, but I'm actually *in* a classroom and a dorm every day and spend afternoons coaching. Barclay's office is bigger than my classroom, and there he dictates letters to trustees, conducts final interviews, and ogles the model of the proposed new art building. As Head of School, there is more to his job than these tasks, but I've been teaching here for four years and not once has he set foot in my room to see what parents are dropping nearly $50,000 annually for. If I were taking folks for the price of a decent Lexus every twelve months, I'd want to be able to talk first-hand about what they're getting before asking them to buy bricks on the Alumni Walk. Half the teachers at most boarding schools think they could run the place better than the person who actually does. I'm not as arrogant as all that, and actually must credit him with inspiring me towards one task this year. In a mid-summer message to faculty introducing the new hires for this fall, he proposed that we all chronicle this academic year with a journal, creating a source for reflection. I haven't kept a diary for years, so the notion has appeal, provided I can stay with it. In the mailroom the day before the pre-opening dinner, I mentioned to Barclay that I'd taken up his idea.

"Peter that's great." He pumped my shoulder. "I think you'll find it a useful exercise. And who knows? If folks hear that Mr. Burnham is writing everything down that happens this year, might keep them on their toes." He gave one of those just-kidding winks that inside guys use as a parting gesture, tightening his school tie at me as he left. Only pre-1960 alumni don those at reunions anymore, and they haven't been worn to class here since the '70s. These days, strict dress codes are pretty much only seen at schools in search of stature to make up for their mediocre academics. To seem egalitarian in the 1970s, some headmaster did away with Griswold's crested school tie; all those little polyester cubs died for nothing. Alumni showed their approval with angry letters in the quarterly and a twenty percent drop in annual fund giving. Eventually the ties returned, and said headmaster supposedly moved on to teach conflict resolution somewhere in Wisconsin.

With its Anglophile origins in the 1800s and dorms courtesy of third-rate robber barons, Griswold School mirrors lots of other New England academies. A few industrialists with deep pockets helped it weather some lean years that saw the ascension of other schools that kept taking kids pretty much only from Boston Brahmin and Philly Main Line families well into the 1970s. This secured their endowments and their caches, even when diversity was becoming all the rage, while Griswold lagged. Being just west of Boston and going co-ed like everyone else in that decade helped, or more accurately, was crucial. Just ask alumni from the Tisbury School in Connecticut, an all-boys citadel that dug in its heels against the rush to accept girls when it was the big trend; it is now an assisted living facility with a bocce court on the former soccer field.

"We have to ask ourselves," Barclay's voice seemed amplified under the tent, and brought me back to his words, "'Am I teaching them because I want to teach…or because I want them to *learn?*'"

"I'm in it for the money." Only Frank Remillard would dare mutter such a banal excuse for humor. Our hale Director of Athletics, Remy nurtures his timeless jock image by offsetting his grey buzz cut with a combination suntan – booze burn.

"Whatever the reason you're here Frank, glad you are." *That* took care of *that*. Barclay's strong suit is not humor, especially not accommodating it unexpectedly. The rest of his remarks were let's-have-a-great-year boilerplate. After polite applause, people drifted across campus under the failing dusk or lingered in small gaggles swapping summer stories. I started for my apartment to catch the Sox-Yankees' game when back towards the tent, a curse of disgust cut the darkening air.

"Really? Him? *Back?*" Schyler Van Wyck, in madras shorts and pink polo, was incredulous, leaning into the face of someone from the Admissions Office. "How *starved* for kids *are* we?"

Schy is a good English teacher, a very good squash player, and looks very, very, very good doing both. An Aryan Adonis, his name on girls' schedules is known to elicit 'I've got Mr. V!' He has *the right stuff*, as some would say: boarded somewhere in Connecticut, then either Williams or Amherst – one of those places with purple, and sailed for fun to put off adulthood a bit longer. Crewed two years within the America's Cup orbit, taught at Cornwall Country Day for a bit, then rolled into Griswold in sockless penny loafers two years ago. Got his cousin-poet laureate to speak on campus last year and spent the start of the summer summiting McKinley – "the *north* face," don't you know. The volume of his voice intrigued me, so I retraced my steps to find out what was up.

"Blumberg, that elongated hairball from last year?" he whirled to me with a look of disbelief. "He's back."

I twisted my face, not recalling the kid, and told him as much.

"You know him: that born-too-late deadhead caught stealing flash drives from the bookstore last spring?"

"Managed to avoid a sport all year?" it rang a bell with me.

"That's him; pale as the day is long as a result; looked like Gregg Allman after a month without bathing." I raised my eyebrows, wondering how he knew who Gregg Allman was. "My dad has lots of old vinyl. So Blumberg: skipped just too few classes to get bounced on that score."

"Yeah," I nodded, "rings a bell. Wasn't he kicked out for something else?"

"Apparently *not.*" Schy shook his head and spat as the Admissions rep took my arrival as a chance to slip away. "Just for the term, for whatever it was, apparently. And now the Cretan is in my dorm."

"Well, next year I'll have him." Griswold insists on dorm changes for returnees. "Cheer up."

"Yeah, right," he huffed. "No cheer with that...*Gee* – zus!"

"Hell, Schy, one kid isn't going to ruin your year...I thought you were steaming over some pay cut or the dining hall going entirely gluten free."

He glared at me, then spat on the grass again. "Trust me Peter: kid's a train wreck. My year already sucks. We're gonna regret this. Admissions is gonna regret it, but...*Christ*...wonderful news on top of dessert tonight." He peeled away with a wave of resignation, holding up a cautionary finger, hinting that his words were prescient.

September 2

THE MORNING FACULTY GATHERING splintered into department meetings followed by lunch, then we had computer training on the new grading system, and a third of the folks bailed before a reception in the Old Library, which now hosts trustee meetings and sports old footballs in glass cases from the days when the varsity played MIT's freshman team. Our nineteenth century Georgian brickwork mirrors a dozen other New England schools set around a green circle with a stream running behind the science building. "It looks like a college," is what people new to this world often say. The girls' dorms, Devine and Emory, are in better shape than the boys' halls, Wentworth and Chamberlain, and as boys seem to have a gene that requires them to bounce lacrosse balls off the nearest wall, this is unlikely to ever change. Dix Wentworth made a pile as a Texas oil wildcatter before the crash in '29, and was thrilled that Griswold took his son in and tried to make an eastern gentleman out of the Midland miscreant. He pledged money for a dorm to beat all dorms – or at least beat the ones at the schools that would not have his boy. Some dry holes meant that the Gothic revival he'd hoped would bear his name ended up being a two-story bomb shelter of which any East German *apparatchik* would be proud. Commonly and unofficially known as '*Net*-worth' as a result, the moniker was slightly too clever to have been produced by any of the current residents.

Across the lane from Wentworth is Emory, a girls' dorm staffed by, among others, Katherine McPhee, a new English teacher this year. I don't know who else applied for the slot, but it was probably never close. A few years out of Simmons College, after a stint at a school in Pennsylvania, she went to Panama for a bit with the Peace Corps, earning her a section of Spanish here as well. In addition to these academic laurels, her *whatever* bob cut and perky assuredness probably iced it for her before the interview was over. She's asked to be called Kat, and was fumbling for a key on a school lanyard outside her faculty apartment after the library reception broke up.

"Ready for the invasion?" I asked as we readied to move our cars to make room for parents who'd be rolling in the following day.

"I better be," she cocked her head and shrugged, "Guess they're coming whether I am or not."

"Are you top floor?"

"Bottom," she shook her head. "You?"

"Top. I got tired of living in the dark."

"Dark?" She swept some hair behind her ears while plucking leaves off the hood of her Civic.

"If you like privacy...or simply don't want everyone on campus knowing when you're having a beer or...What I mean is that kids can see what you're doing all the time, unless you live with the shades down."

"Oh...right. Hadn't thought of that."

"Actually, kids here aren't that fascinated with the personal lives of teachers."

"My boyfriend'll be glad to hear that."

The boyfriend card. Took less than three minutes. Was I flirting or just trying to be welcoming? Women pull it out like putting up a 'Next Window' sign in a bank when you're in line for a teller. Said boyfriend, it came out, is in a doctoral program at MIT after crewing on a sloop from Nassau to Newport in August, I'm told. What a guy. I headed back to my apartment and found a school envelope stuck in the door jam. Figuring it was the notice of my new network password or a small gift card to inspire good will at the start of the year, I opened a Red Stripe and sat down to read the enclosure. Called that wrong.

September 2

Dear Peter,

No doubt you are aware that admissions was especially successful in filling our beds to capacity this fall. Truth be told, some students to whom we offered admission but did not expect to accept it did, which requires us to make room for them; an embarrassment of riches. In order to accommodate these additional boarding students, it is necessary to carve out some dormitory space that has been otherwise dedicated, and part of this plan involves reconfiguring the end room in your apartment as student space. That so many students have chosen Griswold is a testament to the wonderful work that you do, and hopefully you can appreciate that this is a good problem to have. These late admits will not arrive until the weekend, which we hope is adequate time for you to re-align your belongings from the northern most room of your apartment. Storage space will be available if you require it, and your understanding and cooperation in light of this development is most appreciated.

Sincerely, Barclay

I had to read it twice to digest it – with the school year basically underway, they're grabbing part of my home by eminent domain because some kids didn't get in elsewhere and are now coming here. And they – Barclay, really – didn't even have the decency to tell me to my face, but instead has some toady stick a note in my door. What a sneaky, spineless load of crap to dump on someone after he's signed on for the year. Sure I'm the school's tenant, and live here at their whim year to year, so it's non-negotiable at this point. Not unlike telling someone on an ocean liner ten minutes out of port that his second-class room is now a berth in steerage; what can he do then?

I poured a tall Maker's Mark and stewed. This over-enrolling BS was not something that came up today; you *know* how many kids you're taking long before Labor Day. People, or Barclay, sat on this until too late in the summer for me to object. Real nice morale builder before the kids roll in. Doing a walk-through of the dorm this night before the kids arrive, I made a point of leaving every light in every room and common area on. With all this extra tuition money, they can suck on the higher electric bill.

September 3

THE ARRIVAL OF STUDENTS always fosters some nervous energy even in seasoned teachers, regardless of whether they admit it. The campus is manicured, classrooms have been painted, and the dorms look better than they will for the next eleven months. Parents have gone through the search process, and either chose the school, or because a child's name will not show up on a Nobel Prize short list, he or she is here by default. This morning the SUVs appeared, their hatchbacks opened, and the sounds of new and unsure voices could be heard in the halls of Wentworth. Dads, some in blazers, moms carrying shopping bags with items their sons will not use as often as they hope, and sisters or trophy wives drawing stares. You can always tell new students from returning ones. The dress code doesn't matter until the first day of classes and as the returnees know this, they arrive in their best this-old-thing summer garb: $70 pinpoints that have never been ironed and cargo shorts busting with cell phones, with an obligatory tip of the hat to A & F. Meandering from my apartment into the hallways of Wentworth, I passed an open door with only one name on it: Aaron Tang. Inside was a gaunt boy with a Ralph Lauren tie and hitched trousers bunched up with a belt. He was contemplating two duffle bags, a steamer trunk and shipping boxes with Korean characters on them. You could balance a pin on how much Korean I know, but the difference between its characters and Chinese is pretty clear.

"Are you Aaron?" He nodded. I introduced myself and explained that I lived down the hall. Nothing.

"Are you from Korea?" He nodded. *"An yong haseyo."* One quarter of my Korean. His face brightened.

"I student."

I doubt he weighed a hundred pounds wet, and with a pensive look of bewilderment in his eyes, seemed, to use Mick & Keith's words, two thousand light years from home. He contemplated the duffels at his feet like a tenant assessing a ransacked apartment. I got him started on putting some items in a dresser and suggested he knock on my door with any questions he might have, and left him to unpack. The ESL teacher should be able to help him, or else the Admissions rep who said that we *could* help him should be canned and his parents should get their fifty large back. Just because we like to think that we can educate every student who passes through our gates doesn't mean that we actually can.

Somewhat more fluid greetings were repeated up and down the two floors all day. Unlike returning students, some of the newbies wore blazers that they were forced to try on at Brooks or Macy's in August and which, owing to growth spurts, in many cases will cease to fit them sometime around MLK Day. Mothers stand in rooms with armfuls of clothing asking what drawer Tyler or Hunter would like his polos in while dad eyeballs the window shades and bed, wondering if he's getting his tuition's worth. I reminded everyone about the chapel gathering after dinner, and repaired to my incredible shrinking apartment to do laundry.

Opening Convocation was at 7:30, one of those perennials that holds no surprises but carries an air of anticipation all the same. Students and teachers flood the chapel, some still aglow with their summer tans, a few kids seeming six inches taller than they were in June. Girls toss their new bob cuts and wince, explaining, "I can't believe I had her cut it *so short*," while a few boys in madras and avocado look to be just back from their J. Crew shoot. Up in the dais, we were perched between the pulpits, administration on the left, faculty to the right. On the far right was Howard D. Bagwell, who has been teaching here longer than anyone, and has seen it all. "I've *forgotten* more Latin than Cicero *knew!*" he is fond of saying. "Bags" is famously stingy with 'A's in his classes, earning the moniker "Howard D+ Bagwell" among those who aren't as smart as they think they believe themselves to be. Good company if he likes you, a scold if he doesn't. Bags looks like one of those rumpled, cranky solicitors in a BBC series. Next to him was new Admissions fellow who'll be coaching hockey – or more accurately, a former Michigan forward who was good at face-offs and needed a full-time job after he agreed to help coach our varsity squad. A ruddy, go-for-it guy, he seems rather uncomfortable in a blazer and tie, but will look great in the catalog and will no doubt wow all the fifteen year-old girls he'll take on Admissions' tours.

Allison Manville sat between Kat McPhee and me, flattening imaginary wrinkles in her batik skirt. A no-nonsense math teacher whose facial expressions vacillate between deadpan and scowl, Allison seems to have been born cranky and been getting angrier ever since. During her first year here, she announced plans to adopt a baby from China with her life mate. Legally, the school had to give her time off once it was a done deal, but she wanted time off to 'go explore the baby market in Asia.' When Barclay said no, she lawyered up and went at the school with venom; anti-family, anti-gay, violating the spirit of the Family Leave Act and all.

"This is so *narrow-minded,*" she took to saying. "In Sweden and France, when you have a baby..." But since she hadn't been knocked up by Ingmar Bergman or Hollande, it seemed like she was pissing up a rope, and when an arbitrator told her as much – "I *knew* he was a bigot!" - nobody figured she'd be back this year. Word is she's got a Peace Corps application in the pipeline. I tried picturing her and her partner helping to irrigate the Kalahari with little Hop Sing on their backs. Good luck to them.

Barclay took to the lectern, and his sheer visibility drew down the noise in the chapel. Although you can hardly credit him with it, Barclay *looks* like a headmaster, now referred to as a Head of School: tall, salt and pepper CEO hair, laugh lines that suggest experience and wisdom, usually unflappable, and able to discuss Proust or the NFL draft over the same drink. Claire Sears is the perfect Head's Wife as well – a lean rosy-cheeked blonde who seems to know all the students' names, sends birthday cards to faculty members and is said to remind some trustees of a young Blythe Danner.

"Welcome...and welcome back," Barclay began. "This is the hundred and twenty ninth time that a Head of School has stood before the school community to convene a new year of learning and discovery. Only eight other individuals have had the honor of ushering in a new school year at Griswold as I do now. Through those doors," he made a sweeping gesture towards the gothic portal behind the pews," thousands of young men and women have preceded you." Then came the honor roll: the actor, the Secretary of State, the Pulitzer winner. Name-dropping is big at even the best schools; *look* who chose *us!* I didn't have to glance at Bagwell to know that he was engaged in Olympic-level eye-rolling at this point. Much of the address was unremarkable. Kennedy supposedly nicked his "Ask not..." line from a speech at Choate by St. Johns, the headmaster in his day, who is said to have lifted it from Oliver Wendell Holmes, Jr.; being original is such hard work. After mentioning a space shuttle pilot as well, Barclay offered a pretty seamless segue forward. "I am, thanks to the Science Department, advised that the next several nights will offer some wonderful opportunities to view the Winnesook Comet in the northeastern sky, especially with the help of our refurbished observatory, and for those of you wishing to take advantage of this unique window of astronomical wonder, some selfless members of the Science Department have offered to staff the building, so I believe that some extended lights and dorm closings tonight are in order for those who choose to partake..."

Approving applause quickly morphed into the menacing pounding of feet that filled the chapel almost to a slightly alarming level. Simultaneously, dorm faculty shared unhappy glances. With no homework yet, dorm life would not be terribly structured after this gathering, and to be sure, some students probably would head out to – and ideally back from – the observatory beyond the upper fields. On one level, it seemed a very worthwhile diversion. On another, it made dorm parents' job that much harder, and no e-mail had been sent out to this effect ahead of time. Barclay had come up with it on his own, and now appeared magnanimous to everyone in the chapel under the age of twenty. Tucked away in his 14,000 square foot manse, however, he didn't have to worry about taking room check later on. In addition to parsing up some people's living space to others, seems like he's pretty generous with other people's time as well. Making decisions about a realm in which he doesn't toil and from which he is quite removed – must be a first for an administrator.

Outside the chapel afterwards, I chatted up a few seniors as the students streamed into the September evening. With gaggles of kids headed to the observatory, it wouldn't be an early night. I surveyed the night sky but saw no comet; nothing but a ring around the moon. Heading back to my time-sensitive digs, I spotted a Building and Grounds truck with fresh dry wall parked by my entrance, ready to start work in the morning.

September 12

TO WAKE UP IN mid-September and realize that boarding school isn't for you is no doubt inconvenient, but less so than were it February. Two weeks into the year, and two students have bailed already – one due to homesickness, the other is said to have found us too 'old school,' a term often used by kids who are so tethered to their phones that they can't deal when told to put them down in class. Girls' varsity and JV soccer have been thrashed by the Davenport School, and it seems that the fire warning system in Devine is especially sensitive, resulting in early morning false alarms, probably sparked by shower steam. In spite of the inconvenience to the female residents, the sight of forty just-roused girls trying to stay warm in the dawn light has been a genuine source of entertainment to my boys in Wentworth.

An alumnus from the class of '62 who's been ambassador a few times over gave a school assembly talk this week. We don't turn out as many splendid *New York Times* obituaries-in-waiting as we used to, but the ones the Alumni Office can find are often invited back to campus for the '*I* once sat in *these very pews* myself' talk. We get fewer kids than we used to from traditional boarding school zip codes, and international students don't get financial aid; they come paid in full, so in the 1990s, the school went to the far east in search of heads for beds. Parents in Tokyo and Taipei got to say that Yuki or Yao attended a New England boarding school, and Griswold had a tennis team and math SAT scores like never before. One early evening last week in Chambers, a *de facto* teachers' room in the old music building where BYOB gatherings have been known to occur, the State of the School was the impromptu topic at hand.

"That Takashi kid, Christ," Remy was recalling a tennis prodigy from the previous spring. "Serve like a kamikaze and smoked Choate's #1 as a sophomore. Chose MIT over Penn. Techies haven't won a match since Christ was a corporal. Frigging waste." For some reason he was still chewing on the phenom's college choice.

"How can you call an MIT degree a waste?" Mary Carpenter, our ever-polite English Department chair chimed in, looking up from her essays to take the bait.

"An Asian with an MIT diploma...*He'll* stand out."

Chambers is an optimism-free zone. It is to laugh to call it a faculty lounge. Pier 1 closeouts and a *New York Times* daily does not a lounge make, especially since someone always shuts the coffee maker in the room off after lunch. The person whose fingers flick that switch and force the rest of us to survive post-lunch *sans* coffee deserves a bamboo manicure. Remy was holding court securely, lamenting that Asian parents haven't turned up in the Annual Fund ranks.

"All the money we get for the Lees and Kims, you'd think I could get a few scholarships to throw around Everett and Saugus so we could win a hockey game more than once a year," he went on. Everett and Saugus are two towns north of Boston where hockey is a religion. Just to show their spirit, about once each winter some dad there pummels a referee into a coma over an icing call.

"Is that what we want to be?" Mary cocked her head, "A jock factory? With students from…"

"Revere? Everett? What's wrong with that?" A math teaching fellow – Griswold-speak for a student teacher one year out of college we work to death - whose name I haven't learned yet looked up from his green tea to play Devil's Advocate and proud socialist. He actually looks like Trotsky might have at twenty-three, except for the man bun and a thumb ring, which unintentionally create an image of crunchy absurdity.

"No…what I…" Mary clasped her hands to her blouse, doing her best late-career Audrey Hepburn, professing that she was happy with a student body sprinkled with kids from working-class zip codes. "I certainly didn't mean---"

"Well if she didn't, I do." Bags grumbled from behind his *Times*. He's been at a New England school as either a student or teacher 'since 'Bush 43 was using fake IDs to get into bars,' he likes to say. His Charles Laughton face and frame betray more years than he's lived, which is partially explained by his love of Old Fashioneds and a refusal to coach anything since fencing died in the late '80s. "'Judas' *priest;* are we in such straits that we need to go mucking in one of those murky north shore gene pools where all the Mafioso pave over their front lawns in order to find kids who can skate?" He rolled up his Times and pointed it like a cautionary finger at the teaching fellow. "Think *they'll* be able to do your logarithms?" The TF started to raise his finger, perhaps to clarify that only his calculus kids did logarithms, but Bags' blood was up. "And don't start with me about whether I think only Cabots and Lowells can do logarithms. Fact of the matter is – and you ought to *know* it – Wenham and Duxbury, and Fay and Dexter turn out more kids who can at least *spell* logarithms than all those towns with Our Lady of the Tub on every front lawn."

Wenham and Duxbury are two of Boston's more upscale hamlets, while Fay and Dexter are obscenely expensive feeder schools for the 9-12 set, although Dexter added an upper school a while back. Running through Bags' thinly veiled rant on class was a thread of truth. Gone are the days when schools such as ours were brimming with names right out of the Mayflower Compact, yet the schools that still cater to such legacies do have the nicest squash courts and best college matriculation records. The number of *Griswold Quarterlies*, the alumni mag nicknamed *GQ* - *so* clever – that we send to Greenwich, Prides Crossing and Falls Church is less than when Bags started here, and that bothers him. We're a fair school, but there are others that, if a kid got in there, he'd or she would go there instead. Being asked now and again why I'm still here prompts the feeling thirty-year-old females must get when asked why they're not yet married.

"Oh," Bags fished into his satchel for an inter-office envelope and handed it to me. "What's-her-name in Admissions gave me this an hour ago, figuring I'd see you before she did." I put my glass down and pulled out a "Late Admission Notice: Faisal Aboody, freshman. Hometown: Kuwait City, Kuwait.

"What's this now?" I thought out loud, and read the enclosure to the room. "Kids can just start here whenever they feel like it, now or…whenever?"

"Did you say *Aboody?*" Mary's eyes became saucers and she sat up straight. "From Kuwait?"

"That's what it says…arriving between eight and nine tonight. Guess this is my last drink…"

"He was here this summer…wow, they *got* him." Mary nodded with a hint of satisfaction.

"Well, if he was still looking for a school in the summer," Remy held up a clarifying finger, "I'd say *he* got *us*, rather than the other way around…"

"N-n-n-n-o-o-t," Mary corrected him, "if this is the same kid. Kuwait?" I nodded. "That's him," Mary was smiled to herself. "His father was here too. Arrived in the cleanest black car you've ever seen. Apparently he's some minister of something or other there. Long story short: no financial aid form was filled out. Good for us."

"Hell, if you're so happy about it Mary," I stood up to leave, "care to be the welcome wagon tonight so I can have another here?

"Sorry Peter," she raised her glass to me as lame solace, "that's what we English teachers call a rhetorical question."

I headed back to the dorm to brush my teeth and see that Master Aboody's room was ready for him.

September 16

BURNSY! WAIT UP!" SCOTT Paone was running to catch up with me heading to class after lunch today. Like most folks at a school, Scott wears a few hats: Academic Dean and Head Girls' Basketball Coach. He's been here for six years since leaving Thayer, and his easy smile and lacrosse captain looks are assets at Open Houses. Loves nicknames, his of course being Scooter.

"Howzit going Burnsy?" he caught up.

"Fine, 'cept I'm a little late for class, and now I'm probably gonna be a lot late…"

"No sweat," he patted my back as we strolled, "I'll write you a pass."

At times, Scott and I are on the same wavelength and can finish each other's sentences. He's a bit of a paradox, though. A real booster of the school, under the surface I suspect he's not entirely content here. He's not alone in that respect.

"What's up?" I asked.

"Whatcha reading in your Western Civ class? Any fiction?"

"*Pompeii*…later in the year."

"Why?"

"Why? I get kickbacks from the publisher." A stupid question deserves a stupid answer.

"Really," he pressed.

Pompeii is Robert Harris' novel about the area of the Roman Empire leading up to Vesuvius' eruption. Good historical fiction. I had no idea where he was going with this query, and mentioned all this, displaying more patience than I actually had for his question.

"I got a call from a parent about it. Guess she knows the book. You...on pretty solid ground using it?"

"It's a good story. Tells a lot about Rome too. I used it last year. Who's –"

"I don't want to get in to names, but---"

"Oh, *please.*" I stopped in place, halting our little stroll along the path and glared at him. Want to piss off a teacher? Go over his head on an issue without speaking to him about it at all. "A parent goes to you on something– doesn't call me – about a book I'm using, not even now, but later this year, complains to you, and I don't get to know *who?*"

"It's not about you. It's about the---"

"*I* chose the book, and since you and I are having this conversation, it *is* about me."

"I just...I'm in no way questioning your judgment."

"Really? Well you're doing a pretty good imitation of someone who *is* questioning my judgment."

"Whoa, whoa." He held up a defensive palm. "If you say it's worth using, fine. But I've got some noisy parents who---"

"Parents? Now it's *plural?*"

"Well, two. You know how they e-mail each other all the time. I'm willing to – *happy* to – go to bat for you, but give me some good...gimme the reason for it."

I broke my glare at him. "Such as?"

"For one, the book. A lesson plan, showing how it works with the curriculum, and –"

"Look; the Roman Empire. I teach it, remember? First century. Things are starting to turn. They get spanked invading Germany in 9 A.D., Rome burns, and then a mountain blows up. Bit of a pattern, eh? Name of the city wiped out by the angry mountain: Pompeii."

"Fine. Good. Get that to me in an e-mail, will you? But there's, I guess, some sex scene...that's what---"

"It's a few sentences. Maybe a paragraph tops. In a two-hundred - page book. I didn't show them "Caligula," for Chrissake."

"Fine. Just get me the---"

"I will. What about telling the parents to get in touch with me directly? If they had, I coulda put this thing to bed. And you wouldn't have to run after me and make me late for class."

He was nodding with his lips pressed together. He could have told the parents to speak to me first, but didn't. Knee-jerk administrators and school counselors; former teachers who couldn't cut it in the classroom.

"I'll suggest that when I speak with them again," He patted my shoulder the way a coach does when he tells you he wants you to start the game on the bench so you'll be fresh later on. "If you get me that stuff, I'll put this little fire out," and he was off, assuming one of those slightly-hurried gaits that says, 'I've got a meeting in thirty seconds.' Maybe he can pick up a spine at the Faculty Secret Santa this year.

September 18

I NOW OFFICIALLY LIVE in a three-room apartment. Buildings and Grounds sealed off my end room yesterday and while it doesn't drastically change my lifestyle, I resent the hell out of it all. Moving stuff out, I came upon a copy of *Pompeii*, which brought to mind my chat the other day with Scott Paone, fresh from planning his little Nuremberg campfire. In the mail today was my own alumni magazine, dishing forth pics of some new faculty housing and a section of class notes in the back. I don't envy my senior roommate who's now at a hedge fund or the classmate who interviewed Harper Lee for a book, but the quarterly from another boarding school offering a view of life elsewhere timed with my residential downsizing and Scott second guessing my teaching collectively flipped the switch: *I will not be here next year.* I feel about as valued as crab grass on the varsity soccer field, and it's only September. Part of the lure of independent schools is the freedom to teach as you deem best; we pick our own readings and have classes small enough so we don't need to use multiple-choice tests. Once someone starts tweaking your work or second-guessing your decisions, you might as well be at one of those public schools where teachers turn in lesson plans to principals. By and large parents trust us with their kids – and give us tuition approaching 50K as another sign of that trust. Thus, we don't send permission slips out before showing "Schindler's List" or taking a class to the ropes course. Too early to start a search now, but note to self: start tweaking the rez.

September 20

STUDY HALL DUTY IS something about which teachers like to grumble but which can actually be useful for getting work done if you look like you're in no mood for horseplay. I have it on Mondays to get it out of the way. Two hours at night when kids have to keep doors open and...study. To make sure that fun doesn't break out, one sits at a desk in the hallway and strolls about now and again, answering the odd question and making sure that a stoic time is had by all. Between being part tutor and part white-collar prison guard, there's little room for goofing off so it's possible to actually read those essays or correct those tests that pile up. Going walkabout, one gets to know the students a bit – as much as one wants to. My project the other night was Aaron Tang, the Korean with the Chinese name. I've watched him negotiate the dining hall, tray in hand; he doesn't get waved over to the Korean table, the jock and black tables are out of the question, and girls...not quite. He stands there like the last kid to board a full school bus, a school lanyard around his neck and a belt pulled too-tight. If in fact we'll all work for a geek someday, the geeks will work for him.

"Howzit going?" I stuck my head in his room. A single for him was probably not a good idea, for the more socialization the better, but it's only a matter of time before a miscreant at another school gets caught drinking and a mid-year admit fills the other bed.

"Hello," he looked up from his math book. The fluorescent lamp and dearth of wall coverings gave the room a surreal air. Posters paying homage to lacrosse and Jessica Alba are in other rooms, not here.

"How are you finding Griswold? Or haven't you found it yet?" Banter was useless, so I simplified. "Is...school...OK?"

"School."

"School. OK?" The hand symbol. "OK?" A half smile. "Any questions? Problems?"

This went on for a while, him repeating one or two words from each question, and me playing mime.

"How's laundry?" He seemed to favor a few rugby shirts all the time, and with some prompting, produced a pad of laundry slips which I encouraged him to use after demonstrating one.

"Every Monday," I modeled the drill. "OK?"

"OK."

"So...are you making friends here?"

"Friends."

"Who do you...eat with, talk with...other Koreans?"

"N-n-n-n-not so much."

"So...who?"

He tipped his head to one side, looking puzzled.

"Will you go to Boston this weekend?" A wrinkled brow. "Boston? Field trip? Shopping? Saturday. Will you go?"

"I...maybe no..."

"Why not? It's fun." Given the chance, many kids will happily thumb away at PlayStation 3 or War Craft 7 with every free second they have rather than actually *do* something. Great for fine-motor skills, but it fosters socialization skills along the lines of Ted Kaczynski's.

"Listen. I'm chaperoning. You should come. It'll be fun. Go to Quincy Market, the waterfront, Super 88." That got him – a huge Asian market in Allston where kids buy cartons of noodles as if a nuclear winter was on the calendar.

I left him to his math. The problem with enhancing the school's bottom line via international students to the extent that Griswold has is that each group of overseas kids is big enough in numbers that they form their own subculture on campus. The girls from the Dominican Republic, the kids from Taiwan, same tables at meals, speaking only Spanish or Chinese. Within the Asian culture, the hierarchies emerge: age is the biggest factor. In Japan, it's called *sempi kohi*. A third grader walks a first grader to school; the older kid being responsible for getting him there safely and the younger one is responsible for listening to him so that he crosses with the lights. The underside of this is bullying, which at a school can mean a senior forcing a sophomore to make his bed each morning. This is usually age-based, but can spring from class issues too. If the pair ever ended up here, the son of a rice farmer from Tohoku, a rural area north of Tokyo, would perhaps defer to the whims of the son of a Sony exec from Osaka.

Aaron's a freshman from Korea with a Chinese surname, so has no natural niche at Griswold, he's truly an *other*. You can't just force kids to be friends, but you can cajole them to effect congeniality. Down the hall a few minutes later I looked in on an older Korean. A second year junior, he was also someone who might have seemed an oxymoron twenty years earlier – an Asian rebel. He breaks the mold of the dutiful math wiz with the violin case with his Bon Jovi hair and Jackie-O glasses. His peers seem to respect that he's willing to go down his own path, perhaps simply because it would never occur to many of them to do so, and perhaps because at home, dad is said to be a very buttoned up mucky muck with Samsung.

"Does Aaron ever sit with you guys in the dining hall?" I asked at his doorway as he fingered his smartphone.

"Aaron?" He had a far way look and was chewing gum.

"Freshman. Aaron Tang."

"Oh! Orange!"

"Orange?"

"We call him 'Orange.' Orange Tang. You Know. In astronomy we heard that it's what they made for the astronauts to drink. Aaron had a big orange shirt on one day, so..."

Naturally. After a classmate at my school regaled us with tales of his tryst with Honor Balfour, she promptly became known as "On All Fours." There were worse things to be called than "orange."

"Does he sit with guys at meals?" I asked.

"No...I mean, he's a freshman," he shrugged.

"Sure, but you're all 14,000 miles from home, and probably have a bit more in common with each other than, say, you and the theater kids or the choral group? Doesn't being from the same land and speaking the same language count for something?"

"Y'know Mr. Burnham," he sat up a little straighter at his desk, "not all Koreans like all other Koreans."

"Sure. Of course. But could he at least sit with you? At meals? I'm sure you've seen him standing there with his tray. And when you guys get together for ping pong or...whatever, do you ever ask him to play?"

"Well, it's like...he knows we're playing..."

"Sure, but if you were a freshman, would you just walk up to a bunch of seniors and expect to be worked in?"

He avoided eye contact, and finally coughed up a willingness to try to roll him into their fold. We shook on it. As I left his room, I thought to myself there was no guarantee that our chat would do any good, but if I weren't sanguine for a little bit of each day, I'd probably be in another line of work.

An hour later, just after dorm check-in time, raised voices floated up the stairwell. In center lounge, a sometimes high-strung junior from Shanghai whose name I was still working on was pleading his case to Bags, who had first floor duty.

"But... I was *there*. I jus' did not get… the signing…"

"Well," Bags shrugged, "go back and get him to sign it now."

"But he's probably gone. The library…it closed by this time."

"Not yet. If you run, you can perhaps catch him." Spotting me, the student appealed. Bags held up a cease and desist palm my way and interrupted. "Just materialized. *Now*. 10:03.Says he was in the library, but..." he held up a pass with no signature, so the student could have been anywhere.

"Mr. B., *you* know me," he pleaded, "Can you call Mr.---"

"This is Mr. Bagwell's floor tonight. I wasn't here when yo—"

"This is shit! Very shit!" Foot stomping accompanied his cursing in a second language. Good rule of thumb: whenever two people are arguing, whoever swears first is probably wrong.

"Perhaps you mean '*bull*shit,'" Bags held up an instructive finger. "You seem quite familiar with the concept; *say it correctly.*"

The boy's eyes widened. He tossed his head towards the ceiling, spat out something in Chinese and stormed out.

"Anything to avoid walking back to the library, I guess." Bags chuckled. "Think I'll write him up for language." Now, it must be said that this was one of those moments when one must either choose to say what should be said and endure the response, or remain silent and let it play out.

"Where do we get them?" he muttered, looking nowhere.

"Them?"

"Kids who can't follow rules – they're worse, and there are more of them – than ten years ago. Talking back…is this what the Admissions Office gets paid for? Filling our beds and desks with these…these…"

I asked him if he had change for the Coke machine and fished out a bill for the exchange as my exit strategy. Fine line between backbone and temerity.

September 21

TODAY I STOPPED IN at the athletic complex to check on the squash schedule for the winter. Sports are an odd realm at schools. Some institutions have very strong teams in certain areas – in my day, St. Mark's hockey team was a scourge among schools, and rowing used to be that way at Kent. Some folks at schools insist that winning helps generate alumni funds, and that publicity about good teams makes recruiting and admissions easier. Frankly, if a crew team is successful and competes at the Henley in England, alums and parents may get out their checkbooks, but they'll give to the team's Henley fund first, and if anything disposable is left afterwards, then the school – but after one is done paying for the trip to the UK and helping to buy a new boat, the Parents' Fund envelope might not even get opened. Being a good hockey player might get a student a spot at a school that his grades alone would not, but look at the brick and mortar gifts on campuses. In the 1980s it was libraries, and more recently science buildings. Look at the plaques on them; chances are they'd still be there even if the lacrosse and soccer teams went 2-10 for a few years. Do not, however, try telling this to Frank Remillard. Since he became Athletic Director, a number of our teams are finally winners after years of dismal play school-wide. As I strolled past the large window of his office by the Old Gym, I could see Remy shaking his salt and pepper head while someone was pleading a failing case to him. I came up with a question about a winter sport as an excuse to intrude, but never needed it.

"Peter, can this wait?" Remy held up two palms to stop me before I spoke.

"Remy...please?!" Schy was groveling. This may have been a first. Schyler Van Wyck does not strike one as a person who has had to ask for much in life. The sun must have been circling the moon.

"Buck up Schy. It'll teach you humility." Bags was on a couch in a corner, enjoying it, whatever *it* was.

"I don't need humility. I need kids who remember their goggles for matches."

"Problem?" I inserted. I had nothing to lose.

"Lawrenceville and Salisbury," Remy shrugged, "Both schools want a tri-meet in Connecticut for squash. Schy doesn't want to play."

"No, I don't." His arms were in full McEnroe at Forest Hills mode. "We'll get clobbered. Lawrenceville? *Jesus.*"

"Their coach tells me they lost a lot of seniors last year," Remy offered. "So maybe---"

"Maybe pigs can fly. And maybe they didn't recruit from Fessenden and the Casino in Brooklyn. Face it Remy: compared to them, we suck. Suck, suck, suck, suck, suck."

This candor cast a silence about the room for a moment.

"That reminds me," I had a notion. "Are we playing Milton in hockey this year?" I couldn't help myself. Schy glared at me, finding no humor in the reference to Milton Academy's hockey team - oral sex scandal a few years back.

"What?" Schy was not amused, or wasn't getting it. Remy was, and leaned back with a smile. "Good one," he nodded approval.

"I'd have to check. Gotta tell that at the ADs' meeting." Apparently, the Athletic Directors of schools meet now and again in order to…meet; there's probably a lot more to the intricacies of lacrosse nets than I realize. Remy started to rock with silent laughter.

Clearly, this wasn't settled, so I slipped out, figuring that they'd be a while, and that I could e-mail Remy about the girls' squash schedule. I walked slowly, hoping that Bags would catch up with me. He didn't disappoint, and was recalling a more recent scandal at Deerfield as we strolled past the library when some acorns sprinkled onto our heads and the shaded grass beneath under our feet. A scampering amongst the branches overhead ensued, and we both stopped to look up. Given the dearth of hundred-pound squirrels on campus of late, our interest was piqued.

"Jump!" Perhaps Bags only half meant it. Silence. "Jump. Your teachers hate you." His Orson Welles' snarl was not an affectation, and has sent more than a few students fleeing his room in tears now and again. More silence. "Fine stay up there and starve…you spineless waste of pimpled skin."

"I don't have zits." The leaves overhead spoke.

"Zits will be the least of your probl---" I began, but was interrupted by an ungraceful descent from among the turning leaves. After dangling from a low branch, William Blumberg actually landed on his feet, seeming to have enjoyed the demonstration of gravity.

"I was right about the 'waste of skin' part." Bags' muttering was almost loud enough to get him in trouble, but Blumberg was still dusting leaves and twigs off his…clothing. Nobody would appear to have successfully convinced Will that the 1960s were over. Simply put, he looks like a pothead; oily dreadlocks, unwashed Bob Marley T-shirts under an oversized thrift shop duster coat, and a general presence that prompts the question,

This is the spawn of a cardiologist and a Yale prof? If Janis Joplin and Alan Ginsberg had met and produced a son, it would have been Blumberg. He is a core member of a student gaggle that offers a passive-aggressive-dismissive pose to any hint of tradition, authority or convention on campus. They espouse an affinity for Wiccan customs, although this seems an affectation more than anything else. Pentagrams have been carved into trees, and they actually requested use of a classroom during Study Hall before last year's Winter Solstice.

"Hi," Blumberg got to his feet, and reflexively checked his phone.

We both eyed him for a moment, probably wondering the same thing: *how could learned adults capable of dropping fifty large a year for high school have been so ineffective raising a son?* Dressing like a Tom Petty groupie was no big deal; send a kid off to boarding school, and after a month, it often looks as though he never had a mother anyway. The Wiccan stuff was another matter. Teenagers like to shock, but Will and his band of lice carriers were committed; tried to get themselves named an official school club: the Non-Traditional World Tribe. *Nitwits*, to those of us paying attention. Nobody's found vials of chicken blood in their rooms, but they're just weird enough to make you wonder. Ever the politically correct jellyfish, even Barclay chuckled at our re-branding of them.

"Gathering nuts for the winter William?" Bags asked.

"It's an awesome tree, Mr. Bagwell. The branches are like…really good for climbing."

"You're not at your sport because…" I offered this prompt eagerly awaiting a response – and hoping not to seem too impotent in Bags' eyes.

"See, I'm in rock climbing, and the van for the rock wall place left before I got to it today."

"Doesn't it leave at the same time every day?"

"Well, yeah...but today I had to wait for a download, and when it was done, I---"

"Which class was this *download* for?" I asked. Blumberg affected a helpless pose, then coughed up an answer.

"It was music... Nirvana."

"Wonderful!" Bags was energized. "Who exactly? Mussorgsky? Rachmaninoff?"

"Nirvana."

"Well that depends," Bags was having him on, "which *composer* was it?"

"N-n-n-o-o-o-o-o...the band, Nirvana. Y'know?"

Yes, Bags knew, but burned a hole in Blumberg's skull with a glare all the same. These days sarcasm is thought of as cruelty, but Bags ventures where angels fear to tread, and between his quotable wisdom and hunting party threads, is seldom called on it. If they didn't like it, he could leave tomorrow and commence a Salinger-esque existence of rare book collecting in Franconia Notch. He would not, however, be able to whither an acolyte of Satan with his sarcasm once ensconced in the White Mountains, so he was getting it out of his system here and now. He assured Blumberg that an absence for his skipping rock climbing would be reported, just in case his rock climbing teacher didn't miss him enough to bother, and told him to park himself outside of the Deans' Office.

"But I missed the van, so to make up for it I was cli---"

"Don't piss in my ear and tell me it's raining, son. Off with you. *Now.*"

He was off. It would never occur to most of us to be so blunt, but even Blumberg knew Bags' currency here. Respect is nice. *Gravitas* is better.

"If you ever see me being led from my classroom in handcuffs," he began as we walked on, "it might be because that sack of cells was in a course of mine and opened his mouth.

Bring me some books by Christopher Hitchens when you come by on visiting day, will you? Prison libraries are probably hit or miss."

I assured him I would. Recalling Schy's rant about Blumberg being back here this fall, I wished I could be in the Dean's Office for the impending conversation. You have to wonder whether every kid on our Admissions Wait List is as unremarkable a person as Blumberg seems to be, but I just don't see that he's the *enfant terrible* that Schy says he is. One of us is wrong.

September 22

Email today:

Southern New England History Teachers' Conference
Host: The Weld School   April 27-29
  *Call for Papers
  *Teacher Workshops
  *Educational Resource Vendors
Go to our website for more information: www.snehtc.org

These notices trickle in weekly, and as April seems a light year away, the only reason it stuck with me for a bit is that Dave Meeks, who I rowed with a few years back, sent it. He also CCed Barclay on it. Dave is one of my favorite people, and Barclay is currently one of my least favorite ones – odd triangle.

September 23

Email today from David Meeks;

Hi Peter

Hope your year is going well so far – that HIS teacher' conference in April I emailed you about is something I also sent to your Head of School, figuring if I put it on his radar, it might nudge him to approve your coming down for it. Hope so – let's catch up at some regatta this fall.

Yours – Meeks

September 24

EVEN THOUGH I'VE BEEN here for four years, the teacher I'm probably most in synch with regarding school and even non-school things is a hundred miles away in another state. Dave Meeks and I met rowing at a club on the Charles a few years back, and by the end of the first summer there, we could finish each other's sentences. He's parlayed his grad work and yeoman's duty at a charter school where he re-wrote the curriculum into being a department chair at Weld, a gothic citadel of Anglophilia in Connecticut. What are friends for if not an email when you're in a job hunt, so tonight I found his original email and wrote him while running copies off in the print room.

> Dave
>
> Hope this finds you well, and getting some rowing in down there. I haven't been on the water since August, and Griswold doesn't row in the fall. Actually, Griswold doesn't do a number of things, such as trust its teachers with their curriculum or leave their living quarters at a reasonable size...long story short: I'm looking around. We've got a Head of School and Ac Dean who have neither any self-awareness nor appreciation for those of us still in the classroom. As you said once, Q: What do you call a retired educator? A:

Headmaster – spot on. Griswold is run by an aloof idiot who wouldn't know a classroom if he fell into one. I'm wondering whether any openings at Weld are on the horizon...early I know, but figured I'd let you know I'm looking; can't imagine being here in...January, but certainly not next September. Still coming up for the Dartmouth game next month? Let's meet up @ H Sq if so.

Best – Peter

I was proofreading it before hitting 'send' just long enough for a student from my World Civ class to stroll by the faculty copy room where I was running stuff off, see me and remember that he wanted to ask me about the upcoming test in Gilgamesh. *Will there be a study guide?* (No, we'll review in class.) *Does spelling count?* (Yes – this is high school.) *Do I drop the lowest test grade for the term?* (No - unless you want me to drop your highest one too.) Note to self: keep door to faculty copy room closed.

September 25

A T LUNCH TODAY, I scanned the dining hall to see if my plea that Aaron be worked into at least the odd meal with other students was heard. He was sitting with some other kids for once, but only one was Korean; even better. The English conversation would do him good. I opted for coffee in the Teachers' Room afterwards to erase the grime of the grilled cheese in my mouth, and it was there that I first saw her.

Naomi Watts is one my favorite actresses. Seeing her double walk into the Teachers' Room with Carol Dane, Barclay's secretary, was a moment.

"Here's where the teachers read, complain about the coffee and plot to take over the school," Carol introduced Ms. Watts' doppelganger, and after a few seconds it was clear that Kat McPhee was suddenly the second most eye-catching female on campus. "This is Peter Burnham. He chairs the History Department and is a houseparent in Wentworth."

I stood to greet her and offered my hand

"Elizabeth Michaels. Liz." Her clasp had that odd mixture of female gentility and a businesslike demeanor. Her makeup was minimal – or simply very effective by appearing so, I suppose -

and her smile and sky blue eyes betrayed a minimum of charm, nothing more.

"Liz will keep my chair from getting cold come next month." Carol explained. "Comes to us from Portsmouth Abbey in Rhode Island."

Carol Dane has been the gatekeeper outside the Head's Office since before most people could remember. As it is with most folks at an institution too long, she affects a manner which is evident but never articulated: *I'm capable of answering your tiresome request, but honestly would rather not.* She came to be called 'The Great Dane' without affection and has seen people and fads come and go here. She knows what liquor trustees drink, when it's too early on Monday to bother Barclay over a weekend issue and which parent calls should be put through to him. She is what headmasters need and she knows it, affording us her terseness at no extra cost.

"Do you get there often?" Elizabeth pointed to my Nantucket tie.

"Not as often as I'd like. There's a family place in Monomoy."

"Ah! We go to the Vineyard, when my aunt has her month at the house there."

"Liz is..," Carol picked her words carefully, "going to live in North Farmhouse."

North Farmhouse is a white clapboard barn of a place at the edge of campus that would make Robert Frost proud and could easily house a family of six. As did everything she said, Carol's mentioning it had meaning: *It's more than she needs. Perhaps more than she deserves.* They turned on their sensible heels and other introductions were made. The Lord & Taylor fossil handing things off to a Nordic Talbots gal. *Meet the new boss...* It's hard to know which will be the more engaging topic at the faculty happy hour Friday: that Carol is finally retiring and taking her Joan Crawford warmth with her, or that her replacement as Barclay's

Girl Friday is perhaps three decades her junior and will be the solitary resident of North Farmhouse.

October 2

OH, FOR A GODDAMN time machine. Dammit, dammit, dammit to hell. The email I sent replying to Dave Meeks and venting about matters here...I threaded into the original email from him about the conference at Weld...which he CCed to Barclay, to grease the wheels for me to attend the conference...so my rant, intended for Dave, also went to Barclay. Jesus, what a cluster. Barclay's message hit me cold: "Let's chat about how I'm not at all self-aware – tomorrow at 2:15 , my office," his email said. If it hadn't been for those stupid student questions about a test I might have checked the addresses more carefully, but...he's a kid, and it's on me. A goddamn pig's breakfast.

October 3

BARCLAY KEPT ME WAITING a good ten minutes outside his office, as if I needed it to be on edge.

"Peter, c'mon in," he called from inside, not looking up from a screen when I entered and dithered about sitting.

"Sit," he still wasn't looking up, and tapped away for another minute as if I weren't there. After a brief eternity I began checking my phone, which of course prompted him to hit one key on his board emphatically, then pivot to face me.

"Sorry to keep you waiting," he straightened some papers on his blotter, "Punctuality is a casualty of not being self-aware..." His stare was distant, like that of a chess opponent who was pleased with a moderate recovery he'd just made from a terrible predicament.

"I'm," I was truly stick handling in the dark, "guessing you ---"

"Have 'no appreciation for those of us still in the classroom?'" he was clearly scanning a printout of my message to Dave. "Apparently not...at least in one learned opinion of someone here..."

He held it up for me to see, then hunched his shoulders and webbed his fingers, thinning his lips as if he was hurt while contemplating a reprimand at the same time.

"This year has," I ventured, "not begun as I expected, and now, in retrospect, my...sentiments in that...message seem...an overreaction, I do feel as though---"

"Griswold is run by an aloof idiot who wouldn't know a classroom if he fell into one?"

He glared at me such that was I reminded of the courtroom scenes in "Law & Order." He had my words before him, and seemed game to wring every one of them to affect his wounded self.

"Barclay...fine. I wrote it. Clearly. Alright?" I sat up a bit. "I didn't send it to anyone here, actually, and admittedly, I should have proofread it. It was late and ---"

"No proofreading needed Peter. Perfect spelling." He flicked the paper with his thumb and forefinger. "Wish I were...even half as perfect..."

"Look Barclay...I don't know what to say. The...things I mention...my apartment, having my choice of a book mentioned...they give...one," no time to get British on him, "they give *me* a sense of...really not feeling valued here, and I thought that---"

"What about *communicating?* Coming to me?" he directed two fingers to his Barneys' tie, tilting his head as if to suggest I'd not done the most obvious thing to do in such a situation. "I hired, you, remember? Suggested you be one of the chaperones on the Costa Rica trip last year? You were coaching sports *two* seasons until that policy change I pushed through...and you can't even *talk* to me?" His tone was a combination of affected hurt and simmering anger.

"Barclay..," I turned my palms skyward in the universal symbol of this is how it is, "I'm sorry, but in the first month of this year, you'd have to agree, I've been treated pretty...much without much respect for where I live or how I do my job." He sat a bit more erect and raised his chin. "I lost a room in my place, and…it's right there: Scott questioned my judgment using a text. I mean…what's next?"

"Well Peter, Parents' Weekend is next, and I hope that in the course of it, that you will contain your contempt for others here," then he picked up a Mont Blanc fountain pen and began tapping his blotter with it. "But given this…admission of how you feel about…others here, who have been placed in positions of authority by the trustees, who believe us to be of sound judgment, I have to say that…to have a department chair, or even a teacher here who expresses such a lack of confidence in the administration…actual contempt, when you think about it, it untenable." *Untenable?* What does that mean? I know what it means, but what's with the Edith Wharton umbrage? "I wish you hadn't brought it to this point, but given your feelings towards Scott and I, I can't see offering you a contract for next year…"

His words hung there in the well-polished stillness of his office. We stared back at each other, him perhaps searching for a reaction, and me for any clue that this was a joke, expecting him to rock back with laughter in another second, but he didn't.

"You're saying that..," I wanted to be calm and eloquent, both of which seemed a reach at the moment, "because I wrote, but *didn't send to anyone here*, a message, that says how…unhappy I am with how---"

"I'm saying that if you truly feel this way, it's best you move on. Obviously a month into the school year, we'll move ahead to make the best of…the situation. I'll hope that you will conduct yourself professionally and…be discrete with your…contempt for some of your colleagues." The wounded soul act did not suit him. "And in the event that you secure something elsewhere for next year, HR will be happy to confirm your dates of employment here."

This actually seemed to be happening. He sat there, looking for a reaction from me, and all I could do was eye him back. After a good half minute, a thought occurred to me.

"Is Scott aware of this…decision?" I asked, wondering how, if he was, I could make any future double homicide look like an accident.

"I don't see any point in…widening the circle, so to speak. Not now anyway. Obviously once we begin a search, the reason why should…reflect…a normal professional decision that is made at schools where one is employed year to year. I'm not looking to make it a big deal, but honestly Peter, it's clear to me that I don't have your support, or your confidence, so you don't have mine, as I must think of the school and those charged with moving it forward. It didn't have to come to this, but…I've made my decision."

He stood without moving from behind his desk, telling me that our meeting was over. It was the kind of moment when in the films on TCM, Gary Cooper says something true and righteous that deflects the verbal punch just thrown at him. Nothing like that came to me. I merely took the liberty of not closing his door as I left.

October 4

I WAS AWAKE FOR about twenty seconds this morning before remembering that I've been told I'm done in June. It came back like suddenly recalling that you'd had a car accident the night before. My own fault I suppose, but Barclay was...really overacting. If bitching about work was a firing offense, 98% of the workforce would be getting pink slips. I didn't even send it to anyone on campus, and now I'm expected to stroll through the school year with a smile on. If he thought I'd be sending out the occasional rez before yesterday, now it'll be all I do come January; drop into the Trustees' Winter Reception? Nope. Offer to chaperone overbooked trips to Boston? Nope. Ought to be interesting when my position shows up under *Opportunities* on the school's website. Watch Barclay suggest some line about how it's my choice to move on, *taking my career in a new direction*, then when people ask about that direction, if I don't have something by then... *Well, that's an interesting way to put it.* No such thing as a secret at a boarding school. Might seem awkward, and not just for me. As it's October, I'm not panicking yet, and went through classes today like nothing had happened. When the Admissions Office emailed me after lunch about shooting some pics in my classroom for the new catalog, I said sure – be fun to live on in the school's literature even after I'm gone.

October 5

IF FRIDAY LUNCH OFFERS no trace of fish sticks, chances are that trustees or parents are afoot. It being October, Parents' Weekend is at hand. The leaf blowers can be heard everywhere, the brown and white school seal has found its way onto the varsity soccer field, Barclay was spotted in a new suit, and teachers have been encouraged to put forth their 'A - game' lessons for classes that might be visited by families. "Not that you don't every day," Barclay added in his e-mail. Liz, his new aide de camp-in-training, has slid into The Great Dane's role bit by bit as Carol uses up untaken vacation days. Some older boys who have been perched in the anteroom of Barclay's office for some reason are said to have found the brief interlude there less disagreeable than it was with her predecessor.

By early afternoon, the parents were amassing. Prep mobiles have evolved from my days as a student; the Volvos and Wagoneers are now Lexus SUVs and Land Rovers. The entrance of the day, however, was far and away that of Faisal Aboody's father. The late arrival from Kuwait City has disappeared into the freshman class and is barely noticeable in my dorm. In the 1980s, the present king of Jordan had trickled through a few New England schools *en route* to Oxford and the throne of the

58

Hashemite kingdom. As it's still not clear whether Faisal's dad is a sheik or the nation's Finance Minister, discussion at lunch one day focused on whether one can in fact be both. His helicopter landing on the varsity football field – turned helipad seemed to render this burning question moot. Barclay and his entourage stood in formation, their suits rippling under the whir of the chopper as it set down gently on the school crest at the fifty-yard line. Barclay's demeanor became that of a governor greeting Air Force One in his home state.

"Think that handshake will lead to a school gift?" asked Mary Carpenter, as a few of us looked on from the patio behind the science building.

"*God,*" Allison Manville hissed, "what a sycophant." She glared at the scene with contempt, her arms crossed over a pair of tan overalls. Guess she'd be doing some farming after the morning's parent meetings.

"Well...I wouldn't call being respectful to a parent being a sycophant..." Mary didn't bother to look at her as she spoke, and is so delicate that even Allison, Griswold's incarnation of Andrea Dworkin, had to tread carefully here.

"Well," Allison ventured, "would Barclay be falling all over himself with a parent of a kid on aid from Bed-Sty or Roxbury?"

"Lot of folks in Bed-Sty have their own choppers?" I couldn't resist. Allison shot me an I-never-expected-such-a-sardonic-salvo-from-*you* glare.

"*Christ,* Allison," Remy shook his head, "The guy could probably buy Manitoba with petty cash and his kid goes here. Lighten up." He had a way of shutting discussions down with one sentence. That seemed to be *that.*

"Just because someone is wealthy doesn't--" Allison was eyeing the toes sticking out of her Birkenstocks when I jumped in.

"Wealthy? *Wealthy?*" I turned to her and jabbed my thumb in the direction of the varsity helipad, "Forget wealthy. This guy might be mega-rich. George Soros on steroids. Kuwait...get it? And if we get a big Annual Fund gift out of him for moving his son along the educational treadmill, great. Maybe even new nets for your field hockey girls. Would that really piss you off?"

Allison had nowhere to go now, since last year she'd been whining about all the goodies that came the way of boys' lacrosse, hinting at a Title IX complaint. She closed and opened her eyes slowly in that it's-clearly-pointless-to-argue-with-him sort of way, turned on her heels and was gone.

"We enjoyed that a bit too much," I pointed out.

"She can take it though," Remy shrugged. At the chopper Liz was at Barclay's side, earnestly trying to keep her skirt down amidst the waning gale from the blades. Scott Paone was next her and Schy was window dressing, explained perhaps by being one of Faisal's teachers. Stepping off the chopper, the father patted his son's head while shaking hands all around.

"Do you think he's happy here?" Mary nodded towards the gaggle, clearly meaning Faisal.

"Probably as happy as you can be thousands of miles from home at the age of fourteen." I offered. Mary thinned her lips, and seemed to be looking past the scene on the field below.

As the whir of the chopper died down, distant sirens could be heard. The public housing project a mile away can't go a day without a false alarm. Barclay, Mr. Aboody and their respective acolytes chatted on as they strolled from the field, slowing their gaits as a fire engine turned into the school drive. By then a few onlookers were pointing to the smoke wafting out of a second floor window in Wentworth. After a few seconds, I recognized it as Aaron Tang's room.

No school year passes without some unscripted event of note. One year here it was an empty school bus skidding into the pond through the ice. The yearbook had fun with it, coming up with some caption about "dropping off the hockey team," a toned-down alternative to a "Chilly Chappaquiddick" ditty that Scott wisely nixed before it went to the publisher, seeing how some Kennedy cousin was here at the time, *en route* to Betty Ford. With seemingly the entire campus transfixed, the sirens wound down and a fire truck lumbered over speed bumps and slowed to a stop in front of the dorm. Less than two minutes later, the smoke from the second floor window ceased. Liz, Scott and Schy shepherded Mr. Aboody's entourage towards the Parents' Reception while Barclay conferred with the firefighters once they emerged outside Wentworth. There might be a worse time of year for a dorm fire than Parents' Weekend, but I couldn't think of one. Soon word spread that there would be a briefing for the whole school before dinner on "the business in Wentworth."

Taking to the chapel pulpit a few hours later, Barclay struck that tone of cautious relief one hears from governors when tornado damage is less than expected. "As unfortunate as this afternoon's excitement was," Barclay began, "it is a testament to our preparedness for such events that everyone was accounted for in short order and thankfully there are no injuries to report." Polite applause, which grew louder as people noticed the fire chief by the door of the chapel, still in his battle gear, "Damage would appear to be limited to one student room, and while the causes are under investigation, a resident of the room will be made comfortable elsewhere tonight."

By dinnertime the story was that some replica of a Korean flag had been set afire and papers on a desk caught on as well.

"I don't understand it." Mary shook her head as a decompressing bunch of us flopped down in Chambers for our standing Friday night bull session. This is known of higher up the food chain, but never spoken of.

"What's to understand?" Remy shrugged. "Boys play with matches. Or these days, probably a lighter."

"But why...?" Mary was perplexed. In an oversized wingchair she looked right out of an Agatha Christie drawing room.

"Christ," Bags spat, fixing an impatient glare at nobody in particular. "Do we actually have to analyze it? Nobody was hurt, and it's Friday night."

"It doesn't add up," I offered, nursing a Coke on the couch. "He's not a great mixer. The other Koreans really haven't taken him into their ranks in...what? Over a month here. And soccer...guess he's no Maldonado. But taking a lighter to a makeshift flag..." I shook my head at the theory.

"Weirdness takes many forms at school," Mary seemed contemplative, "the Unabomber went to Harvard, after all..."

Kat McPhee appeared at the door, fished a Diet Coke out of the fridge and gently took the other end of the couch.

"A bit excitement today, eh?" she offered. "First a helicopter, then a fire engine...this is a *fun* school. So...now what?"

"Aaron, it was his room, is bunking with another student for now." I shrugged. "Discipline-wise...I don't know. I really don't think he was behind it, but..."

"Pardon me for saying so," Bags was speaking to nobody in particular, "and this doesn't mean I think he's a bad kid, because I don't, but he's weird."

"He says nice things about you," I threw out. "Show me an adolescent who *isn't* weird. Even the Stepford kids who take three AP courses...how normal is it to spend half your Saturday nights doing homework and every summer studying marine biology or BC Calculus?"

"Maybe he wants out," Mary wondered, "I mean, half a world from home at fourteen. Does he *want* to be here?"

"Like that's a first." Bags was chewing an ice cube. "But be clever about it will you? Chip Bohlen hated St. Paul's, so one day made a condom into a balloon. Batted it around the old library there. Not quietly either. That was inventive."

"Really?" Kat wrinkled her brow. "When was this?"

"Oh, 1920s I think. Maybe earlier."

"So...what happened? To Bohlen?"

"Ambassador to Russia. Under Ike, I think..."

"No. At school? With the condom thing?"

"Oh. Kicked out. Just before graduation. A hundred years ago, that would do it." With genuine *schadenfreude*, Bags then recounted the more recent rape scandal at St. Paul's, and before that how the Rector's pay ended up on the front page of the *Times*, Rector being St. Paul's–speak for Headmaster.

"Are you on duty tonight?" I pointed to Kat's Diet Coke, recalling that some of the new teachers had headed for a tavern for dinner.

"No. My boyfriend took me to a wine tasting last night. I didn't quite like it. Think I'll take a day on the wagon...Not a great time..."

"You didn't like...the event?" Bags was transfixed.

"No, the event was fine, but the only wine I liked was some red from Australia."

"Where *was* it?" Bags sounded like a Mensa convention had been held and he hadn't been invited.

"The Union Club. In Bost---"

"I *know* where it is." There was a bitterness in his tone, suggesting an insult, that seemed to kill the conversation. I hadn't eaten yet, and as the chatter seemed to have jumped the shark, I bailed for dinner.

In my dorm's lounge, those students whose parents hadn't taken them off campus for the night and the international students with nobody to cart them away were slouched about on butcher block furniture affecting an interest in some meaningless event on ESPN when I meandered through after dinner.

"So Mr. B...." a Chinese student fighting with the Coke machine that had eaten his change piped up as I entered, "is Aaron history?"

"No, Aaron is Korean. The Crimean War is history." Sarcasm is a double-edged sword with students, but here I felt on safe ground.

"Come on," he was incredulous, "I mean, there was a fire."

"You should be a detective," I offered. This was met by quizzical look.

"So...Mr. Burnham..." Sitting up from a couch before the TV, Isaiah Franklin was intent on an answer, turning his attention away from an English Premier League soccer game on the screen. A sophomore from Brockton, a hardscrabble city halfway to Rhode Island, he'd left most of his street threads at home and went for cred via the hip-hop-prep look: backwards hats and pants that would fit Orson Welles with A & F tops and polo shirts with popped collars. For a young man of color, he is a salad of sartorial references. Some call him an Oreo, a student of color who's white at heart, but he straddles this fence well.

"This is major. If he were a brother..." At this the white kids watching the game eyed each other as if Al Sharpton had just walked in.

"Are you saying that..." the Coke machine fighter glared at Isaiah "kids from Asia get special treatment here?" This was going to be better than ESPN.

"You were here last year." Isaiah sat up straighter and eyed both of us. "Remember...what was his name...that kid from Philly?"

I couldn't remember his name either, but had an image of the student he was thinking of. Such a student is what happens when an idealistic Admissions Director and a myopic basketball coach conspire. Once admitted, requests of the young man to comply with dorm policy, especially at night, were always met with emphatic pleas for late lights. It was he who insisted that the life of Frederick Douglass would indeed do as a topic for a non-Western civilization paper. He liked to mention that his uncle had once met Henry Louis Gates. Caught drinking in the fall, he really fell through the ice in April when he called a black teaching intern a "fucking Uncle Tom" for marking him late for class. Truth be told, they were a slew of offenses just under the reporting radar that came out at his hearing. Personally, I was impressed to learn that he actually understood the concept of Mrs. Stowe's character. The students of color protested with a day of silence and last word was he was making folks at Canterbury School rethink the merit to their quest for a power forward.

"Is he getting kicked out?" Isaiah was dying to know.

"I don't know as it's clear what really happened yet." I wasn't just being judicious; this was true.

"My cousin had a roommate at his school," a student spinning a Frisbee on his finger while eyeing the game on TV jumped in, "Had a little barbecue on a ledge outside his window. They almost kicked him out, but his folks made a huge donation to the Parents' Fund, and he got to graduate." Perhaps true, and repeated each year at schools here and there very quietly. Fair? No. Good for schools' bottom-line? Absolutely. I have no idea whether Aaron lit a fire in his own room, but parents' largesse has been known to play a role in how such matters have been decided in the past. I lingered for a bit, just to make sure that the discussion didn't escalate, and after the battle with the Coke machine seemed lost and Manchester City scored a goal, I slipped out.

October 6

THE PARENT MEETINGS TODAY were true to form. Even though *Sean has always earned all 'A's before your class* and *Calista honestly is paying attention while doodling* were heard, with time, one learns delicate ways to convey mediocrity.

"To date, Stephanie's work hasn't been as strong as I'd like. She's hovering just below a C minus, but some serious studying before the next task would surely help."

"I have no doubt that his 58 average is not a genuine reflection of Josh's real potential, but proofreading his essays more would be a good way to start turning things around..."

"From his comments in class, it is clear that Jeremy is one of the more thoughtful students in his section. I hope he begins to find more of the homework worth doing, so we can get him into the passing zone in terms of his average in the class."

Not being on duty after Saturday conferences, I didn't feel compelled to stay on campus for the games against the Westgate School. A gift card for the Harvard Coop from a thoughtful parent made a trip to Cambridge seem a good use of the afternoon. Heading out, I gave two seniors a start in a parking lot where they acted as if they'd been expecting privacy. In coats and ties, a tad dapper for a Saturday afternoon, they were getting into a car with what looked like college catalogs in hand. One was Dickens Matthews, the Head Proctor in the other boys' dorm, but I've never had the other one in class and his name escapes me. A Troy Donahue clone with a varsity swagger, he loves to twirl his keys on a lanyard as he strolls about. Cool without being arrogant, girls always seem in the orbit of this gentleman jock. The Pepsodent smile looks all the better with the Oak Bluffs' tan, and he's never in a hurry anywhere. Owing to a twisted ankle, however, no soccer for a while. Dickens is a senior from D.C whose poise is so complete that his fellow black students don't call him out for *acting white* when he schmoozes with the faculty and flirts with the Oyster Bay debutramps in Devine.

"Word, Mr. B.?" one of them called out.

"The word is Cambridge."

"Not gonna stay and see soccer beat Westgate?" Dickens asked.

"Has anybody *ever* seen soccer beat Westgate?" The school playing us is heavy with post grads and its nineteen year-olds usually prevail on the playing fields. "You're bailing too?"

"We've got...off campus permission," Dickens was checking his wallet.

"Bit overdressed for pizza..." I thought out loud. A pause, and they eyed each other for a response.

"Double date," the Troy Donahue type offered. "Simmons College girls," he added.

"College girls. Right." I was dubious, but actually indifferent. They yucked at that more than they needed to, piled into a waiting car and were gone. Not being on duty and with a gift card to use, I followed them out the school gate and they turned right while I headed east, not giving them another thought. I'd devote Sunday to starting in on the résumé.

It was one of those yellow and blue afternoons at Harvard Square that made meeting occasionally dour Dave Meeks a pleasure. We met at Riverside Boat Club on Memorial Drive. Being chair of the Humanities Department at The Weld School in Connecticut was a nice jump from his urban charter school. His red flattop and beard suggest more than his thirty years but his ragg sweater over jeans looked more grad student than department head. As I'd sent him the email that rendered me unemployed come June, I figured I could recount the tale and see if his school might have any openings on the horizon. Service at the Chinese place we started at was so good we hadn't really caught up by the time the bill came, so we continued over pints at a watering hole that we frequented after rowing practice years ago, Cum Laude Come All. Between tales of races past, Dave kept dropping hints that all was not well at his school. Weld is one of those gothic citadels that dots the Connecticut landscape. Founded by some brother-in-law of a Roosevelt, a fact the school trades on whenever possible, its spires and Service of Nine Lessons and Carols at Christmas places it at the vortex of perpetuity, Anglophilia and money.

"So what's new at..." I was searching for a certain characterization of Weld.

"Harrow on the Housatonic?" he tipped his mug back.

"Very clever."

"Yes, we pride ourselves on being clever."

"I detect...dissent?"

"Ever read that John Cheever story, "The Swimmer?""

"No...but I saw the movie with..."

"Burt Lancaster."

"Yeah." David knows his celluloid. "Even better. At the end, he's locked out of his house, but then we see inside, there's nothing there. Empty." I nodded. "That's Weld." He drained his pint and signaled for two more. "Great kids, mostly, good teachers - many of them anyway - and a year-end faculty party that genuinely says 'thank you.'" Being at a place that is currently balancing its books by trolling Beijing and Seoul for warm bodies, all this sounded pretty good. Inside I was pining to hear that a colleague of his in the Humanities Department had experienced an epiphany and would be leaving in June to work on a lobster boat.

"But..." I nudged.

"It – Weld – is a *brand*. The Latin quotes over the doorways, the 'a life of service' crap, 'truth matters,'" he made quotation marks with fingers in each hand. "The parents buy it, especially the ones on the Philly Main Line and the alumni in *Swellesley*." Swellesley is pejorative for Wellesley, a leafy town west of here with long driveways leading to homes owned by Celtics and Bruins, and usually the teams' owners too. "But behind the curtain, it's a farce. A well-manicured, legacy-infested farce. I mean...I know: stuff happens. That coke scandal back in the '80s at Choate, Groton had that sex-hazing thing a few years back, and that drama teacher who, where was it---"

"Ick. Yeah, I get it," I waved off more examples. "No place is perfect. Every school has its warts."

"No place is perfect, sure." He started in on the new pint, squinting with some bitterness as he spoke. "Well, we've raised *im*perfect to an art form." He tipped his glass and continued with an allow-me-to-explain look.

"Last year at the very end some kid's laptop went missing. Not unheard of. By May kids don't lock their doors, and get careless. Thing is, this junior has all his work and term papers on his desktop. Nowhere else. Stupid? Yep. But it goes missing finals' week. Eventually some proctor finds it under another kid's bed while looking for a lacrosse stick he lent out. Also finds a few iPods that had gone missing and a bottle of Capt. Morgan. Freaking jackpot. Slam dunk. Kid's gone. Doesn't even take finals. Nice and neat. Then, this fall, kid shows up - in my Post-War U.S. class. I had to look at his name twice to believe it." He shook his head and guzzled a bit. "This kid...a sniveling streak of piss from the Bordeaux region of France. His roommate, some equally sneaky shit from Seoul was in on it too, but he didn't return. Quite a rap sheet."

"How did the French kid turn up again?"

"Turns out he wasn't expelled. He was *allowed to withdraw*," again with the quotation marks, "with the option to reapply. Which he did. With the blessing - perhaps the nagging - of our Head of School." He raised his glass in a mock toast. "So come Labor Day, the kid's back again. Hardly missed a beat."

"Yeah, we bounced a kid last year in March, and he got the same deal." Blumberg's tumbling out of that tree came to mind.

"Here's the kicker, though," Dave turned to me for the footnote, "Last week, same kid sneaks back on campus late under the cover of darkness, without signing out, mind you, and returns stinking of...let's just say that the Seagram's family is quite solvent thanks to him. Then he lies about signing out with me. I get called the next day for a meeting in the Head's office on a Sunday. A *Sunday*. Kid's dad has promised us a new scoreboard in the gym. Funny timing, yeah? The teacher who caught him coming back drunk is the varsity b-ball coach; he doesn't like it, but he can live with it, *and* the new scoreboard. Spineless shit. Seeing that I'm kind of wound up, the Head pulls me aside and says, "I thought you might like this." Hands me a copy of *The Rector of Justin,* signed by Auchincloss. I get one of those pats on the shoulder and looks that says, *We're all part of the same team here right?* Bottom line: in-school suspension."

"Nasty pill to swallow," I offered, and started in on my next pint.

"Yeah, right? I know that's how the world works, but I always thought that with a long waiting list of kids in the Admission

Office, we could afford to tell miscreants to piss off. Shows what I know."

"Hmmmm...I suppose, such...occurrences allow the school to be able to...afford to be picky about other things such as---"

"Yeah, well we're not. For me, the rub is the kid whose folks *can't* give us a turf field. When *those* kids get caught, they're on thinner ice than George Fortesque Maximillian...whoever." I couldn't help but smile at his reference to *Rebecca*. "Look at your little *alma mater* down the street here," he gestured in the direction of the Yard. "I saw a statistic somewhere: forty-one percent of Harvard undergrads there are legacies. You can't tell me they're all brilliant. No offense, pal."

"None taken, but...think of what you get from...some of that. An endowment in the millions. *Billions*, here." I turned it back on him. "Your *old* squash courts are nicer than our *new* ones. You might not have them by only taking valedictorians who play the cello and speak three languages."

"Sure, sure, but...to be so, baldly for sale...and then we get this Anglican wisdom in chapel. The Book of Common Prayer in fortune cookies."

"Well, the chosen frozen look after their own." I shrugged.

"Chosen frozen," he gave into a grin, "I like that." He clinked his glass to mine.

We meandered Brattle Street for some air before parting, and the right moment to ask about a history spot there never arose. Damn frustrating, but I suppose not inquiring left me with a bit more dignity intact for the time being. I'll see him in two weeks for the Head of the Charles anyway. I made for the Coop with my gift card and bought some books that, truth be told, I probably won't crack until Christmas break. I also bought some résumé paper.

October 11

SCHOOL THIS WEEK HAS been uneventful, save the smoke damage crew in Wentworth, and whispers that someone other than Aaron fired his room. No names, at least not around teachers. I left the digging to others; Scott Paone can play CSI. Yesterday I loitered near his office after lunch just to see about getting sub coverage for some classes at week's end. He'd had just gotten off the phone, and perched behind his desk in his starched blue shirt with pumpkin motif bow tie, he looked baffled. I also noticed Mary Carpenter in there, and this intrigued me.

"Their Head of School?" Mary sounded incredulous. "*Really?*"

"Really. Barclay was out, so I took the call. Lucky me..." Scott rolled his eyes.

"What did he want? Oh, wait – it's a she, right?" She removed her reading glasses and sat down in a window seat. I lurched into the doorway, and wasn't waved away.

"Right. A rather officious woman, too. Caroline...something or other...I'll get it right before I get back to her."

"Who is 'she?' I leaned on the door's polished molding.

"Head of Westgate." Scott shook his head. "Not happy."

The Westgate School twenty miles north of here with a tad more *elan*, a lot more post-grads (read *jocks*) and a much larger endowment than Griswold.

"Didn't they fare pretty well here last weekend? Their soccer and cross country teams seemed..." Mary's gentle, declarative manner, even when stating the obvious, was always positive and never at anyone's expense.

"Here we got beat, but there, it was another story." From behind the door Remy piped up, perched most casually in a school captain's chair. "Our JVs were on their campus...boys' and girls' soccer both won, and field hockey spanked them 10-2."

"I gather she didn't call because one of their fans left a water bottle here," I inquired.

"N-n-n-n-n-o-o-o-o-o..." Scott shook his head gazing at his desk blotter. "Seems that Saturday afternoon, their Admission Office there was expecting a family – Newhouses. The media people."

"Oh yeah. Gave a communications school to Syracuse..." I offered.

"That's them. They've got an eighth grader looking at schools." Scott was drumming fingers now. "Anybody know about one of our kids having a sister there? At Westgate?"

"Rings a bell..." I allowed, and it was if someone was striking a match that no one had been able to light yet. "Rings a bell."

He eyed me with a hint of suspicion. "Did you know she does her community service in their Admissions Office?"

I offered up a deadpan look to his rhetorical question.

"Well, she does. So Saturday afternoon when the Newhouses show up for their tour, they are met in the parking lot by two dapper, eager beavers who hurry them right into a tour. Showing them the whole place – but putting an odd spin on things. Coloring everything...in comparison to us." He rose, and began gesturing with his arms, mimicking a tour guide.

"'This is the Bateman Library. Thirty computer terminals, wi-fi too, 150,000 volumes of books...almost as many as Griswold. And this is the gym – three basketball courts and a pool...not Olympic size like Griswold's, but there's talk of a high diving board next year. Here's the English building – bit drafty in winter, but you learn to wear sweaters. Over there is the school telescope – same model as the ones they have at Griswold.' That sort of thing...'" Silence, but few corners of mouths began to turn up. "Heading down to the playing fields, they observed the score of the field hockey game – something like 8-0 us at the time – and mentioned that it was par for the course when Westgate played us. They pointed out that this shouldn't be taken seriously however, since the varsity was playing at Griswold, owing to the great condition of the fields here, and that Westgate's varsity was actually having a winning season this year."

"But...Westgate has...nice fields...don't they?" Mary walked this thought out carefully.

"N-n-n-n-o-o-o-o..," Scott corrected her, "Westgate has *very* nice fields...and more of them than we do."

"S-o-o-o-o..." I had no idea where this was going.

"At the end of the tour, the guides take them back to Admissions, say that they're not part of the interview process, wish little Newhouse and his parents good luck and scram." Grins are on most faces at this point. "Their Head of School dumps this all on me over the phone. I'm like, 'So, you'd like me to do *what?*' She goes into this thing on how the family spent half the interview asking about us. She's fit to be tied." He turned to me. "Burnsy: did anybody sign out with you on Saturday?"

"I wasn't on duty, but...why?"

"Yeah, but…since it was boys, I just thought you might have…Sunday night, a student at Westgate didn't log off from her computer there, and someone read some message on her facebook page about some stunt at Admissions the day before by some of our kids."

The light finally came on. I let out a howl that made Mary jump in her chair. "Y-y-y-e-e-s-s-s…" Eyes came to me. "Saturday, as I was heading out, Dickens and one other kid, they were headed somewhere. They were in coats and ties…" I replayed the scene of the two well-dressed boys leaving campus for vague purposes when I went to Cambridge.

"That. Is," Remy was parsing his words with a methodical cadence, "The. Funniest. Thing. I've. Ever. Heard. It's brilliant. Sheer *brilliance!*" That it was. Clever. Subtle. Bloodless. I didn't think such gifts were still in this lot of students.

"So, what are you going to…" Mary curious.

"Do?" Scott turned his palms up, "I don't exactly know…*what* to do." Back at his desk, he sat forward, hands forming a cathedral. "What's the offense? They didn't steal the school flag or spray paint the mascot statue. Caroline what's-her name's knickers are in a twist, but…not sure how you'd file this one."

"It's not like Newhouses signed up for a tour here later that day, right?" I wondered.

"I wish, but no." Then Scott eyed me in that impersonal way that makes you forget you ever attended the same Christmas Party as him. "Why didn't you press them Saturday? If you saw these guys heading out…didn't it raise any flags for you? Two cocky seniors heading off campus in coats and ties on a Saturday?"

"You're right," I straightened up, sensing that this discussion was about to go south, but for all I know, maybe Barclay has told him I'm done in June, so what do I have to lose? "Two kids dressed nicely headed off campus Parents' Weekend. And I let them go. What was I thinking?" Scott didn't know what to say to that, and gave me an *unfortunately-I guess-you're-right nod.* I headed out, pleased with myself and knowing I was right, but wondering whether I'd heard the last of it. That Scott thought I should have acted upon…I don't know what, was ridiculous. Those kids pulled a darn clever stunt, and I'm supposed to explain why I didn't grill two guys because they were in blazers? I headed to my room and started typing.

2012-Present	**Griswold School** Lexington, Massachusetts
	History Dept. Chair & Teacher, Girls' Squash Coach & Dorm Parent

Filling in my duties, other jobs and degrees, I began to envision how great it will be to tell folks in the spring how I'm headed somewhere else.

October 16

I N WORLD CIV CLASS we're looking at who ruled the roost in Greece and why. Stumbling into the concept of an aristocracy, most students rejected the idea of it as a good way to run a society...

"That's kinda dumb," someone said, "letting someone rule just because his father did. Look at Bush."

"Yeah, but he got elected."

"No," one of our rad-fems in a Che t-shirt offered, "The Supreme Court put him there." The conscience of the junior class, she's an emphatic vegetarian who insists that none of her clothing comes from sweatshops. This line of discussion went on for a bit, until I lost interest in the direction and steered it towards other aspects of an aristocracy, such as attending certain schools.

"Like...here?" a few asked at once. I just shrugged.

"This place isn't like...I mean, some of the kids here...they aren't..." a ruddy soccer star had to choose his words carefully.

"Aren't what?" Ms. Che fixed her gaze.

"C'mon, you know." The soccer star almost bothered to look up as he spoke. "Everybody had to take the SSAT to get in, even if their dad went here." The SSAT is the high school equivalent of the SAT, the latter of which was created to foster a meritocracy instead of bloodlines at schools.

Ms. Che was all in now. "And they'll probably get into their dads' colleges too."

"Or their mom's colleges…and the dumb ones will join the all-blonde sororities there." Our soccer star even stopped doodling to make this point.

"Now that's sexist. Just because someone is…" Ms. Che was grasping for the right word, "not unbearably ugly by your ridiculous standards doesn't mean there's no brain upstairs, and that she shouldn't be here."

At the end of the table, a future trophy wife that some have taken to calling 'Illegally Blonde' was suddenly more engaged in things than she had been all term. "In fact---"

"So if your face doesn't look like the surface of the moon," another female jumped in, "and you have a sense of style, you're stupid, *right?*" All their heads swung to the soccer stud for his return.

"No, I'm not saying that…but, c'mon, you can't tell me that…."

In my own head, I started ticking off the names of those here who I'd bet wouldn't be here if they'd checked off the financial aid box on their applications or weren't legacies.

"So, following your logic," one girl tossed her head and tucked some golden locks behind an ear, "the kids who most deserve to be here are the goths, the punks and the hip hop - gang banger wannabes. The kids on aid with no family connection to the school, who are just…random…"

"N-n-n-n-o-o-o-o," Ms. Che was choosing her words as she went, "but look at those lacrosse jocks who got busted last year. And those sailing kids who got caught smoking. I mean, afterwards, they didn't even care. They *knew* they weren't gonna get bounced, or that daddy would get them in somewhere else if they did. And they were like, cookie cutter school catalog models. And I know for a *fact* that two of the kids were legacies here."

"Fine!" another slapped her notebook shut. "Forget families...who've given money to this place. Just take people who can pay now. You want Snoop Dog here on Parents' Weekend?"

"Why...Snoop? Because he's black?" Isaiah Franklin had that look: *you opened a door, now let's see you walk through it.* Headed for a nice intellectual cul de sac, we were.

A shabby-genteel maiden in a bob cut and Barnard sweatshirt leaned into the conversation. "My grandfather went to some school in the 1940s. He once told me that forty kids from his class got into Yale – and that Yale told his headmaster they could take four more, and that he, the *headmaster*, could *pick them*. Is that fair?"

"Bet he didn't pick any brothers," Isaiah was probably right.

"Probably didn't have any brothers there in those days, anyhow," someone added. The anecdotes went on. This cousin, that school. Eventually I pulled it all back to the Greeks and we looked at the city-states of the period we were covering before breaking. Nobody seemed happy with everything that was said, but since they did all the talking, I was fine with it.

Heading to lunch I saw Aaron Tang shuffling along, scrutinizing something.

"What's new?"

"Math. Test," he hissed, "not good." He showed me an 88 on an Algebra I test.

"That's a B+," I patted his shoulder, "That's not bad."

He stuffed it into a book under his arm and kept shuffling. With a half hour for lunch, I didn't have time to be a social worker, so just dove in.

"How did that fire start in your room?"

"The fire was on."

"The *bedroom* was *on fire*. Yes, why?"

"Not sure."

"Well, what do you think happened?"

"I already tell Meestah Paone." His English was coming along, slowly.

"Good, but I haven't seen him yet. And since we live on the same floor, can you tell me?"

"My door is not…I lose my key."

"S-s-s-s-o-o-o-o-o…what does---"

"I don't lock door. Never. I in gym when they tell me, fire. In my room."

"So, you're saying, you weren't even there."

He shook his head. "In gym."

"And…who knows you leave your room open?"

He shrugged. Half the kids don't lock their rooms, and then they're floored when money disappears from a desk drawer.

"So, Mr. Paone knows all this?" He nodded. "OK. Listen, don't sweat a B in Algebra. We'll get to the bottom of the fire thing."

"Bottom?"

"We'll find out…what happened. Don't sweat it just now."

"Don't sweat?"

"Don't sweat…don't worry." I mimed wiping a dripping brow.

"OK," he half smiled, and I headed for lunch.

The library can be a good place to shut out the world. Kids now can't sneeze without texting five friends and posting it on Facebook, but have never heard of the Dewey decimal system, so the place is usually a tomb during classes. Last period of the day I'm cloistered at the back in a wingchair with *Harper's* and Scott Paone finds me.

"Hi Burnsy."

"Scott..." I nodded.

"What's new?" Small talk. We're not quite beer pals these days, so I know something's on his mind. I avoid eye contact until he gets to it. This could be what is meant by 'passive aggressive,' but I was alone in the back for a reason.

"How's that lesson plan on Rome coming?"

"Rome? That's weeks away."

"Right, but remember we spoke last month about a book you were gonna use?"

"Sure. *Pompeii.*"

"Well..." It was fun to make him ask. "You were gonna get me the plan...for how you're gonna use it?"

"Right, but we're doing Greece now. Won't be cracking the book until...December maybe."

"OK, but I was hoping to let that parent---par*ents*, know..."

I wasn't going to help him out. So it *is* a parent, not two or six. Not that there couldn't be two nuts around who want another Monkey Trial or little Vonnegut-style BBQ with some of our texts. I felt a tad chagrinned making Scott's task a chore, but then recalled that he's one of those educators who jumped into Administration as soon as the chance came, and has notions of what should happen in an ideal classroom, which he probably never created himself, since he was measuring the windows in his office for drapes before they announced he had the job. I used to ask folks in his spots if they missed teaching, but found that most of them gave the same answer. 'Actually,' some like to start, affecting some sage look, gazing off into the distance, 'I think I do more teaching *now* than I did in the classroom.' How lucky for us all.

"Scott, what *is* it you want to let them know? That I'm not showing "Sophia Does Sicily" to the kids?"

He offered a polite acknowledgement of the levity, then peered over his glasses. "I did ask for it...a few *weeks* ago."

"Yes, you did. And since we haven't even gotten to Alexander's march to India, Rome is still months away, and I honestly haven't planned the exact lessons yet. I might just cherry pick chapters from it. Maybe only excerpts. Why do you need it now?"

"Mrs.," he caught himself, and started again. "The sooner I can give these squeaky wheels some grease, the less likely it is they'll go to Barclay."

"Barclay? Let them. Or let *her*. They deserve each other."

"Whoa," he sat back a bit, "What's that about? Look, nobody wants to...Simply...certain parts are..." he pinched his lips together, searching for the right word.

"Scott. It's like this. If there's a kid in that class, who has a friend who has a friend who downloads and shares hip hop, *any* hip hop, they're getting stuff a hundred times raunchier than they'd find in a two-sentence brothel scene in some relevant historical fiction."

"True," he nodded and raised an excepting finger, "but they're not paying tuition to have you err just this side of Lil Wayne or Nas. They expect better."

"And they *get* better, and it's not..." I looked away, and realized that as an administrator who didn't teach or coach, there was probably nowhere he absolutely had to be right then, and so he could go on and on like this. I told him I'd get him something by week's end.

Following a nice read spoiled, a run on the cross-country course seemed a good way to clear my head. The school course meanders around the campus and through the woods, and with the team at an away meet, would be pretty quiet. For all the tasks and little mushroom clouds that this place provides on a regular basis, running through its woods on a blue and yellow October afternoon makes it all tolerable. It's the petty pestilence from administrators who are detached from the classroom and dorms that had me thinking about another school even before the meeting with Barclay a while back. This crap is everywhere, but here, it seems like expecting support from the higher ups is like expecting Bill Clinton to pass up a strip club.

One of the cross-country course's distinctions is McKinley, the sarcastic moniker for a 150-meter incline at the two-mile point – our own version of Heartbreak Hill. Summiting it, so to speak, I came upon a sight: a small gaggle of the Goodwill-clad students in a circle on a little knoll just over the crest. Blumberg was there, in vintage rags and Rasta hair, flanked by four other waifs who, by their appearance, seemed to have the same tailor and hairdresser. Under the tilting birches, on a forest floor of foliage, they had cleared some ground and within the circle of dirt before them sat a small pile of leaves. All had sticks in their left hands, pointing to the center of the circle. My timing was not to their liking.

"Hi guys," I caught my breath," What's up?"

Five statues, surprised to the point of speechlessness. The NTWTs, living up to the pejorative morphing of their name, dropped their branches, and one by one they eyed Blumberg, imploring him by telepathy to be their spokesman.

"We're just..." his eyes darted about in a decaffeinated panic, "...into nature."

As he spoke, barely visible ribbons of smoke rose from the clump of leaves inside the circle.

"How was lunch?" Admittedly, I was toying.

"Lunch?"

"Looks like you've been cooking...correct?" Five deer caught in halogen headlights.

"Isn't there, like, an amendment," one of the garden variety deadheads began, "about, freedom of worship?"

Waving the constitution at a teacher of AP US History. Brilliant.

"Sure is," I nodded, "and the thirty-second amendment discusses willful destruction of nature." I could almost hear their sphincters tighten.

"We didn't kill it. It was already dead," one of the waifs turned his palms up in innocence. *Shit.* All I wanted was a quiet run in the woods, and I end up stumbling into some squirrel crematorium run by a pubescent witches coven. Might as well be on duty. So I marched them back to campus and to Scott's office, gave his secretary the Cliff Notes version of it and figured I can still get a loop in before dark. Reaching for the door to leave the Admin Building, it occurred to me that the dunking stool in Salem was probably a good idea whose time had just come again.

October 21

I T IS NEVER QUITE clear when summer *de facto* ends in New England. You can still get some nasty bee stings in October, but I spent a few Halloweens trick or treating over a dusting of snow in New Hampshire. Rowing offers something the thermometer does not. On the twisting ribbon of water that separates Cambridge and Boston, the Head of the Charles has been around since the 1960s, morphing from a chummy three-mile chase upstream among local oarsmen to a relatively dry *madi gras* of preps and world-class rowers on the third weekend in October. Once the domain of schools, colleges and boat clubs who would imbibe after their races with such WASPy decorum that the Cambridge police didn't care, the banks of the river between Boston University and the TV tower past The Stadium are now blanketed with and meandered by every person who's ever bought something in Freeport, Maine. The rowing, now over two days, is more serious than ever. Under crisp fall skies, the youth fours, veteran singles and national team eights round turns and thread arches, endeavoring to not turn their oars into fiberglass driftwood at the more perilous bridges. In spite of the explosion of rowing over the years, the crowd is still reliably well-scrubbed, in spandex or Princeton sweats, in search of former classmates or a hot pretzel at the next bridge. You can see the transitions within a few steps: high school rower, college oarsman, club man – Vesper, Riverside, NYAC - and eventually, parked on some Orvis blanket along the riverbank, in too-short khakis and weather-beaten cheeks, the flinty Brahmin cheering on offspring as they pass under the Weeks Foot Bridge. I've let my boat club membership lapse and settled for watching the race this year. I met up with Meeks by Cambridge Boat Club, which spawned and still manages the race. Our chatter was brief before he dug something out of a pocket.

"Might want to get in touch with this guy, about his boss," he handed me a slip of paper as we found a patch of grass on the Cambridge bank. "He went to Weld. Came back last week to talk to some classes. He's an aide to Kirk Mayhew. Big muckymuck at the Commerce Department, who I guess went to Griswold."

"Could be," I eyed the name and e-mail address, " I'm not up on the alumni stuff."

"Anyway, this guy told me this sort of on the QT: Mayhew's thinking about running for the senate. Wants to raise his profile back here, though. And would probably like returning to his old school for...whatever."

"So, have him back to..."

"Talk. He's at Commerce so, maybe to an economics class, or about public service. My school loves tapping the alumni vein whenever possible."

"Can't say I've heard of him."

"Nobody has. That's why he's said to be willing to start small. Griswold would probably treat him like a conquering prodigal son. I mean, jus' 'cuz you can't name the number three person in a cabinet level department doesn't mean he doesn't have...'something on the ball,' as my mother would say."

I nodded, eyeing the paper.

"Anyway. Call him. Or not."

"Thanks."

"My Head of School was tickled that his aide spoke to our econ sections. He's basically a glorified gopher for a bureaucrat, but a great name-dropper. Worth an e-mail. See if you can get his boss to come back to his old stomping grounds."

"Yeah...might be fun," I nodded.

"Brownie points anyway. Good to remind people of it come contract time next year."

"Y'know," I kept my gaze on the race going by, trying to seem casual, "come contract time, I'd like to bring up that I'm signing a letter somewhere else next year. Maybe they'd counter offer, but I doubt it. I need a change."

"Really?" David seemed surprised, pursing his lips out from his short red beard. "Gee, I figured, being a department chair and all, you'd stay put and wait for some dean to move on..."

"Me? Hell no. Who wants to be a dean? Sit in an office and meetings all day, and pull in teachers to scold them for not letting a kid re-write a paper..."

"Yeah, but at least you don't have to *read* all the papers. It can't be that bad at Griswold."

"It's not...bad...I just...I'm looking for better." I resisted looking at him, not wanting it to be too obvious that I was fishing.

"Hmmm..," he stroked under his chin and waved at some woman he seemed to know in Cornell shorts. "No place is perfect. Hell, I know two folks who left Taft last year and didn't even have jobs to go to. Just wanted out..."

"Sure, but I've been there four years, and..."

"Huh. Well, if you want to put me down as a reference for your rowing experience, happy to be one."

"Thanks," I turned to him. "I'll take you up on that."

"I'll keep my ears open, too," he offered. It was a start.

We watched the singles and crews go by and talked of our own races here. Sometime after four in the afternoon the Championship Eights came up river. National teams, college crews, and club boats with folks in them who can't let go of being twenty-one years-old and having an old Olympic team pullover in the closet. Like the sun, they disappeared to the west, beyond the Elliott Bridge and into the failing New England afternoon.

October 26

I'D FORGOTTEN THE CRUMB of info Dave Meek's slipped to me at the Head until a news item on the *Globe's* website mentioning the Commerce Department caught my eye, nudging me to fish out the crumpled reminder of a few days ago. I sent a message to the Weld alum whose name he wrote down, and got an email back the next morning. It began with a boilerplate recap of recent laurels of note at Commerce, as well as some news. "Secretary Watson's surgery makes it prudent for him to take a leave of absence while he addresses his health. With Undersecretary Boyce on leave to tend to personal matters, Kirk Mayhew has been named Acting Commerce Secretary by the President. Mr. Mayhew's experience and vision will no doubt serve him and the Department well in his new capacity for the foreseeable future."

A search revealed that Undersecretary Boyce was currently in negotiations with his counterparts at the Justice Department regarding images found on his laptop following a trip to Thailand last year. The aide at Commerce noted that Mayhew would in fact be in Boston next month for 'a major policy speech,' but would love to find time to visit his *alma mater* during the trip. I ran this past Scott Paone at the faculty table during dinner last night.

"Super! Outstanding! Let's make it happen!" What a go-for-it guy.

"Isn't that really," Allison Manville piped up without looking at me, "the domain of the Alumni Office?" It was hard to imagine her really caring about such distinctions. More likely, this verbal spitball was simply her noisome causerie of the day, available to anyone unlucky enough to find himself in her bitter orbit.

"If Burnsy has a rapport with this fellow's aide," Scott was very matter of fact without looking up from his plate, "I say let him run with it. When would this guy be coming?"

Suddenly questions about it began flying around the faculty table. *Who would he be speaking to? Are you looking at the whole school or just a few classes? I'm taking my oil and watercolor students to the MFA on Pearl Harbor Day; I hope it's not the 7th...* Amid the flurry of priorities which started bouncing around the circle, the notion that no good deed goes unpunished came to mind, and it occurred to me that for all her grumpy bonhomie, Allison may have stumbled on something. I slid it over to the Alumni Office the next morning. Even a stopped clock is right twice a day.

November 3

THERE'LL ALWAYS BE TEACHERS who make bad decisions - showing R rated films to fifth graders or taking too few chaperones on field trip, but at independent schools, teachers are vetted like nowhere else. After a phone interview, if you make the cut for the next step, you're invited to campus to meet a bunch of key people at the school and teach a sample lesson to a class – which is observed by a department chair, a few deans and anyone else who's free at the time. After all that, if there's a decision to extend an offer, it's along the lines of, *You'd teach three sections of Algebra II, two of pre-Calc, be a dorm parent, coach swimming and baseball, and find an activity you can run – the school paper, yearbook or the gay-straight alliance.* If references check out, you receive your 'letter,' detailing these tasks with a salary. If you have a good year, you'll receive another one in the spring, an offer to stay on. In public schools, with union contracts, unless you slap a kid or have a child with one, you can pretty much stay there for life. At private schools, they can just decide to not extend an offer, and cook up some reason for it. Sometimes, for financial reasons, the goal is to really just hire a 22-year old college grad and park him or her in a studio apartment, shedding the more expensive faculty who need three bedrooms and health insurance for a family of four. By and large, if someone gets hired by virtue of having run this gauntlet, it says that his judgment and professionalism are trusted. By and large. All of this was turning over in my head when I dropped by Scott's office yesterday with my *Pompeii* lesson, doing so at the end of the day so I could use a pre-season squash meeting as a reason I couldn't linger.

"The idea of the book is to give the kids a good sense of the period with some sound, historical fiction," I offered this as I handed a hardcover copy with a lesson outline in it across his desk. "and to color in the picture with the reality that in the first century AD, things started to go downhill in the empire.

Scott raised an eyebrow.

"The Roman one."

" 'Course." Scott thumbed some post-it marked pages as he tilted back in his chair, pursing his lips like an editor scanning galleys.

"Where's the passage that...has probably prompted...all this?"

"Post-it number twelve."

His eyes moved over the satanic verse, which discussed the search for an aqueduct official in 79 A.D. Pompeii, a search which led to a brothel where a patron is channeling a Jesuit priest from Boston two millennia in the future with the assistance of a young boy.

"Kind of... R rated," he huffed.

"Not to kids today. Not if they have cable or listen to rap. Which is to say, to all of them."

"But parents don't---"

"Yeah, I know. They don't send their kids here...yaddah yaddah...but it's two sentences in the whole book. And here's the usefulness of it: the empire is huge – edge of Scotland to Africa. Nine A.D. Roman legions get spanked in Germany. Back home, some rather sketchy characters rise to the top. Caligula for one.

Makes his horse a senator. Then there's Nero. Kills his mother to solidify his power. And *sang* mind you, didn't *fiddle* during the fire. Blames it on the Christians. We hearken back to Socrates in our study of Greece, recalling how all failing societies love a scapegoat." If Scott was going to quash things, he was at least going to learn something in the process. "By 79 A.D., some of the aqueducts around Pompeii start failing, and just for good measure, Vesuvius blows. We cover all that, and the book has a nice narrative of it all. Does that one passage suggest decadence? Yes. Was Rome becoming decadent? Absolutely. Fat, dumb and happy with itself. I want them to see that we can learn from history via literature, not just textbooks and some cable channel."

He was nodding, but still hard to read. His white pinpoint had a perfect roll in its collar that flanked his budding second chin. After a moment, he sat up and slapped the book closed.

"Y'sold me Peter. I think it works. It fits."

"Oh," I was expecting more of a fight. "well...good."

He nodded slowly, looking at the cover.

"I rather wish I hadn't needed to make this case though..." I cocked my head a bit, "like I'm some purveyor of porn."

"I do too, frankly," he stood up, "but we serve many masters here. Give some of the squeaky wheels some grease, and they'll be quiet. Play it out like you laid it out. "

"So...we good?"

"Yeah...we're good. I got your back." He shook my hand like I'd earned something even more than his trust. I suddenly had time for a run before the squash meeting. I took to the cross-country trail with a bit of a kick, still somewhat pissed that I had to prove anything to him, but happy with the outcome. Since becoming a dean, his mom has taken to oil painting with the help of a wealthy muse – new life-mate in Rockport on the north shore, and he's moved into the house in which he grew up in Lexington. Early forties and he still lives at home. No coaching responsibilities and doesn't come to games or plays either. A most dangerous place to be at four in the afternoon is between him and his car – which still has a college sticker on it.

Running the cross-country course, I reached the crest of a hill and came upon a scene right out of the start of *Law & Order SVU*. Curled up at the base of a white birch on a bed of leaves was Faisal Aboody. The green cargoes and yellow fleece he lives in left no doubt.

"Faisal? Faisal?" Nothing. *"Faisal?!?"* I kicked his foot and he jumped, prompting me to jump. His *where am I* look soon focused on the leaves where his head had been, whence he retrieved a Smartphone. He started checking the screen intently. Until I let loose.

"What the hell are you doing here? Trying to get hypothermia?"

"N-n-n-o-o-o Mr. Burnham. I was…I fell asleep."

"Why the devil are you doing it out here?"

"No sports today, so I---"

"I *know* there aren't sports today, *thank you*. But why are you here? It'll be dark in an hour, and it's thirty-eight degrees."

He tossed his head about, as lost as he could be, and babbled something about it being the quietest point on campus, and private. I could feel my calves tighten, and realized that I was probably more pissed at having my run interrupted than I was at him dozing *a la* Thoreau.

"So, why Faisal, are you sleeping here?" Recalling his dad's entrance Parents' Weekend, I figured he'd already learned how to sleep on a helicopter. For a fleeting second, it occurred to me that his father could probably buy Temperpedic beds for the whole school and not notice the dent in his checking account. "I know you're not drowning in homework. Don't you sleep at night?"

He shook his head.

"Why not?"

"My friends. In Kuwait, they are awake then. It is the only time I can speak with them."

"What time is that?"

"Two or three o'clock our time."

"What? They call you *then?*"

"Yes. I set my alarm. On my phone."

"You set an alarm every night to wake up and talk to your friends?"

He nodded.

"What about e-mail? Can't you do it that way?" This was logic - always a curve ball to teenagers. He shrugged.

"Faisal, you can't give up sleep to talk to your friends. It's not...healthy."

He wasn't contrary, just matter of fact and still half asleep. I told him I'd be back to campus in twenty minutes and that I expected to see him in his room when I got there. He nodded and lumbered back the way I came. I headed on, trying to run off some leg cramps.

"And you did nothing about it?" Mary Carpenter was incredulous at the brevity of my chat with Faisal, which I recounted at dinner that night. "Recalling his father's grand entrance Parents' Weekend, seems maybe...a bit more attention would be---"

"Hey," Schy jumped in, hands in the air, "What would you suggest? Opening doors at two in the morning to see if there are flashlights on under the covers?"

"So we...do nothing?" Mary hadn't expected such a tone.

"We? *We?*" Schy was itching for a bit of a tangle. "Remind me which dorm you live in."

Mary sat up straight and stabbed at her carrots. When phrased as an interrogative, English teachers call such a construction a rhetorical question. She lives in a five-bedroom Tudor in Belmont with her husband, two sons, a Border Collie and a photo of her meeting Toni Morrison.

"Look," I wanted to lower blood pressures around the table, "if we wanted to, we could probably go from door to door with glasses to our ears each night in the wee hours. Nothing good happens after midnight, right? But something does. Me sleeping. I'm not about to play hotel detective and be bleary-eyed all day just so Johnny will roll over and go to sleep." Reason can be a real discussion killer. After a minute, Mary spoke without looking up from her plate.

"So how do...how can the students be---"

"Stopped? They can't." Schy was down a few decibels from a minute ago. "They drag their groggy little heads to class and doze through it – or oversleep altogether. They miss review sessions, bomb tests, and figure it out for themselves. A few warnings at report card time. That'll do more than me playing midnight rambler up and down the halls."

"If Faisal flunks out," Mary cocked her head in a slightly smug way, "how will that building or whatever get built?"

"Good point," Schy nodded. "Guess we'd better get used to the classroom space we have for a while. Or...Barclay could check on him. Nightly." He rose with his tray and was gone. He does know how to make an exit.

November 13

WHETHER HE'S HOMESICK HERE or something else, our favorite Kuwaiti national remains a real cipher. He's seemed a bit morose since his father choppered away on the Sunday of Parents' Weekend, and more so since I interrupted his slumber in the woods. There's a sense that certain aspects of school life are quite foreign to him, such as clearing his place at meals and having to wait to use a shower. A bit of a loner, he never tries to catch up with a pack ahead of him *en route* somewhere. The *News* link on the school's website is chock full of photos from Parent's Weekend, and those of Faisal's father stepping out of his copter and beaming at a reception afterwards are featured a tad more prominently than others. At lunch today, Scott cornered me just as I was set to leave. We sat in a corner of the emptying dining hall.

"How does Faisal...seem Peter? In the dorm?" Scott was making a steeple with his hands while looking down, as if his wheels were already turning. I offered the best thumbnail sketch I could, but he seemed pretty grim after my account of his cat nap in the forest.

"Any...visitors that he has, on weekends? Anybody sign him out?" Scott was now working a spot of food on his tie. "Any contact at all with...anyone not from here?"

"Not that I've seen," I shook my head. "Keeps to himself, and hasn't asked for permission to sign off campus while I've been on. Why?"

Scott shot glances to his right out the window, as if searching for a cue telepathically to clue me on whatever he was turning over in his head. After a minute, he leaned in.

"Following his visit here Parents' Weekend, Faisal's father received...a disturbing message. Someone, according to the text of it, objects to Faisal attending Griswold. Or any school in the west, basically. 'Swimming in the pool of the infidels, embracing the enemies of Islam,' that kind of stuff. Could be a homegrown issue. Dissent, fundamentalists...that part of the world can be a real onion."

"So, how does this impact...us?" My palms were turned skyward. Never covered this in Ed School.

"Keep a sharpened eye on Faisal, in terms of who he communicates with, leaves campus with, that kind of stuff." Scott was ticking off items as he uncurled his fingers. "Check the dorm log, maybe even have a look at what sites he's on in the computer room when you're on duty."

"So, are...we, they...looking for someone here? In Kuwait? How do we know---"

"We don't," Scott shrugged a bit and rolled his eyes in resignation. "For now, we're just trying to see what we can see from this end. And letting the appropriate authorities know if anything...emerges here. We're putting a security guard a hundred feet up from the school gate in case any unwelcome vehicles appear. Between that and Faisal having a pretty tight schedule here, we ought to be set, and don't need to fret about..."

"About?" I wondered aloud.

"Well, we obviously want to make sure that Faisal is safe here…"

"Kidnapping?" I was louder than I intended. "Are we looking at…*that* maybe happening?"

"We're not looking at…" he was fingering his coffee mug, eyeing it as if the right word lay at the bottom of it, "anything in particular, but we're being cautious. Anyone who turns up here who isn't a visiting parent, a ref for a game, a family expected at Admissions or dining hall delivery, they don't come in. We've got campus safety posted at the gate with two-way radios if anyone…forces the issue. Just…have your antennae up for…anything out of the ordinary." Scott was shooting me a super-serious, DEFCON 3 look. "Better to err on the side of caution."

"Wait a minute. Is this a…a…security threa—"

"No," he was emphatic while endeavoring to seem calm. "*we*… we're just in the loop, with his father's security people, and he's in your dorm, so, now you're in the loop too. We're buttonholing a few others here. On the QT. Don't want to start…any unnecessary concern. Any questions Peter?"

I shook my head slightly without breaking a glare at him. He seemed to be fishing for more of a buy-in from me on all this, and I couldn't help but wonder if Barclay had told him of my uncertain status here. This is not to say that I'm indifferent to Faisal's safety here, but if any of this makes Barclay's job harder, more of that.

November 22

VACATION SIGN OUTS ALWAYS have a bit of don't ask – don't tell aspect about them. A few campus shuttles take students to Logan and South Station, some kids go home with roommates, but some, mostly internationals, sign out in small groups to local hotels. If they're eighteen or over with ID, the places are happy to swipe their folks' credit cards, but nobody thinks that they sit around for days playing Trivial Pursuit, watching The History Channel and drinking Snapple. Last year a student took an obsequious entourage to his home in Grosse Pointe for the Thanksgiving Day football game in Detroit; dad chartered a plane, so that they thankfully wouldn't have to fly first class with the dreaded public. The other day as the students were set to leave, I parked myself in the Wentworth lounge for the afternoon of departures for sign outs, and Faisal came by with Toby Weeks who was going to introduce him to White Plains and turkey with stuffing.

"Any holiday like Thanksgiving in Kuwait?" I chatted him up a bit at my door.

"Our holidays are not as this one." Faisal's initially sculpted black mop was now a bit unruly over his dark face, his big brown eyes offering no more expression than a passport photo.

"You'll like it," Toby was fingering his Smartphone, "My uncle finished restoring an old bi-plane. Gonna take us for rides after dinner."

"Wow," I hoped my envy would spawn excitement in Faisal. "Any…other plans?"

"Probably go into the city. You been there Faisal?"

"What...city?"

"*The* city. New York." Toby offered that Gotham-centric *as-if-any-other-place-deserves-to-be-called-a-city* indignation one finds in teenagers.

"Yes. Several times. I was taken to a store for clothing for here."

"Yeah, one or two stores there," I noted their contact info, which was Toby's folks. "Have fun boys."

The upscale cars, taxis and chartered buses wound down to the school gate and disappeared, leaving in their wake that heavy silence that settles like an invisible fog on a campus once the reasons we are here have departed. Ahead lies a seven-day teenager-free zone.

November 30

A T THE END OF Thanksgiving break, a distant knocking woke me way too early on the Sunday morning the kids were due to return. No reasonable person would be calling at such an hour, so I rolled over. Then the person's persistence sent me flying towards the door spitting profanity under my breath.

"Mr. Burnham?" A fiftyish Asian fellow in a glen plaid blazer, white button down, pressed grey flannels and the shiniest black shoes I've ever seen was looking at me hopefully. "I am Dr. Ji Jeong Tang. Aaron's father." He nodded slightly, as much of a bow as a westerner gets. "I am sorry to be unannounced. Have I disturbed you?" Perhaps the Nick Nolte mug shot look gave me away. I mumbled something about not getting dressed better just to grade papers and invited him in.

The small talk while I made coffee was useful. Dr. Tang's father was at the UN in the 1960s and thought Eaglebrook in western Massachusetts was a good place for his son – as did Jordan's King Hussein for his son. After Northfield Mount Hermon School, Dartmouth College and NYU Medical, my guest settled in Seoul and became one of Korea's foremost authorities on skin cancer. In spite of this laurel, he tried to affect comfort sitting on a steamer trunk in my living room. I chose a mug with VE RI TAS on it. Parents in East Asia will set themselves on fire if they think that doing so will get their kids into an ivy.

"So, you see," he looked up and smiled with some humility after spinning his bio, "I know what a good education can do for someone. Aaron is shy, and perhaps has fewer friends than others...here. He is content with this he says. But..." He looked away a bit, as if shamed by his son's persona. "I understand that after the...incident in his room, you were very kind to him."

"Incident??

"The...fire,"

"Right. 'Course. No problem. It would shake anyone up. It was nothing, really. I felt bad about his clothes getting smoke damaged." Enough people confirmed that he was indeed elsewhere when it started, so while it wasn't solved yet, he was in the clear, and Wentworth boys had taken to locking their doors again. I brought him a pizza once the smoke damage crews were done, and put in a word on his behalf with Scott.

"He liked the pizza," Dr. Tang smiled, "and you played chess with him afterwards. I wish I had been here to do this." He uncrossed his legs, suggesting he was getting to the heart of the matter. "My position in Korea keeps me very busy. I'm afraid that I don't have...the time to...be with Aaron that I would like to have." I nodded. "I was hoping that this chess experience could, perhaps become a regular...occurrence, with you."

"Well, I'm always game for some chess. If he sees me and we're both free, I'd be happy to have at it with him."

"I was hoping for something more...scheduled." He was agonizing over his words. Like folks I met while traveling in Japan, he was endeavoring to get a point across without saying it too directly. "Perhaps, once a week?"

"Well, frankly, it would be best if he found someone in the dorm to play with. That could help a lot on that front. Building a circle of friends and all..."

"Yes, but he finds you a good...person. And I happen to agree with his judgment."

"Well, I'm flattered, doctor. Really. He's got the makings of a fine young---"

"You see, his mother and I are...not together. And he has not...responded...well, to this situation." The chess set on my coffee table was in plain sight, and still on my first cup of coffee, my grey cells couldn't come up with another valid reason to say 'no.'

"I know you are busy, and I value your time, so I would like to pay you. Would say, $100 a week be satisfactory? For chess and...discussion? The latter would be good for his English, of course."

Being flattered was edged aside by being materialistic. For the first time in three years, I'm hoping to spend the summer working on my skin cancer while sailing and studying the effects of alcohol on the human body instead of teaching summer school. If I make a change school-wise, this little stipend would help pay for the movers as well, but it honestly seemed somehow...unethical to be paid for so basic a task as chess and conversation. I told him as much and he raised a cautionary finger.

"Aren't there teachers who tutor...for extra...income? That is not unethical, would you agree?"

An hour and another cup of coffee later, I could probably have come up with a valid rebuttal to this, but I was not firing on all eight just yet. It also occurred to me that the good doctor had probably thought this through a bit ahead of time, and that his thinking at any hour of the day was probably better than mine. An adage from my side trip to Seoul while in Japan also filtered through my brain: in East Asian societies, *many items and acts are not considered to have value unless they are paid for.* The doctor could see he had won.

"Aaron must not be aware of this *arrangement*, however. Please." Fine. If his son will benefit from chatting and capturing my bishop every Saturday, there's no need for him to know that it was his father's idea, and certainly not that there's a financial dimension to it.

December 6

EVERYTHING IS RELATIVE, SO in hindsight, school life prior to Thanksgiving seems nicely unremarkable, especially now. In that sliver of time between classes and sports today, Scott appeared at my door.

"Peter, got a few gentlemen here like to talk about Toby Weeks' Thanksgiving trip. Did you sign him out?" I nodded and eyed the four humorless men flanking him, two in identical charcoal suits, white shirts and slightly different foulard ties. The twins had olive skin and offered pleasant but business-like smiles. The other two seemed like cops in a buddy film: one lean, one stocky, off the rack suits, poly ties and earpieces. I told everyone that as afternoon practices were at hand, Toby probably wouldn't be in his room. They'd already been to his room and knew this. Scott asked again about his Thanksgiving departure.

"Yeah...he went home, as I recall," I offered. "Might be able to find him at practice. He ---"

"Faisal went with him, right?" Scott asked, "Did he check out with you or someone else?"

"He...checked out with me. Same time. Went home with Toby. Amtrak to Stamford, usually. They came back together too.

Faisal said it was the first time he'd had turkey. Took a cab from South Station Sunday – Faisal paid - because they mis---"

"So..." Scott turned to the four other men, all of whom looked like they'd been sent by Pall Bearers 'R Us. "Let's step inside, okay?"

At my kitchen table, one of the off-the-rack guys laid it out.

"These gentlemen," Off The Rack #1 gestured to the olive-skinned foulard twins, "are with...the Kuwaiti equivalent of the Secret Service. We're with the Department of Homeland Security. Seems that a threat was received in Kuwait City recently that referenced Faisal Aboody being here at Griswold. Seems that a person or party, as yet unknown, objects to the young man attending the school, and---"

"Excuse me," one of the olive-skinned, foulard twins raised a palm, "I do not mean to interrupt, but I do not understand this use of your word 'seems,' but does it question the facts? I assure you, our government has received this information. If you doubt that---"

"Just an expression. Sorry," OTR #1 waved off concern. "We understand the facts as they've been explained to us."

"E-e-e-e-h-h-h good." Foulard Twin #1 sat up a little straighter. "And to clarify: the communiqué expressed displeasure with Mr. Aboody attending *any* school in the US. In the west. It is not only here."

"This ought to ring a bell with you, Peter." Scott turned to the suits. "As the dorm parent, Mr. Burnham was made aware of this matter when the school was. In a general sense."

"I gather...there's..." Rather new territory for me, so I trailed off.

"My government has received a specific communication about this matter. It was very clear about Mr. Aboody's attendance here. Yes, his schooling at any place in the west was also said to be unacceptable. But the specifics of this communication are cause for great concern."

"We..." OTR #2 was pulling up an image on his phone, "have a copy of it, which---" At this OTR #1 casually shot him an ambiguous look, prompting OTR #2 to tuck his phone back into his breast pocket and relay the essence of matter rather than show it to me. "The...concerned parties reiterated dissatisfaction with the young man's going here, but also conveyed an awareness of his movements. This...raises the level of the threat."

"Threat?" I asked. The use of this word changed everything.

"Apparently," Scott broke in, "they're demanding---"

"Sir," OTR #1 cut Scott off with a raised palm and definite look, "if you'll allow us to share what is essential, we'd appreciate it. We know our job, thank you." He turned to me with a stoic glare of aplomb. "It would appear that Mr. Aboody's movements are known to those who are expressing this demand to his father's office. The latest communiqué they received referenced his travels in New York City over the Thanksgiving break. We understand that he was in the company of a Toby Weeks during that period."

"Right." I nodded, "He went home with Toby. Lots of international kids do that over breaks, 'specially short ones. They signed out together."

"Right. Did you notice anyone else about as they departed. Anyone who, didn't look like he belonged here? Anyone you hadn't seen before?"

"They were...alone. It was...the Tuesday before the holiday. The dorm was pretty much empty by then. Late afternoon."

"Please try to remember sir." One of the foulard twins had a wounded look of concern in his eyes.

"Really. It was just them. And they got the shuttle to South Station. Amtrak. I...assume."

"As*sume*?" Foulard #2 hinted at disbelief. "So you didn't actually *see* them board."

"No, but..."

"We can check the shuttle list." Scott dared.

"We'll do that," OTR #1 winced, then unpeeled the onion a bit more. "Mr. Burnham, there's an aspect to this matter that enhances our...joint concern." "Whoever is taking issue with the Aboody's decision to educate their son here has stated that the young man should be withdrawn from school over the holiday break. Or else."

"Or else...*what?*" I wondered aloud.

"Not sure. 'Cept that there's a suggestion that...'unhappiness will visit his family.'"

We all sat silently for a few seconds, chewing on the phrase without looking at each other.

"Maybe Toby Weeks saw someone." OTR #2 raised his eyebrows hopefully. "He's not...in trouble, but you can appreciate how him being with the young man is of interest to us."

"I think I know where he'll be," Scott offered. "The gym is not far from---"

"We hope you appreciate the gravity of the matter," OTR #1 glared passively, "and that it is...delicate. Not a topic for lunch table chatter. But if you notice anything, or remember anything..." He handed his card across the table, then pulled it back to circle the .gov email address on it. "Don't be shy."

"Mr. Burnham," one of the foulard twins cocked his head for emphasis, "Minister Aboody and the family are...distressed on this matter, as you can expect. We are hopeful that there can be help." My assurances to everyone were getting to the point of repetition when Scott offered to take them to the gym in search of Toby. Manly handshakes all around. *Jesus.* One minute I'm planning the afternoon's squash practice and next I've got

Homeland Security and some prince's bodyguards in my kitchen. Where's Jack Bauer when you need him?

December 8

THIS MORNING I RECEIVED an email to drop by the Alumni Office - the Undersecretary of Commerce for Intellectual Property, ne' Acting Secretary of Commerce was coming. Kermit Coffin Mayhew is an endangered species: the New England patrician who has opted for public service. His family goes back to some of the earliest Europeans on Nantucket in the 1600s, some of whom parlayed whaling profits into Boston real estate while folks in the Adams clan did other things with their time. Swamp Yankees – WASPs who settled more than fifty miles from Boston in colonial America - made good. After Griswold, Williams and Yale Law, Kirk, as he preferred, passed on the eastern, old-line firms to instead help the nation of Bhutan reform its justice system with the Peace Corps. Later he became an advocate for the environment and consumer matters, making his name with a huge class action case against the maker of a faulty infant car seat. An old alumni quarterly had him on the cover afterwards: toothpaste ad smile, great hair, eyes suggesting that he was always up for a game of touch at Hyannis Port.

"Mmmmm," an intern in the Alumni Office eyed the photo while I lingered at her desk.

"Down girl," her boss didn't bother to look up. "He's married."

"Natch," she sighed. "or gay."

"What's the game plan for...." I didn't even know when he was coming.

"A week from Friday," the intern began, "we figure he'll meet with Barclay, then go to an Econ class, the school assembly, then your Politics & Gov class. Lunch with some faculty – you, for instance. Then some Q & A with a selection of faculty and AP Gov students."

"When is the Assembly?"

"D block."

"Really?" I raised an eyebrow, which said it all.

"Problem?"

"Allison won't like that." Ms. Manville's inflexibility with all things that impact her classes in the slightest is legend. Anything which disrupts her schedule – which includes a D block class – is taken as a personal affront. "This'll put her in a foul mood," I cautioned.

"How'll we tell?" Pretty clever for an intern, but I waved a 'now, now' finger at her.

"Will this all be---"

"Y-e-e-e-s-s, Peter," a hint of exasperation was evident in her tone, "you'll get an e-mail. Don't you always with our events?"

"Yes, but what I'm wondering is, will *everyone*, kids included get it, or just us?" She gave me a constipated face, suggesting no clue as to my point. "It just might be nice if...he didn't get cornered by some gaggle of crunchies who want go all *occupy* on him.".."

"What...I don't---"

"Remember when that coffee big wig spoke here, and some kids got all twisted and rude about Fortune 500 corporation wages in Bolivia?"

113

"Vaguely...weren't they pretty much anti-everything?"

"Trade-wise, yeah," I shook my head. "Said it wasn't free trade if slave wages are being paid. Democrats Against Foul Trade, or something, they called themselves."

"That's right," she nodded, "I remember thinking it was weird; some bright kids in the group..."

"How bright are kids who come up with the acronym D.A.F.T?" The intern's boss chuckled. "Bit of unintended symmetry in it, don't you think?"

"Bit of stupidity is more like it."

December 9

GIRLS' SQUASH IS UNDERWAY. We share the courts with the boys who Schy coaches. He's got a few phenoms this year – a kid from Philly and two brothers from Pakistan. Squash is one of those diversions that breeds in those who are good at it an air of *us-ness* as opposed to everyone else, especially on the court. Kids stick with it for life, and the more competitive ones like to affect a manic intenseness as they play *in the zone*. College rosters are full of kids from New England schools, Philly and the Asian subcontinent. By senior year, some boys get very McEnroe about things, seeming to not be aware of supporters on the other side of the court's glass, on which they wipe their sweaty palms, rather than on some cloth nearby. I have yet to regret my switch to coaching the girls since Schy expressed a preference for the boys' team.

"Mr. Burnham, when are we gonna pick captains?" one of the girls asked during a break from practicing serves.

"Early next week."

"Why? Why not...today?" she insisted. Some of our kids haven't been told "no" or "not now" too often.

"I've got a whole practice in mind. It'll keep, won't it?"

"But our first match is next week." Give her this – she can read a calendar. She didn't like my verdict, so huffed and sighed, then resumed slapping a ball against the far wall. Schy sauntered over from the boys' courts in a 2003 Bear Stearns Tournament shirt. His gait was unhurried, and he eyed my girls practicing as if contemplating a mixed match.

"Plans for the weekend?" he asked while watching them.

"I'm on duty."

"Too bad," he snapped his fingers and bounced a racquet off a knee. "Buddy of mine got this condo at Sunday River. New snow yesterday. Got a deal on lift tickets..."

"You wanna cover my duty, I'd love to go." I shrugged.

"Couldn't you swap with someone?"

"Maybe could have Monday, but *now?* Doubt it"

"Pity."

"Yeah, well, Penn Squash is at Harvard for a match Saturday, so one of my activities is to take a van of kids to see the match. Kids like...these." I nodded to my girls.

"Penn huh?" He rubbed the racquet under his chin. "I'd like see that, but..."

"I've seen Penn's women's uniforms," I smirked, "you *would* like to see that." At a tournament hosted by Trinity last year, the consensus was that they'd been designed by Victoria's Secret and deemed too racy for the remake of "Baywatch."

"Well...Sunday River still sounds like more fun," he turned on his heels and waved his racquet. "Let me know for sure at dinner...prime rib tonight." That reminder alone nudged me to the dining hall after showers. The best diet around academy-wise, namely fare that will keep you from wanting to eat too much of it, is at a school north of here that is so renowned it can afford to have awful food, which it does; there's a reason beyond genetics that certain famous alums from there are rather lean fellows. Conversely, for all its splendor by a huge lake, a certain school in

New Hampshire is basically a hockey factory for kids who read below grade level, but it has great meals, at least when we eat there after a game or match. The popular notion of boarding schools as they are often portrayed is like Brigadoon; so idyllic that it doesn't actually exist.

December 11

A S IF WILLED TO do so by the Alumni Office, the morning of Kirk Mayhew's visit broke clear and crisp. Two inches of snow had blanketed the school overnight, the covering being quite preferable to the un-raked leaves that remained underneath. The dining hall was a bit tidier than usual with the servers wearing boy scout-like kerchiefs in school colors. Someone actually found some bunting for the entrance to the chapel. A memo had gone out suggesting that folks give a bit of thought to their dress for the day. Such pleas must be offered carefully, so as not to suggest that people ever look anything but professional. A crunchy member of the math department is one of the unspoken names in mind with this reminder. His overalls and gray ponytail would prompt anyone who encountered him at the school gate to think that the campus was the setting for a re-make of "The Grapes of Wrath."

"Look," Remy once offered after his third beer one Friday, referring to the crunchy math guy, "it's great that he knows the 47th problem of Euclid and all that, but does he have to look like a farmhand moonlighting at the town dump *every freaking day of the week?*"

Mary Carpenter was in her perpetual Katherine Hepburn weekend garb. Our bohemian folks were another matter. In addition to Allison & friend, there's a lacrosse coach who teaches English, as opposed to a teacher who also coaches, and if you saw him on campus, you'd probably mention to him that the dumpster behind the dining hall needed emptying. A few years ago, after several 0-12 lacrosse seasons, it was decided that the reality of his coaching skills eclipsing his teaching ability wasn't a reason to not hire him at the time. Three hundred pounds if he's an once and covered with tatts, he seems best suited to sit atop a zamboni. Chatter was that someone put a necktie in his mailbox before the Mayhew visit.

After breakfast Liz was already darting around campus, clipboard and cell phone in hand, helping everything to fall into place. Her determined gait had an extra purpose in it as she plowed through last-minute worries, scowling at the few unshoveled walks that B & G hadn't yet reached. Liz has that perpetual tennis partner appearance. She probably looked the same at twenty-five and will not appear much different at fifty. Her evenings working with Barclay have inevitably sparked gossip, mostly with those who have the time for it and secretly resent her put-together carriage. Truth be told she does turn heads, but not by being a knock out, simply by not being dowdy and lumpy, which is enough to set her apart from most females on campus. Wrap around tartans and frosted lipstick aren't sexy – unless most of the other women at school look like they're headed for a yard sale in Maine. This would not, however, include Kat McPhee. The mildly-perky, spoken-for first year has smitten a number of her male students with her well-scrubbed cheeks and friend-of-your-older-sister manner. There's a lifeguard stand in Chatham next summer with her name on it. Allison Manville hates her.

At 9:15 the carillon bell called the campus to the chapel. The schedule had been tweaked after an endless e-mail loop of bitching withered the Alumni Office into submission. Faculty sat on the left side of the dais with administration and staff to the right flanking a podium with the school crest. The first dozen or so rows of pews were seniors. Peering out from behind the organ pipes, Liz caught my eye and waved me back there.

If he hadn't, Kirk Mayhew should have rowed in college. In a navy suit and perfectly dimpled power tie, he was what my aunt would call *strapping*. Although the center of attention, his anchorman face betrayed a sense of ease with the bustle about him. A few girls from Devine who were his campus chaperones genuinely seemed to be ogling him in spite of the age difference. I got the *damn-glad-to-meet-you* grip from him which would no doubt be offered a thousand times at rope lines in the near future if his political ambitions play out.

"Liz tells me we have a favorite place in common." His eyes were friendly, with that official, slightly detached gaze that public people cast to the unknown individual. I drew a blank until he pointed to my Nantucket tie.

"Oh – 'course."

"Where are you?" he asked.

"Monomoy."

"Nice there. We're over at Tom Nevers. Don't get there as much as I'd like..."

"Who does?"

"Well, with summers off, do you get down much after school?"

"Well, I usually teach summer school or---"

"*That's great.* Griswold is *lucky* to have you. Will I see you at lunch?"

Liz jumped in to say that the schedule might allow some downtime later, but that we could talk about this afterwards, so I slipped back out into a faculty pew. Perhaps it's natural to assume that teachers spend the ten weeks before Labor Day in hammocks or under umbrellas. An unabashedly lazy art instructor once told a dinner guest of mine that the three reasons he became a teacher were June, July and August. Such folks don't do the craft any favors.

Taking to the lectern, Barclay quieted the assembly. At times such as this, with the whole school seated as orderly as Roman phalanxes and class banners dating back to the 1880s overhead, it felt good to be part of Griswold. Barclay called for student and faculty announcements.

> *Amnesty International will meet in the library at 5:30.*
> *Key Club will not meet this week. Check e-mail.*
> *A laptop left in Emory's lounge last night has disappeared.*
> *Could whoever mistook it for his or hers please return it?*
> *Boys' squash will be dismissed early for their match at*
> *Belmont Hill.*
> *The bookstore is closing at 3 PM today.*

This last point was met with spontaneous applause, the rapier-tongued matron of it being the scourge of loitering students and civil people in general. Barclay then introduced our guest, reciting his record while a student here and beyond, noting his current duties, which include crafting US trade policy, and citing a *BusinessWeek* article that called him one of the "Fifty Beltway People to Watch Next Year."

"It's worth noting that his *gravitas* has even inspired the loyal opposition to express itself," and he gestured to a D.A.F.T. poster being waved by a few students down front stage right. Sadly their unkempt appearance was not obscured by their placards denouncing *foul* not free trade, NAFTA, globalization, and generally anyone who doesn't ride a bicycle to work and smoke hemp. They raised and rattled their signs in acknowledgment. For people so miserable over the state of

121

affairs, they seemed downright giddy. "Enough of me," self-deprecation does not suit Barclay, "May I present the next...fill in the blank: Kirk Mayhew, Griswold class of 1989."

The place erupted in applause, more so than the polite response one would expect for a bureaucrat. Tamping down the approval, he beamed and waved a bit, and the prospect of seeing that face on the Sunday talk show circuit seemed quite real.

"I can't tell you what a thrill it is to be back at Griswold today," he began, offering up some archival anecdotes from *back in the day*. Then we had 'what I learned here' and the need to drink deeply of the experience.

"It may not be most welcome to hear that you have an obligation to put this opportunity to work for a good greater than your own, but life is really a series of just that; obligations." His style was quite natural, no notes. Realizing that he could be heard away from the pulpit without a microphone, he took to meandering a bit, striking a conversational tone by posing questions and having students respond, setting the bar rather high for a commencement speaker in June. Even as he slipped into asides about trade and fiscal policy, you could hear a pin drop. He descended the steps, leaving one foot up on the dais, noting how life is just a series of steps that we either choose to take, or not. Strolling over towards the D.A.F.T. bunch, the hempies eyed each other almost nervously.

"Ronald Reagan liked to tell the story of two men shoveling out a horse stall," he went on, "and in spite of their efforts, there was still---" and as he mimicked someone shoveling, he spotted what looked like a crumpled dollar bill on the floor of the center aisle. What unfolded next took perhaps seven seconds, but never made the papers as it exactly happened.

Kirk bent over to pick the bill up, but as he did, it suddenly scooted off the floor and between some pews, as if on a yo-yo string. The morning light was streaming in at just the right angle so that from my seat, I could see it glistening for a half second like a fishing line reeling in the bill. Kirk stretched further to grab it as it flew out of reach, and in doing so lost his balance, as a swimmer bent over on the starting block might when the starting gun is delayed. His head struck the small granite row marker noting the class or alum who donated that pew, and he toppled onto his left side. A few seconds of gasps and nervous chuckles followed, all of which were quickly sucked back in, and concern took over the room. His right arm reached up towards his head, then fell back onto the brown runner and was still.

Barclay nearly collided with the school nurse as they simultaneously reached Kirk and kneeled over him, speaking into different ears. People rose, necks craned and everyone spoke in the hushed tones. After the 911 call, Scott approached the mic and asked teachers to repair to their classrooms for their D block classes until they get an email to do otherwise. *Now.*

People third in line at the US Department of Commerce are not afforded Secret Service details. Outside the beltway, you could perhaps fit everyone who could *name* the number three at Commerce into my apartment; he's probably lucky to have a driver. The wheelman, a lanky redhead in an ill-fitting suit, hovered about his charge as the gaggle around him shifted in constrained unease. Students filed out looking over their shoulders, and in what seemed no time, a siren wound down and a gurney appeared. The EMTs took over as Scott kept waving us out with impatience. Off to the side on the dais was a circle of grim faces, arms folded, thumbs and fingers jabbing the air to make points. It looked like one of those grainy Kennedy White House photos of the ExCom during the Missile Crisis. A last glance over my shoulder revealed Scott walking with purpose towards Remy and a math intern who were both flanking Will Blumberg. This was all pretty unscripted, so the kids in my classroom could wait. I brought an alum here who was now being wheeled out with unsmiling urgency, so I wasn't leaving. Approaching the trio, I saw Remy's hand on Will's shoulder.

"What's up?" I asked.

"This is...kind of a matter for Barclay," Remy winced, suggesting that I'd be fenced out of the matter.

"Does it have to do with what just happened?"

"Most definitely."

"Well, I'm the reason Mayhew is here, so I'd kinda like to know...whatever..." I wasn't budging.

"Well," the math intern – I must learn his name - was too young to be politic, "I saw him. Right in front of me. I was late so I sat in with the kids." He eyed Will. "You want to chime in any time on this?"

Will's eyes were darting about in a distant way, as if hoping that the sprinkler system would suddenly let go or that some overdue bomb outside would finally detonate. Remy nudged him with a stern finger in front of his eyes, and gritted his teeth as he spoke. "You really don't wanna make this worse by pissing us off with some 'who me?' attitude."

"It..," Blumberg was reaching for words, "Jesus f---"

"Watch ya' mouth you sad sack of cells." Remy tugged at his arm and Will went limp for a second, at which point the math intern reached into his own blazer and fished something out.

"Had this in his pocket." He held up a crumpled, fake dollar bill with a barely visible fish line attached to it at one end and a finger ring at the other, then handed it to Remy who pulled the bill from the ring and the line extended. When he let go, it snapped back.

"What's this about?" Barclay appeared, eyeing everyone, desperate for information.

"I think Mr. Blumberg has something to say," Remy was not the good cop here. In point of fact, there wasn't one.

"Is that so?" Barclay folded his arms over his chest.

"I might be able to shed some---" the math intern began, but Barclay cut him off.

"Hold on," Barclay's palm silenced us all, and with his other hand he dug out his phone and turned away for a minute. If constipation had been one of Will's problems that morning, it probably no longer was. He almost inspired sympathy, looking helpless and hopeless at the center of a newly - formed and unfriendly universe, displaying all the composure of a paranoid hippie in a pre-Miranda police station.

"This is not the place," Barclay whirled back to us, "or the time. I need to get to---"

"The media will get wind of this. Fast." Scott Paone fingered his phone, his face betraying DefCon 4. "Given who he is, could be a news crew here eventually."

"Jesus, Mary and..." Barclay rubbed his brow and suddenly Liz appeared at our small circle. Barclay turned her way and spoke without looking her in the eye. "Since we don't know anything yet," he shot a glare at Will, "something...general, innocuous. An alum of the school," he circled his hands before him, as if coaxing the cover story out like a magician pulling a chain of kerchiefs from his mouth, "...in a newly- appointed post, maybe...collapsed. From exhaustion...we *think*. Nothing concrete. Keep it vague."

"I think there's more to it than that," Remy snapped.

"Well, they don't need to know that – not *now*. But by Christ," Barclay's George Clooney eyes were laser pointers on Blumberg's, "I *will*."

"Best to, if I may," Liz was thumbing her phone's screen, "keep it general. If it's not exhaustion, and we say that it is..."

Barclay nodded in agreement, and said something in a hushed tone that she absolutely understood, but that nobody else could hear.

I got someone to cover my class and became part of the troika shepherding Blumberg to Scott's office along with Remy and the math guy. We plodded along in silence, all of us in unchartered waters. As administrators are wont to do, Scott tried to tighten the circle when he arrived.

"I think we're good. Burnsy. You don't need to be here. Remy and ---"

"I'm responsible for Kirk being here," I offered with a deadpan face, "I'm not going anywhere."

He pursued his lips and looked away. "True enough." He didn't need one more battle just then, and could perhaps tell that this wasn't negotiable. He squeezed behind his desk and smoothed out his tie.

"So...Will: things seem centered on you," Scott began.

Blumberg sat motionless next to Remy while I stood by a window trying to will the kid's head to explode with my thoughts.

"Will: talk to us," Scott implored. Nothing. Remy fished out the gag bill-on-a-string and placed it on Scott's desk. "Shoved that in his pocket right after Mayhew went down." The math guy who'd slipped into a corner confirmed that he'd seen it all. Scott eyed the intern, who continued. "He… pulled it out of his pocket earlier. I didn't make anything of it. I was behind him – Will, that is. I couldn't stop him. But when Mr. Mayhew fell, he shoved it back into his pocket."

"Real Einstein," Remy scoffed.

"Remy, that's..." Scott was about to admonish him. Not allowed to call stupid kids stupid anymore, *don't you know*. No matter how stupid they are, they or their stupid parents are always smart enough to take offense.

"Scott...*Mr. Paone*," Remy was having none of it, "can we not wet-nurse this one? A Secretary of Commerce is in an ambulance because of him."

"*Acting* Secretary." Will muttered without looking up.

"You picked the wrong time to crack wise smart ass." My words got his attention, and with them, Scott realized that he was the only one in the mood for some Ed School, esteem-preserving, discipline-with-dignity bullshit.

"You'll be happier later if you talk now," Scott entreated him. I'd have been happy to grab him by his dreadlocks and swing him over my head, but my cell phone rang. It was an 800 number, some marketing call. Between the second and third rings of the phone, I had a brainstorm and went with it, phone in hand, loudly.

"Yes? Hmmm...I see. Mr. Mayhew's blood type? I wouldn't know...Someone in Washington, I suppose..." Everyone was transfixed, and in a pause, I mentioned that I was fielding questions from someone at a hospital on the other end. For a second, a scare went through me that Scott would ask me to put it on speaker, but if I kept the ruse going, he probably wouldn't interrupt. "Sure, but, I don't...you could try the Nantucket phone book, but in December...How should I know? I never heard of someone being allergic to anesthesia...Look, they must operate on people who can't tell them that all the time...Ask the driver. What? Well, he's federal after all, so yeah, FBI makes sense, I guess." I shot a glance at Blumberg, as if what I saw would determine my next answer. "I don't know. It's really for Barclay to call the school's lawyers, but they're mostly business law, aren't they?...Whoa, whoa there," I held up a palm to no one in particular, "that's above my pay grade. The *school* posting *bail* in the event of an *arrest?* How should I..." Out of the corner of my eye, I could see the remaining signs of life drain from Will's face. "Hey, it's like they say: 'if you cannot afford an attorney...' I'm not working that angle right now, y'know? Fine. Let me know." The telemarketer at the other end had given up a minute earlier, convinced he had dialed incorrectly, or that his interlocutor was clearly off his meds.

"Who...was that?" Scott was beside himself.

"Later." I folded my arms. A page had been turned.

"Look kid," Remy leaned in close, "D'yu hear that? I've seen kids in all types of jams. You're not the first, but you *are* in this crap up to your ears...Some free advice? Get in front of this. Now. You *did* hear that call, right? You weren't caught skipping class..."

Blumberg's knee was about to bounce out of his jeans. I half expected a puddle to begin on his chair. My evil side was enjoying this part of it. Scott looked skyward for a sign, then leaned forward.

"Who do your folks use for lawyers?" he asked. Nice. Bad cop, worse cop.

"Those court appointed hacks," Remy huffed, "the ones usually right outta law school? Couldn't help you beat a parking ticket."

"Al-*RIGHT!*" Will doubled over, head in hands. His tussled Rasta mop was a good metaphor for his life at the moment. "Christ!" he sat back, head up at the ceiling, eyes, closed. "It was just a...a joke, y'know? I didn't mean for...I didn't think---"

"Yeah, why start today?" Remy snorted.

"Remy..." Scott cautioned him.

"This vermin is...He injures a public servant who's an alum, just for kicks. What the...*it's not like he farted in Chapel f'Chrissake!*" He jabbed a hitchhiker's thumb in Will's direction. Somewhere off campus, a siren came and went. Nice timing.

"It wasn't, like," Blumberg pleaded, "intentional...what happened. It's funny when someone reaches for---"

"Funny? *Funny?*" Remy was close to frothing. Kojak on Red Bull. "What in that defective mind of yours were you thinking? This isn't the locker room – not that you've ever *been* in it to *know* that. This was a *school assembly*. With a *guest*. A government official. Who *went* here. Long before you were even..."

Scott tapped his desk with a pen, and once sure that Remy wouldn't finish the sentence, buzzed his secretary and asked for the number of Newton-Wellesley Hospital then focused on Will.

"Mr. Burnham is going to take you to your room." He was pragmatic and exacting. "Do you have a cell phone?" Will nodded. "Hand it over." Done. "You are to give Mr. Burnham your laptop and have no contact with anyone. *Anyone.* Is that clear?" Blumberg forced a nod. "A proctor will be outside your door – which is to remain open. You can sit, sleep, and *think,*"

"*That'd* be something new..." Scorsese must get Remy for his next film. Scott ignored it, not missing a beat.

"If you are not concerned about your situation, just ignore one of the things I've said. Doing so will provide you with a whole new universe of meaning to the word, 'unhappiness.' If everything I've said is clear, move your head like this." He nodded slowly. Will followed suit.

Heading to Wentworth, I didn't feel obliged to break the strained silence. I found a proctor, grabbed Blumberg's tech toys and left for my classroom, where Kat had rolled her kids in with mine and had a discussion going about books that had been made into films. Two satellite trucks were already lurking down at the school gate. It was before my time here, but I suspect that September 11th must have been a bit like this on campus - the contingency for such a situation wasn't in the school handbook. The kids hypothesized to the moon and back. *An epileptic fit? A cerebral hemorrhage? A flashback, triggered by his drug use when he was a student here?* Movies such as "Vantage Point" and "In the Line of Fire" were recalled. From the ridiculous to the sublimely ridiculous. We kept the discussion on movies until lunch, then the schedule reverted to a normal day, so to speak.

That afternoon I took my squash team to the Dana Hall School where they eked out a win due in no small part to the flu making the rounds on the Wellesley campus. It was hard to care though; the plasma screen in the gym lounge had a shot of Griswold's gate. *Breaking News*. On the bus back, I received a text sent to all faculty and staff saying that a Disciplinary Committee would be meeting on 'the day's incident' at 8 PM the following night. After we unloaded the bus, I decided to look in at the hospital before dinner. *En route* to my car, Kat McPhee asked where I was off to and came along. On the way we found the story on NPR:

"Circumstances at Commerce thrust Kirk Mayhew to the top job there, but he was reported to have been at the school this morning as an alumnus, not in any official capacity. A graduate of Griswold, Mayhew was offering a speech to current students when he collapsed. The Acting Secretary was rushed to a local hospital where his current condition is not known. There is no comment from the school thus far. The Secret Service and FBI are said to be investigating."

"That'll be good for admissions," Kat shook her head and squinted into the failing sunlight.

"Well, Choate survived the coke bust years ago. Groton and St. George's have weathered some pretty creepy stuff too..."

"Creepy stuff?"

I recounted as delicately as I could some sordid doings that no doubt caused trustees and admissions folks to lose sleep at both schools .

"Ick!"

"Maybe explains why FDR, who went to Groton, preferred the sitting position for much of his life." It was as close to humor as I could get.

"My boyfriend," in case I'd forgotten that she had one, "I think almost went to...what's that school in Connecticut, where Kennedy went?"

"Choate?"

"Yeah...wasn't there something there years ago?"

"Back in the '80s, some kids got caught coming back through JFK with enough coke to keep Amy Winehouse happy for a year. They all went to Choate. Not the best publicity."

"Rod says the art building is nice. His cousin or something went there. Bit of a *toff* as the Brits say."

"You're an English teacher. You know what Fitzgerald said about the rich..." Turned out she didn't, but she knew *toff*.

The state troopers flanking the hospital room door told the story. In the corridor, some Washington types were chatting intently in hushed tones. In pinstripe suits and wing tips, they looked ready to be stand-ins on "Meet the Press." Some younger types in North Face coats with iPads were reporters. I approached one of the pinstripers and introduced myself.

"S-o-o-o-o-o-o...you work where...this happened?" He let a glare hang there for a bit, with eyes courtesy of Bethlehem Steel.

"I teach there, yes." He chewed on this for a bit. *One of* your *kids did this.* He went back to his iPhone without a word. He must have known we were there to check on Kirk, but offered no hint that this would be allowed. After a truly eternal minute, I ventured a bit.

"Is it possible to---"

"No visitors," without looking up from his screen, "Only family." Kat had already begun to edge towards the elevators. On the way back to school, she pulled up the details from a news story on her phone. Kirk had suffered an epidural hematoma as a result of blunt force trauma to the skull.

Back on campus I rifled my three-ring binders, trying to figure out where I'd pick up in class the next day. By 10 PM I was needing air, and heading by Devine saw Kat's light on, so I knocked. Being greeted by a Simmons sweatshirt and the smell of gin made this the highlight of my day, which truly needed one. She waved me in and held up her glass, inquiring if she should fill another one.

"Sure."

"This place..." she was fishing for ice in the kitchen, "...is never dull."

"Sometimes I wish it was."

"Were."

"Were?"

"I'm an English teacher, 'member?" She handed me a jelly jar with a line on the rim and flopped onto her couch.

"Anything on the news?" I asked.

"I haven't checked," she tipped her glass back, "Probably." She nodded toward her TV's remote, and on CNN, someone from Mass General was saying that if Kirk landed on his forehead, he might have ruptured the meningeal artery. She went on that if blood was collecting between the skull and the dura, the membrane between the skull and the brain, the pressure that this could be creating could be 'extremely serious.'

"*Gee* – zus..." was all I could muster.

"Well put," she raised her glass to me. "Freaking bizarre were the words I had in mind. I mean, I know this place isn't exactly a stepping stone to Skull & Bones or Tiger Inn, but Christ...*some* of these kids...Where the hell do we get some of these...excuses for students?" She drained her glass.

"From people with murky gene pools but good hedge fund statements." I squeezed down the world's worst gin. She rolled her eyes and got up to fix herself another.

"Y'know, in the fall, when someone said that this place had some real...pieces of work, I took it with a grain of salt. I figured; kids had to submit grades and SSAT scores to get in, they all must have something on the ball. Why else would parents drop fifty large on their future, right? But..." she sat up and bored in, "I've got these two girls upstairs. One of them, Kendall Stends? Last month I hear a bunch of guys referring to her as Kendall *Benz*. We had a cake for her birthday, so I asked some girls if she got a Mercedes for it. I know her folks are loaded, right? They just laughed. Turns out it wasn't B-e-n-z, but *b-e-n- d-s*. Apparently she does that a lot. *Bends*. Then there's Gina Ambrosia. Even the girls have a name for her: *Gina* – as in *va*-gina. Sounds like she fights the dogs for fire hydrants. Jesus..." She folded her arms over her chest, as if to defend her own virtue at the moment.

"Well, it takes two, so---"

"I know, I know...and these guys will do anything with their junk. But these girls don't have to...*give* it away...like seconds at the dining hall. Kendall is in my honors class, f'Chrissake, and it'd be nice if every time I call on her henceforth, I didn't have this image of her on all fours..."

"Look, all you can do is all you can do," I shrugged. "You can get the nurse to do a talk. The dangers of sex and all...but...unless you show them a PowerPoint on the microscopic aspects of gonorrhea, they're gonna do what they're gonna do."

"Eeeww!" she wrinkled her nose.

"See? Might work."

"Thanks. I was gonna ask if you wanted t'get a pizza – dinner sucked...but, think I'll pass after that image."

Hard to tell on that one, but with her grad stud reporting for duty each Friday, it probably would only have been pizza. I finished my drink and made to leave.

"Another? You're not on duty..."

"No thanks," I declined, "Gotta write a test on the Punic Wars. Hannibal and all that."

"And a drink is gonna make you misspell 'Punic?'"

"After this conversation, I just might. Besides, Barclay's probably gonna want to meet with me tomorrow. Be nice if I didn't smell like a Kennedy. Rain check?"

"Whatever" She waved me off and reached for the TV remote.

December 12

THE ADMINISTRATORS WERE EARNING their pay last night, their offices all lit up, a first for that hour. Bagwell's apartment over the Admissions office was also aglow. His take on events of the week would be rich, so I knocked and was growled inside, where I found him in a cardigan with Latin tests all around his feet.

"What's new?" I asked, finding a chair.

He shrugged. "Far as I know, we're still open for business. Quite a cock up though. Mary says it's on the *Globe's* website. Friend of mine at Thayer called about it." I flopped into a chair and eyed the dark TV in the corner. "Seen Barclay's e-mail?" he muttered without looking up.

"Not yet? Good reading?"

"Boilerplate," he furled his brow, "There's something annoying about a washed out teacher adopting a tone like a White House Press Secretary."

"Barclay washed out of teaching?" I'd never heard that, so this was intriguing.

"Well, think about it," he turned to me and held up an instructive finger. "After becoming pretty well-versed in a certain subject, learning how to work with young people and amassing all

135

the resources that help you teach, you give it up…for an office, meetings all day, maybe the chance to dole out discipline or ask people for money…Think about it: if you were really good in the classroom, and effective there, if kids responded to you, why would you leave it to sit around suspending kids, going cap in hand to donors and drafting strategic plans?"

"Well," not being about to knock off the points of his logic, I defaulted to the obvious. "I expect the money's a lot better."

" 'Course it is, Peter, but there's a lot to be said for liking what you do." He eased himself into a burgundy wing chair and squinted a bit, suggesting that what was coming was his silver bullet of common sense. "Look around the dining hall at lunch someday – check out the tables where we are, faculty, and then have a look at where the administrators are. Notice their faces, Barclay, Scott, Admissions staff, that new head of IT. See which tables are emitting more laughter, or are simply smiling more. Lemme know what you notice."

I wanted to pursue this thread, but just then his phone went off. "Remember: email," and he waved me out.

Back in my flat I read it.

> *TO: All Faculty, Staff, Parents and Friends of the School*
> *FROM: Barclay*
> *RE: Mayhew Incident.*
>
> *As you may already be aware, an incident on campus this week has resulted in the hospitalization of a visiting alumnus who is also a government official in the Executive Branch. Kirk Mayhew '89 is the Acting U.S. Secretary of Commerce and graciously agreed to return to campus for a school- wide address to discuss the merits of public service with current Griswold students. In the course of his visit, Mr. Mayhew was injured in a fall and taken to Newton-Wellesley Hospital. At this writing, the full impact of his fall is not known, but the school is in constant contact with the hospital and is confident that he is receiving the best care possible. We can all be most proud of the level of his service in the*

Administration, yet it should also come as no surprise that his station in government will mean considerable media attention directed at Kirk as well as Griswold. As such, I wish to clarify matters prior to the feeding frenzy that the press can be counted on to engage in until this matter has passed.

The School is reviewing events surrounding Mr. Mayhew's incapacitation to determine what form of an institutional response is in order. As matters progress, this office will inform members of the Griswold community, with an eye towards protocol, reason and confidentiality. Please respect the Mayhew family's privacy during this time and allow the School to pursue matters as we best can, understanding the need to consider the interests of all concerned. Please keep Kirk and the Mayhew family in your prayers, and thank you for supporting them and Griswold by honoring the sentiments of this communication.

I'll give him this: the man can write. That said, the entire imbroglio is one more arrow in my why-I-want-to-leave-Griswold quiver, which would mean not having to explain why I'm not being asked back here. For all I know, Bill Buckley, arguably Millbrook School's most famous alum, was perhaps nailed with a snowball when he returned to his *alma mater* one day, but this event is unsettling, fouling my sense of the place. I also don't want to become a dean and it's been suggested that the history curriculum is as broad as it should be, so running in place here doesn't quite take one's breath away. Not sure what's next, except that I'm not getting a gold watch from this institution.

December 15

I T IS SAID THAT the last time anyone actually *trotted* at The Frost Trot, the faculty –staff holiday affair, was in 1962, and that was only because half the faculty were, to use father's term, *overserved*. This was explained away afterwards as a delayed exhale after the missile crisis a few months earlier. Older faculty who weren't even here then have passed other versions along. For several years, there had been an aching among the faculty and many alumni for the Headmaster at the time to step down. The situation, or perhaps simply the manners of the day, kept everyone from overtly trying to make it happen.

"Konrad Whistler," Bags' exhaled the name one rainy afternoon in the Teachers' Lounge. "Gone by the time I got here, but I heard the tale a million times. Came to the school during the Depression and somehow got tapped to take over in '33 when Cutler had a stroke. 'Roosevelt, Hitler and Whistler all came to power the same year' the joke went. Biggest horse's ass this place has ever seen, so I've been told. At the top anyway. Least that's what the old guard – old in *my* day – said. First he killed interscholastic sports. Riding up to Andover to play squash while a quarter of the country was in breadlines was wrong, it seemed. Tweaking this and that, he turned the place into a virtual plebeian stable out of Dickens by the time the war came. Then he went ass over teakettle to get Jews in here after the war to atone for 'one of our type' – a Grottie - as president, ignoring the Nazi camps. All quite noble really, but...they didn't want to come here, really. 'Specially after he practically turned the place into Putney." Putney is a crunchy school in Vermont where students are graded on milking goats. "Why would Jewish kids from Yonkers want to come here to do chores? Even though he watered down the church school angle, all the kids here had fathers who played golf at clubs that Jewish dads couldn't get into. Then he decided to make room for them by turning down legacies. Said they'd get in elsewhere, but that those schools wouldn't take Jews, so we had to do something. Pissed off a lot of alums. One boy – woulda been third generation or so – did go elsewhere. Middlesex, Mount Hermon, some place with an "M," and then Princeton where he rowed in the US eight in the Olympics. Turned up on Bobby Kennedy's staff at Justice a few years later. His father sent a news clipping of it to Admissions – along with the copy of a thank you note for a $50,000 gift he'd made to the school that *did* take him. That tore it for the Trustees in terms of Whistler – and he didn't help himself at their fall meeting by quoting John Dewey and that quack who ran Summerhill, that *whatever* school in the UK. They let him say that he wanted to start a book over Thanksgiving so wouldn't be back afterwards – you could do stuff like that without an act of Congress in those days. Some dean became Interim Head. Hell, some teachers had even stopped taking attendance – a real trend in the '60s. So when the Christmas Party came – you could still *call* it that then – people really cut loose. Emptied the bar. Got real Yeltsin. I came years later and they were still talking about it then." Bags laughs to himself whenever he finishes this tale.

The "Trot" has become more of a mid-year faculty party once the kids leave for the holidays, since anything remotely alluding to

Christmas is *verboten* these days. We actually moved to a *Secret Snowflake* gift swap two years ago after someone decided that *Secret Santa* had too many exclusionary overtones, and I've opted out of this 'community building' exercise ever since that silliness. A few door prizes are given out at the fête, and cocktail napkins say 'No Shop Talk.' Held at a local hotel, the affair is slated for the weekend just after fall finals. I received an email reminding me that I hadn't RSVPed for it. I'm actually looking forward to it even though I'm told that to call what I did two years ago at it *dancing* is generous.

During lunch on the Tuesday, Mary Carpenter was feeling torn. "Couldn't it...be considered...in bad form to...have a party if he's still in the hospital?" Kirk Mayhew's status was making the Boston papers daily. Remy was having none of it.

"We can't stop living just 'cuz some little shi---...twerp took twice his daily ration of stupid pills one day." He was stabbing his salad and not looking up as he spoke. His knack for putting a period at the end of a topic remained intact. *That* took care of *that*. Mary affected a pout, chin in palms, eyes closed, pursed lips.

"Do you...is it necessary to use those words?" Mary politely grumbled, at no one in particular.

"Which words?" Remy was matter of fact.

"'Stupid.' And 'twerp.' Is it possible to see it as a...a..."

"A *not-so*-stupid act?" Remy was giving no quarter, head down, still defoliating his plate. "Sure. Fine. I'm sure the police have another term for it. Feds too."

"We're talking about a boy," Mary was pleading with her palms skyward, "not even old enough to...to vote. Obviously he felt frustrated at not being able to expr---"

"You *are* joking, right?" I've always gotten along with Mary, but unlike many matters in life, this was black and white. Her comments burst the glass on my bullshit meter. "There's a man — an alum, a government official — who took time out of his schedule to come here – who's *still out cold,* thanks to that...kid. Were you there? *Christ.* What about owning your own actions? Hold up a sign, write a letter, give him the finger, sure, but---"

"The *finger?*" Mary recoiled.

"Nobody ever ended up in a coma because someone flipped him the bird," Remy wagged a reminding fork in Mary's direction, and slowly her face and shoulders sank with an exhale of defeat. She was hoping to play T-ball and found herself in Triple A.

"My mother saw the story on CNN," Schy appeared with a tray and sat down. "Can we skin that little shit? Alive?"

Remy offered him an air pound, and they bonded over their agreement on torture.

"Schyler, please," Mary was Henry Fonda and we were three angry men.

"Where is Cousin It anyway?" Schy had adopted Remy's caricature of Blumberg as the hairy creature from "The Adams Family."

"Home for now," I offered. "His lucky roommate has had a single since the day after the incident."

"Cousin It," Mary bristled. All very unprofessional. Tough shit.

December 17

STROLLING CAMPUS BEFORE 8 PM tonight I ran into Bags on a snowy path in front of the library.

"Who'd 'ja get to cover?" he didn't bother to make eye contact.

"Cover what?"

"Your duty? You slacked off, because..."

Christ. It was my Study Hall night. I'm a bit young for a senior moment, but with the mess this month...I grabbed some papers to correct and headed for Wentworth. The academic stretch between Thanksgiving and Christmas is always rather porous in terms of work; kids are thinking about nothing but the next break, some teachers slack off because...kids are thinking about nothing but the next break. Not the time to ask for ten-page research papers, so Study Hall can be less than monastic on these nights. My out of breath arrival in Wentworth's lounge was met with blank stares.

"You forgot, didn't you?" Allison looked up from a table of tests she was grading.

"Forgot..?"

"Remember? Tonight I'm here and you're in Devine? That whole byzantine switch because...I can't even remember why..."

"Oh." A whisper of recollection came and went. "Oh!"

"All set," she waved me off, "pretty quiet there-I strolled over earlier," and her cell rang. After a few words she covered the speaking end. "Can you just...hang here at the desk for a minute while I take this. Then you can head over there?" I nodded and she slipped into a computer lounge to talk.

Isaiah Franklin was sprawled on a lounge couch. He could usually be found there when ESPN had a basketball game on – which is to say he seems genetically conjoined to it from November through April. Ten minutes to Study Hall, he was still beached three feet in front of the dorm TV, his head propped up on one arm. Having forgotten the re-worked plan for my duty, I didn't think it polite to ask Allison why he was still watching the box, even though TVs usually go off at 7:45. Not because I cared, I asked the score. Two schools I'd never heard of were three points apart. A one-time baller, Isaiah's skills and girth kept him from the Griswold varsity and their clique this year, but he's an officer in a student group that advances minority concerns, and he has *presence* as those of the stage would say.

"So Mr. Burnham – what's up with Blumberg?" Must have been the end of a quarter in the game.

"I dunno, Isaiah."

"C'mon...what's gonna happen to him?"

"That's not up to me."

"Yeah, but...waddya think?"

"Well," I slid myself onto a butcherblock end table of dorm furniture. "I wouldn't want to be him...let's put it that way."

"Isn't this, like, criminal?" He sat up, his eyes brightening.

"Y'know, Isaiah, there are different layers to it, and I---"

"If he were...if it were *me*, what would happen?" My wrinkled brow nudged him to explain. "Not saying I would, but like...if he were...I mean, does his dad have that news company?"

"N-n-n-o-o-o-o. that's *Bloom*berg. B-l-o-o-m..."

143

"Oh. But...he's still kinda..."

"Kinda what?" Where *was* he going with this? He sat up more, feeling he'd been given an inroad.

"Y'know how we get, like, Rosh Hosanna off? And Yom Kippur? Well, we don't get the King holiday or Easter..."

"We have *events* on the King holiday. We don't sleep in, true, but we honor the day with events that remind us of his work. And Easter – that's a Sunday. If you wanna go home that weekend, you can. What's your point?"

"No, I'm jus' sayin'...."

"You're not saying much – yet." Where the hell was Allison? "Get to it."

"Fine," he whipped his barrel frame around. "If he were---" and he stopped. A student from Taiwan entered the room to warm something in the microwave. Isaiah assessed the situation, and at this point probably wished he hadn't opened that door. Not exactly the audience for a Sharpton shtick. "F'get it." He turned back to the game.

Schools are just microcosms of society, so racial and ethnic issues have no trouble making their way past the school gate. In October there'd been a minor dust up with the JAGS – Jewish Association of Griswold Students, known to detractors for various reasons as Jaguars - and the BLUDs, Blacks & Latinos United for Diversity. Both wanted a function room for the same time one weekend; the school's own little version of Crown Heights. There were grumblings of past offenses by students of each ethnicity and how each had been punished, and feelings lingered. If anything, the school usually errs on the side of leniency with regard to discipline compared to a decade or two ago. Kids are quick to find cause for any such decision to be disagreeable, or more accurately, unfair to the teenage mind.

"Whaddya 'xpect? She's from *Jew*-ton," was overheard in the dining hall after one disciplinary decision came down. Whether it was the girl's faith or her being from the town of Newton which rankled the commentator was not clear. Teachers also grumble that certain decisions are made with an eye towards third and fourth chances as opposed to policy. Of course now and again there's the legacy or full-tuition kid who gets off lightly; *Tapper would probably be gone if his dad hadn't gone here and he weren't from Deluxbury*, a reference to the south shore town of Duxbury whence some spawn of the *noveau riche*. At a well-known New Hampshire school a few years back, after some sixth formers – seniors – were caught at a year-end beer blast, a few family assurances to double the Parents' Fund allowed their kids to graduate, so it's always case by case.

"Every incident is a unique, as is each student," Barclay likes to say. This went over like a lead zeppelin with most faculty two years ago when a junior from Bed-Sty was found with liquor *and* a girl in his room. Somehow he skated, and the only people pleased were a few coaches and the BLUDs, the student group founded in response to the matter. The hilarity of the name was too much for anyone to suggest a change. Schy actually started a whispering campaign for another group: Campus Realm for the Inclusion of all People, the CRIPs. He proposed a softball game between that group and the BLUDs – and in the event of a tie, a snowball rumble to settle it. Barclay got wind of it and that was the end of it. Forgetting for a moment that I'd like to see one of the icicles from over his outer doorway descend into his skull, he probably made a good call on that one.

Allison mercifully reappeared in another minute and I headed to Devine.

Every campus has a dorm that tour guides show to families visiting the school. At Griswold, it's Devine. Grey and earnestly gothic, it became the first girls' dorm when the school went co-ed in the '70s, and thankfully nobody has been foolish enough to turn it over to boys. No generic, dorm-issue butcher block stuff in these common areas; *actual furniture*. The mantle of the seldom-used fireplace is flanked by photos of teachers and housemothers past as well as some antiquated field hockey sticks. I dropped my books at the duty desk and a freshman girl agreed to fetch the evening's proctor. A minute later Madison Jackson appeared. Two last names and both of them presidents, she'd had presence on campus since her freshman year, in which she also made girls' varsity squash, and honestly I'm glad she's stuck with it. A mildly obsessive diva with an air of self-assuredness, she says and does things that, if they do not always meet with approval, are seldom questioned. Specially-made veggie burgers at brunch and spontaneous sign-outs are not unreasonable to *her* it seems, but are requested in a passively entitled manner suggesting that she's not used to hearing 'no.' She waltzed into Devine's lounge, tying up her long, blond mane as she spoke.

"So what's the deal Mr. Burnham?" She studied some split-ends between her fingers rather than look at me. "Can seniors watch TV tonight? During Study Hall?"

"Why would that happen?" My nose was buried in a grade book. Two can play that game.

"Cuz...we're gonna be in college next year. We need to learn how to manage our time without artificial constructs like Study Hall." She made quotation marks with her fingers to underline her contempt for the routine.

"Learn how to manage it starting tomorrow, will you?"

"No, really. Think about it. One year from now, I won't even be *having* this conversation. I'll be---"

"All the more reason to not practice it now."

Big sigh.

"Ms. McPhee once told---"

"Madison," I looked up with my best weary eyes, "be a good proctor and take check, will you?" She whirled around in disgust and was off, and the incident promised to afford me some chilliness from her during squash practice the next day. Truth be told it was probably my fault she attempted this at all. Last spring in ECON she didn't have a paper done on time. It was Friday afternoon and after class she came to me to grovel, stumbling upon an undeniable truth.

"You're probably not gonna start reading them tonight, Friday night, right? So if I, like, email it to you at say, six o'clock, or after dinner, is that OK and, y'know, not late? I mean, think about it. If you have them all when you start reading them, do a few hours matter?"

"That's not the point Maddie. You were 'sposed to turn it in during class, and if I take it late with no penalty, how fair is that to the kids who stayed up late and did it on time?" She pursed her lips, and out it came.

"I can't be judged by what others do or don't do." It was as if this teenage Morgan Fairchild were channeling Ayn Rand. We went on like this for a bit, all the time the fact that I truly *wasn't* going start reading them until Sunday circling inside my head. Friday afternoon is a good time to request things of teachers. I granted her the extension, with notice that I'd be grading with a slightly higher sense on expectations *and* shaving points off for tardiness, given the extra time. She took it as a win but shouldn't have, as the late points changed her grade on it, but it wouldn't surprise me if she thought that what did the trick was her too-small rugby shirt and cocked head when she said, *pu-leeeez?* Later it occurred to me that her 'I can't be judged' comment was probably a writer's line from some movie she'd seen. She might not try with it with Mary or Kat, and perhaps saves the head-cocking for male, bachelor teachers. At least this evening, there'd be no TV.

A fellow new to the Building and Grounds Department appeared in Devine's lounge as I settled behind the desk, mentioning that he needed to tinker with the dorm furnace. All was nicely boring until just after nine, when a dull, metallic *thunk* with no lingering ring penetrated the hall door. Stepping outside, the clear night air reached into my lungs and the moonless sky offered up more stars than one would expect so close to Boston. A cabinet official was in the ICU across town owing to events a few hundred feet away, but the crisp darkness made the Blumberg messiness seems miles away at the moment.

All tranquility is fleeting. The campus is bisected by a ne'er do well stream spanned by a stone bridge. Careening across the bridge at the moment was a jet black Land Rover which seemed to be out of power steering fluid. Soon it was clear that it was headed for Devine in a manner that would have made Lindsay Lohan proud. I edged behind one of the granite pillars on the dorm's steps, hoping that Newton's laws of motion had not taken the night off. In spite of what seemed to be the best efforts of whoever was behind the wheel to send it off the road, the vehicle wound its way to the turnaround in front of the dorm, where it plowed into the back of the Building and Grounds truck, which kept it from overshooting the pavement and de-barking a white birch at the circle's edge. It was one of those crescendo crashes, the crunch of which seems to silence everything for miles, as if nut-gathering squirrels and all the cars on Route 128 froze to take notice.

"Mother of *G-e-e-e*-zus!" an unreconstructed New York twang spat out, "That's *it!* You're taking Drivers' Ed. No argument. Even if I have to get your *father* to help out!"

The hatch of the B & G truck was punched in a bit and the Land Rover's black hood now formed a low A-frame of shiny tin in front of the windshield. Headlight glass was sprinkled underneath. Out of the driver's side stepped Vanessa Radzwill, a two-year junior. Jet-black mane, Burberry scarf, skintight jeans, Park Slope haute, an Olympic-level narcissist. She'll do fine in the world, assuming a perpetual demand for clueless trophy wives.

Mom spilled out the other side, masked with Jackie O. glasses, scarf and Prada bag swinging.

"What a...Did I *not* say *brake?*"

"Mother: it's winter! There's like...*ice!*"

"Hi, I'm Peter Burnham," I edged down the steps. "Is everybody---"

"Hey," the pseudo-Jackie O made a discovery as she studied the glass-sprinkled snow under her spiked heels, "Says *fire lane*. What's this truck doing here?"

"There is a heating problem in the dorm Mrs..."

"Radzwill. Call me Deidre." She removed the shades. "You...a-a-a-h-h-h...I know: my doortah's teachah... last year? I remembah now."

Seamlessly she broke into a charming smile. Either she had Vanessa when she was fifteen or she'd found the best nip and tuck man in the city.

"This is pretty unfortu---" I started.

"*Christ.* I *asked* Tony to teach ha how to drive last fall. East Hampton. October. Pretty quiet then. Safe, y'know? Does he do it? *Course* not. Like his fund will collapse if he doesn't spend twenty hours a day obsessing over it. So *this* happens. Were you even *looking?*" She shot a world-weary glance at Vanessa.

Bill Murphy, head of campus security, rolled up. A retired Boston cop with a bitingly arid sense of humor, he isn't above an air of self-importance on occasion. This was one such occasion.

"What have we here?" He clicked his tongue "All-night bumper cars?"

"Hitta truck parked in a fire lane," Mrs. Radzwill gestured to the school truck as if a dog had just left something warm in that direction. "How safe is *that?*"

Bill eyed the kissing vehicles, sized up the mother and daughter and offered a deadpan that spoke volumes when told who was driving.

"Mr. Burnham: can you add anything to the story?"

"Story?" the mother was on fire. "What do you mean 'story?' Do you mean to sug---"

"Just an expression ma'am. Just an expression." Bill sent a cloud of blue exasperation into the night air and dialed the local police in order to get it reported. Vanessa was beside herself, rolling her eyes and shaking her head. Back inside a dozen girls had gathered by the dorm entrance and were sputtering, but not too quietly. Mrs. Radzwill was already on her cell phone and couldn't hear the not entirely muffled comments at the doorway.

Her mother's such a bitch.

Oh, not like her right?

Watch her get a car for graduation anyway.

She hasn't even started college apps yet.

What place would take her?

With a wave over my head I shooed the girls at the threshold away from the doorway, confident they would simply watch the scene from somewhere else. Bill had his hands on hips in that 'all right folks, the show's over' way that police do. Once the town cops came, I went inside and considered the homework I'd promised to give back in the morning.

December 18

FACULTY MEETING - CLIFF NOTES version: Blumberg on suspension until further notice. Mayhew family expresses no interest in getting legal just now. Local police will nudge TV trucks from school gate when time permits. Administrative committee to review disciplinary steps in cases of harm to visitors who are presidential cabinet members.

Like finding a $20 bill on the sidewalk, Liz tapped me on the shoulder on the way to the general school meeting after the faculty gathering with a message; police wanted my statement on the Radzwill accident. Don't want to keep The Man waiting, so I headed out to the police station, missing Barclay's wish that the entire Griswold community have a safe and happy break. Devastated.

December 20

IT SEEMS THAT AMONG faculty, The Frost Trot was actually looked forward to this year. Maybe just to see people dress up a bit. Maybe to see if any spouses are more interesting or better looking than their teaching halves. Maybe, after a dorm fire, Kirk's fall and mother-daughter bumper cars outside Devine, people just wanted to clear their heads. Bacon-wrapped shrimp and a cash bar in the function room at a hotel a half-mile from campus awaited us. Late in the afternoon before the fete, I stopped by Bags' apartment to return a book. He was getting a head start on the evening and asked me to join him.

"Ever had an Old-Fashioned, Peter?"

"Can't say I have."

"We'll fix that." He set about at his dry sink in the corner and came over with two tumblers you could barely see through. "Good for a cold night." We clicked glasses and I squeezed down a swig of sweetened kerosene while he emptied half of his. "That Korean boy was looking for you... the one you tutor and play chess with?"

"When?"

"Err... yesterday. Before dinner. Must've been one of the last kids to leave campus. Sorry."

"Wish you had told me..."

"Slipped my mind," he shrugged, "So damn polite and afraid to impose, he doesn't really make an impression to remember."

"Did he... say anything?"

He shook his head and fished a package from the kitchen. "Gave me this for you." An exquisitely wrapped something the size of a softball. "Nother?" I shook my head, loosened my collar, and found myself eyeing his ascot. As contemptuous as Bags can sound regarding affairs such as The Frost Trot, his tartans and neckwear suggested otherwise.

"Got a date?" He settled into the couch.

"Nah. I asked a friend I taught with in Japan, but she's busy."

"Friend?"

"She's at a day school in Boston. Lives near Fenway."

"Give her another call. Y'never know...Plans change."

"N-n-n-n-n-o-o-o-o...I don't want to deal with the 'Who was that girl?' tomorrow."

"Oh c'mon. Our dull little lives would be enriched by some gossip, even it if isn't about Barclay."

"Barclay? And...?"

"Oh grow up," he scoffed. Clearly I haven't been paying attention.

"Hmmmm...in a small place like this, fooling around could be rather...self---"

"Destructive? Good Christ boy - you could teach psych." It occurred to me that if his opinion of Barclay was as low – or venomous – as mine, it might be worth letting him in on how this would be my last Trot. I wondered whether he'd know any folks worth speaking to at other schools. As I worked up the nerve to spill it all, his phone rang, and for ten minutes he spoke in a hushed tone with his back to me. When he was done, the moment seemed gone. He snatched my glass. "Call Remy will you?" he threw over his shoulder, "He'll have to drive us."

In spite of candy cane toothpicks in shrimp and a few pairs of go-to-hell pants, nobody appeared *overserved* in the Charles River Room of the Colonial Inn. The music lent itself to the kind of dancing that adults can do without looking entirely epileptic, and if the season and fare annoyed the pagans and the vegans on hand, they kept it to themselves or stayed away. Kat was quite the vision with both her hair and her hemline up, even if she was on the sturdy arm of the brawny brain from Memorial Drive, a ruddy, intense-looking fellow still with a sailing pallor, nursing a bottle of Beck's. After Bags' rocket fuel, I stuck to the pinot noir. Crunchies like Allison were scarce; obviously there was a Bernie Sanders fundraiser at the same time as this fete. Liz's green strapless number drew an amusing mix of looks; stares from husbands and glares from wives. After drawing the tickets for the door prizes, she drifted off, claiming that she felt a cold coming on. Schy showed up in a fire engine red blazer and on his arm was a lithe, dark lovely in a quasi-tutu who looked fresh from some hip-hop awards show.

"Nice that his folks let him take the help," Bags chortled. Mary Carpenter glowered at him, then gave in begrudgingly with an agreeing smile. Remy and Bags were rehashing some ancient school scuttlebutt when I realized that chasing an Old Fashioned with wine is a bad idea. Mixing can send one's head swimming, and "Rocking Around the Christmas Tree" wasn't helping. Not having won a door prize and finding the shrimp pretty sorry, I decided to bail, hoping some night air would clear my head. I told Remy I'd hoof it back to school.

It was one of those still, frigid winter nights when two blocks into the hike, I wished I'd worn a heavier coat. Through the barren trees, the lights of the school came into view, and a path through the woods offered a shortcut. The recent thaw had left the snow on the cross-country course at no more than a few inches. I ducked into the trees, and after a bit chose a good spot to write my name in the snow, and midstream I saw a figure headed my way. Between the crunching of snow underfoot and a determined gait, he was oblivious to me behind a huge tree. The moonlight caught something glass-like in his hands; that he appeared to be carrying either crystal candlesticks or large icicles seemed odd, but I was honestly too cold to dwell on it. The students were gone, and I really didn't feel the need to trifle with someone who was collecting bottles in the woods for the deposits. His dark shape trudged up a slight drumlin toward the school grounds, and after a minute I began to follow, hopefully out of his sight. Making my way slowly between the trees, I pulled up to keep a discrete distance when I heard him slip and fall on an icy patch. Under the blue- white moonlight, I saw him pull himself to his knees.

"Judas Priest!" cut the night air. He'd fallen in his tracks, and was now studying the damage beneath him, which seemed to include his hands. None of this summoned the Samaritan in me. Nothing good happens in the woods at night, not in winter anyway. Once he pulled himself to his feet and plodded on, it occurred to me that the same path in the dark wasn't perhaps the smartest route. I retraced my steps and settled for the shoveled sidewalks to the main entrance to campus. Sometimes the long way home is the best.

January 9

I SPENT THE BREAK at the family home south of Boston, and brought the package from Aaron with me. It was a Christmas tree ornament; a glittering sphere lashed with gold and jade strands that looked more like a Fabergé egg than something to hang like tinsel. A note from him thanked me for my tutoring him and our chess games. A second note from his father expressed a profound sense of gratitude. He graciously overemphasized my impact on his son, whose note I read a second time. I pictured him at his desk in Korea over the break, laboring over each word and letter, his lamp and clock radio perhaps being the extent of his workspace clutter. Passing his room now and again before the students returned, I'd hear the clock radio's alarm announcing urgency at odd times of the day to no one, and without anyone to turn it off. Some mornings I tell myself I'll get him to try the music feature to add an aesthetic sliver to his Spartan existence here. As students now use their phones as alarms, I find his choice for waking up downright quaint.

Over the holidays a few Boston TV stations made sure the break wasn't entirely Griswold-free, however. In a "year in review" news segment New Year's Eve, one channel replayed its reportage on the Mayhew incident. In early January another station reported that the president had appointed a college chum of his as Acting Commerce Secretary in Kirk's absence, which, he added, "we all hope will be short-lived." Meandering Boston socially during the party circuit between Christmas and New Year's, where I teach came up now and again.

"Griswold... why do I know that name..."

"Wasn't there some shooting there?"

It was like telling people after Katrina that I was Chief of Staff for the mayor of New Orleans.

The first day of classes after a break is like trying to start an engine that has been dormant for six months. First night dinner is perennially a McLaughlin Group-like food fight of one-upmanship of who had the more amazing vacation. A gaggle of rested and refreshed lads from Chamberlain were swapping tales at a corner table.

"That's nothing. Turks and Cacos, right? There's no drinking age. So my folks are out golfing, I swim up to the bar - *swim*, mind you - and have four Red Stripes for lunch."

"What's that – fish?"

"Whadayu – *retarded*? Beer, for Christ's sake - from the Bahamas." Least he got the hemisphere right. I didn't feel compelled to correct him.

"Sounds cool, but Aspen was..."

This seemed to be repeated again and again around campus that night; girls sticking phones in front of each other's face to share the priceless pics of to-die-for fun. A quiet hippie from Maine returned, without his past-the-shoulder blonde locks, sporting instead, a Brad Pitt just-woke-up cut.

"What gives?" I pointed to his ears, which I hadn't been seen since the previous school year, as I strolled through Wentworth's lounge.

"Had a deal with my dad," he kept his eye passively on MTV. "Anything below a C last term, and," he mimicked scissors with two fingers.

"So, what class was the legal tripwire?"

"Trig. And French."

"French? Didn't you go to Paris last summer?"

"Yeah, but that was for some art classes..."

"Oh..."

On the third night back, I thought of checking in with Aaron. Heading down to his room outside the north end of the dorm, I saw his light on. Closer, from a snow bank by his window, I saw him near a desk, scratching his head then sniffing his in hand, as if wondering what the barber had doused him with. He seemed a bit taller, as boys will after three weeks away, and a shaved bowl cut gave him a renewed geekiness. Heading back inside, I tapped on his door, and waited while some dresser drawers were fumbled with. Cracking the door, he peered out at me like a hunted suspect in a bad TV show.

"Happy new year, Aaron."

"Happy... new year."

"You don't have a girl behind that door, do you?"

"Girl?" He was about a light year from getting the sarcasm.

"You seem worried... about opening the door."

"Oh...no. Sorry." Late in the fall, he was moved in with Sean Reagan after Sean's roommate, depending on which tale one chose to believe, either found the academics here not as challenging as he'd expected or admitted to sprinkling Viagra he'd ground to powder onto a classmate's potatoes. I wasn't on duty the weekend he disappeared, so didn't concern myself with which story was closer to the truth. Moving Aaron in there seemed a good idea. Between this, osmosis and our weekly chess sessions, his English was getting better, and he was less of a sore thumb socially.

"How was your break? Vacation?"

"Oh... my family went to Singapore."

"Nice. What did you do there?"

"My father had a medical conference, so we visited places and went to shopping."

"Went shopping."

"Huh?"

"Went *shopping*, or *went to the shop*. Remember?"

"Ah. Yes, sorry."

"No biggie. Where's Sean?"

"I don't know," he looked around the room, hands in his back pockets.

"Room looks good," I nodded to the South Korean flag poster of Yunjim Kim, the female character in the old TV show "Lost" who is a big star in Korea. He nodded. "We still on for chess Saturday?"

"Y-y-y-y-y-e-e-e-s-s-s-s-s."

"Good. If you're still reading *The Giver* in your English class, bring it with you if you have questions, okay?"

"Okay." He forced a smile. His teacher had them reading Lois Lowry's book which was several leagues over his head. There was a slightly rank odor about him that I couldn't place, and wasn't bothered enough about it to explore.

For a reason I still don't know, heading into the night air I was suddenly nudged from somewhere inside to go to the hospital and see how Kirk was. It was really out of the blue, but seemed practical before the term got thoroughly underway. Given the chronic ADD of the media, the Mayhew incident seemed to have receded from the airwaves. Driving there through the newly plowed streets, it occurred to me that guilt probably sparked the trip.

Nice not to see satellite trucks in the hospital parking lot. Outside Kirk's room sat a lone policeman on a folding chair. In the small world department, he was the officer who took my report when I had to offer my two cents on the Radzwill bumper car incident a month earlier.

"No change," he shook his head with a deadpan look, "nonresponsive. They've got another word for it. Boils down to a coma."

"Shit," I shook my head.

"Shit is right. Nice family. Great kids. Wife is"... he made an 'OK' gesture with raised eyebrows, suggesting that she wasn't just polite. "Young guy too. Freaking shame."

"Mmmmm. Sure is."

He went on about some car crashes he'd worked with victims who ended up in similar stages of nothingness. Tales that would almost make you stop driving.

"So...what's the deal with...the...suspect..." I lowered my voice. "You know, legally."

"The kid? Over my pay grade. I heard someone saying that the family wasn't out for blood. *His* family, that is." He jabbed a thumb over his shoulder at the room behind him. "Which I don't get. Off the record? 'Cuz I'm on-the-job? If I weren't, and someone put one of my family in a coma? I'd skin him alive and wash him down with kerosene." As I was conjuring up the imagery, he reminded me again that it was all hypothetical, him being on-the-job and all.

Heels on the linoleum floor behind me didn't sound like a nurse's footsteps. The cop stood as they came closer, and I turned to see Mrs. Kirk Mayhew with two cups of coffee, one for the sentry.

"I hope I got it right - two sugars, no cream?"

"Perfect."

"Sally Mayhew," she extended her hand.

"Peter Burnham."

She had that look so common in blondes with year-round tennis tans, suggesting anything from thirty-five or perhaps fifty years; *classic* looks, as mother would say. Her camel hair steamer coat, silk blouse and pearls suggested that she wasn't in the habit of fetching coffee for policemen, except maybe the crossing guards outside the club at Junior League functions. Her mane was early Donna Reed. Somehow I'd missed the wood paneled Wagoneer in the parking lot.

"I am...at Griswold." This felt like admitting to having scored a seat in one of the *Titanic's* lifeboats.

"Yes. Yes, you are." Her eyes suddenly bore a hint of sympathy, sensing the yoke by association.

"I can't tell you...how...I'm the one who invi---"

"It's..." she placed a warming hand on my forearm "It has been hard on all of us."

"Yes, but I can't help but think that..."

"Please, Mr. Burnham, don't try to own this. You asked him to speak. At *his* school. Perfectly reasonable. There is no way you could have...no way..."

"Well, that's very... gracious of you. Please, Peter."

She forced a smile, sighed and looked at the closed door behind me. "It is...what the given day has given us. Kirk likes to say that. Too often, actually." Her jaw tightened, then she closed her eyes and caught herself.

"What about visitors?"

"He..." she stopped to take a sip of coffee as if for strength, "doesn't respond. Yet. But it's good of you to...let's go in."

The fluorescent bulb behind the wooden beam over the headboard was the only light in the room, and sprayed a frozen glow over a motionless figure under an oxygen mask and four or five monitors beside the bed affirming life. Even in a coma, his hair was press-conference perfect.

"I like to think that... as long as he's like this, he's not in pain." She thinned her lips and bucked up.

"That's a good way to look at it."

"How is...the boy?" She looked away towards a darker corner of the room.

"Not at school. I gather, it's more of a legal matter now."

"I...I don't think...if it's a boy with bad judgment...I suppose I shouldn't say it. But...I don't think that Kirk would want him...overly punished." She sipped. "That's probably not a word - or term. Overly punished."

"Don't worry. I'm not an English teacher." I bumped her elbow as I turned, forgetting for the moment that she was wife of a cabinet official. She turned and smiled.

"I…would like to be kept apprised of the boy's status. Kirk is a forgiving sort. Gosh knows I've given him..." She caught herself and straightened a bit. Looking at her motionless husband, she didn't really appear to see him.

"I'll...see what I can learn." A real moonscape in terms of conversation. Best to follow, rather than try to lead. Kirk's vitals continued to spike in blue and green lines. Behind one of the monitors were some crayon pictures with 'Get Well Daddy' at the bottom as only a second or third grader can scratch it out. Focusing on these posters, I was seized by the desire to hear bad news about Will Blumberg upon returning to school. To learn that he was dragged by his lice-infested dreadlocks into the woods and kicked repeatedly. I wished that his family had fallen into that nasty financial abyss of 'too middle class for financial aid from the school but too poor to pay for it by themselves.' Every teacher has felt this: a kid who brings more misery than joy to his world, and who specializes in poisoning things around him. Most teachers know a kid like that. If they say they don't, they're lying or they're no longer educators, but administrators.

"I want to let you have some time with him. I gather things are..."

"Unchanged. Static. That's it, static. Kirk...likes to teach the girls a new word every day. One day they came down with sweaters on. Hair every which way. Kirk spent time teaching them other meanings of the same word. He was even late leaving for work that day." She almost gave way again, but steeled herself.

"If there's anything I can do... or... tell the school..."

"Thank you. Thank you Peter. Kirk loves Griswold, and I know he wouldn't le...*won't* let this...matter spoil his... feeling for the school."

Her cell phone ringing was a good point to leave. Forgetting myself at a couple of intersections prompted a few horns when I missed lights that had turned to green on the drive home.

January 10

ALWAYS NICE TO HAVE first or last period of a day free. Now is when jobs for next year start to appear on school websites. I honestly haven't had a conversation with Barclay since our October meeting, and can now start putting this place in my rear view mirror in earnest. It was actually a passive aggressive streak that I'm not too proud of that nudged me to drop by his office to let him know about my visit to see Kirk in the hospital – not to update him on anything, as he ought to drop by there regularly himself. If he wants to freeze me out of this place, I'll at least let him know that I've been in touch with people who matter. After breakfast I knocked on his ornately carved office door, as there was no sign of Liz as gate keeper. It was ajar an inch, so hearing nothing after the second rap, I stuck my head in. Barclay was on the phone, but waved me in.

"So... I don't get it. We weren't going to serve champagne anyway...I know, but principle isn't... maybe they're behind the wine glasses. Did you look there?" He leaned back in the chair and ran a hand through his Romneyesque schock. "Well, as you say to Judd when he can't find things, 'they didn't just get up and walk away by themselves'... Last time? Probably when we got that grant in the fall...Look, there must be some place online to find them. We can't be the only people with that style...check...fine...love you." He replaced the receiver and sat up. "Champagne flutes...Judas Priest." Looking up, he fixed a generic stare on me, then forced a weak smile and raised eyebrow, as if to ask 'what's up' without having to say so.

"I saw Sally Mayhew last night," I offered in my best deadpan. "Thought you'd wanna know."

"Yes. Yes." He gestured for me to sit. "How did that come about?"

"I dropped by to see Kirk, and she was there."

"Did you see the bouquet from the school in his room?"

"No. I don't think they allow flowers in ICU rooms."

"Hmmm," he wrinkled his brow, "How is she?"

"As...you might expect. A trooper. But human."

He frowned and pumped a fist into the other hand, then winced for a few seconds, eyeing his palm. "And Kirk? No change?"

"Comatose."

"Mmmmmmmm"

"She asked about...Blumberg."

"Mmmm."

"She's quite...undemanding, given the... situation."

"Undemanding?" He arched an eyebrow

"She's not out for blood, so she says, and I tend to believe her."

"Hmmm. Very...unselfish of her. Noble."

My grandmother loved to talk family history, referencing *The Boat* now and again, the one that landed in 1620, yet for all that dusty WASP stoicism, I wonder if somewhere way back there might be some Irish blood, for I can indeed hold a grudge. Getting the gate for next year in October, I'm having *very un-Christian thoughts* about Barclay, as mother would say. Cliff Notes version: if he were rolling around on the floor on fire, I wouldn't piss on him to put him out. But with no sign of flames, I just offered things up casually, content to seem indifferent to information that I was willing to let drip. Truth be told, I liked being able to convey a personal interaction with someone that he probably should be in touch with daily. I gathered from his unfamiliarity with the situation, that he is not.

"She specifically said she doesn't want him, Blumberg, drawn and quartered, so to speak. Says Kirk wouldn't want that either." He was still eyeing his palm and said nothing. "Problem?" I pointed to his hand.

"I...grabbed a mug right out of the microwave. Really hot. Stupid."

"Right. Well, that's how things are, it seems."

"Right. Good of you to look in on him. As to Mr. Blumberg, he isn't back yet. We've required him to see a psychiatrist. Still has a few more appointments. Depending on what the shrink says, he might be back, or not. Not something that'll happen quickly, I'm sure. Frankly I think we can make the case for expelling him, but I don't want to make it by *fiat*. Having him back with Kirk still in the hospital won't do, however, and would get the satellite trucks back at the gate..."

"Well, I've told you what Sally said about him."

"Sally? Quite inside the circle now, aren't we?" *Damn right you capricious sack of shit.* He cocked his head, as if this realization knocked his thinking a bit. "I know we've..." he massaged his bandaged hand while he searched for words, "we had a bad patch in the fall, Peter." I was happy to sit there and let him go on rather than make it easy for him by jumping in. "Thanks for keeping me posted. And for visiting him. I should get there myself this week."

"Might want to have them look at that hand when you do." With nothing more, I rose and headed for my classroom. Checking my email, I found one from Scott Paone.

Peter –

Thanks for the lesson plan on the section of Pompeii we spoke of... it does indeed speak to the decadence, which was enveloping Rome. During that first century. You're good to go. Think about this though: could you assign the book in sections and have your page numbers skip over the nasty passages? Just a thought - I think doing so would still preserve the integrity of your intent.
Scott

You're good to go Peter. Just don't go there. What a weasel. If he'd honestly come out and said don't use it, I'd respect him more. But this slippery BS calls for a truly passive aggressive response.

January 16

S HOW ME A TEACHER who shows entire films in history classes, and I'll show you a lazy history teacher. No need to show all of "Ben-Hur," as the chariot scene gives the idea of the Roman Empire's scope. A few kids always hold on the myth that a stunt man died in the filming of it. After we watched some clip of it this week, I handed out the assignments on Robert Harris's *Pompeii*.

A few students were already complaining about the task at hand. "Why do we have to read a whole book about a volcano erupting?" was the most banal question, and came from a junior who thinks that the "Matrix" films are collectively the eighth wonder of the world. Bright, articulate, and consistently hyper-cynical in an effort to seem mature.

"Because it's not simply about a volcano erupting," I offered.

"Well, it's not like a battle or something," he shrugged, "where someone won and someone lost."

"You don't need armies clashing for history," I offered. "Natural disasters impact things."

"Like when?"

"Well, look at Katrina." I sat back. "Hurricane hits New Orleans, and the government's response - or lack of it - undercuts its credibility to the country and the world."

"Fine. One case." What a contrary little bastard. Why *ever* would his folks want him away from home at boarding school?

"The Mongols - conquered everything in Asia but Japan," I offered, "and why? In the thirteenth century, a typhoon destroyed their fleet as they were on the verge of invading. And they never got there."

"So what's this volcano do?"

"Turn a few pages and find out. Here are the writing prompts. The idea is to develop a narrative about first century Rome as you read. But take heart: you don't have to read the whole book. There are a few parts you can skip. Some pages aren't crucial to the story, and I've indicated them on this handout. They're numbered, with the page numbers too. Most of these passages involve side plots, so spare yourself. Number seven is definitely off limits. Don't trouble yourself. In fact, you are *not* to read it. *At all.*"

"Mr. Burnham, are you, like…" Several students now had wrinkled brows. "censoring our, y'know, reading?" *You know.* Conjunction. Often pronounced y'know. Used when the speaker wishes to be inarticulate.

"No," I shook my head. "Not at all. That…would be wrong"

"So how can you tell us not to read something?"

"Easy. Don't read that part."

"Why are some parts on this form labeled 'don't need,' and one part is 'definitely avoid.'?" A four-year senior wondered.

"Look, I'm trying to save you some work. And part of your souls."

"What?"

"Nothing," I waved off my aside.

"How about a book burning?" someone suggested. "We can bring marshmallows."

"Yaaaahh, dis is a goot idea." Another student piped up. "Ve can make zhe smores for za fraulines." I couldn't help but smile at the German accents.

"I'm just trying to spare you a bit of homework. Of course," I threw my hands up and looked helpless, "if you choose to ignore my instructions and read a certain passage on your own...I mean, I can't lean over your shoulder as you turn the pages. Far be it for me to monitor your reading." A few were now exchanging intrigued looks and grins. "*Very* far be it."

January 19

ARON DROPPED BY FOR chess and conversation today. He actually won our third game. I'm afraid I've mentored him a bit too well, and find myself spending some of our time running possible lessons for the week ahead through my brain when I should probably be studying the board. When he leaned over for checkmate, I caught a distinctly unpleasant whiff of him. It was as if he'd recently bathed with the cake of soap from the bottom of a urinal. A minefield, but I had to.

"How's the water in the bathroom down the hall these days?"

"Water?"

"Sometimes in winter, it takes forever for the water to warm up. For showers. Then there's a big rush for them. In twenty minutes all the hot water would be gone."

"No problem...I think," he cocked his head.

"So you're able to get hot water? For a shower? Everyday?"

"Yes. No problem.

"That's good. Make sure you get in there early."

"Okay." He resumed his focus on resetting the board and I let the hygiene matter go. Playing chess with Aaron on Saturday mornings was hardly something his father had to pay me for, but the good doctor is no poorer than he is stupid. Chatting up his son actually is a bit of a chore though, which makes me feel better about cashing his checks. As he aligned all the pawns, he had a question.

"Do you know Estabrook?"

"Is...he a student here?" I wondered.

"I...don't think so...the...school."

"Oh. Estabrook. *Academy?*"

"Yes!" He was suddenly lifelike.

"Sure - it's in New Hampshire."

"Is it... a good school?" he desperately wanted a positive answer

"A *good* school? Well, it's not a bad school, really." I reached for that boilerplate admissions statement. "There's a right school for each student. Why?"

"A Korean student is there. He is from my town." So are most of the Koreans in America. His town is Seoul; population eleven million. One quarter of the nation's citizens. There's a kid from there at another school in New Hampshire. Small world.

"I expect there are a few students from Seoul there." Just then, a knock at the door and Bags blew in, arms full of books, and Aaron jumped a mile.

"Relax. I'm not Kim Jong Un." Bags threw out, then unloaded his arms on my excuse for a dining room table. Aaron got the Korean name, but nothing else. "I was going to toss these books – thought you might want to browse them first."

"So it is a good school yes?" Aaron continued.

"Well..."

"What school?" Bags' hearing is extraordinary.

"Estabrook. In New---"

"I *know* where it is…"

"Aaron was asking about it."

"Why?" He was sorting books on my table without looking up. "Found that Willa Cather first edition for you." He waved a small green hard cover over his head.

"Maybe," Aaron jumped back into things. "I would enjoy going to school with someone there. Next year."

"Why would you do that?" Bags was in full Charles Laughton mode now.

"So, it is…not…a good school?" Just then his cell phone rang. Bags took this as a good time to bow out with a half wave.

The common perception of Estabrook is that it's a jock school in a great setting by a huge lake. You can get bounced out of just about anywhere else and still go there. If you can skate or sink an outside jumper, you can get kicked out of public school and go there. Such schools serve a purpose: there are kids with attention issues who can do well in the right school. If such a kid can develop a slap shot into a laser, he or she has a shot at certain colleges that would otherwise be out of the question. With the democratization of college after World War II and the mad rush to go coed in the 1970s, campuses were flush with first-generation boarding school students, but not all of the kids were destined for a prize ceremony in Stockholm. Most schools realized this, and some carved out niches for themselves as alternatives to training future Whiffenpoofs. There are artsy schools, ski academies, tennis academies, and the artistic ones send budding Van Clyburns or Yo Yo Mas to conservatories. If a family has the tuition dollars, there's a school for their kid, even if he will never come to terms with differential equations.

When Aaron was done with his call, I tried to frame the matter for him. "You don't want to go to a school just because someone else goes there." I knew that if Aaron found suburban Boston seemed unwelcoming, rural New Hampshire would be a desert for him. "Are you unhappy here?"

"Not unhappy. Maybe…not the most happy. Sorry."

"Don't apologize - that's okay. There are days I'm not happy here also..."

"Really?" His eyes widened in disbelief.

"No place is perfect. Nice campus, lousy teams. Good teachers, bad food. Nice dorms, middle of nowhere. The trick is to find some good things about where you are, or make things there better - and to not think everything to death. Don't think too much about whether something isn't exactly as you'd like it. Nothing in life is." He nodded and squinted, as if chewing on my words. "There's a saying: the devil you know is better than the devil you don't. It means that, even if you don't totally love something, at least you understand it, but something you don't yet know, you might like even less; you just don't know."

"There's a saying like this in Korean too. My grandfather often says it." He zipped up his oversized North Face parka and nodded as a sort of a bow as he left. He seemed to leave more confused than he was when he arrived, as ten minutes later I realized that he'd left his phone on my coffee table. I'd get it to him later – the bus for my team was pulling up in front of the gym.

January 23

OUR SQUASH MATCH LAST weekend was at Chiswick; close enough to eat lunch here and then travel. The Chiswick School sprawls across a great lawn up from a crossroads in a quaint town full of *shoppes* an hour west of Boston. Founded as a church school in the 1800s, for years it was a home away from home for Boston's chosen frozen, St. Paul's being too remote in New Hampshire to be fashionable and Middlesex seemingly too secular. In the 1980s it suffered a student sex scandal that would have made Bill Clinton proud. The tweedy teachers and *forms* rather than grades persist though, and its squash courts are spiffy. A few Cabots and Armours still clutter the class lists, suggesting that the same DNA is tearing up the playing fields as it was a century earlier.

Squash remains a club; either you're in it or not. The glass back wall of the court itself offers a partition of more than one kind, actually, and the tight-lipped intensity of the competitors enhances this. To be sure it won't be found at PS 112 or on the back streets of Newark, and it breeds prodigies in certain athletic clubs. Scores of kids pick it up before they can ride a bike. This produces 10-year-old phenoms from Brooklyn's Casino or Boston's Union Club who get carted around to tournaments up

and down the East Coast for a month of weekends each year. Their rail shots and drops seem effortless and they tend to judge other people by their abilities as players. The ranks of my girls' team are not brimming with such *enfant terribles*, but a few do affect a myopic intensity accompanied by Steffi Graf temperaments, which help us hold our own on the court. Teams rank their players, so that their number ones play each other, their number twos play each other, and so on. Our number one is now Madison Jackson, an Aryan ice maiden from Shaker Heights. Her corner of the squash bus - and wherever she reverts to her intra-absolute self-zone - is a bubble of texting and gazing out the window, keeping all at bay with an arctic, aloof demeanor that would make Grace Kelly seem warm and fuzzy. Quietly, I think she still held a grudge from the evening of my duty in her dorm when I said 'no TV.'

At Chiswick we took to half the courts, as their girls were already warming up. The gallery for spectators is basically a causeway overhead between the facing courts. It was already buzzing with idle boys, who didn't have a game that day, but knew that the girls in squash skirts did. The pre-match chat from the co-captains was pretty perfunctory, but I always enjoy listening to them before putting some icing on it.

"Anticipate," Maddie pounded her fist into a palm at the center of the pre-match scrum, "*where* is her shot going to *go?* Look at her *feet*. The angle of the racket. Get there *before* the ball does. And forget the boys up in the gallery. If they're here on a Saturday, they didn't even make a team." Lot of warmth, that Maddie. Hopefully she'll go into nursing.

The matches began, and the early ones went quite well for us, then the momentum shifted, and when it came to the fourths and thirds, Chiswick took each of our girls in three straight. Our number two, Cheryl Powers, stepped into the court while tying up her hair. She and her opponent split the first four games,

building the focus for the final one. A few volleys in, Cheryl stood at the T in the middle of the court while her opponent dropped the ball right above the tin. The tin is the foot-high base of the wall at the front of the court, above which all shots must land. Returning your shots after they hit the wall is the task of your opponent, and the idea is to make this impossible. A drop is when you just kiss the ball with your racquet rather than smack it so that it taps the front wall and dies there. As consistent as her opponent was at this, Cheryl seemed unable to adjust her game to it.

"*C'mon*, Cheryl!" Maddie had her hands on hips and was in full Sharapova-Joan Crawford mode. "No gifts. *Get* that next time. *My little sister* could get that." Heading back to the glass wall for the obligatory wipe of the hand on the glass, Cheryl eyed Maddie for a second as she brought her hand downward to remove sweat. She kept one finger extended a second longer than the others, which some of us caught. Cheryl looked down at her racquet, spoke to herself, lost the next point, then proceeded to smoke her opponent, sending her to chase the ball's shadow for the final points. It was almost like rope a dope. They shook hands when it was over, and Cheryl made it a point to reach for a towel before acknowledging Maddie's high fives. Eyeing the Chiswick girls, I could see that they had expected an easier time of it, and were puzzled at how we were holding our own against them. Their number one was a gal from Zimbabwe, six two if she is a foot. Fifty years earlier, the only people at the church schools who looked like her were serving food or folding laundry. Since New England schools are probably not foremost in the mind of 17-year-old girls in Harare, probably some Chiswick alum traveling in Africa saw her one day at a club owned by someone in Mugabe's family. She gets a nice American education, Chiswick gets an amazing squash player and a bit of color for its catalog.

Finally, the number ones took the court. Maddie's opponent probably broke a sweat while beating her in the first match, but not much of one. She basically controlled the T, planting herself in the center of the court and went one way or the other to return Maddie's shots, starting out with 15-6 and 15-9 wins.

"Play *your* game, *not hers,*" I told her before the third game. "Send it to the corner to make it die there. Get off the tee. *Drops.* That's your game." She nodded and wiped her red, glistening face, betraying nothing.

Like someone who knew what she had to do all along, she followed the game plan, dropping her head with each point, slapping the ball with her racket to the floor six times before each serve. After an endless volley for game point to clinch the third one, she wiped her brow and dropped the towel at my feet. The fourth match began as a seesaw, and by the time it was 10 - 10, it was clear that this match would end up in both schools' papers next week, possibly in the yearbook write-ups as well. Lost on no one was the reality that someone had to lose quite soon.

Maddie found a second wind somewhere and got to places on the court faster than the ball. A burst of cheers at each point was followed by a sputtering of encouragement from each side, then hushed silence reigned, as if it were the 18th hole at St. Andrews. At 13-10, Maddie seemed in charge, tuning out the noise. Awaiting the serve, her opponent looked as fresh as she did in the first match. After sixteen years under Mugabe, this was probably a stroll for Ms. Zim. After a half-minute-long volley - a genuine eternity in squash – Maddie sent a return towards her opponent that she probably could've hit - but she was just close enough for the judge to call a let; Maddie's position on the court was so close to where Ms. Zim's racquet would have smacked the ball that she prevented her opponent from hitting it - she otherwise would have.

"Let," the referee was matter of fact.

"What?" Maddie was livid. The call gave her opponent a do-over while some of our girls, including the one on the court, thought Ms. Zim could have it hit it, but didn't, and that the point should be Maddie's.

"Let." The ref repeated. "Chiswick serve, from the right."

Mouth open, eyes like daggers, Maddie turned away tossing her blonde ponytail with as much contempt as any middle finger. Another long volley; Maddie dropped one just above the tin, but Ms. Zim saw it coming. She slapped it against the wall and sent it well behind Maddie. A textbook kill shot, there's nothing to be done at such times. There are some kill shots even Jonathon Power can't get. Miss Zim now had her number, and just repeated the sequence of shots, pushing ahead to 14-13.

"Maddie," Cheryl bellowed, "no gifts." She and I exchanged looks. She needed to know that I didn't like her timing, but inside I smiled.

Maddie returned a serve nicely, and had her opponent covering a lot of court, tiring her a bit. In a nice move, her opponent raised her racket as if to send a bullet to the wall and instead dropped it just above the tin, not moving afterwards. Maddie sprinted up front, slapped it back, hard enough to arch back to the glass. She'd done so twice before, something boys love to do, but rarely seen in girls' matches at this level. Maddie can be her own worst enemy with her blood up, and was here as well. The ball sailed two inches over the glass and into the crowd.

Ms. Zim reached skyward with both arms as if preparing for chin-ups on an invisible bar, then pulled them down by her side, fists clinched. It looked as though she exclaimed *yes!* at the moment, but the eruption from her teammates and the crowd drowned it out. The two shook hands and exited the court, repairing to two very different team benches. Maddie buried her face in a towel, and everyone knew well enough to give her space.

As the girls gathered their gear, she emerged and called for the team huddle. She gave the obligatory *we did our best* speech, eyes down the entire time. "These guys smoked Miss Porter's last week. Seeing how we almost had them today," she held up two pinching fingers in a *this close* sort of way, "we should definitely own Porter's on Wednesday. Bring it in." All right hands went to the middle of the huddle, and the Grizzlies' team cheer preceded the drag to the locker room. As I lingered to check for all our gear, the Chiswick coaches – a salt and pepper spinster north of fifty and a Nordic deb-jock killing time before grad school – came over to chat.

"Your gals are pretty game," Salt and Pepper offered. "They were right in it all the way"

"Your number one is something," I answered. "What year is she?"

"Fifth form... no, fourth actually." In Anglo-prep-speak, either a junior or sophomore; school records from Zimbabwe can be so confusing, don't you know. The small talk always turns to who else you've played and swapping scouting reports. I did a bit of fishing to see whether any faculty had already announced that they were leaving at year's end.

"Heard there might be a change or two in the History Department here..." I tried to sound quite casual. I hadn't heard anything, but such a prompt can get people thinking about who might not be returning.

"Hmmm..." the deb-jock tilted her head and eyed her colleague, "you think Sandy's gonna finally pack it in?"

"I dunno," Salt and Pepper shrugged, "what's-her-name grumbles and threatens to retire every year...She's got issues with...an administrator here, but you didn't hear it from me. If *he* left, she'd stay, if he stays..." She shrugged again. "Where'd you hear this?"

"Oh you know," I hoisted an equipment bag onto my shoulder, "people talk at conferences, and lots of times it's just talk, but you always wonder…"

Back on the bus, with hair still wet from showers and cell phones out, talk turned to the dance that night. The consensus was that the DJ at the last dance was lame. The lack of testosterone makes coaching girls preferable to the Schy's team. Be it a ref's bad call, some other perceived injustice, or simply a loss, boys can own it for two days, sulking and bitching about it, like McEnroe with nothing else to do. Half the time it's someone else's fault, of course. With girls, by the time the bus is halfway back to school, some of them can't tell you the final scores of their matches.

I'm usually happy to let wayward phones remain wayward, but the largesse of Aaron's father nudged me to return the one he'd left in my apartment. Trudging down the hall, I stuck my head into the room and found his roommate Sean Regan twisting the top onto a bottle of baby shampoo over a bucket; odd but innocuous. He did, however, go into mild convulsions when he heard my voice. A bit of an under the radar kid, his curly red hair was under a backwards Mets' cap. His slim form keeps him at the JV levels for sports, and while he's never been in any of my classes, I've heard he's content to get by.

"Hi Sean."

"Hi… Mr. Burnham. What are you…"

"Just looking for Aaron "

"Oh… he's not… I don't know…"

"No sweat. Don't forget to use conditioner."

"Huh?"

I pointed to the nearly empty shampoo bottle in his hands.

"Oh…yeah." The odd little moment was just weird enough that I forgot why I'd gone there and headed to dinner, still with Aaron's phone in my pocket.

Saturday night is a pretty quiet meal, with some students signed out, and others content to order pizza later. Parking at the faculty dinner table at this time affords its unique form of depression; *this* is my Saturday night? I had a nasty cold, which ruled out one of Bags' Old Fashioneds. Over pasta with marinara sauce, Allison and Scott were flushing out the matter of how our students are too focused on goals, often forgetting process.

"It would never occur to most of these kids to pursue something they actually liked, unless they were *convinced,* or convinced their *parents*, that it would offer them real security." Allison was scanning the thin ranks of international students at tables, and a smattering of day students waiting to be picked up after their games.

"Don't knock material security," Scott was making a pyramid of his carrots. "And clothing is great now and again. Our kids are just more practical than say, a Jackson Pollack or Herman Melville. Did you know that Golding's *Lord of the Flies* was rejected by twenty publishers before it saw print? That's no fun."

"I'm not saying that they have to go out and try to become world-famous artists." Allison was resting her chin on upturned palms now, her elbows on the table. "But even the theater kids - some of them have real talent, but wouldn't dream of pursuing that stuff in college. They couldn't stand the idea of having to wait tables for ten years, hoping for some callback from some "Law and Order" clone or summer stock. They want everything *now.*"

"Lots of kids from schools like this have become pretty famous actors," I offered, uninspired by the assortment on my plate. "These are exactly the kind of kids who can afford to pursue something like that."

"Who *are* you talking about?" Allison was incredulous.

"Well, James Spader was at Andover," I was ticking off names with my fingers, "Laura Linney at Northfield…Huey Lewis went to Lawrenceville and quit Cornell to play music. It happens"

"Well, how common is it though?" Ever practical Scott.

"The two actors in "Fatal Attraction," that movie years ago," I recalled a factoid from somewhere, "this is weird - Michael Douglas and Glenn Close: they were both at Choate, almost at the same time. Coincidence? I think not."

"So... you think Choaties are destined to kill each other's rabbits after sex?" Schy, who'd to that point been working a salad, chimed in. "I like it. Could be a new reality show."

"And Sam Waterston went to Groton," I remembered, "There's another"

"So did that big green guy in "The Munsters," that goofy '60s show," Schy is like an encyclopedia of this stuff. "Cotty Peabody must've been so proud." Endicott Peabody founded Groton and had a knack for molding his boys into men who ended up in presidential cabinets, as well as one fellow who got to call the White House home and now sits on the dime.

"Peabody died a while before TV came along, old sport," Scott had a ring of assuredness about him. "They can't all become crippled four-term presidents."

"What about Howard Dean?" Allison was popping grapes in her mouth. "I met him once. Did he go somewhere?"

"Oblivion." Schy did have good timing. "Before that, St. George's."

"Nice campus, there," Scott nodded. "Kind of a happy, little place with happy, shiny people."

"None of the *wrong* kind, you know," Schy affected a mock lockjaw - yacht club drawl.

"This from someone who goes to Myopia," I pointed out, mentioning the polo club north of Boston named for an ocular malady that he suggested he'd been to once or twice.

"Once. I went *once."* Then he went with it, back into a lockjaw, "and they *ran out* of mint Julips. Can you be-*lieve* it?"

Checking e-mail after dinner, there was a message from Sally Mayhew.

> Dear Peter,
>
> Your concern for Kirk in the wake of this incident has been genuine and most appreciated. This is why I feel the need to share with you the developments on this front. Yesterday, doctors again worked to reduce swelling inside Kirk's skull. Based on data this morning, apparently they were not successful. The complexities of injuries to the brain are more than I can correctly detail here, but at the end of the day, doctors are less than sanguine about him regaining consciousness. Simply put, the swelling within his skull has forced the dura inward, creating more pressure on the cerebral cortex than his brain can bear- it's as simple as that. Some time ago, Kirk and I prepared living wills, expecting that they might be good to have in 30 or 40 years. We both included wishes not to be sustained in a persistent vegetative state, which is how Kirk's doctors have described his condition. We will be arranging to have Kirk's wishes honored in the most peaceful and compassionate manner in the near future. I thought you would want to know, and will be in touch when matters take their course.
> Best,
> Sally M.

I sensed it was a form letter of sorts, but nice to be in the loop all the same. I'd been to the hospital a number of times since we'd met, and apparently word of this had reached her. It would've been quite nice to have something very responsive to kick at this moment - ideally, the groin of a certain long-haired ne'er do well from Connecticut, but that's unprofessional, of course. I wasn't quite sure how to respond, so it didn't entirely bother me that Aaron's cell phone went off just then. Not finding him in his room earlier, I hadn't left it there. Heading over to Wentworth, I found the Saturday night drill in full swing: guys digging out clean shirts and crowding mirrors to sculpt hair. A few steps before Aaron's room, a desk chair exited mid-air into the corridor wall. It tumbled to the floor, but didn't break up like the saloon chairs in western movies. It was chased by a dresser drawer full of socks that didn't weather the trip quite at all well.

"You *dick!*" was followed by more clunking of furniture and bodies. Inside, Aaron and Sean had turned the room into a small, smokeless version of Dresden, and were trading lousy wrestling moves. This wasn't horseplay; it was a hockey fight in a 10 x 14 dorm room.

"Break it up! *Now!*" This was my outside voice. A headlock and cursing persisted. "Break it up *now* or be *incredibly* unhappy tomorrow!" This was my outside voice when barking into a headwind off Cape Cod. Each was waiting for the other to relent. "I do *not* need this shit on my off duty Saturday night!"

Profanity from a teacher is often a showstopper. A floor prefect appeared, followed by half the dorm, and slowly headlocks subsided.

"First, get this crap out of the hall. Next---"

"Mr. B," Sean started in true schoolyard fashion, "he---"

"*Next,* shut up. I'm not on duty tonight. You'll see a new concept of pissed off if I have to spend more than the next three minutes here." I tossed Aaron's phone on the bed, and turned to the prefect. "Clear the hallway and call Mr. Remillard. He's on duty. Fighting, damaging school property. He can add to the list."

"He ruined my laptop!" Sean exploded, rummaging around on the floor to find it. "*Look*it! Fu---," he caught himself. "Freaking *ruined.* Look. A new Dell this year. I've got *work* on here! On the *desktop.*" He tossed it back to the floor. The keyboard was smothered with a mucky, yellow liquid. "And *he* did it!" He jabbed a finger at Aaron, whose eyes were daggers right back at him. "Go 'head. *Tell* him."

"Quiet Sean."

"But he---"

"*Shut up!*" Not my most professional moment. "Aaron?"

"He…" fumbling for words with a twisted face, he patted his bowl cut, "My hair." He smelled his hand and winced.

"What about it?" He eyed the doorway, thick with spectators, and I waved the stragglers away, closing it.

"He…" This moment was the reason the phrase pregnant pause was invented. "He went in my shampoo. And I used it."

"Went?"

"He…" Looking about frantically, seeking a word. Failing that, he simulated urinating.

"It…washes out…" Sean shrugged in a sort of *it's not that bad* way.

"And what to help wash out? *Shampoo?*"

"It's not like it costs you money. That lap top was---*Je*-sus!"

"So…" I turned to Aaron, "when did you figure this…*how* did you figure this out?"

"In the lounge. They were laughing. And…they told me, after they said I smelled…"

"And they told you, Sean did it?" He nodded.

"So you poured the shampoo on his keyboard?" He nodded again. "And you found your computer that way? Just now?" Sean nodded.

"Is what Aaron heard true?"

A Hobson's choice. Sean was turning his head to everything in the room but my gaze. "Mr. Burnham," Remy appeared in the doorway. "Little redecorating?" He surveyed the shit storm at our feet. Not being on duty, I was elated to hand the situation off to him and go nurse my cold in peace.

January 24

Dear Dr. Tang –

Aaron may have already contacted you regarding recent events here at school. I happened by his room as things erupted Saturday, and thought I'd share my understanding of things with you. It seems that on a dare (challenge) - from others, Aaron's roommate added his own urine to Aaron's shampoo bottle in their room. A very foul and unkind act indeed. When Aaron learned of this, he poured the shampoo into his roommate's laptop, ruining it. This came to a head Saturday in the form of a wrestling match in their room, which I broke up. I expect that this chain of events will result in some administrative response, impacting all involved, but such decisions are not in my hands. My current understanding of the matter, however, is that Aaron did not initiate the trouble. I will try to make this clear to others as they decide on a response. Aaron is most welcome to discuss this matter with me as it proceeds. I will keep you posted.

Sincerely,
Peter Burnham

Dear Mr. Burnham,

Thank you for your e-mail of last night. Aaron's mother and I were aware of this troubling experience to him, but he would not share any details such as you have. We would like more knowledge of the matter as it is possible. We are glad you are involved and that Aaron can speak with you. Please keep us informed as soon as possible.

Ji Jeong Tang
Director of Reconstructive Surgery and Dermatology
Young Nam Medical University Hospital
1-11-14 Dae kwon Il Taegu, Korea

Schy nearly brought his orange juice through his nose when I recounted the matter over brunch Sunday morning.

"Wow. There's a cleverness in that whole chain of events, y'know?"

"I can't believe you're impressed with this?" Allison looked wounded. "How is a fight great?"

"Not that," Schy pushed his tray away. "The symmetry of it. Reagan whizzes in shampoo, Tang uses the same shampoo to trash his computer. The circularity of it is very tidy." Inwardly, I understood his comment. "Satur*day*, Satur*day*, Saturday *night's* alright…" Schy started up with Elton John, which fostered a lethal stare from Allison. "You're no fun." He muttered with a shrug, which did not suggest surprise.

"D.C. tomorrow after classes." I offered, as I'd already heard from Scott. "I'll need coverage for the first half squash," I was looking at Schy. "If the case runs long…" Disciplinary Committees seem to inspire wordiness in people.

"No sweat, I can get your girls started on some drills," Schy picked up his tray, "just give me the details afterwards." Schy knows that the content of Disciplinary Committees is confidential, meaning it will not be all over campus for at least half an hour after it ends.

188

January 25

THE MAJOR SCHOOL RULES at Griswold, not unlike the whims of adolescents, have been evolving for over a hundred years. As of now, the following infractions loom large on the radar:

Theft
Alcohol/drugs
Honor code
Willful injury to others
Inappropriate personal contact or communication
Behavior inconsistent with community
Violation of the Acceptable Use Policy of technology

Typically, a first offense results in a one-week suspension and a second means expulsion. Some schools treat persistently self-destructive behavior as a symptom of a personal problem rather than an offense, and alcohol awareness programs take the place of suspensions. Someone at my old school dubbed this approach 'Betty Ford Country Day.' The idea of healing kids dealing with an issue rather than just whacking them is noble; to treat every infraction as a symptom of a greater issue requiring 12-step meetings in the chapel basement is another matter. Sometimes, the application of rules seems as consistent as who gets stopped for speeding on Route 128. When decisions came down at my school, however, it always meant a visit from the parents.

"What'll your folks do?" My roommate asked his cousin our senior year after he was suspended for drinking.

"Obviously they know...dad's here. Let's see...they'll shake their heads, put a little blame on themselves, and shake their heads some more between sips of Mount Gay tonight." He was stuffing items into the duffel bag, having to pack for an involuntary week's vacation. "Probably have to see a shrink. Maybe I'll get to chill at one of those cushy places - you know, deluxe detox. Maybe I'll get James Taylor's old room at McLean. Y'know he wrote "Fire and Rain" about someone there?" McLean Hospital is a psychiatric mecca outside of Boston that also deals with substance abuse. He slung the bag over his shoulder and sauntered out to his awaiting father.

DCs are Griswold's way of looking at each case as a 'situation.' No outcome can be predicted, but if a student is before one a second time and shows no remorse for his actions, it's safe to say that the following day he will not be down for breakfast. Six theoretically disinterested members of the community - three faculty and three students - sit on the committee, which is chaired by an administrator, usually Scott Paone. They have everyone's version of events and kibitz to come up with a recommendation, which Barclay can follow or not. No action, a letter in a file, suspension, expulsion, or some Calvinistic dictate, like washing school vehicles every Saturday for a month, although there's less and less of that these days. Aaron and I were first before the committee. After they asked Aaron for his version of events, they turned to me. I began with my encounter of Reagan and the bottle of Johnson and Johnson.

"Are you sure it wasn't Sean's shampoo?" a student asked.

"No, but given what happened, connect the dots."

"So...it's possible that the shampoo you saw him with was his?" the same student.

"Look," a matter of fact math teacher, rolled his eyes. "We've got an admission he used Aaron's shampoo bottle as a bedpan. Got that?"

"I just..." the student had passed the point of accuracy and had arrived at anal. "I simply want to clarify that---"

"It's clarified. Don't watch so much TV." The impatient math teacher had heard enough. "Peter...Mr. Burnham, can you add anything else?"

"I know it seems childish to get into 'he started' stuff, " my fingers were quotation marks, "and the response, resulting in damaged property, is more quantifiable than say, soiled hair. But there's an aspect of...almost lewdness in urinating in someone's shampoo, which was the catalyst for why we're here."

"Doesn't lewdness suggest something... sexual?" The same pedantic student, clearly a future member of the ACLU, was at it again.

"Y-y-y-e-e-s-s-s...Perhaps lewdness is not the right word."

"How about perversely unsanitary?" My math colleague framed it nicely, and I was done.

Sean and his advisor were next. Outside in the hallway, Aaron sat on a deacons' bench. I pumped his shoulder as I headed off to squash. Should have taken another route. Barclay's door opened and a lean, fair - haired fellow who looked like a Brooks Brothers salesman stepped out, looked my way, turned and headed in the other direction. Barclay spotted me as I passed and called me in.

"That was some fellow from Kirk's office," he rubbed his brow, for want of a better reflex. "They are going ahead with...maybe you've heard..."

"I have..."

"Yes...his *aide de camp* called you by name...doesn't get much more inside than that..."

I did my best to not blink as we eyed each other. He was the one who said I'd be done in June, so if he didn't like it that and aide to our most famous alum knew my name, good.

"Is there a question in there?" What did I have to lose?

"Look Peter..," he raised a finger as if to suggest a salient point was at hand, and maybe because just then, I folded my arms and cocked my head like one of those ridiculous models in a full-page *Esquire* ad, he thought better of it. I've started searching school sites for positions, which I may have been doing anyway, even if he hadn't been such a hyper irrational dick over my email in October. Got to admit, too, for all the unknowns before me, it'll be fun to watch him stroll candidates through here in the spring for my job, knowing that he's hoping nobody tells them that contrary to the cover story he'll offer, that I have not in fact *chosen to move on*, and that he's a capricious SOB who got bent when he read someone else's email, which is what I'll put out there quietly once my job appears under "Employment" on the school's website.

"Peace for him, I guess," I wanted to wind this up.

"And a shitstorm for us."

"Do the Blumberg's know?"

"The Blumbergs...I couldn't give a rat's ass what the Blumberg's know. They know how to raise a kid to the verge of voting age who...They know how to be so vacuous that thanks to their kid's actions, our neighbors are on a first name basis with people from CNN and Fox News." He ran fingers back through his graying mane. "Not the most professional response, I know."

"Any word on when she...you know, the process?" End of life discussions aren't my forte.

"Soon. Good if they did it Friday night. Bury it in the news over the weekend. Maybe we'll get a nasty blizzard," he glanced out the window at some flurries, "and all the weather on the news will fill the air time until the lottery numbers, and it'll be on page three of the *Globe*."

"That'd be nice," I muttered, feeling odd speculating in this realm at all.

"But," he thinned his lips, "…I'm afraid we'll be back in the headlines. Above the fold, this time."

He wrinkled his brow, gazing at the paperweight on his desk. "If Blumberg sets foot in the state of Massachusetts, I'll get a restraining order against his coming to campus. And if he violates it, I'll drag him up to their little vacation dacha in Vermont and dangle him by his feet over the Quechee Gorge myself." He was pretty unguarded here. Maybe he figured he still had me by the short ones to the point that he doesn't need to worry about me quoting him to others. "I'll have External Affairs draft a statement for when things---"

"Sorry to interrupt…" Liz on his intercom. "Your 3:45 is here."

I turned and left without a word.

January 26

Feigning confidentiality, such communications are not meant for students, but the idea of a secret at a school is laughable. By lunch, common knowledge mutterings over the disposition of the matter sprinkled dining hall chatter.

"Whadja expect? He's Asian. Nice work if you can get it…"

"If Sean was a brother…"

Not unlike a tie in a hockey game, the outcome of the DC is always pretty unsatisfying.

Dear Dr. Tang,

I expect that you've been informed about the outcome of Aaron's DC. Personally I feel that Aaron was the more wronged party in the matter, and that his punishment might have been less than what he was given. My sense, however, is that those on the DC felt that the issue of the other student's

computer had to be addressed. While I understand this decision, it doesn't mean that I also agree with it, but would appreciate it if you not share my opinion with others. I feel that Aaron will bear his consequences well and that a change of roommates will help things take a positive direction here. Please be in touch as you wish.
Best,
Peter Burnham

In addition to a nice work out, cross country skiing is a good way of coping with winter, especially if your digs don't have a fireplace and the artwork about the walls will never show up at Sotheby's. I was out on the backside of the X-C course, enjoying what is as close as we get to powder in New England, when Kat Mc Phee passed me.

"Bend your knees, Petey!" She glided by.

"You first." She tossed her head back as if laughing, then disappeared over a hill between the brown, barren trees. Back on campus, I dropped by to give her a chance to apologize for passing me. She chuckled and started to make coffee.

"Is this place always so juicy?"

"Juicy?"

"Well," she flopped into a chair, "everything over the past few months. DCs, attempted assassinations, demolition derbies between parents and B & G trucks..."

"Life happens...here, it's just all in a fishbowl."

"Fun place. I can't wait for spring. But, I mean...kids whizzing in shampoo, tripping up a cabinet secretary, you couldn't make this stuff up."

"Well, it has been a rather...busy year...but there's stuff like this at every school. You just don't hear about it unless you're there."

"Sure," she turned and pointed to me with a sugar spoon, "but what's next?"

I shrugged. "Who knows? Maybe Jimmy Hoffa will turn up in the lower lacrosse field."

"Who?" Why I inserted American labor history from the 1970s into a discussion with an English teacher is beyond me.

"Famous missing person-years ago."

"Couldn't have been too famous," she shrugged, "How's squash?"

"Good. Fun. Doing better than we should. No real head cases this year."

"No? You could always take on Ms. Radzwill - she's only doing fitness this term."

"I don't know if there is enough of that," I pointed at a Smirnoff poster in her kitchen, "in all of Russia to inspire me to do that."

"How'd that car thing with her mom before the break work out?" she asked.

"I guess the insurance companies are sorting it out with the school. Mom quit talking about the truck being in a fire lane after Scott asked if there had been any alcohol at their dinner..."

"Yeah, I heard that. But that was days later. It's not like she'd show it."

"Scott suggested he might call the restaurant to check the bill."

"Ouch." She winced. "Remind me not to piss *him* off. Wasn't he already on your case too about some parent?"

"Made me give him a whole lesson plan for a book with one paragraph set at a whore house."

"Maybe you softened him up for me. I want to use a Philip Roth in the spring. Some..." she flattened her hands, palms down, and tilted back and forth, "some parts of it could be dicey."

"Which Roth?"

"*Portnoy.*"

196

"For sophomores?"

"Don't make a face like that. He's got a distinct style. Very American."

"*Playboy* is a very American magazine, but…"

"Are you a prude Peter?" She flashed an inviting grin, then rose to fetch the coffee.

"Ever read his *Great American Novel?*" I asked. She shook her head.

"What's the title?"

"That's it. *The Great American Novel.* Clever. Really funny. And safe."

"I don't want safe. Not a priority."

"No, but when you're making someone else's kids read it, the law of large numbers says you're bound to encounter a few bible thumpers."

"Hell," she threw her head back, "when I was at school, we read *Lady Chatterley*. Senior year *The Canterbury Tales*. Ever read those?"

"Sure," I leaned in, "but years ago, you didn't have parents calling every time a teacher looked at a kid cross eyed. We had a teacher pull a gun on a kid in class, it never came to anything."

"A gun? A teacher? You are joking."

"Middle of class. Really…"

"How…why…" she handed me my coffee and pointed to the cream and sugar with a look of disbelief.

"It was pre-Columbine, so not the big deal that would've been later on."

"Why would a teacher point a gun at a kid?"

"English teacher. Junior year. We were reading, *Billy Budd* and this one kid - Rudy Gutman - starts trying to draw analogies between the captain of the ship and Hitler."

"Was the captain anti-Semitic?"

"I don't even remember. But Rudy was just not shutting up. So he got on this ridiculous tangent, and Kingswood, the teacher, tries to rein him in. No luck. He's just going on and on - bringing in Kristalnacht, everything. We're just looking at him, wondering what he was on. Finally Kingswood – who's also the boy's swimming and crew coach - pulls out a starter pistol. Uses it in races, and trains it on him. Rudy freezes midsentence and Kingswood just says, "D' ya feel lucky Rudy?" – right outta that Clint Eastwood movie.

"No way." Her mug was poised before her mouth agape.

"Way. When we figure out it was a starting pistol, we just lose it. It was classic. I mean, here I am, talking about it all these years afterwards. The point is, none of us – well, far as I know - rushed to call home and tell our parents that Kingswood pulled a gun on a kid in class. We saw it for what it was. A stunt. No long term psychological damage."

"Wow. Fun class."

"Yeah. I still remember it, and that was the book in which I learned what a phenomenon was."

"Oh?"

"Yeah. An extremely rare incident or event, but one which can transpire, nevertheless."

"How did that come up?"

"When Billy Budd was hung, his body---"

"Hanged," she corrected me.

"What?"

"Never read it, but he was hanged?"

"Hung, yeah. What?"

"Pictures are hung. People are hanged."

"Wow. You're ...anal."

"No...just a native speaker of English. Anyway, go on. What happened to Kingswood?"

"Nothing. He retired a few years ago. Married some hardware heiress and lives on Bermuda."

"Hmmm…" she cocked her head, "Guess he… felt lucky."

January 31

ARCLAY WASN'T TOO FAR off hoping that some breaking news might bump Kirk's odyssey from the front pages. Thursday night in Providence, a lineman for the New England Patriots was in some club at 2 AM. Gunfire breaks out while he's getting a lap dance from some *unknown female*. He bolts and is clocked doing 97 on I-95, and the woman plays 'Do you know who I am with?' when the cop comes up to the window. Turns out she's the daughter of the woman who taught Marion Barry how to smoke crack in a police video years ago. That would've been good enough. But she supposedly had a part in some MLK ceremony last week in Boston. Her story changes when that news gets out. Suddenly the story involves the cop making a racial inference during the matter. That sound of a credit card people heard was Sharpton booking tickets for Boston. This matter involving sports, sex and race was a textbook media maelstrom that squeezed Kirk's passing to below the fold in the *Globe* Saturday morning. *Mrs. Mayhew expressed an intention to honor her husband's wishes. "We thought a great deal about this before making these plans. Kirk lived his life with dignity, and his fate needs to also involve dignity."* The article noted that life support would be disconnected at some point, and that a memorial service in

Washington and north of Boston were in the works as well as plans for a remembrance on Nantucket in the summer. I sent Sally a note and a small gift to the ASPCA in his memory. Kirk made headlines once spotlighting animal abuse in the food industries, and such donations were requested in lieu of flowers. The Patriots' lineman's news - the "Bronco Brouhaha," as a local TV station put it – kept satellite trucks busy somewhere other than at the school gates. With word of Kirk's fate, faculty at dinner that night were pretty quiet. I went to my apartment and watched "The Departed." Again.

February 3

EVERY SOCIETY HAS ITS icons of beauty; often they're movie stars, sometimes they're athletes. For better or worse, we seem unable to ignore these salient symbols of physical perfection, who at some point probably reconcile themselves to being subjects of ogling by both sexes for life. Some schools more than others seem sprinkled with heavy quotas of well-scrubbed kids with great teeth whose coloring and tossing of hair suggest summers by salt water, riding in open Jeep Wranglers. Of this ilk, Griswold has at least one specimen who causes boys to be a bit less attentive in class than they should be: Lettisha Cathcart, a.k.a. Tish the Dish among our hormone-heavy lads. Tish is a junior who might have been kept back three or four times. This is offered not as a reflection of her intellect, but rather because she could perhaps pass for twenty-three years old and maybe a Fox News anchor. She uses this gift to her advantage whenever possible. Which is often. On campus she's usually at the center of a small entourage, acolytes hoping to pick up some of her glow. Her hair twirling and head tilting are said to get her extra helpings in the dining hall. At games, fathers steal glances at her. Girls and mothers mutter about a budding trophy wife. To be sure, good things will happen to her. Perhaps she'll be a TV weather girl a year out of college, or a hostess at La Cirque. Party photos in *Boston* magazine and *Vanity Fair*. In twenty years, she will be backing an SUV out from in front of *shoppes* in Wellesley or Stamford or some other *townne*, heading to the local day spa on time. It is no secret how good looks allow those who enjoy them to make unreasonable requests effortlessly and to have them granted, simply on the basis of appearance, while those of us less blessed have queries turned away.

A week ago an email from Tish's adviser mentioned that next year she was hoping to take *Honors Global Issues*. The class is commonly subscribed to by two types of students: those who are emotionally invested - as much as any teenager will be in matters such as genocide and fair trade - and those who still need a history course to meet graduation requirements and want the H before the course name on a transcript. Tish is definitely in the latter category. This is not to say that she has an echo chamber between her ears, but it is safe to say that she will not walk at graduation with a gold *cum laude* tassel dangling from her mortarboard. I told her adviser I'd think on it. After squash practice last Friday, Lettisha spotted me on a path outside the gym and headed my way.

"Mr. Burnham!" Tish was walking towards me on the path from her dorm. The narrowly shoveled lane put us face to face, as waist-high snow banks on all sides made anything else impossible. Tish is not in the habit of calling out to others, no more than Reese Witherspoon calls out to reporters at film premieres.

"Hi Tish."

"You have a minute?"

"Sure."

"You teach *Global Issues*, right?"

"Right."

"Well, I'd like to take it. Next year."

"Super. Great to have you."

"At the honors level."

"Okay..."

"You mean, 'OK I can' or 'OK you heard me?' "

She leaned forward and raised her eyebrows hopefully as a cold gust tossed her hair back a bit.

"I think it's great you want to take it. It's a fun class. Important too."

"Yeah. S-s-s-o-o-o...Honors..."

"Right. How did you do in my class as a freshman?'

"I...I gotta 'B'. I had mono that winter, but... I really liked your class."

"If you've got a B average in the humanities, no problem. Otherwise, it's sort of up to your current English and history teachers to recommend you for honors classes."

"Yeah," she pursed her lips, "I spoke to Mrs. Carpenter, my adviser. She said to ask you."

"How are you doing in her class?"

She cocked her head a bit with the wincing smile.

"I got a B in the fall. I think. And...I got a 90 on the first test this term."

"Nice. So...your average is probably..."

"P-u-u-r-r-r-o-o-o-o-o-o-bably.... good. But, I've missed some homework. I had a cold a few times."

"Well, the College and Honor courses cover the same content."

"I just *know* I can do it." She flashed the kind of smile seen on patrons calling on a storeowner five minutes after closing, imploring the proprietors to reopen for them.

"I know you're capable Tish. I'm not an ogre in Honors, but there is more writing and the tests are...It's not just writing. It's writing analytically."

"*I* can do that." It was if she was trying to channel both a girl scout in earnestness and a Cosmo cover with her fixed glare.

"I...bet that you can. And---"

"S-s-s-s-o-o-o-o-o..."

This is never fun. If it was all on the level, namely if her grades warranted it, fine, but that she was asking me suggested that her grades didn't make the case by themselves. Regardless of the student, inherent in the teacher, perhaps in any person of authority beseeched by others, is the sense that it is infinitely easier to say *yes* and move on. Obviously, however, there are ripples to doing so.

"How about...we see how you do for this term?" I returned her imploring glare.

"So, if I get 'B's ...of any kind...?"

"B+s would be best...a B- would give me pause...and if you started in the 'College' section and found it too easy, you could always move up."

"Yeah ...but," she indulged in two Tishian gestures: twirling her hair and biting her lip. Truth be told I happen to think she may be able do the honors work, but if not, sending a student down is much more involving than moving one up to honors; the *I'll try harder* and *It's just that I lost my notes* excuses and pleas are endless. If she were a candidate for the course, it would be because of her grades, and we wouldn't be doing this, but she's on the cusp. Candidly though, now I did not want to appear susceptible to her charms, so mentally I was digging in my heel even harder.

"Let's see how the term goes and be sure to ask me after the break...you know where my classroom is right?" Her disappointed sigh sent a quick, white puff into the dusk air, suggesting this – a *no* - was a somewhat alien response to her appeals. I pumped her shoulder lightly for encouragement and squeezed by on the path.

"Ok-a-a-a-a-a-a-y-y-y, Mr. Bu---"

Just then I found a nice patch of ice that sent me forward. A reflex made me grab her sleeve, and losing her own footing on the same ice, she came down on top of me. For two seconds, a whole sea of awkward engulfed us as we were nose to nose. As we pulled ourselves up, I asked her more times than was necessary if she was okay and apologized. All the way back to the dorm, I cursed Building & Grounds for their stinginess with rock salt.

February 6

FEBRUARY AT A SCHOOL in New England is, to paraphrase Tom Paine, a time that tries people's souls. The weather keeps kids in the dorms, prompting faculty to confiscate countless lacrosse sticks and hot plates. Roommates get on each other's nerves and at each other's throats, and when faculty get sick, others have to sub for them. This fosters a bit of resentment - first among the frequently drafted subs, then everyone.

"Christ," Bags spat one day at lunch. "Hasn't anyone here ever heard of a flu shot?" Kids start asking for extensions on work, while mentioning in the next breath that they're headed to Aruba for March break. At the all school meeting yesterday, Scott Paone was presiding and called for announcements. A few hands were up.

"Mrs. Carpenter?"

"The trip for Walden leaves at 7:30 tomorrow - so get to breakfast early and dress warmly."

"Mr. Remillard." Scott nodded at him with a hint of weariness.

"Boys' basketball: you'll be dismissed early today for the game at Tabor." *Whoops!* from the varsity and JV. "But you're still responsible for any work assigned in classes you miss. So check your class websites, and be at the bus at 1:15." Some hisses and sniggering followed.

A student volunteered that a Friday showing of "Do the Right Thing" will have an admission charge of two dollars, which will help fund the culminating event for Black History Month

"BHM! BHM!" Scott patted down the chant from one distinct area of the student seating, and offered some parting wisdom on avoiding the school pond, the ice on it looking deceptively thick. Black History Month is a perennial opportunity to give dedicated attention to certain aspects of a heritage that have received short shrift or been downright ignored in years past.

"Mr. Burns," Isaiah Franklin stopped me as I posted BHM event notices outside the Moody Student Center after lunch, "how come brothers get only one month?"

"Well, Isaiah, I teach history all year, and---"

"That's your job - and it's the shortest month too." He was more curious than annoyed.

"Isaiah, I didn't pick February. I was out of town for that meeting. I suspect...someone who's black did." He kicked some plowed snow at his feet and looked away. I'm not going to pretend to know what it's like to be him; a black scholarship kid at a largely white school, where fifty years ago, you might have found six students of color in the whole school yearbook. Some kids think he's here due to his skin color only, others think it's because of his skill as a point guard until his girth slowed him down. Kids at home call him an Oreo and clerks at the mall follow him when he's in a store, while Aaron and Sean go unnoticed. As nuts as Sharpton is, he strikes a nerve in Isaiah, and for all the yuks Dave Chapelle and Chris Rock provide, there's some truth in their rants too. The midwinter chill had thrown a blanket of quiet over the campus, and we stood there, our breath evaporating into the blue stillness overhead, trying to sort out a footnote to four centuries of problems. It was one of those rare teacher - student moments that will stay with me.

"Isaiah, as for the month, don't go all grassy knoll on me."

"Grassy…what…?" he wrinkled his face into bafflement.

"Conspiracy theory. I can't imagine some old white guys from Scottsboro sitting around a table with calendars saying, 'Hey, let's give them the shortest month!' There are groups in this country who don't have a month…I guess you could call this some kind of progress, yeah?"

He nodded obligingly, and I half wondered if he was about to break into that great, disarming grin of his that told you he was pulling your leg, but it never came.

"Look, you want to help change something?" I pointed to another flyer I'd just hung on the corkboard. "There's an Amnesty International meeting Thursday. We're gonna do some letter writing about South Sudan and the Nigerian school girls. These are still issues that matter. Forgotten by many, but trust me; you wouldn't wanna live there, either place." He gave it one of those uninspired, suspicious looks. "It's a matter of race too, you know. Over there. A lot nastier than lunch counters and water fountains." He raised one eyebrow skeptically. "Genocide, Isaiah, genocide. We're not talking about the fronts and backs of buses here. This is nasty stuff, and even after the election and a new country of South Sudan, it's nasty."

He wrinkled his brow and shifted on his feet.

"Thursday. 6:30," I cocked my head, "My classroom." He nodded. I offered my fist to him to pound. A foolish successor to high fives, it prompted a grudging response from him, after which he promptly checked his phone and headed off.

February 10

I'VE NEVER BEEN QUITE clear what it is that makes someone want to be a Head of School. The big house? The salary and perks? The yearly trip to Asia? Obviously, if you've got a package like one Head did at a school in New Hampshire - so good that it got him canned eventually - it can be sweet while it lasts. A century earlier, leaders like Frank Boyden and Cotty Peabody could mold a Deerfield Academy and a Groton School; they became *their* schools. Now people with egos like that run for president, regardless of whether they should. Barclay did it by the numbers, rising elsewhere and having a well-groomed way about him that all CEOs seem to glow with. He and I manage to avoid contact whenever we're in each other's orbit; I'm certainly not going ask him to reconsider, and I can't imagine that he'd have anything to say to me. I can hope that if they post my position under Employment on the school's site, that there'll be a buzz of curiosity. *So, are you just gonna teach, not be a department chair? Are you taking a sabbatical? You're not leaving, are you?* I think I can answer these honestly without my tail between my legs, but how the school will spin it is another thing...and since there's no such thing as a secret at a boarding school...

Campus is one place where in winter, no news really is good news in winter, for cabin fever, falls on slippery walks and getting back late from faraway games all put people in foul moods. A few teams are headed for league playoffs, yet my girls prefer not to clutter exam week with double-elimination rounds at the New England Class B Squash Championships, thank you. The stage production of *Our Town* was actually darn good. The snow has been piling up, but Buildings and Grounds always find a place to put it. Saturday the hockey teams were at away, which meant that the rinks would be free. Being on duty, I offered to cover a free skate, which meant sitting in the stands reading essays while a few kids show up to do twirls.

An empty hockey rink is one of those silent mausoleums to past glories. In addition to the banners of opponent schools, the NEPSAC championship flags are mute reminders that the boards and nets have seen a lot of excitement over the years. Black and white photos outside the locker rooms, and more recent ones in color, reflect the evolution of equipment as well as the mercurial lengths of teenage hair. It started snowing again overnight, which made it easy to opt for rink duty over driving kids to a mall. I unlocked the place after lunch and a few girls showed up and started spinning like third stringers for Disney on Ice; quite impressive really. A few freshmen boys showed up, whipped out cell phones, and soon the penalty boxes and benches were jammed with 15-year-olds who probably didn't realize that the tan limbs they were mesmerized with were actually skating leggings. My clipboard list had the group at twenty.

"Mr. Burnham" someone called up to the stands, "we gonna have school Monday?"

"Why not? It's not my birthday."

"The snow. It's still coming down."

"It's winter. That's what it does here."

"Yeah, but it took the hockey team three hours to get to Northfield."

"Don't get your hopes up. We're a boarding school, remember? Besides, the school recently put in heating pipes under the road and paths. It'll all be gone by Sunday night." There are always a few who fall for something like that, so it took the shrewder ones among them to dispel the notion that we now have heated walkways on campus.

Just after four I announced that there was a half an hour of ice time left. A moment later, a noise like a slap shot cracked the cold, fluorescent air. Free skates are hockey free, so I scanned the ice looking for sticks. None. Then another crack and the light over center ice flickered. The dozen or so boys in the penalty box had lured the Michelle Kwans their way, and one by one their heads turned upward.

"Off the ice!" I howled.

First it seemed as if the quartet of public address horns were being lowered over center ice in a halting motion, until it crashed to the face-off circle. On top of the dark hulk fell some snow. For two or three seconds the arena was still and silent. Then the roof began to unzip with a muffled tearing sound.

"Off the ice!" I was perhaps never louder. *"Now!"*

Down poured the previous week's accumulation, covering the ice in a matter of seconds. As the tear spread towards the northern net, snow fell like soap suds, stopping just over the goal line.

"Get under the stands! *Under the stands!*" They perhaps could have heard me back in the dorms. Overhead, another row of lights flickered and died, and as if a pair of invisible hands were at work, the roof over the other half of the ice opened and a white avalanche descended methodically with a deadening thud, covering the sounds of falling lights and tearing sheet metal. The stands on both sides of the ice were untouched, as were the bench and penalty box areas. Across the way the students' mouths and eyes were wide and frozen as they scurried for cover.

"Heads up!!" at the top of my lungs. "Stay under there." Uncharacteristically, all the students complied.

They didn't cover this in Ed School. Being the only adult there, I started running through my head what the faculty handbook might say about such a situation, trying to figure out step one; little more than a broken window. When it seemed clear that the building had completed its transition to an open air rink, I made my way over to the other side of the ice.

"Mr. Burnham, my hat's out there," someone piped up. Kids were already on their cell phones, reporting and photographing the matter breathlessly. I took a count, all were accounted for, and we shuffled up a path under gray skies with large flakes still blowing down around us. Teenagers are quick to call most developments of this magnitude *cool*, but here, they seemed to sense that this was different. This was a school building they had been enjoying until a few minutes ago. I flagged down a Building & Grounds truck plowing some driveways and asked him to rope off the rink and call the fire department. The kids splintered away to dorms and the Moody Student Center, and I headed to Barclay's house. The snow was now blowing sideways, almost obscuring the orange glare of campus lights in the failing afternoon. Kat was trudging back from cross-country skiing, so I filled her in and asked if she'd seen Barclay.

"His wife's got a thing at Smith this weekend. Probably there."

"Then why," I looked over her shoulder to the house on the hill, "is there a light on in the house?"

"I dunno, and I'm too cold to care. Later."

Elliott Cottage is the Head of School's reward for wearing the heavy crown – 'cottage' in the modest Newport sense of the word. A large brick colonial with black shutters and a portico, it stands just distant enough from other buildings and uphill to remind all just who dwells there. The walk had not been shoveled since the morning. If Scott was keeping Barclay's study warm in his absence, I could hand the matter off to him. Two rings of the doorbell, and there was that distant, indefinable hint from within that someone was there. A third ring, and *voila.*

"Peter." Barclay took my measure for a second, his face betraying nothing. "I'm guessing," he eyed the weather over my shoulder, "this isn't about me writing you a reference…"

I hadn't expected that, so took the silence to size him up. He looked disheveled and knew it. The executive coiffure was askew, and he was barefoot.

"Trying to get forty winks," he winced, "Bear of a week." He ran his hands back through his hair and yawned. "This…must be…important. Who is the Duty Dean?"

"Remy, but I just came from the rink. The roof gave way. During free skate."

"W-w-w-w-w-w…once more?" He stood there for a moment absorbing my words. His wrinkled khakis and untucked blue oxford contributed to the sense that he was truly bewildered. "Judas Priest. Judas freaking Priest." He closed his eyes and clapped his ears, as if to keep his head from exploding. Some snow from behind me blew into the front hall. I stepped in and closed the door. A second later, somewhere else in the house, a door gently latched. Barclay raised his eyes to meet mine.

"Windy out there. Good thing you closed the door." His tone was an octave higher. "Anybody hurt? There aren't still people there, right?"

"No. Everyone's out, and okay." I fumbled.

"S-s-s-s-o-o-o-o-o-o…" he went into contemplative mode, arms crossed.

We stood there in the front hall of the house as the gray afternoon outside dimmed. Orientals covered the wide pine boards underfoot, and some of the fading light was picked up on a well-polished butler's tray by an umbrella stand. This house had seen a lot of Lemon Pledge over the years.

"I told B & G to mark it off, somehow, and call the fire department."

"The *fire* department?" He twisted his face. "What the hell for? Nobody was hurt, right?"

"Right, but...I dunno... it just seemed like, collapsed buildings are sort of their thing."

"Maybe so, Peter, but that's my call, or...well, not yours." I affected a bit of contrition with my body language, but it was disingenuous. "There's a chain of command you know. Maybe at another school you can..." At this I tilted my head, wondering if he was really going there at this moment. He sensed as much, and pursed his lips, thinking. "Who'd you say is on duty?"

"Remy."

"What are activities tonight?"

"A...trip to a Northeastern hockey game, open dorm in Divine. Poetry slam too, I think."

"And you said, nobody hurt right?"

"A few kids were there, but not hurt. Everyone's out, but... it's a sight. Like someone took a can opener to it."

He stepped back and sat on the stairs behind him. He rested his chin on a covered fist. Elsewhere in the house, a door creaked and a cell phone's ring tone sounded, but was quickly silenced. Barclay thinned his lips, and behind his eyes, seemed to be wishing that those two noises hadn't drifted downstairs.

"Can we patch together something else off campus? Some other activity in Boston? Be nice to have the kids not crawling around the site all night."

"I don't know as anybody will be venturing far tonight. The game might even be scrubbed. Still coming down out there."

"When it rains," he rose and put his hands on his hips. "See if you can find Remy. Ask him to throw a movie on in the auditorium after dinner."

"Sure…"

"If you or he can manage it, give me a call before the fire department turns up. We ought to have someone at the gate, just to wave off the newsies."

"I wouldn't imagine there'd be too many out tonight…" I had started to turn towards the door.

"Regardless. They'll be here. If B & G has made the call…" I nodded. Beyond his instructions, this was above my pay grade, which was fine with me. He said he'd be in his office in half an hour and to check e-mail at 6 PM. I closed the front door behind me and stepped back into the swirling cold. Never had to tell a Head of School that a building had collapsed before, but I sensed that it should have somehow gone differently from how it transpired.

The Northeastern game was played, which in spite of the driving, was still preferable to babysitting the Seth Rogen movie Remy offered. Turns out that Griswold didn't have the monopoly on Chinese construction in the area, as a number of other roofs caved in as well. Sundays on campus are pretty sleepy, so it didn't bother me at all when Bags dropped by after ten for coffee with his *New York Times* in hand, fountain pen at the ready for the crossword.

"Bit of excitement last night, eh Peter?" he offered as he fussed with my Keurig.

" 'Fraid so. Glad I'm not A.D. today. Wouldn't want to sort out where the hockey teams will practice tomorrow."

"I wouldn't worry about Remy. He'll get the teams skating somewhere, even if the rink is still a sledding hill tomorrow. He might be rather slow about it, depending on the housing situation."

"Housing?" I settled on the couch and grabbed a section of the *Times*.

"He was grumbling about their house at lunch the other day. They want more room. Liz has a whole house to herself that's bigger than theirs. Remy has...let it be known that if they don't get better housing, he might...stick his finger to the wind, job-wise."

"Bit of a ..."

"Threat?" Bags doesn't mince words. "It might work. He's the A.D. with a family, but..."

"But she's only a secretary, and single," I added.

"Correction," Bags held up a clarifying finger, "She's *Barclay's* secretary. And single." He let it hang there and eyed me as the Keurig topped off his mug.

"S-s-s-o-o-o..." I ventured, "are you saying that there's somethi---"

"I'm saying that...logic alone does not dictate how things go here...at a*ny* school, but especially not here."

Sitting there for a minute, it occurred to me that Bags was one person I could tell my plight to, but I honestly did not know what his reaction would be...sympathetic? Would he put in a call with a friend at another school for me? Or would he think me a twit for sending an email so clumsily? He's still a bit of a cipher to me, so I held the thought.

Outside, a few stray flakes blew around the clearing day. Some of the paths on campus were still being plowed and small gaggles of students could be seen meandering towards the new open air skating facility, tossing and kicking snow at each other as they went. A few high-end cars were outside the registration building; perhaps some trustees were already on the scene. A lone figure began scurrying along the path away from it towards my dorm. It was a familiar figure in a dark green parka. A minute later, Aaron was at my door. Bags is not one for small talk with students on a Sunday morning...actually, ever....so nodded, promised to return the mug and left.

"Hal – loh, Meestah Burnham."

"What's up, Aaron?"

"I haff ...an ... envelope...here. With me."

"C'mon in." He sheepishly accepted my offer of tea and perched himself on the edge of my ottoman, massaging a flat parcel in his lap.

"My father, he...want for me to go to another school..." He dropped his head and looked away, as if he was telling a girl that he was breaking up with her. Such news is never a revelation to teachers. A trustee at my school sent his son to some single-sex place in Connecticut, and lots of headmasters' kids don't go to mom or dad's school.

"He *wants*, you *want*...agreement. I want, they want, she *wants*, remember?"

"Yes, sorry. Wants."

"Did he say where?"

"A few. Estabrook... Brooks...Port... I can't remember the--

"Portsmouth Abbey?"

"Yes."

"Nice place – right on the ocean in Rhode Island."

"Really?" He brightened a bit.

"Well, this is a nice school too. But, you can certainly apply elsewhere; no law against that."

"Law?" His face tightened.

"Rule. No rule. It's fine." He exhaled and nodded. "I will miss you - if you, get in and go somewhere else, of course." I didn't see any point in telling him that I was leaving too.

"I will miss you too also, but…" He fingered the envelope on his knees and gingerly reached for his tea. "I must have a recommending letter not math or English. Another person. My father said you are a good person to ask."

"Well," I sat back and forced a smile, "technically, I'm not. I'm not a teacher of yours." I looked at the Common Application form. Great invention. "I guess I can do it as your dorm parent…sure." He breathed and patted his chest. "The deadline was in January. There'll be some late fees, and you never know."

"My father says he knows. No problem."

"Okay, sure. Actually, lots of schools have rolling admissions, in spite of what they say. You should be all set. So how's dorm life. And Sean???"

"Okay." He cocked his head to one side in that *not perfect but tolerable* way.

"You've both got new roommates now, but are still on the same floor. So when you see each other, no problem?"

"No problem." He nodded vertically the way non-native English speakers do when agreeing with a negative statement.

"Good. Yeah, I can do this rec. No sweat. I can get it done in a day or two."

"You are a good teacher. I do not want…I do not think these schools have teachers better than you."

"Don't worry about it," I pumped his upper arm and rose, "There are lots of good teachers out there. Don't feel bad about this. Lots of kids transfer colleges too."

He rose and nodded. In spite of our chess and tutoring, he still didn't know when or how to shake hands.

February 15

UNTIL NOW I'VE BEEN pretty lazy on the job search front. Whenever you're not looking for a position, you hear about one, so I've sort of figured that word of mouth would send news of openings elsewhere to my ears or inbox. Sometimes colleagues you've met at teachers' or coaches' conferences learn that someone is leaving their school and decide to let you know about it. Maybe they think that providing a candidate for the position will reflect well on them, saving the school the cost of a search firm. I've been hoping to avoid such a business myself, but at this point I figure I have to bite the bullet and get my résumé into one. STEAG is the Schools, Teachers, Educators and Administrators Group, a placement firm out of Connecticut that has established a record of helping people move to and among independent schools professionally. Like other firms in this game, they enter into an agreement with schools to try to find the right candidate for positions that need filling. If the candidate they bring that way gets the job and stays for a certain period of time, the firm collects a nice fee. There are some lesser-known companies like this, and they all strive to convince people seeking jobs that they are working for them when in fact their bread-and-butter is meeting the needs of the institutions. STEAG actually helped me interview at Griswold years ago, yet I've been hopeful of not having to go back to that well again. As it's mid February and I've got no nibbles yet, yesterday I contacted their Boston office and submitted an updated résumé and application. Recommendation letters are good for five years, so the ones I have are fine, but I did have to update my reasons for seeking a new position.

Seeking a more rigorous academic environment.

This is always a safe one, adding that you've proposed some AP courses but had few takers.

In search of a school with more opportunities for inter-disciplinary collaboration.

Some administrators gobble this one up – visions of the astronomy teacher working with the music department on a project involving stargazing while the school orchestra plays Holst's composition "The Planets."

Once when reviewing applications for a history position at Griswold, I noted in one candidate letter that he was interested in moving from a day school to a boarding school so that he could get to know the students in a more encompassing environment. Noble, but also quite possibly bullshit. To live at a school, be able to walk to work and not pay a monthly water bill has appeal, but no one in his right mind seriously *wants* to take up residence with forty-five teenage boys. It's what one does until housing higher up on the food chain becomes available. In two weeks in Hartford, STEAG is hosting schools to interview candidates in a few of the conference rooms at convention center. Note to self: get a haircut.

February 17

TRADING WEEKEND DUTY EARLIER in the year meant I had it again this past weekend, which in the wake of the rink cave in, seemed somehow unfair, albeit also my own fault. Saturday I received a text from Dave Meeks that he'd be nearby Sunday night, so once my duty was over at the dinner hour, I headed to Boston where we met at some generic Chinese place downtown.

"Why do they cover the tables with this clear plastic stuff, even though there's a tablecloth under it?" Dave asked as the beers came.

"Keep the cloth one clean," was all I could muster.

"Sure," he raised an expecting finger, "but doesn't the kitschiness obviate the intent of having nice table cloths?"

"Look, China makes 80% of what's sold at Wal-Mart. They hold a huge chunk of our debt and slaughter babies that are born girls. Good luck getting them to take culinary design advice." Nice to put a question of his to bed with the facts.

We couldn't be so pedestrian as to order a Pu Pu Platter, so we did the whole eight dishes thing. For as long as I've known him and for all our ties, David is someone whose company can tire you out. Sometimes it's like we're both on the same PBS interview show but he is by far the more interesting guest. This time, I was determined to match him in aloofness. When he suggested going elsewhere for a nightcap, I feigned disinterest.

"Like to, but I'm covering someone's first period tomorrow."

"So dedicated."

"Someone's gotta work...the Chinese debt and all," I reminded him.

"Well, technically I *am* working. Tomorrow and Tuesday. "

"Technically, the Ivies don't give jock scholarships. So what's up?"

"A bit of a shakeup at Weld this winter. Some e-mails - which should have gone to *Reply*, not *Reply All*, a trustee backed out of a major gift...long story short: I'm splitting the Academic Dean job with someone else at Weld. Bit of a promotion, I guess, but we're job sharing it. So it's not a total vote of confidence."

"Congrats, I guess..."

His red buzz cut and loden sweater reminded me more of a lobsterman than a dean. He nodded and sat back with a not quite self-satisfied look.

"But...always shoes dropping. It's like a chessboard."

"Sounds like you're on a good square." I offered.

"I guess so...very nice." David loves metaphors. "So there's this two-day workshop at Hereford for incoming administrators." Hereford is a day school north of Boston.

"Nice place, Hereford, "I nodded. "I interviewed there once."

"Yeah. Day school, so they're putting me up at the Marriott."

"Great. Let's go trash the room Monday night."

"Will do...but first..." he squinted at me, "what's up with Barclay?"

"Barclay. As in my Head of School?"

"Yeah. Aside from the fact he probably wishes he was on sabbatical this year - Mayhew, the hockey rink..."

"Yeah, maybe our sailing team will hit an iceberg for a hat trick," I offered.

"So... is he looking?" His face betrayed nothing, affecting a stoic inquisitiveness. Good start for an administrator.

"Not as far as I know, but that's not very far"

"Hmmmm...."

"And...you ask because..."

"His wife is talking to folks at Weld about a position. Something in External Affairs. Job doesn't even exist yet. I don't know if it's a done deal, but... she's visited twice, and the chatter is, something's in the works."

"Well, it wouldn't be unheard of for a couple to be at different schools for consulting or something..." I shrugged.

"Sure, but a Headmaster's wife? What about the whole school hostess thing? St. Paul's paid that bishop's wife thirty-two large to serve tea until word of his deal got out. A stag Head of School? Kind of odd."

"Well, Griswold is kind of an odd place. And you know more than I do. She's not much of a presence on campus as it is. But, this Academic Dean hat, or new half-hat of yours – you like it?"

"I'll see how it goes," he tipped his head with a bit of resignation, "I'd still like to keep my hand in and not have to give up all my classes...which...if it becomes permanent..." I wanted him to ask me if I was thinking about moving on, but he didn't, so over the last course, brought it up.

"Lemme know if anything opens up in History, will you?" I tried to seem casual about it.

He nodded while chewing, as if not surprised, but also not excited at the idea of me being there as a colleague of his, which was disappointing.

"Will do...," he cracked a fortune cookie. "No telling yet..."

"You...want a rez from me?" Hell, he could have at least asked, rather than make me pander.

"Sure. I mean...I can keep it handy."

"I'll email it to you tonight."

"Sure. Good. I'm not back there until Tuesday night, but I'll get it."

He picked up the tab as part of his conference per diem, and the entire evening was as satisfying as a birthday card without money in it.

February 19

LETTERS FOR NEXT YEAR - teaching contracts – aren't out yet and people are starting to talk about it, especially those who've had a lot of sick time or who couldn't get the technology to work when a department chair came to observe a class. I covered the library during Study Hall Tuesday and lit into a kid who was wasting time as noisily as possible all evening, and afterwards headed back a long way around to clear my head and swung by the rink. The gray shell seemed to grow out of the snow and the yellow DO NOT CROSS tapes rippled in the night wind. A letter tailored to some alumni who've made the NHL has gone out, and the hope is that we'll end up with a new rink bearing one of the stars' names.

Even in the darkness, the faint images of the scoreboard and the championship banners could be seen, as could an eight – foot mound of snow spanning the blue lines. A few steps from the entrance, a small orange light brightened for a second, then went out. No good deed goes unpunished.

" 'Scuse me." I approached. A dark figure in the stands took another drag.

"Hi Peter…. it's me." A lighter flashed, and offered of a dim glow under Kat's face. She was perched at the end of the stands.

"Please don't alert me to the fact that I'm smoking, all right? I'm pretty intuitive about that sort of thing." Tightening her folded arms, she drew on the cigarette again. The glow lit her face for a second and then it was dark.

"Reliving hockey memories?"

"Hardly. Just seemed like no one would be here. And my apartment has got smoke detectors."

"No sweat. I thought it was kids."

"N-n-n-n-o-o-o-o-o," she blew out of a corner of her mouth. "I'm no kid."

"Everything…"

"Okay? Yeah, sure." Her tone was one of someone who had taken a hit; flat and hinting bitter. A long drag.

"Really? If this is 'okay'…Grad school news?" I'd heard she was applying.

"Grad school? No. Just…no."

I only go where I'm invited, but when someone who's run half marathons is smoking in a collapsed hockey rink...

"Listen, I'm pretty much done with duty at 10:30," I started to turn away. "If you want to drop by for…. well, *you* can have beer."

"Thanks," the glowing tip lit up her face like a Christmas card from Philip Morris. "I started in on some Capt. Morgan before dinner. Then forgot about dinner. Found some port for dessert though. Felt like I was channeling Amy Whinehouse."

"Doesn't have to be beer. Coffee might--"

"Peter," she flicked her lighter so I could see her no-nonsense glare, "stop. It's okay. I'm not up for Mr. Bagwell's acerbic wisdom tonight in case he drops by." Darkness again.

"Well," I started to turn, "if you change your mind…"

"Peter," she called out after I'd taken a few steps toward the doors, "I'm sorry. It's Rodney. Fucking Rodney. And…a fucking undergrad. Rodney is fucking a fucking undergrad. She even had on my fucking T-shirt. Fucking ballsy, yeah?"

As she explained it, the girl is in his study group. Some Thai prodigy.

"She probably clips his fucking toenails, too. So fucking demure…embarrassed when I caught them. He does this whole fucking Robert Bly meltdown, in his apartment. He's in his fucking boxers, trying to sound rational."

"Sorry to hear that…really, I am."

"Pretty fucking unethical too," she flipped her hair back and lit another. "Sure, Thailand is like the world's whorehouse. No news there. And TAs doing undergrads? Not the first, I'm sure. But he'll be the first one to make the news this week. From his study group. He's fucking toast. I'm gonna spray this all over MIT. By the time I'm done, he'll be lucky to get a gig as a substitute math tutor in Chelsea."

"Wow. How did you---"

"Maybe I'll even call the *Globe*. They love that kind of stuff. They broke the whole priests molesting kids thing, y'know…you saw that movie "Spotlight" right?" She clasped her head, elbows on her knees.

"You gonna be okay…to teach tomorrow?"

"Oh yeah. No sweat. Already *into* my hangover. I'll be fine. Thing is," she flicked the ashes from her cigarette. "I took this job, mostly because he was at MIT. I had offers from Ethel Walker and St. George's. *St. George's*. I could have coped with living next to Newport with a view of the sea, y'know?"

A beam of headlights flashed through the doors and was gone.

"Sorry Peter. I'm just… really shitty company right now."

"Yeah, no big deal. Give a call if you like." She nodded without looking up. I strolled over and pumped her shoulder lightly and left. So Rod was test-driving a younger, foreign model. In fairness, I've only met Mr. Knightley twice, and as mother says, it takes two. The idea of whom he would leave Kat for was intriguing. Her well-scrubbed, rosy cheeks and strawberry blond hair pulled back still has boys bumping into each other when she passes them in buildings. "Wow," they still say when she's out of earshot, "can you believe she's a teacher? I wonder what she'd be like." No idea how close he is to finishing at MIT's Sloan School. Wonder if he did a cost - benefit analysis like a good economist, or did she just look too good after a case study to not give it a go? Who said economics was boring? Father liked to quote Oscar Wilde with stuff like this. *Some people know the price of everything, and the value of nothing.*

February 21

JUST BEFORE ROOM CHECK last night, Scott Paone came knocking, waving a 9 x12 manila envelope as he entered and made for my couch.

"First of all Peter, understand: for various reasons, some people are seeing this, some aren't. You are, but based on what I just said, don't assume someone else has. Loose lips, yeah?" Opening the door at 10:15 never pays off.

"The Homeland Security guys got this to us yesterday, and they hope that it'll underline how important it is that we have an eye out for anything that could lead to...anything." He pulled out a sheet of paper which had on it text which had been copied, scanned, and re-printed enough times that it had that look of a high-tech, pirated memo.

> *To the Enemies of the Prophet Mohamed*
> *As patriots of Kuwait, we continue to demand that our youth*
> *not be poisoned with the teachings of those who wish violence*
> *upon Islam and our Arab brothers and sisters. A most visible*
> *example of this is Faisal Aboody who is made to attend the*
> *Griswold School in Massachusetts. Kuwait has excellent*
> *schools and America continues to wage war against our*
> *Muslim brothers and sisters. You can no longer ignore our*
> *demand. We state that Faisal Aboody must return to Kuwait*

and his brainwashing at his school must end. If he is not promoted to the next grade at a school in Kuwait for next year, his current school will regret this. We are not terrorists and this will happen when there are not students there. Do not forget this! Allahu akbar! Long live Kuwait!!
The Patriots of Kuwait

It was as if a curtain had been drawn back and suddenly removing our shoes in airports made some sense. It was one of those documents that gets passed around conference room tables in federal buildings and inspires the creation of task forces and Venn diagrams on office white boards. It took two readings. Somewhere in buildings near the Smithsonian and Washington Monument, twenty-first century G-men are reading our school's name and considering it a…target?

"Scott, what…am I…supposed to do with…with knowing this? Jesus Christ. This is…like a movie. *Christ*. Tom Clancy stuff. Why…"

"Not a movie Peter. It's here. Us." He slipped the copy back into the envelope. "New territory, that's for sure. So here it is. Our friends from after Thanksgiving? The Kuwaiti security guys? They might be around here, on campus. Looking for…what we can't see…dressed as educational consultants. That's their cover. If they approach you, fine, obviously you're on board. But don't you approach them. *Kapisch?*"

"Yeah. Sure. Does…Faisal know…about all this?"

"No. Not the essence of it. Basically he's been told that…he needs to report any contact he has with non-school people, which we tell all kids on campus, but we just reiterated it with him. Don't want him to think that there's a horde of talk radio listeners hiding outside the school gate. So, hopefully his antennae are up. Who knows…"

"This is just a tad…no, *more* than a tad…this is above my pay grade Scott," I sat back. "Frankly, yours too. We're *teachers*, f'Crissake."

"Hey," he stood and patted me on the shoulder with the envelope. "No argument there. But…he's here," he gestured towards Faisal's room down the hall, "and the feds are on it. Like that British thing during the war: *Keep Calm and Carry On.* Just…putting you in the know."

Nice news just before bedtime. I wonder if Scott is *in the know* that owing to Barclay's whim, I'll need to start packing in early June. With each passing day, this reality inches a little bit more to the surface of my consciousness. For all the convenience of being able to walk to work and not mow a lawn that living at a boarding school affords, it only affords you this and a roof over your head as long as you work there. Finding a place to live after Griswold, somewhere, wouldn't be an issue, but paying the first and last month's rent and a security deposit without a job is another matter. *The* matter. I don't wish Griswold ill, but also have no idea if I'll even be here when all this boils up, which honestly puts at all a bit off-center on my plate right now.

February 28

THE STEAG PLACEMENT FAIR takes place over Friday and Saturday at a hotel in downtown Hartford, perhaps because Connecticut and western Massachusetts are the center of the boarding school universe. There are workshops and presentations offered as diversions for between interviews that one can sample: "The *New* New Technology for the Classroom," "Bringing 21st-century Diversity to a 19th century School" and the like. Personally I find the best professional development for teachers is to observe other teachers doing their jobs very well, and then return to the classroom to try to incorporate those good practices. Otherwise, it is perhaps most useful to partake of a conference or workshop at the start of the school year when you can apply some new ideas early on rather than try to change gears in late winter. A daylong set of seminars on different perspectives on East Asian history filled my professional development dance card for the first day, so for Saturday, the focus was interviews. STEAG had taken over a large ballroom on the hotel's second floor and had set up one of those reception tables with swag and 'Hello' stickers at the door. They'd forwarded my résumé and recommendations to a number of schools that were said to be looking for history teachers for

September, and three of them had representatives there with whom I had interviews scheduled. A blue blazer and repp tie seemed more prudent than a suit and something with a Harvard crest, if only to go for a more youthful approach without dropping the H-bomb beyond the rez. As is often the case, it seemed like every college senior in New England was there looking for a job, so this 30-ish department chair might have already looked downright middle-aged and overqualified compared to the still-using-fake-ID crowd.

My first interview was with Gunnar Hall, a coed school between Hartford and New York where suspicion is that a female history teacher is off to coach D1 field hockey at Lehigh in the fall. All I remembered from watching some games there years ago was that there was a wall around the campus, and in the middle of Connecticut, I couldn't figure out why. The Academic Dean from there and I had a nice chat, and that we know some of the same people at other schools warmed things up nicely. She liked the idea of the electives I've developed at Griswold and suggested that it would be possible to introduce similar ones at Gunnar. When we got to the part of why I wanted to make a change, she shifted a little bit in her chair.

"We've got some great kids…who want to be challenged…but are you looking to run all AP classes and push the kids to get fives on the tests?"

"No. Not at all," I waved off the notion, "but I like to…help kids get their fingernails dirty with what we cover. I'm not a fan of multiple choices tests or…"

It went like that for a bit, with me needing to reassure her that I wouldn't start looking for another job in October if none of the students seemed destined to win a Nobel Prize. It seemed like I put her fears to rest, and she mentioned a couple of possibilities in terms of faculty housing and how the squash program could use a hand as well. This is usually when talk turns to the possibility of visiting the campus someday and teaching a sample lesson to a class.

"Oh, one more thing," she sat up straight and leaned in, "What do you know about field hockey?"

"I know it's kind of a religion in the fall for some," I offered, "my sister played it for four years at Northfield and my mother played at Winsor."

"Good! So you know the game. Ever coached it?"

It took a bit of restraint to not label this a rhetorical question. She had my rez, and on the STEAG application I'd indicated everything I had coached or could help out with; squash, rowing, sailing and cross-country. Field Hockey was nowhere to be found, so why ask me?

"Well, I've never coached it," I sat back a bit "but couldn't tell you how many games I've attended over the years. You can't help but pick things up from them..."

"True, but...the thing is, this teacher we may lose, she also coaches field hockey, so we need to fill that slot too..."

"Well, as I said, I've certainly..." and I trotted out the same line again, quietly boiling inside: *do you want a history teacher who can help run a practice and blow a whistle afternoons or do you want a coach whose idea of teaching is showing Ken Burns films all term?*

We parted warmly with her tossing out the, "I'll email you this week if we want to have you visit us." I wouldn't be holding my breath for the call, and consoled myself by recalling that two kids who'd been kicked out of my school ended up there; no use leaving a third tier school for a fourth tier one anyway.

An hour later I was across the table from my counterpart at The Dunworth School, a small coed place near New Haven I'd never been to but whose recent claims to fame are a huge athletic complex given by the head of JP Morgan and a du Pont Library. In the same sports and academic league as Gunnar, it's a cozy place where you can let the world go by and nobody's going to demand that you offer Advanced Placement European Studies or teach the *Illiad* in the original.

"So...," the fellow began, "is Barclay Sears still at Griswold?" His ski bum coif and sweater made me wonder where he'd met the big man.

"Well, he was yesterday, so I suspect so. How do you kno---"

"He ran a seminar one summer at Columbia. I'm doing a doctorate there. Pretty interesting guy."

"Yup, he holds the reigns, and we're still ridi---"

"How are things there? At Griswold?"

, This is always a challenge; if they were perfect, we wouldn't be having this conversation, but how to make it about how I'm looking to bring some useful experience to some place else rather than simply trying to flee a bad situation, perhaps of my own making?

"Pretty fair...I feel like the history curriculum is as broad as the higher-ups want it though, so---"

"We did a total re-working of our curriculum two years ago," he spread his arms like a Pentecostal preacher, opening up and revealing a few holes in his ragg sweater, "Thank God that's done. We think we're set for a while." Translation: we don't *want* your electives in our catalog, thank you. Truth be told, a guy who shows up to interview people in a moth eaten sweater and went to the Chris Mathews-Diane Rehm Interrupting-Is-Good School of Conversation isn't interested in hiring anyone. I cut my losses, pointed to my rez before him and asked that he be in touch if it works for them. For a few seconds he was clearly surprised – not used to having the person looking for the job walk away, but I didn't see the point.

"Say 'hi' to Barclay for me!" he threw out over a limp handshake, forgetting that he never even mentioned his own name.

The third interview was after lunch with a school whose name brought a smile to my face. For a number of reasons, Estabrook is a school I can't see myself at, albeit on a charming campus on a New Hampshire lake. If they are indeed looking for a history teacher, it's either because someone there is tired of dealing with IEPs – Individual Education Plans, to-do lists for teachers dealing with less than stellar students, or because long winters in a small, northern New England town have become too much for a teacher in search of a social life. Still, that the school is on Aaron's list of places to which he might transfer gave me a chuckle; if we both ended up there in September, that would be a hoot, but I couldn't see it. Trading one mediocre setting for another isn't worth the whole interviewing and moving process. I stuck a note in the school's lobby mailbox saying I couldn't make the 1:30 interview but thanks anyway.

Outside the hotel, the February thaw seemed to have ended, and under a grey ceiling, the wind whipped through downtown Hartford. Disappointing to be sure. I licked my wounds with some overpriced coffee then stopped at a mall in Farmington to justify the trip by getting a shirt at Brooks.' Heading back to school, I was reminded of something Meeks had said years ago while wondering whether he'd get the job at Weld. "Problem with us is that you can't swing a dead cat without hitting a history teacher looking for a new job, and 99% of us are white males." I hate it when he's right. I was pretty happy with myself a few years ago when a black female out of Bryn Mawr accepted a spot in our department as a sabbatical replacement, but when we tried to keep her on the next year, she begged off, having too many better offers.

One of the nice things about teaching at an independent school is that it doesn't require jumping through those hoops for state certification or a license – a master's degree is often the coin of the realm. Most teachers at private schools, like me, *aren't* certified, and yet their degrees could get them college jobs as well...maybe not like me. The sticky side of this is that without that little state-issued cert, working at public schools is out, so they're not even on my radar. I had a ton of teachers at school with more degrees than they had children, and they could have been at a college as easily as where they were, but would never even have gotten a call back at the local public school.

February is far from the end of the hiring season, but it hasn't been a big bowl of encouragement thus far either.

March 8

ASIDE FROM EXCURSIONS I'VE pulled together, I've never managed to endear myself enough to the people who take students to Europe on school trips to become one of the chaperones who goes along for free. It's fun to meander Prague or Venice on someone else's dime and be thought of as a selfless teacher willing to forgo his vacation to shepherd students around these places, until, as happened two years ago, one of our kids was caught shoplifting at the Louvre' gift shop, so it's not all postcards and selfies in front of landmarks. Nantucket seemed a good place to be over the March break; no internet at the house so no temptation to check for school messages, and the dearth of Land Rovers off-season is quite pleasant.

Like most summer places on the island which go back a few generations, *Wychmere* was built by my great-grandfather whose success at his calling made upkeep and taxes mere afterthoughts. As offspring opted for less lucrative vocations, it became necessary for them to pool resources when a new roof was needed or a chimney required pointing. Over time, doing so wore on some, but I'm happy to kick into dad's share of ownership for my week or two in August. Those from Philadelphia or Maryland who whined in disbelief that a *septic tank can actually cost that much* eventually sold their shares in the place, feigning the remoteness of the island and the rarity of their stays. Cost may have been an issue as well, but while he was with us, such matters probably never worried former Tom Nevers summer resident Kirk Mayhew.

All I brought to the house were some books and a pound of coffee, since my cousins seem to spend the summer drinking nothing but decaf. Just being able to read and not have to shave amidst the solitude for a week down here is a tonic. Mother wouldn't think of coming here before June, and the cousins in Delaware imagine it to be like Greenland until July 4. Near the new yacht club is a kayak rental place with off-season rates posted. Paddling through the moorings of the six-figure toys bobbing sleepily at high tide in the summer, I wonder what it is like to spend the GDP of Lesotho on a weekend diversion. My day sailor, a Rhodes *19'*, which can host five or six people plus me, must look cute to Senator Kerry, who, thanks to his second wife's first husband, has a $7 million tub nearby, but it's honestly all I want. The hyper rich are forever finding new uses for disposable income.

"More money than brains," the guy in Hyannis fixing my timing belt once said, "whole Nantucket crowd." I learned long ago not to enter Bob's Super Lube a few blocks from the ferry in a seersucker blazer or ask him to hurry my oil change so that I'm not late for the clambake at the yacht club. Once I asked him to elaborate though; did he really think you could be stupid and get as rich as some people there were? "By and large, yeah. One of the Kennedys rolled a Jeep over there years ago. Put some girl in a wheelchair. He walked, 'course, and that Matthews guy from cable TV? 'S'posed to be a news guy? *Loved* Obama." In terms of the borderline ridiculous, I will grant him that the backyard 'cement ponds' seem a bit much. Pools…at houses by the sea;

God's way of indicating that some people actually fit Super Lube Bob's description of residents here.

It being March, instead of rigging the boat, I spent the first afternoon here food shopping, slowly rumbling along the cobblestone streets in a Jeep Cherokee older than I am. Coming out of the Stop and Shop, I felt a tap on my shoulder.

"*BURN*-HAM!" Steve Kuhn was described at my last school reunion as a blonde Belushi. His Williams sweatshirt did nothing to hide the beer belly he'd started at college. He is said to have worked their alumni directory to death as he climbed up the mutual fund food chain.

"Yeah, I'm still at Fidelity. Client Services," he pumped my hand, "You still teaching? Wow. That's great."

Secretly, I have no doubt that he couldn't fathom why people would dabble in something that would not reward them with six figures and require anything other than Paul Stewart threads. His apple cheeks hinted that he either sails or skis. A lot. He was at his in-laws place over in Cisco, out of town towards the western part of the island.

"Hey, you going to the *Andrea Doria* thing tonight?" he asked.

"Thing?"

"At the Athenaeum." The island library. Looks like it belongs above Arlington National Cemetery. "Some guy, gonna talk about his book on the *Andrea Doria*. Wine and cheese. Screw the cheese, right?"

"I hadn't---"

"Be fun. Nothing else to do here in March." The perpetual fraternity brother, no expense spared nor no excuse accepted in pursuit of a good time. Perhaps half a dozen times since school, I've found myself on a balcony or in a noisy room with Steve in a sea of Soho cups; one time in Park Slope, another in Brighton near BC. I once saw him vomit on the steps of a tennis club in Brookline.

241

Two hours later, I was listening to a nephew of the captain of the ship that took on the survivors of the *Andrea Doria*, an Italian liner that collided with another ship off shore here in 1956. The details of the event were not new, but the shiraz was just old enough. Keeping up with Steve on this score was an engaging endeavor. An accomplished if shameless gadfly, he drops names the way Boston's Hancock tower used to drop windows. After a few glasses, he asked me if I knew anything about teaching in Abu Dabi.

"Afraid not; Japan yes, but that's it in terms of overseas. Why?"

"I got a cousin teaching history in Connecticut who just took a job there. Could be fun, but I think he's got it pretty good already."

"What's he teach?" I asked.

"History, at school…Walton? Walt? Some place with three indoor hockey rinks…"

"Weld?"

"Yeah, that's it. Don't know why he'd give that up, but…guess he likes sand…"

The loudest land-based ship's bell on the eastern seaboard gave off an unruly clang, and we were told to find our seats. The bizarre nature of the *Andrea Doria* event should, on some level, place it in the stupid column of seafaring lore. All of the North Atlantic to sail in, with radar and men on the bridge, and two ocean liners collide. Like going into an empty room and breaking something. The liner and a smaller ship, the *Stockholm*, met in a fog bank south of Nantucket one night in 1956. One of the ships that responded to the SOS was a freighter, the *Cape Ann III*, and the captain's nephew was telling the story via PowerPoint, offering the impression that of all the vessels which came to the rescue, the *Cape Ann III* distinguished itself most, don't you know.

"In spite of coming to rest 160 feet under the surface," we were told, "the ship is pretty much cleaned out in terms of salvage." Nevertheless, a young salt in a red beard and Irish fisherman's sweater was perched at a side table with some brochures on his treasure hunting enterprise.

Steve started critiquing the presentation as soon as it was over, but I couldn't even hear him. Weld, where Meeks works, is losing a history teacher and I find out about it from someone else.

"Want another?" Steve tipped his empty wine glass.

"Hell yes," and we camped out near the treasure hunter's table. Somehow we fell into small talk with someone who knew David Halberstam from summers here and has a cousin who was kicked out of Griswold in the 1940s.

"So Burnsy – you up for dinner?" Steve is always *up for* something. We were pulling our coats on as the salt and pepper crowd in baseball caps stepped past us into the winter air blowing in off the North Atlantic.

"Well, I've got a steak at the house – gotta cook it tonight or it's gonna spoil."

"Yeah? I've had steak all week. Ha'bout swordfish? There's a new place off Fairgrounds...some people I know opened it," Natch. He went on about how the owners used Italian marble from the same quarry that yielded the makings of the forum in Rome. Do you put that on the menu?

"Yeah, maybe a raincheck," I begged off. "I'll be here through Saturday though." For putting up with his running it out so much, albeit well-intentioned, I felt entitled to a small lie about my dinner plans. Once I defrost the steak, I eventually *will* need to eat it.

"Sure. They gotta single malt scotch there you'd sell your mother for. Call me OK?"

We shook and he bounced into the night. Deep down Steve is a nice guy, but someone best taken in small doses. As they said with Reagan, 'there's no *there* there.'

Nothing like a slaughtered mammal seered over hot coals. Seafood prices are pretty mercurial since it seems there's always an issue with getting it out of the ocean here. One year it was the scallopers, whose job was made harder – and product pricier – due to a rather curmudgeonly harbormaster who supposedly hated commercial fishermen. *On Nantucket.* Another year, folks in 'Sconset, where houses on a bluff will tumble into the sea now and again, wanted to dredge the seafloor off their end of the island to shore up the bluff there – but the area they wanted to dig up was a prime shellfish bed. After dinner, the wine had worn off enough that I went for a drive out to Sankaty, the eastern light. On the way, I took a detour to Tom Nevers, having a hint of where the Mayhew place was. Crawling past the alphabet streets on the right then circling by the old bunker, I headed as close to the sea as I could, and found the mailbox on the right. A weathered-shingle colonial with saltbox extensions on each side, the green shutters flanking the windows had the letter M carved into them. Through a large picture window, some adults were in an animated discussion. Out of nowhere, a twenty-something hulk with a ruddy face and buzz cut tapped on my car window.

"Can I help you?" he asked without expression.

"Actually, I…visited Mr. Mayhew when he was…I'm over in Monomoy, but I teach at Griswold, where, he ---"

"Were you…at the…school where…" he jabbed a finger my way as his wheels were turning.

"I…yes, and at the hospital, Mrs. May---"

"I'm sorry, what's your name?"

When I told him, he asked me to wait a minute and ran inside, returning with an envelope for me.

"Didn't mean to scare you. Sorry sir." As he bounded back to the house, the porch light winked off and on a few times, and from the picture window I could see a woman wave to me. I tucked the envelope into my pocket until there was some light to read it by.

Twenty years earlier, thanks to my impossible nagging about it during dinner, my aunt drove me out to Sankaty Light in a gale blowing horizontal rain. Heading back there this night seemed…a better idea than returning to my underwhelming book at the house just yet. In 2007, the lighthouse was actually moved back from the bluff, buying it a fifty-year stay before it topples into the North Atlantic to join the weathered houses in 'Sconset that will no doubt precede it there. Like a good lighthouse should, it stands just out of reach, a golf course to the left, dune grass and a 75' drop to the right. Its height and stoic silence suggest a reassuring permanence; its beam telling all ships, or none at all, that land is near. Miles off shore, in the direction of Europe, the beam scatters over swells and white caps that vanish with no one knowing they ever existed. There is something admirable in such a beacon's consistency. I sat on the hood of the Jeep a while, just watching it slice the March darkness, regardless of whether some trawler headed for Georges Bank needed it. The caution stretched out over the surf below into blackness, and for a while I felt serenely and completely untethered.

March 13

AFTER A WEEK AT the house, I needed both a reason to shave and a conversation longer than the island Stop & Shop check out variety. Memo to Mary Carpenter: Henry 'I want to be alone in the woods' Thoreau was probably a bit nuts. It wasn't until the ferry ride back to Hyannis that I fished out the envelope I was handed at Tom Nevers.

A Celebration of a Life

Kermit Coffin Mayhew

Public Servant   Devoted Husband & Father   Loyal Friend

Let Us Remember Him on His Day March 19th

and Always

Edgecomb   'Legger'sWay   Beverly Farms

Cocktails 5 PM Regrets Only

"The unexamined life is not worth living." Socrates

Mother once said that the time between a person's passing and his service are often in proportion to his station; the more important the individual, the more time between the death and the encomium. Such certainly seemed to be the case here. That the date was not far off suggested that me receiving the invite was prompted by my skulking in front of the house on island, but here it was nevertheless. Picking what appeared to be his birthday for the service had some cruel symmetry to it, but not my call. I slipped back onto campus under the cover of darkness with a day to kill before the fete. I was fishing for a reason to contact Dave Meeks, and on Harvard's website I found the date of the Adams' Cup, a race between Penn, Northeastern and the school up the river from it in Cambridge. I emailed him to see if he was free for it. A Quaker as an undergrad, he still had more of a soft spot for Penn than Cornell where he did his master's. He got back to me before midnight.

> *Peter*
> *Think we have a home race that weekend–if not, let's do it.*
> *Some break. Was here on campus for half of it and tomorrow*
> *I'm at Hettinger School for a regional thing. Are you free?*
> *Is it June yet?*
> *Meeks*

A third tier school north of Boston, Hettinger keeps to its dress code and Episcopal roots to compensate for the fact that nobody there got into Westgate. It's carved out of a self-consciously upscale hamlet near Beverly Farms where I'd be later that day for the Mayhew affair, so I got back to him and we set it up to meet after he was done on the same day I'd be headed to Edgecomb.

In the mailroom was the usual week-long vacation pile up. In a pleasant surprise, a duplicate invitation to the Mayhew fete had arrived as well as a letter from Seoul and a notice from the Coop in Cambridge informing me that a Harvard captain's chair had been ordered for me and would be delivered in 7-10 days. As the kids say, WTF? An inflated pizza box addressed to me was a puzzle, but three minutes and 600 Styrofoam packing peanuts later, a Samsung laptop emerged. Spanking, hi-end, and a letter from Korea.

> *Dear Mr. Burnham,*
>
> *Thank you for your help with Aaron's applications to other schools this term, and all your assistance in the dormitory matters. We were pleased to learn that he has been accepted at Estabrook School, Master's and Hill. We expect that he will make his final decision soon. We are grateful for all your work with him and wanted to express that to you.*
>
> *Aaron told us that you once mentioned buying a new laptop this summer. I hope that you will soon realize that you do not have to. He also said that you went to Harvard but I did not see a Harvard chair in your apartment. I hope that the one which arrives for you will be comfortable.*
>
> *Aaron tells me that you have lived in Japan. I would like to invite you to learn more about East Asia and come to Korea this summer. Aaron says that you often teach summer school. My brother-in-law runs a small language school in Taegu, a city less than two hours south of Seoul by train. He is always looking for good teachers and I think that you are one of them. Would you like to visit Korea this summer and teach at his school? You would be paid fairly and we would like to introduce you to our country if you have time. If you have other plans, of course no, but as they say, if this "sounds like a plan," please let me know. Thank you again for all your help with Aaron. We hope that he has many teachers like you at the next school.*
>
> *J.J.Tang*

Guess I need to make room for some new furniture.

March 19

TWO TOWNS OVER FROM Beverly farms sits Hettinger, with its white clapboard buildings and brick Georgian faculty homes surrounding a common on which only seniors are allowed to tread during spring. The school's view book could pass for an A & F catalogue. A coke bust and teacher-student scandal in the 1980s brought it down a few pegs, but that the approach still looks like the 18th fairway at Augusta suggests that it has weathered these storms intact. I arrived on campus late afternoon and thumbed yearbooks in the Teachers' Lounge where Meeks said he'd find me.

"Any coffee left?" Dave sauntered in sporting a tweed blazer *sans* tie, every bit the budding administrator. Pity.

"Church coffee." I pointed to the cream to fill it in. "Hot water with brown food coloring." He collapsed into a leather wingchair.

"Y'know, there are days in this job that you spend more time with adults than kids." He was speaking to no one, his eyes closed. "Is that teaching?"

"Big news flash. More of the same for you."

"Yeah, but why are some…educators such…" he offered his palms as if to surrender.

"Because the stakes are so small."

He opened his eyes and glared at me. "Who said that?"

"In various forms, probably lots of people. I've heard it attributed to everyone from Isaiah Berlin to Woodrow Wilson."

He prattled on about school life. The smells of dust and old book bindings seemed to color our elocution with Somerset Club *elan.*

"How was Nantucket?" he asked.

"Nice. Lonely."

"Nice. Wish I'd been there."

"Yeah. Well, there's room." Without looking at him, I tried to sound as offhanded as possible. "Waddju do over the break?"

"Interviewing. More exhausting than it ought to be." He looked at me a moment, perhaps trying to size up what I might know, or be wondering. Then he crossed his legs and was a tad more professional. "Had some interviews. In my department, some guy's girlfriend made partner in some law firm and is headed for Dubai or Abu Dabi or some place."

"Didn't know they had lawyers in those place – does she know sharia law?"

He nodded and chuckled. "They'll have at least one lawyer in June, I guess. The word came down: need to fill the job *with an eye towards diversity."* He made quotation marks with both hands. "Translation: hire a black Hindu – a one-legged, transgender one if possible."

"Can Hindus be transgender?" I was half serious. He cocked his head.

"I dunno...probably a light bulb joke in there somewhere. Anyway, in case you're looking, that's why I didn't call you. *You're not diverse.* Actually, I'm not either. Sorry."

"Me too. Woulda been fun."

"Yeah. We could row a double in the mornings. And I think we might be losing a squash coach too."

"Don't tell me that!" I held my head. "I've got the poor judgment to be a straight, white male – damn it to hell."

"Hey, it's the way of the world. Four hundred years of domination, you – *we've* got the bad timing to be in this game when they decide to bring our schools into the twenty-first century. Sucks, but waddaya gonna do?"

We meandered over to the gym and watched baseball players taking batting practice in a cage. When he heard why I was due at the Mayhew affair later, he was surprised.

"Sounds odd. You bring him into the school, some kid gets stupid, the guest dies, and you get invited to memorial service for him? At his house?"

"His wife has...sort of the big picture. She knows it wasn't the school... just some lower form of life that got past the Admissions office. He went there after all, and got some alumni award once."

"Still..." We watched the Hettinger batters and agreed that we were glad neither of our schools would have to play their varsity this spring. Before we parted, Dave was vague on whether we could meet for the crew race in April, reminding me that I affected an interest in it earlier. He patted my shoulder, lamenting again that I was "just too pale" to make the cut for the round of history interviews at Weld. Back in my car I fished out the GPS and set it for Edgecomb.

Once part of the town of Beverly, Beverly Farms is one of the more ironic names around, even for New England; like stumbling upon an abstinence chapter in Intercourse, Pennsylvania. Most of the farming that endures there consists of harvesting grand pianos from carriage houses for them to be made into sideboards for dining rooms. As a tack shop in town suggests, a few horse farms remain. Lots of homes can't be seen from the street, and if you see a Buick with an 'I brake for beer' sticker, it's passing through or belongs to one of the landscapers; aside from the odd Escalade, it would be the only American car you'd find, unless Ford bought Jaguar and Land Rover and started making them here when I wasn't looking. When grandmother heard that an obnoxiously snobbish cousin had moved there, she rolled her eyes.

"Judas Priest - as if he's already not bad enough. Every family there loves to discuss how far back they go. It's nauseating. He once insisted that he had to get into Cambridge to buy some underwear at J. Press...God...wish he'd bought one of their overpriced ties so that I could have strangled him with it." Grandmother is now limited to one Manhattan before dinner.

Not to be outdone in the name department, by say, Manchester-by-the-Sea, Prides Crossing is next door,

"Prides Crossing!?" a girlfriend once asked me. "Are you serious? Sounds like a TV show..." Back in Beverly Farms, the train depot in town is one of the oldest landmarks. When Oliver Wendell Holmes received a missive from a friend one time with the letterhead Manchester-by-the-Sea, he wrote back with the return address, Beverly Farms–by-the-Depot.

Edgecomb is a three-story manse of weathered shingles on the way out of town, closer to the sea than the road. A crushed - shell drive circles the lawn that even in late March looked ready for croquet. It didn't seem right to be fashionably late to a celebration of life. One of Kirk's brothers-in-law was greeting people in the front hall. Off to one side, the gatekeeper from my drive-by at Tom Nevers was quietly but frantically trying to point another guest into a sunken living room while simultaneously thumbing an iPhone. Wide yellow pine floorboards were covered with braided rugs, and a mix of chintz and tick upholstery somehow worked nicely while sextants and black-and-white photos made up the well-bred wall clutter. A yawning fireplace framed a perfectly burning log, and in front of it stood the widow, nursing white wine in a simple navy dress with pearls. Her hair was behind the ears and her sharp but feminine angles gave her more dignity than sex appeal, but the latter was still there, in a Presbyterian sort of way. The fifty or so people there were very well-scrubbed; men in club ties with drinks in hand and women straight from Talbot's. It looked felt like a political fundraiser, albeit a very subdued one.

"Peter," Sally glided my way and extended a hand. "So glad you're here. I wish I'd known you were on the island last week. It's so quiet in March, unless you like to talk scalloping all day. Please, get yourself something for the toast, and I'll catch up with you later." She rested her hand on mine for just a second. Perhaps this charm was simply the innate skill of a political wife, like remembering names and keeping to one glass of wine at official functions.

The adjoining study was a stroll through Massachusetts and national politics of the last of century. Kirk's father was a governor and an ambassador a few times over. Photos with Eisenhower, Kennedy and Queen Elizabeth among others were in no particular order, and were broken up by colorful, more recent shots of the Figawi Race, a regatta on Nantucket that Ted Kennedy seldom missed. Another showed Kirk surrounded by bone-thin children in Sudan during a fact-finding tour there. Around the corner and back into the main room, a large picture window offered up the black North Atlantic.

"Too cold for a dip." A tweedy fellow with a weathered sailor's face joined me at the window.

"Maybe wait a few months, eh?" was all I could manage. He was a warm salt, with wispy eyebrows that Robert Frost would envy. His hounds tooth blazer and repp tie suggested he was on familiar turf here.

"There's a polar plunge in January. At West Beach. Done it every year since '54 until last year."

"What happened last year?" I wondered.

"Cruise to Barbados," he scoffed. "Promised the wife."

"Sounds," I was fishing for something to say, "more fun than hypothermia."

"You haven't met my wife. *Ha!*" He emptied his glass. "Did you know Kirk?"

I explained my presence as briefly as possible.

"Rather...damn awful." His well-groomed, self-assured way offered a sense that life has gone much as he'd planned. I doubt that he's spent many of his days slogging through endeavors with the likes of the Blumbergs of this world. We were in a room which I sensed was similar to ones he's been in all life. He insisted I try his rum concoction – 'my family drink' he added, as he waved to one of the caterers with a tray and ordered me one. Rum and something imported from Trinidad. Pretty unremarkable, but then his type doesn't go in for Southern Comfort, and I was too embarrassed to admit that the Burnhams don't have a "family drink." The buzz on my cell gave me an excuse to duck out. A text from Kat.

Hi – B a ref for a job elsewhere? I'll explain later. Plz?

Happy to, albeit like hearing your brother found a $100 bill.

No prob G-luck.

Stepping out to check messages in the night air would've had a chill about it were not for my new friend's rum-flavored anti-freeze. I meandered around to the front just in time to see a bottle green Bentley glide up the driveway. I affected a phone call as it crunched over the shells to a stop. A quartet emerged: a weathered fellow in a Mac, his wobbly wife and a younger couple who sparkled in a way suggesting that this wouldn't be their last stop of the evening. The thirtyish woman glittered a bit too much for the occasion, her blonde coiffure suggesting that somewhere, a Fox News show was missing its anchor. Her date's bow tie was a bit much with his Nantucket Reds; was he headed for an inauguration or a boat auction? He'd have company inside, where he could find all different shades of red. It took an evening of studying this from a wicker couch at a lawn party on island one summer to discern the irony. Some of the older men have had their reds so long they've worn to a light pink, the cuffs often no lower than ankles, suggesting that they've had them since their teenage growth spurts, but can still get into them. Imitations of the more vivid red, not the heavier cloth of Murray's originals, can also be found. This second choice actually suggests a very secure Islander who doesn't need to prove anything by his threads, so just pulls on the closest pair of pants before the party, which might indeed be knock offs from some catalog. Brooke Astor, it is said, served S.S. Pierce bourbon to her guests; she was *still* Brooke Astor.

Back inside, the glow of the fire, the sparkle of the glasses and the gentility of the chatter made it hard to recall that a man's passing was our *raison d'être*. In time, the remembrances were called for, and the college days, summers sailing, the first campaign for district attorney were all recounted with anecdotes. An accused embezzler told of being exonerated thanks to Kirk's pro bono work. Each accolade was met with raised glasses. The stream of tales suggesting selflessness, public service, integrity and overall perfection left one feeling quite the underachiever.

Sally Mayhew was a model of composure as she thanked everyone for coming. "If Kirk were here tonight, I know what he'd say: write a check to Save the Children and Friends of the Bay in that order or there's no more booze!" The laughter exceeded the humor, but such was the atmosphere. At the door, Sally gave me a Republican hug.

"Will we see you this summer?"

"Hope so."

"Better!" she raised a warning finger, jokingly.

Outside I found myself next to two twenty-something fellows, blazered fraternity brothers perhaps, or teammates of a sort at one time. They were sharing passport stories.

"So'd you like Bangkok?" one asked the other.

"Mmmmm…Seoul was more interesting, from a history standpoint. But Thailand is, like, a theme park for sex the size of New Jersey." A green light went on in my head.

"Excuse me," I jumped in, "I couldn't help overhearing - you've been to Korea?"

"Yeah," the taller of the two nodded. "Good time."

"I might be headed there this summer - mind if I pick your brain?"

"Sure."

I explained the offer from Aaron's dad to my new friend; he was a couple of years out of Syracuse and after year in the Peace Corps in Kazakhstan, he bummed around Asia and was now freelancing for some local papers with movie and club reviews while trying to decide whether to apply to law school or continue adrift.

"Kirk had a BBQ for all past and present Peace Corps folks last summer. He wrote me a recommendation for it. Wow. Can't believe he's gone…"

I offered my connection to the event, but he wasn't the curious type, and instead seemed happy to let me talk him up about Korea.

"I've been offered a job there - the summer. Not in Seoul – some other place: Taegu?"

"Sure, Taegu. It's on KTX. The train system. Doing what?"

"Teaching. English."

"Yeah – they love American teachers. *Really* love ones from Boston or the ivies. Korea is like," he loosened his tie, affecting an 'old hand' pose that didn't quite work. His good looks and well-moused hair probably open doors for him here and there, but he was too young to be sage. "Korea is like the ugly sister of Asia. Mind you, the chicks aren't ugly, but Japan is, like, the New York of the region. China is sort of…US in the 1890s, 'cept for the big cities like Shanghai – but huge, and growing at like 10% a year. Then there's Korea; if the country were an American beer, it'd be Rolling Rock."

"So…working there…" I asked.

"Yeah. Well, I was in Seoul, but it's not a huge country. I was blogging for some cousin who runs a travel website. Stayed with people from college. Friends of friends. Spring to early July, got out just before rainy season. You want to avoid that if you can. Rainy season. Ninety-five degrees and 105% humidity for half the summer. The rest of the time, it just rains."

"Did you learn the language?" I wondered.

"Seoul…" he cocked his head and winced, "you could probably get around without Korean. It's like any other big city, but…"

"But…what? I mean, I figure I should at least get a Berlitz book or something."

"Yeah, absolutely. But, it's weird. I've been to a lot of places and, don't get me wrong. There are great folks there. I had some good times. The folks in Japan and Vietnam were… overall…friendlier. Like when you're lost or trying to buy something."

"So… does it sound like, worth doing?" I still couldn't envision it.

"Good money?" he raised an eyebrow.

"That… remains to be ironed out."

257

"Uh – huh. Well, do yourself a favor. Go online and find out what English teachers are getting paid there these days. Just so you know the ballpark. If you can grab some free time, see the DMZ, hit some beaches on weekends. Yeah, it's a good gig."

"Well, I lived in Japan for a few years," I offered, "so I have some idea about pay and all."

"O-o-o-o-o-h-h-h," he was suddenly a tad impressed, "Japan, huh? That's kind of the gold standard of teaching in Asia, so I wouldn't try to do apples to apples with Korea. Might not want to preface every conversation over there with that bit of information, either," he was shooting me a wise eye. "Koreans, a lot of them anyway, look at Japanese the way some older Jews might look at Germans old enough to remember the war. Nasty occupiers…treated them like the shit on their shoes. Mentioning Japan… it's just not going to endear you to a lot of people."

He and his pal checked phones about their next destination, and we started for our cars when he had another thought for me. "Get your school to buy your ticket to Korea. Round trip."

"Is that..," I hadn't thought of this, "not pretty standard? My school in Japan covered it. Are schools over there tight about buying the ticket up front even if they hire you?"

"Well, in China, some are…and I know one in Korea that made a friend of mine teach three months with good evaluations before they reimbursed him." He pulled a ski parka over his blazer and checked his phone. "If a place can't buy you a ticket up front, wouldn't that make you wonder about…getting paid? I mean, it's not like they're worried about you going to some Better Business Bureau in Seoul or getting a lawyer, right? Good luck pal. Have fun."

He patted me on the shoulder. I thanked him, and strolled over the crunchy white gravel to find my car.

March 21

LWAYS A GOOD IDEA to keep a low profile on campus as the new term starts. Don't want to encourage any ad hoc meetings scheduled by a peer who had a brainstorm over the break for realigning our interdisciplinary benchmarks; Ed School b.s for tweaking our classes for next year, which everyone does anyway. The gym seemed a good place to hide for a bit the day before students returned. Silly me. Seconds from a clean getaway into the weight room, the new Admissions Assistant called out to me from the far doorway. A thirtyish blonde with an athletic build, she is sweet with a few extra pounds; cheesecake we used to call them. She always means well, but did not have the antenna to discern that a teacher in the weight room over vacation is not anxious to be part of a school tour.

"Mr. Burnham," she was headed towards me with a determined gait, a mother and reluctant teenager a few steps behind. She offered some names that had no chance of staying with me. "They are from Albany, where he is in the eighth grade, and they're looking at schools." We exchanged pleasantries, and she proceeded to offer a familiar tale. The young man shows real potential as an artist and loves to read. He finds groups intimidating, and likes sports, but would like to be better at them.

His demeanor in the course of this told more. A shaggy beetle haircut and cargo pants under his blazer and a jellyfish handshake made it clear that this excursion was not his idea. He kept looking away as if he couldn't wait for it to be over. Probably happier sitting in his room drawing than kicking a soccer ball around with others come fall sports, and his sleepy eyes suggested genuine indifference to this mission. This is not to say that there is not a place for such young people in society or at Griswold. Maybe I was just as detached when my folks dragged me around to look at schools. I probably at least looked people in the eye. His mother went on to explain that he's quite bright, but that his current teachers have yet to understand his *learning style*. Our super-positive Admissions Rep jumped in to note that my own classes involve a range of strategies: films, Power Points, lectures, presentations, group work, audio books.

"Wow," the mother affected the kind of excitement parents do when they want it to be contagious with their children. "Doesn't sound like your teachers this year, does it son? Sounds like you really try to reach the kids?"

"Well, mixing it up makes it interesting for me too," I offered, "What kind of sports do you like?"

"I dunno," he shrugged, trying to step on an ant nearby.

"What about your cross-country time?" His mother nudged his shoulder. "Tell Mr. Burnham how much you shaved off your course time over last fall." He muttered something about minutes, but then added he didn't think he wanted to run anymore in school.

"Not competitively anyway..." Cross-country is perhaps the most solitary sport you can engage in at school. The only thing less competitive is Ultimate Frisbee, in which opponents apologize to each other for scoring.

"He likes history," his mother, again, "Tell Mr. Burnham about your grade on the Robespierre project."

"I got an 'A.'"

"Nice job," I run through the French revolution in about one week.

"If you're lucky, maybe you'll have Mr. Burnham for a teacher next year..." Mother was quite bubbly.

"If you want to show them my classroom, I don't think it's locked." I smiled at the Admissions Rep and they were off.

In the middle of doing curls in the weight room, an incongruous sound on a deserted campus rang out again and again. *Crack. Crack. Ping. Crack.* I headed down to the batting cage, and at one end of the mesh tunnel was the automatic pitching machine, spitting out fastballs every eight seconds or so. At the other was Remy, bat high, on his toes like a coiled spring, until *thwack. Thwack.* He was sending frozen ropes back in the direction of the machine faster than it was pitching them. His clenched face bore slightly more determination than Pete Rose ever did. If a major-league scout saw him - and if he weren't forty-three years old...He was in some zone in there; not sure he saw me when I came in, but after each swing, I detected an almost reflexive profanity being muttered.

Thwack. "Bastards." *Thwack.* "Sonsabitches." *Thwack.*

When the bucket on the machine was empty, he stopped to gather up all the balls he'd sprayed around into a plastic milk crate.

"You playing summer ball?" I asked. There are a few adult teams around here. He took a break from dropping balls into the milk crate with the label *Theft of this Container is a Crime* and looked up. In a sleeveless sweatshirt and UConn shorts, hands on hips and glistening skin, he looked like a sparring partner in a boxing movie, with a glare, as if daring someone to take a swing at him.

"Like to play the freakin' bongos with a few heads." He spat on the floor as if getting rid of snake venom.

"Heads? Whose?"

"Freakin' got my choice, don't I?" He resumed tossing balls into the milk crate, and I fished a few to keep things going. He loaded them into machine again, but stopped short of turning on the feeder. "Y'know, Chrissie, right? My oldest? Eighth grade at the Shaw School? Won the VFW essay contest this year. Plays basketball and softball. Got the French award too." From a rolled fist, he was uncurling a finger for each laurel. "Got into Westgate, Choate, Northfield and St. George's. Waitlisted here. *Waitlisted*. Where I freakin' work f'Chrissake. And gets in everywhere else. 'Course doesn't get any financial aid from those places. Sucks to be white and middle class sometimes."

"That's...bizarre." Spontaneity is not my strong suit.

"Yeah that's a start. I've been here seven years. We didn't have an intramural program for all the spazzes who can't make competitive teams when I got here. Now we do. Basketball was a laughingstock; our varsity played Concord's JV. Didn't even have a batting cage f'Chrissake." He raised his arms in a *look at my creation* way. Then pointed over my shoulder to the gym wall. "Those Class II champs banners there? How many were here ten years ago? I'll tell ya' how many: five – all from the 1980s. Now, they have to take the old ones down to make room for the new ones each year. And *this* is the freakin' thanks I get."

"I don't get it. She's obviously capable, if she ----"

"Capable? She's a machine. More on the ball than half the twits here. She's *forgotten* more about softball than that dy--," he caught himself. "that bitch I hired to coach last year knows."

"Remy," I looked around, a bit worried, "volume."

"I don't care. Let 'em hear me. Tight ass Bowdoin shits." Since Scott arrived here a few years ago, it has seemed that a lot of the new hires have been from his *alma mater* in Maine. Some of them shouldn't even have made the interview cuts. The backlash is to the point now that two department chairs won't even call candidates for phone interviews if they went to Bowdoin.

"So…they have a reason?"

"Oh sure, just what they trot out to all the sorry suckers. " He made quotation marks, with fingers on both hands, "'An *unusually large pool of qualified candidates* this year.' A candidate – I *work* here, f'Chrissake I'm the freakin' *Athletic Director*. She's a fac brat. *Jesus,* Mary and *Joseph."*

About half of the faculty children go here, but I've never looked into how that happens. Some math teacher's son goes to the local high school 'because he's a handful' as Mother would say, and why be embarrassed by sonny at work? A science teacher here has a daughter at Interlochen, the art school in Michigan, from which she'll probably go to Oberlin or Juilliard; damn amazing on the piano. Those fac brats who *do* become our students know more about the place than some teachers: which doors have faulty latches, who's on the wagon, where the really dead wireless zones are. Remy's daughter has done summer work in the Development Office and babysits as well. At a faculty meeting last year, a confirmed spinster who was childless and never met an item on a buffet table she didn't like proposed closing a hole in the budget by having faculty pay half the day student tuition for their own kids. Mary carpenter doesn't have kids here, but stood up to offer perhaps the most impassioned thing I've ever heard her say.

"If one of my peers, a *colleague,* has a child who wants to learn, I'm happy to have him or her in my class. I'll make room. She could have my chair. My kid probably *babysat* that kid, or vice versa. I'd be happy to have 'em. You want to balance the books on the backs of people who happen to have a family here? You really want to *do* that??" Applause. Some standing. That took care of that. But the bean counters have another view. Every spot taken up by a fac brat is one less spot for a kid whose family might be coughing up the full 50K.

"Christ. What are they smoking in Admissions?" Remy was now tossing a ball up and down in one hand as if preparing to hurl it through a window. "Course they got room for some other kids here. These bowling pins who washed out of elsewhere. Folks drag their kids around here, saying he's a *kinesthetic* learner; doesn't *perform well* - quotation marks with fingers - on written tests. Doesn't *respond* to verbal cues in class. That's not his kind of learning style or intelligence. *Bullshit.* Called being a teenager. Or just plain lazy. Christ, you show me a kid who does cartwheels at the notion of an exam. There ain't one. But admitting they don't like them makes 'em *special* now." In point of fact, Chrissie is everything her father said; bright but not bookish, athletic but not obsessive. In short, well-adjusted. It would be nice to use that term more often when describing kids.

"Truth be told Burnsy, even if they changed their mind, I don't want her here. Not now." We headed under the concourse that runs over the squash courts and into the gym, so he could lock up the balls and bats.

"Twits," he went on. "*Fine.* See how far your *learning style* gets you. Ten years from now, at the town dump, the twits they took instead of her can tell me where to put my glass and where my tin goes. Get this: Admissions brings this kid around today, with his mother. Says he likes cross-country. *She* said. *He* didn't say boo. She says he might like to try baseball in the spring. Do I think he can hit a baseball? I don't think he could hit water if he fell out of a boat. But if they do a teenage remake of "Rain Man," the kid's a shoe in for the lead."

As he finished speaking, a distinctly unnecessary and intentional throat clearing came from overhead.

"No, you don't have to be on the squash team to use the courts. Any time they're not busy with practice, students are welcomed to use them." Leaning over the railing from the squash court concourse, the Admissions Rep and her two charges, mother and son, were staring down at us. "Isn't that right, Mr. Remillard?" The two adults glared at Remy with a mixture of shock, anger and disappointment. The Admission Rep broke the silence. "How about we see a dorm room?" After an eternal ten seconds, she ushered them along the concourse and out of sight.

March 23

THE STUDENTS ARE BACK, lacrosse sticks are out and the shoes are dropping. Some seniors who got in early decision months ago are now having second thoughts about those commitments. One girl applied only to Amherst and got in. A four-year girl got in only to a state school in New York, while Dad's a legacy at Brown and mom's a Smithie; must've been a fun spring break at that house.

Retention is a big deal at schools - getting sophomores to come back as juniors and so on. There are always a few who are asked to not return in the fall; *you can finish this year, but you'd probably be happier somewhere else.* The odd student gets convinced that some hockey factory in New Hampshire will get him to the NHL and now and again there's an actor who forgoes senior year to embark upon a career; it worked for Uma Thurman, but probably has not worked for a thousand others. Sitting at lunch the yesterday with some Admissions staffers, I was curious about the numbers for next year.

"Looks good," one of them was picking things out of her salad. "A bit overbooked, but that's where we wanna be."

"Anybody bailing?" I asked.

They offered a few names that didn't surprise me when they were mentioned, owing to notoriously bad grades in a few cases and that in others, kids said that they found our academics too easy, perhaps hoping for a more rigorous brand of school, if not actually harder courses. I asked whether any freshmen weren't coming back, trying to suggest that this was a purely random line of questioning.

"A few...question marks. But deposits to hold spots are due in a week."

"All the international kids returning?"

Two of them eyed each other as if silently debating to divulge something. "Pretty much." They resumed work on salads.

"Well, just so I can whittle my classes down if any have already signed up for them, spare any names?"

A Senior Admissions Officer laid down her fork and clasped her hands before her. A fifty-something model of efficiency and perfunctory politeness, her Helen Mirren coiffure is turning gray gracefully.

"There is, I gather you are aware, a student from Kuwait whose return is a matter of phone calls and more e-mails than I care to remember. And it is still...unresolved."

"Unresolved...at this end, or in Kuwait?"

"Kuwait and..." she shook her head with hopelessness, "...elsewhere." She held a palm-down hand over her head to suggest that the decision was above her pay grade, then pointed in the direction of Barclay's office. I wasn't curious enough to darken his door on the matter.

March 26

SCOTT CALLED A LUNCH meeting regarding the Faisal matter in his office today, which meant filing in with our trays from the dining hall. Bill Murphy of Security, Liz, and I were there, which seemed a bit thin people-wise. As we were all attempting to negotiate lunch on our laps, Scott – nicely ensconced at his desk and able to eat with more ease, don't you know - informed us that one of the Homeland Sec agents who visited months ago couldn't be here so would join us by conference call. "Some developments with the Faisal matter, apparently." Scott was fiddling with his phone to get the speaker working.

"Where's Barclay?" Murph was buttering a roll.

"Another meeting," Liz was checking her phone. "It was on his schedule weeks ago. Couldn't be helped. I'll take notes and brief him." At this Scott pursed his lips a bit, perhaps wondering if his own take on things wouldn't suffice for Barclay. Murph eyed him, then Liz, then me, raising an eyebrow. When his phone rang, Scott told the caller he was putting him on speaker.

"Agent Dealey," Scott began, "with me here are Liz Michaels, Mr. Sears' Executive Assistant, Bill Murphy, Chief of School

Security and Peter Burnham, Residential Faculty of Faisal's dorm."

"Very good," the speaker squawked, "This is Paul Dealey of the Department of Homeland Security in Boston. Reviewing my notes…I believe I've spoken with each of you at one time or another. Hello." The voice harkened back to the fall meeting in my kitchen. He proceeded to recount the matter of communiqués and responses to date in one of those distinct governmental voices that offers up official-sounding legalese in a drinks-Bud-from-the-can, hockey-dad tone, creating the suggestion, wrongly or not, that he is more comfortable with the *Boston Herald*'s sports section than the vernacular of federal statutes.

"The latest communication received by Mr. Aboody's office in Kuwait City continued to reference the younger Mr. Aboody's attendance at an American school. As of now, a pattern as to the origins of these communications has yet to emerge. They continue to be hard copies mailed to Mr. Aboody's office from various locations: Kuwait, New York, Boston, Kuwait obviously these persons of interest either have the means to move about freely or have cells in different locations."

"Cells," Murph huffed. "Wonderful."

"We cannot confirm the existence of cells, but the postmarks of these communiqués suggest that possibility."

"Agent Dealey, this is Scott Paone. You suggested earlier that some more…detailed information has been received?"

"That's correct. According to Mr. Aboody's security team, a communiqué of…four days ago received by local mail service in Kuwait. The…Patriots of Kuwait, as they call themselves, have reiterated their demands about the young Mr. Aboody's schooling, but have now made known some specific actions they intend to take in the event that their demands are not met." The four of us eyed one another slowly as the air left the room and we absorbed syntax previously heard only on television.

"Hello?"

"We're here, agent." Murph scowled. "'Demands' isn't a concept we deal with a lot at our end. Just taking it in." I spite of years at Griswold, Murph was grounded in his Roslindale roots, a working class neighborhood of Boston that will probably show up in a future Mark Wahlberg film if it hasn't already.

"Understandable. Of course. As conveyed to Mr. Aboody's office, and I'm summarizing, these 'Patriots of Kuwait' stated that if the younger Mr. Aboody is not withdrawn from Griswold by August, it will bring a response from them."

"Did..." Liz removed her reading glasses, "Did they explain the significance of...August? Things are pretty set in stone at schools by then."

"It's actually not a random date...but rather a sorry anniversary in Kuwait, actually. But that's the best guess of their security team as they explained it to my partner and I."

"My partner and *me.*" Liz offered.

"'Scuse me?"

"Nothing. Sorry." Once an English teacher...

"It is in fact..." Dealey could be heard shuffling papers at his end.

"It's the month that Iraq invaded Kuwait in 1990." At last I had something to add to the meeting. "The thing that triggered the whole Gulf War. 'A line in the sand.' Bush One."

Scott shot me a wink and Murph squirmed in his chair.

"That would appear to be the essence of the month's significance," Dealey again. "The details of what that date is to involve are not clear, but it is suggested that Mr. Aboody's office and Griswold will be visited by unhappiness then if the young man is still enrolled there at that point in time."

"'Visited by unhappiness?' What the hell does *that* mean?" Murph's blue eyes were now steeling. "I get visited by unhappiness when I open my kids' phone bill. Are we talking about a fork in the gears of the dining hall's dish machine, C-4 in the science building, some cyber monkey wrench to the school's server or what? Cops guarding open manholes are more useful than this."

"Mr. Murphy, I'm guessing. Yes, that's correct. The suggestion is vague, to say the least. The security folks in Kuwait are attempting to ascertain the origin of the letters, but that's what we know, and we deemed it important to share this with you."

"So," Murph was rubbing his temples with both hands. "Pardon my French, but what we're left with is...there's a thirty-one-day window during which we could be *visited by* some shit storm of an undetermined nature. Am I hearing you?"

"At this time, this is what we have."

"And..." Scott was now hunched over the speaker of his phone, "what would your advice be to the school now, in light of this?"

"There are standard steps that can be taken in cases where an increased threat level is evident for a given target."

"Target. *Target.*" Murph huffed. "Nothing standard about this."

"Well, we appreciate that this is a unique situation for you, but I assure you that there have been other situations of a comparable nature, and we have a protocol to address them."

"Are there steps at this time that you would recommend we adopt?" Murph clicked a ballpoint pen.

"We'll be sending you a PDF file with suggestions for now. Given the time frame at hand, and for reasons which, collectively, do not raise the nature of the threat to an imminent possibility...we're comfortable with... leaving it at that for now. At this point in time."

"Well, I'm just *tickled* that you're *comfortable,* Agent Dealey. Stick another J. Edgar Hoover pin on yourself." You could take

Murph out of Roslindale, but you couldn't take the Rosi out of Murph. Liz shot him daggers.

"Apologies, Agent Dealey." Liz spoke up. "This prospect is wearing on some of us more than others. We know you're doing the best you can with us in mind."

If looks could kill, Murph would have been arraigned for murder that afternoon. No love lost there.

"Understood. Please take note of the protocol that will be forthcoming. When we know more, we will share it with you as needed."

Scott concluded the call and exhaled audibly. Liz was tapping furiously on a laptop, Murph was scribbling on a yellow pad and I had what I thought was a brainstorm.

"It seems that at some point, Faisal is going to become aware of all this. We can---"

"Peter, this doesn't involve Faisal." Scott shook his head. "This is between his family, some…malcontents, and us, or for now. Homeland Secu---"

"It damn well *does* involve him," Murph was still scribbling. "He may be a minor, but has anyone let him know that this circus is whirling around him?"

"Such decisions must ultimately rest with the family," Liz didn't look up. "What Faisal thinks is, sorry to say, not as important as what his father thinks. We can't broach the issue with the student anyway without the family's permission."

"Wait a minute," Murph clicked his pen and jammed it into a breast pocket. "We are a…a *target*, to use the term of Elliot Ness there a minute ago. We need permission to…Frankly, I think we're past this. Look. I'm no stranger to situations. I didn't spend twenty-nine years on the force writing parking tickets. But this kid is the elephant here. Every year, some kids don't come back in the fall. Lots of reasons. If, for some reason, grades, drugs, whatever, he's one of them, this is all moot. Why can't we just talk to the kid?"

"Yeah," I was glad to not be alone on this. "Who knows? Maybe he could even...tell us, or the feds something. Right now there's not much information out there. We don't need a family's permission to speak to him. Ask him if he feels safe here, if anybody has---"

"No, Peter." Liz tapped a few keys on her laptop with purpose, then removed her glasses again. "Perhaps technically, we don't. But, frankly, we're not talking about some kid from Vermont caught drinking in his room. You were here in October. His father, and others in Kuwait now have us on their radar. Beyond what that could entail, we can't lay this in the lap of a teenager. Homeland Security is involved. This is not a matter for someone who has lights out at 10:30."

"I have to agree with Liz," Scott was nodding. "Besides, how would he fare moving forward with this knowledge on his plate. I don't see it as...helping."

"But we ask kids all the time, 'How's it going?' 'What's new?' What's wrong with that?" Like everyone, I hadn't touched my lunch. "Maybe he knows something he just can't share with his fa---"

Scott and Liz were shaking their heads without looking up.

"So we sit on our hands and wait for some PDF file?" Murph tightened his lips to a genuine grimace.

"Look Bill, this is what they do." Scott gestured to the phone. "They know how to handle it. Better than we do anyway. Let's see what they say."

The same points were tossed about the room for another ten minutes, and when it broke, we all peeled away, turning in untouched lunch trays, anxious to breathe the air outside again.

March 29

S O FRIDAY NIGHT I'm on duty and checking doors when I find some duct tape over the latch of a gym entrance used only by visiting teams. Inside by the boys' locker room exit I find a kid who I don't know slouched to the floor, back against the wall, nodding his head to his iPod.

"Odd place to listen to music," I offer, starting with something light, as there's a chance that looks don't tell the whole story. His eyes were closed as he fingered his way towards hearing loss; I could hear it ten feet away. Some Ear, Nose & Throat folks will be quite rich off this generation of music lovers. He still didn't even know I was there. "Hey!" I yelled, as an unnerving volume seemed in order. His start was more than just surprise.

"Oh!" He rose, letting the ear buds fall away. "I..." Being inside a locked school building on a Friday night, he'd have to make this good. "I just wanted some... privacy." His eyes recalled the page in that childhood book, where Mr. McGregor encounters Peter Rabbit.

"In a locker room?"

"Yeah but...it's away from the dorm, you know?"

"How did you get---"

"It was…open." His looks suggested Kurt Cobain at fifteen years old; not a board of health issue by himself, but the people who do photos for the school catalog weren't chasing him down for shoots either.

"You *found* it open?" I titled my head, "Final answer?"

"Yes. *I found it open Mr. Burnham!*" Suddenly his voice was a great deal louder.

"First of all, Mr. Murphy of Security doesn't carry around all those keys for exercise. And now, why are you speaking like we're on a runway at Logan?" I could almost see the blood leave his face. At this, he hitched his shoulders and it seemed clear that any constipation he might have been suffering from was about to pass. It suddenly dawned on me that as he stood, he positioned himself as if to prevent anyone from passing him and opening the door to the varsity locker room. I waved him away from it, and he shrugged, for no apparent reason, except that he was no doubt regretting the decision process that brought him here at this point in time. I pushed past him and into the locker room. Once inside, there was that indescribable perception that I was not alone. In the farthest bathroom stall, sneakers were visible just below the door.

"Come out with your pants up." Nothing. *"Today."* After the longest twenty seconds in someone's life, the banal, metal *click* of a stall door cracked the fluorescent air, and out squeezed Toby Weeks, Faisal's Thanksgiving host. We locked eyes, and he had that holding-his-breath look Bogart has just after Claude Rains says "Major Strasser has been shot."

"I had to go. To the bathroom"

"In the varsity locker room at nine o'clock on a Friday night? Toby, I was born at night, but not last night." Just then a distant door slammed – probably his lookout hoping to flag down a passing motorist for a ride to Canada. Toby rubbed his stomach, then, bouncing ever so gently onto the floor behind the toilet seat was a tortoise shell headband. Invisibly, Toby's stomach imploded. He was at once the most defenseless and indefensible soul in the eastern time zone.

"I'll count to five." Father did a lot of counting when I was young. Apparently we all become our parents. "You don't want to be in there when I get to five." Nothing. "One. Two." Under the stall partition, a dark, woman's shoe was dropped to the floor. Then another. Small feet slipped into them with the help of a clumsy hand at the end of a bare arm. The sound of clothing being adjusted was the only noise about the room until the stall door creaked open again. Head down, Faith Marks sheepishly stepped out, and with large, brown, forlorn eye, pleading mercy. A dark bob cut, freckles, turned up nose and braces, she clutched her pale elbows as if suddenly cold.

A slightly immodest legend in school, Faith is one of those students who is so far from being self-aware that you wonder if it's intentional indifference or whether she's on the autism spectrum. Upon her sixteenth birthday, dad rolled onto campus in a white 350 SL, promising it to her upon graduation. Incremental sources of resentment piled on after that. Over Christmas break the chatter was that at a ski lodge in Stowe, she was agreeable to sharing her natural gifts with more than one fellow present to the point that by mid-January, the boys who partook of her good nature in Vermont were seen yelling, "Have faith!" as they spotted one another on campus afterwards.

"Let's... go." I gestured to the door, "Mr. Paone's office." The Duty Dean would take my statement, and keep them there until dorm closing. Equally horny but more sapient couples might have taken to the woods, given the season. In light of the perfectly inverse relationship between hormonal surges and brain functions, this oversight was not a surprise. Such incidents are to be confidential when faculty stumble upon them, and presumably students would not advertise their transgressions, the better to protest innocence before a Disciplinary Committee. It is however, easier to keep a priest celibate at a Boy Scout sleepover than it is to keep things under wraps for long. By Sunday brunch it was out, and after speculation as what Toby's fate would be, talk then turned to Faith.

"Geez," Schy shook his head without looking up, "I wrote a college rec for her."

"Good call," Remy put his coffee down and eyed Schy. "Smack yourself with one of those polo mallets later today, will you?" Schy was off to Myopia again, so took the ribbing with pride.

I'd let it be known that I'd be in the library for Sunday afternoon duty, which can usually be counted on to be dead. Outside, lacrosse balls and Frisbees were airborne, and a few couples affected studying on blankets, sporting the first shorts of the season. When the library door opened and closed, I figured it was either a geek looking to bury his head in an AP chemistry study guide or a couple seeking some privacy in the upper stacks.

"Heard I'd find you here." Kat was still licking her wounds from being dumped for the TA from Thailand. Gone is the perkiness of last fall; in a flannel shirt, jeans and a bandana, she looked as if she was working a yard sale outside of Portland. I chalked up her pallor to rum and Newport Lights, which a few whiffs of her flannel suggested were vices that had become habits. "Too nice to be outside," she sighed, flopping onto a burgundy wingchair, swinging her feet up onto the matching ottoman.

"I'll get my fresh air in a few months," I shrugged.

"Oh yeah. The Vineyard."

"Nantucket," I corrected her.

"Right." She scanned the New Fiction shelf, as if she came in to do so. "S-s-s-o-o-o-o..." She turned towards me and joined her palms as if planning to pray. "I wanted you to hear it from me...not...the gossip mill." She then let out a breath. "I'm leaving. In June. Not teaching. Just here." Now this was a bolt. Truly, I was flattered that she was telling me in this manner, but I suppose a bit of me was, for no good reason at all, feeling a bit jilted. Some indefinable nag, like hearing that a good roommate is transferring midyear. I had no claim on her, and certainly hadn't offered any hint that I wanted one, but there it was. The girl you didn't ask to the prom going with someone else, and an unjustified glimmer of feeling cuckholded is born.

"Wow." Inside my head I was scratching at my brain, trying to will myself to affect happiness for her. "Sort of...out of the blue. Sort of not. Is this...your idea?" Such things are never clear at schools where one's work is year to year. If it's not your idea, you still have to affect that it is, suggesting that you're *pursuing new interests.'*

"Yes. Definitely yes. Mine."

"Well good then. Great!" We shared an air pound. "What's the plan?"

"I'm headed to Weld. English. *Duh*. Juniors, and a Brit Lit class. No Spanish."

Not too often, a friend's news touches a place just below the sternum, ginning up a mixture of envy and impending loss that makes any well-wishing truly disingenuous. You don't refrain from doing so, but it is as heartfelt as a "thank you" to a highway toll collector.

"That's great." I pumped her arm. "Nice school."

"Yeah. I met some guy there who knows you."

"Dave Meeks?"

"Yeah. That's him. Says 'hi.' How d'you know him?"

"We rowed together, once upon a time. So...was there a last straw here?"

"This-s-s-s...year," she closed her eyes and tossed her head back, as if absorbing news of an unexpected car repair. "Everything..."

"'Course," I nodded, "And Weld...you could do worse."

"Yeah. Seems like a great place. Far from Cambridge, anyway." The thought of Rod Knightley having a lithe undergrad proofread his dissertation between karma sutra recreation was apparently too much.

"How was Barclay with the news?"

"Kinda...at first, he was like, 'well, if it's best for your career, we want to support you, but of course, sorry to lose you, yadda, yadda...' When I told him *where* I was going, it was weird. Like someone flipped a switch. Suddenly he was really just...sort of forcing himself to keep the conversation going. Did he...get fired from there or something?"

"Hmmm. Far as I know, no, but all Heads of School know each other, so...I dunno."

"Weird. Really weird. Anyway, I'm here until they've got my apartment ready. So July anyway. They're *paying* for my move."

"Nice. Damn nice."

"So. You know." She stood up, and behind her bandana, retied her ponytail without thinking about it, the way women do. "You've been really nice to me this year, Peter. I mean it. A big help."

"Hey, happy to be." For want of something else to say, I stood. "Now I'll have to buy my own hard stuff."

"Don't worry," she waved a knowing finger. "I'm not packing more than I have to, so come by and finish it. Everything must go."

"Yeah? Great fun. And...," I suddenly remembered, "there's some workshop there this term I'm 'sposed to go to. At Weld.

Gotta leave early to get there, but in case you want to…look around again…"

"Really? When? I'd kinda like to…see my room and apartment, if I could get coverage for the day…"

"I'll check the date," and with that, her Brandenburg Concerto #2 ring tone went off. She checked to see who was calling, waved and was off.

April 2

SENT EIGHT MORE RÉSUMÉS out last week – five to schools with posted positions and three just on hope. No callbacks from the STEAG interviews. Should probably stop checking my in box every hour hoping for word.

April 3

A T THE START OF TODAY'S 20TH CENTURY History class, Dickens Matthews waltzes in, and without a word, Isaiah high-fives him as he plunks down next to him. Dickens has straddled things nicely here; a go-to guy for the students of color, he seems as at home at the Westchester table as he does among the wearers of do rags.

"Better learn to ski, bra." Isaiah shook his dropped head. Puzzled looks were exchanged, and Isaiah obliged us with a *this guy* thumb at Dickens. "Man's going to Dartmouth." Dickens affected a search in his backpack for some quite elusive notebook, sheepishly avoiding eye contact as Isaiah went on, "What's Mr. Potatohead say?"

Dickens shrugged and cracked his notebook.

Mr. Potatohead is Isaiah's name for his neighbor in the dorm, a PG hockey star out of South Boston who seems to live up to the 1970s stereotypes of his zip code. His nickname might come from the shape of his head and his glasses that resemble the features in the children's game; I doubt that our students think enough about history to tie it in with his Irish heritage. Griswold was his ticket out of Boston schools, where the differences between the publics and the parochial ones have become quite blurred over time. His pallor, buzz cut and street smarts are vintage Southie, and he would seem to have forgotten something, namely that were he not the skater that he is, he'd be back on L Street, meandering Whitey Bulger's old haunts. Nevertheless, he seems to feel more entitled to be here than the student heading to Hanover, shooting Dickens odd looks whenever he makes an announcement at a school meeting. Not lost on me too were some emphatic statements he made about affirmative action in a fall class of mine. Dickens is by far the better student of the two, as well as the better person. He's actually a legacy here, his father and grandfather having graduated from Griswold, but while I know this from meeting his parents, he never advertises it himself. Honestly I've never heard Dickens refer to his embittered neighbor by the nickname favored by others, as if doing so is beneath him, and I doubt he'll start now. No need to shout when you're right.

April 4

FINALLY SOMETHING MORE THAN a nibble on the job front: Blodgett Ohlmsted School in Connecticut called three days ago. Near South Woodstock – does every state in New England have a town named Woodstock? – it's a school on a par with Griswold but seems better endowed. The website notes trustees with names like Chip and Cornelia and the kids appear more desperate than most to look like L.L Bean models. Unlike Griswold it's got a rowing program, and while I currently only coach a sport one semester, picking up crew in addition to squash there might be fun, and it wouldn't hurt to get my hand back into the sport for some future gig elsewhere. After a twenty-minute chat with the Dean of Faculty, she said they'd email me by Friday if they wanted me to visit the school.

April 12

BLODGETT OHLMSTED WAS in touch and asked if I could visit towards week's end. I had a hunch that Thursday might be Senior Skip Day when my classes would be pretty light, so I assigned some research to the classes I had the day earlier and headed south, wondering how many jokes about "B-O" folks at the school endure in the course of a year.

Unless you're on one of the interstates, being anywhere in Connecticut is generic; postcard towns that end in – ford or -ton with white steeples, a hardware store and revolutionary war markers on a common. Blodgett – nobody uses the full name – is as quaint and polished as its website suggests, and is going about the search process carefully; before inviting people to teach a sample class, they want to meet and pass candidates around. The Dean of Faculty was a middle-aged bio teacher whose childcare for the day apparently bailed on her, for in what was a first for me, she had her three-year old hanging all over her during our forty-minute meeting. It was very humanizing in cute, tiresome, unprofessional sort of way.

"We're looking for someone to...sorry, *no* honey, put that down...to cover three sections of US His – Max, *honey?* What did I say? – US History, and then an elective of your choosing. I see that East Asia is – sweetums honey, can you come here? Sit with mommy a minute while I talk to Mr. Burnham, okay? *Please* Max, sit." She at least wiggled in that the opening in the History Department was the result of a colleague who was heading to law school.

She passed me off to a student who gave me a tour, a three year senior from Stamford who is the captain of the girls' crew. There's nothing to not like about the place – it's a cookie cutter school with some traditions and supportive alums, and while they don't send as many students to the most competitive colleges as a few other schools do, they don't seem to attract the kids like Blumberg; if they do, they hid them on this day.

Next I met with the Athletic Director, who knows Remy from way back. "Good A. D.," he nodded with an inside joke smile, "Keep him if you can." It sounded like squash and crew could be on my plate if I ended up there, but there's no shortage of crew coaches these days, so there's always the chance of getting stuck with intramural soccer in the fall. This fellow handed me off to the head of the English Department, the only person I met all day that I honestly didn't like. Perhaps a bit younger than me, we met in his office, where he proceeded to kick back and rest his bare feet on a desk, affecting some *ennui* at everything from teaching to literature to me. I wondered if it was some kind of test, like those interviews in business where a candidate is asked to open a window on the thirtieth floor of a skyscraper just to see how he responds.

Over lunch, the History Chair asked me how I'd feel about no longer being head of the department if I were hired.

"I like teaching, and while it's been gratifying to put my stamp on the department with some new electives, I don't need that reinforced continually, and I probably wouldn't miss the extra meetings. As long as I'm in the classroom, I'm happy." He nodded as if my answer surprised and impressed him.

I met with the dean again before leaving, who explained that they'd be bringing a few other folks to campus this week and would be in touch about re-visits after that. Heading back to my car, I replayed the day in my mind, wondering if I seemed desperate and hoping I didn't drop the H-bomb more than once. Some folks from Harvard really try to work it in whenever they can: "Raining pretty hard today." *Yes, it rained even harder during Class Day exercises at Harvard.* Understandably, this wears thin. Being there, I looked at this dorm and that building heading to my car, imagining myself living there and walking that way to class, wondering where one goes to get a Connecticut driver's license.

April 17

A FORMER TEACHER OF mine once described spring at a boarding school as silliness at sixty miles per hour. Revisit Day brings kids accepted for next fall to campus. Girls wear clothing their fathers surely don't know they own. Frisbees and pathos from year-end break ups fill the air like black flies in New Hampshire. Aaron Tang seems to have found his niche, in part thanks to Ultimate Frisbee. The sport draws those who've found team sports and haircuts not to their liking. 'Touch football for vegans,' Remy calls it. Aaron seems a natural. Last spring half the team was caught smoking pot and had to miss a tournament at Darrow School, which seemed to bother absolutely no one. Aaron remains the demure, head down bookworm who'll fade from the memories of many folks at year's end. Thankfully one cloud has lifted: in the course of Toby Weeks' involuntary vacation for his locker room – love nest stunt with Faith Marks, he coughed up that it was he who started the fire in Aaron's room back on Parents' Weekend. The details remain fuzzy, as exactly what he said didn't trickle out from the shrink his folks sent him to when he got suspended for the locker room business, but the official version came from Scott Paone's office via the school counseling staff. After a month or so, lots of students either stop locking their rooms while others lose their keys and don't want to report it and pay for a replacement. It's not clear which was the case with Aaron, but it was known that his room was never locked, and whispers have included that Toby liked a girl here from Japan and that in his Asian History class, Japan's treatment of Korea while occupying the land inspired him with a way to impress his woman from Tokyo. Another version is that he simply did it on a dare, but regardless, apparently his parents informed the school of his deed after he spilled the details at home and he was allowed to withdraw from Griswold. A dare when I was at school usually took the form of either jumping into the Connecticut River from a high branch or working profanity into a class discussion guided by an especially prudish teacher. Using zippo lighters on another kid's room never entered the equation, but that's progress for you. I emailed Aaron's father the news, who appreciated it, and expressed what almost seemed like irritation when I mentioned his son's enjoyment of Ultimate Frisbee.

Even in this tofu of sports, the zeal with which Aaron chases the disc is something his father has perhaps never witnessed. A believer in upholding the model minority myth that shrouds Asian students, perhaps understandably, since it got him where he is today, tennis was what he'd hoped Aaron would do this term. His mother arrived on campus rather unannounced today, and when I stopped by Aaron's room, she was busy reorganizing it while yammering into a razor phone. She cut the call short as I entered, and quickly offered that Dr. Tang wanted to take me to lunch at The Melting Pot, a local bistro kept in business in no small way by Parents' Weekend, commencement and reunions. While the doctor had mentioned that they were not together, apparently they communicate.

"Aaron seems good." He smiled across the red tablecloth as we sipped what seemed like tap water in chunky goblets. "He is...happy, yes?"

"Yes, I'd say so. He likes Ultimate, and seems to have his circle of friends."

He nodded. "I almost wonder if...his future at Griswold...could be a good thing."

"Well, it could be, sure. But...there are other plans, right?"

He sighed, and polished his knife with a napkin. "My own plans have caused me to make plans for him." He placed his hands palms down on the table, as if bracing himself for his next words. "I will become a post-doctoral fellow at New York-Cornell Medical this summer. It is also a teaching opportunity." His plain, flat face and swept-back mane were flawless, but at this moment he betrayed the slightest hint of ambivalence, almost chagrin. As glowing as this new mantle sounded, he seemed not entirely at peace with it. Even more than in America, in East Asian societies, there are those matters of which everyone knows but no one speaks. This begrudging admission of his still was quite a feather in his cap it seemed, so I congratulated him as our lunch arrived. "As you know, Aaron applied to many schools this year. With your help, for which we are grateful. My new position will take me to New York. I have...found a school for him there. A school which is right for him, I think."

"Good. Horace Mann, right?" I looked up while nibbling some steak fries.

"Yes, but I've asked him not to speak of it yet." He began picking at a chicken salad before him. Koreans and Chinese are knocking on the doors at so many schools that some academies have unwritten quotas of these students that they will not exceed. If Dr. Tang had indeed found a spot for Aaron somewhere, he'd done well.

"So you'll be in Manhattan?" I offered. "My uncle is a doctor there. You'll have to meet him."

"I would like this to happen." His face brightened. "This summer, perhaps you have plans, yes?"

"No...not yet." My deadpan was met with his own rumpled brow, until he realized that he had not elaborated on an earlier suggestion.

"I see...have you had a chance to consider what I wrote to you about? My brother-in-law's language school in Korea?"

As I nodded while chewing, I had a moment of clarity. "Yes I have," I put down my fork. "And I was wondering: were I to accept such a position, and were it to work out well, would there be an opportunity to...teach beyond the summer?"

At this the doctor's eyebrows rose above the rims of his glasses and he set down his silverware.

"Well," he cocked his head a bit, the way people do when some news they've heard is better than expected. "I'm sure that my brother-in-law would be...most interested in any arrangement that allowed for someone of your experience to be part of his school."

Until then, the notion had never occurred to me, but it's April, I want to eat after June, and schools in this hemisphere just aren't beating down my door.

"So...my wife's brother is the director of a school in Taegu. It is a city away from Seoul. South, maybe two hours by train. It is a special school. We call it *hogwon*. You might call it a language school, or a tutoring academy. Students polish their SAT and TOEFL testing skills. They attend after school and on Saturdays. A few come to the US for home stays in the summer, and some go there during the summer. To brush their studies up. High school and some college people." Amazing how in spite of his laurels and learning, he could still mangle a simple idiomatic phrase.

291

"Sounds like quite a spread."

"Spread?"

"A...big range. Of levels."

"They are not all in one class," he held up a clarifying finger, "and this summer one particular college student will be studying there alone. She is a...small celebrity, we might say."

"Celebrity?"

"She was a star on TV as a girl. KBS is a popular channel in Korea." He offered the title of a program as if it would mean something to me. "She later became Miss High School Korea." He went into explanations of the school, thoughts on tutoring the former Miss High School Korea and teaching an SAT prep class to others, mentioning an apartment near the school as part of the remuneration. He had nothing more specific to offer on this matter. "Perhaps," he was tidying his plate, "you can negotiate this with Sonny. He is quite reasonable, and we are most grateful for your help with Aaron." An aversion to negotiate *anything* is one reason I prefer to drive a Volvo half my age rather than engage in the process of buying a new car. A promise of contact information was made and our talk went in other directions, generic to the point of banality until he pressed me. "I am curious, however, Mr. Burnham."

"Please, Peter."

"Very well, Peter. I of course love Korea. It is my home, but here, you are a department chair. Is there a reason you would leave all this? Leave Griswold?"

I held up a finger to indicate that I'd answer as soon as I was done chewing. That and a swig of water gave me time to think. I knew that graduate degree would come in handy some day.

"Well, as you know, my second master's focused on East Asia, and after that I spent a few years in Japan. I feel as though I need to learn more about another part of East Asia first hand, and this sounds like a good chance to do that."

He was quiet for a bit, then nodded. "An autodidact. Very commendable. Let me contact my brother-in-law about this...interesting idea." Things were left loose when we parted on campus, save for a business card on which Dr. Tang scribbled some e-mail addresses. Summer in Korea. Maybe a year. *Kimchi* and a rainy season. Weighing this prospect consumed the rest of my weekend, after I looked up the meaning of *autodidact*.

April 19

ORE OF A LANDS' End model than a Fox News babe, Kat still knows that others will assume her to be clueless in certain realms, such as car repair. Auto mechanics look at females like her the way Sylvester looked at Tweety Pie, so last Saturday, she asked me to come along to a dealership in Newton to make sure she did not pay $700 for a new thermostat in her car. In the service area of the place, I was nursing church coffee and skimming two years' worth of *Car & Driver* issues when a familiar voice wafted around the corner and through the fluorescent light; it was a fragmented conversation, suggesting the speaker was on a cell phone. The service waiting area was five steps from the sales realm, and meandering over, I spotted a familiar pair of trousers in a chair, the face hidden by a glossy brochure on a new two-door chickmobile. *Faisal.* His matted, whatever-bowl cut was anonymous, but the orange high tops and camo hoodie – his latest trademark ensemble – gave him away.

"Faisal?" I was truly hoping I was mistaken. For a second, his eyes suggested a pleasant surprise, being recognized by a familiar face. This faded as quickly as it appeared, and he sat up straight as I approached.

"What's up?" I asked generically.

"I signed out," he offered with a hint of defensiveness. His widening brown eyes suggested a cornered animal.

"That's good. What are you doing here?"

"I'm...sixteen." As the words left his mouth, I realized that this discovery would ultimately result in more involvement on my part than I wanted to commit to on an off-duty weekend.

"That's nice, but wha——"

"I can drive. I have an international license." Ever so slightly, the glossy brochure between his fingers began to quiver.

"You're not...just tell me." He remained frozen. "To-*day.*"

"I have the funds to purchase a car." Very matter of fact. "It would allow me to visit my brother at college." Fayed Aboody is at Williams. It was as if I'd discovered him with a rod and reel fishing in a toilet; stupid on a number of layers.

"You can't have a car at school. Boarders *can't. Period.*"

"But," he finally let the brochure fall to his lap, "it will not be my car. It will be my brother's"

"Is he here?" I waved my arms to suggest the entire dealership.

"He is at college. At Williams College. But there is no Honda dealer near where he is now."

A *Honda*. His family could probably buy every dealership in New England out of petty cash. Why he wasn't at the Lexus dealership down the street was puzzling, but not something I needed to explore at the moment. I also wondered if his brother's attendance at Williams had inspired the kind of scare we'd been getting about Faisal. The Homeland Sec people never mentioned the brother in the States.

"Faisal, I can't believe we're even having this conversation." Truth be told, I was hoping my glare at him would wither his resolve, if not singe his forehead. At that moment, there were no lug nuts being tightened or hoods being slammed. The plasma screen TV over the coffee maker had some NASCAR pre-race huddle on mute. Kat eyed me cautiously, and a few others waiting for their cars appeared rapt.

He turned away and fished his pockets. "I want to call my brother."

"Yeah," it occurred to me, "go ahead." As he began working his phone, a twenty-something salesman with a buzz cut, shiny red face and thirty extra pounds came bouncing towards us. The absence of a neck made me guess that buying clothes is not always easy for him.

"So: Fade. Face, sorry. It is Face, *right?* Did I get it right this time?" He juggled guesses at the correct pronunciation with his hands, suggesting he'd accept whatever he was told.

"Faisal."

"Faisal. Right. I got your color. Midnight – with the sunroof and spoiler." He cocked his head and turned to me. "Are you with him?"

"You could say that. Where...is this process?"

"Process?" He wrinkled his brow at what seemed to be a new word.

"This young man is a student at Griswold. He would appear to have...not familiarized himself with school policy on cars." The salesman's face suggested he'd just smelled something unpleasant. "It's a boarding school," I continued. "Students who board – *live* – there, can't have cars." In a matter of seconds, the glow of an impending commission left his face.

"But," Faisal was honestly not at the table at this point, but was trying desperately to ante up. "I have already said, my brother---"

"Yeah, he did mention that." Buzz No Neck was attempting recovery. "'Course. Your brother. He'll have to take possession. We're just gettin' the ball rollin,' so t'speak."

"His brother will have to roll it himself." I shook my head. In the corner of my eye, I saw a mechanic who had entered the room and was showing Kat something small in his blackened fingers.

"Wait!" No Neck held up a pleading palm. "Lemme get my manager." and he turned.

"Look," my clenched-teeth tone stopped him. "This is over. Nothing you did." Faisal's eyes honestly seemed to moisten at this. I pointed to the bank of chairs by Kat, and he shuffled off, as if just declared 4-F by the army the day after Pearl Harbor.

Faisal had to cool his heels until Kat's Accord was $238 better, prompting him to sulk into his phone all the way back to campus; apparently he'd taken a cab to the dealership. He failed miserably trying to glare me into guilt via the rearview mirror when I threw over my shoulder that Scott Paone would be in touch.

"Am I...is this...a DC problem?"

"That's up to Mr. P."

"But he will listen to you. If you say bad things, he will believe them." As much as Ed Schools are factories of feel-good bullshit, a course on how to forgive student-prompted adversity or simple brainlessness might have been a good class to audit. At this point, I proceeded to tear him a new one, wheeling around to the backseat just inside the school gates to let him know how happy I was to spend my Saturday morning explaining school policy to a local merchant. A blue and green spring day had broken over the campus, and yelps from a distant lacrosse game wafted through the fanning leaves overhead as we rolled on.

After we dropped Faisal outside of Scott's office, Kat had a question. "What if his dad bought it for him, and the school really wanted dough from the family?"

"Good question," I admitted. "Rules are rules, except when a wealthy parent is involved..."

"So," she continued, "if a kid comes back to campus smashed but dad owns General Motors..."

"Well, a school can always use new cars...actually it's a publically held company so it'd be---"

"Seriously," she turned to me after turning off her car, "If a kid's folks take him out to dinner, and, it's like, a Jewish ceremony or something..." This actually rang a very distant bell, something from years ago I recounted for her. During my senior year at school, my roommate's dad took us to dinner. Dad was from Hong Kong. No drinking age, I was told. Part of growing up. Rum and cokes until we barely had room for dinner. By the time we were back on campus, Yeltsin would have been proud of us. With a few minutes left in Study Hall, we felt compelled to advertise our condition outside the library with our best Sinatra. Years later, how we knew the lyrics to "Three Coins in the Fountain" remains a mystery, as did, at the time, why we were shooed back to our rooms and had hot coffee forced upon us, but no consequences to speak of. Later when I asked my roommate about the lack of repercussions, he mentioned that whenever the school's Concert Choir toured Asia, they stayed at one of his dad's hotels. I doubt there was a room bill afterwards, or at least there wouldn't be now. That was the end of *that*. Kat rolled her eyes at the tale, muttering something about *quid pro* quo and an old boyfriend from Taiwan.

April 23

E-mail from Dave Meeks:

Peter -

The SNEHTC is here next Friday. Mostly a Conn. thing, but if you can get away for it, I'm host and we could catch up. Attached is the program. Let me know.

Meeks

April 29

THE SOUTHERN NEW ENGLAND History Teachers' Conference is a day-long workshop on novel concepts for those educators interested in professional development as well as a better than average lunch. Quite a bit of social studies teaching ideas actually do get shared, but whether folks genuinely put them to use the following Monday is another matter. The best way to become a better teacher is to see a superior teacher at work, and then mirror whatever will work in your own classroom. That said, on top of the chance of picking up a new idea, the prospect of catching up with Dave added some reason to the notion of going. Kat couldn't get away for the day to see her new home, but he who travels alone travels fastest.

Griswold looks like a boarding school. Weld looks like a boarding school to the extent that movies about boarding schools are filmed there. Ivy clings to gothic archways and slate gables so as to suggest that all those who darken its environs will ascend to places of ivy upon commencement. The workshops were surprisingly useful. "Why Teach the Vikings?" "Social Media & Learning." "Africa: Denial." Even academicians can get their fill of such notions, however, so a reception in the wood-paneled Dean's Room at five was quite welcomed. Eakins-esque prints -

originals? - and oils of headmasters past glowered down on our plastic wine glasses, suggesting muted umbrage at our repose with their stoic glares. Some teachers had bailed earlier to beat traffic, but for those of us who remained, the open collars and 'Hello' name tags gave it a class reunion feel. People familiar with such environs winced here and there as others, probably newbies, verbally ogled the oxblood wingchairs and first editions on the shelves. Dave appeared and mentioned dinner at The Bottleneck, a former town library a half-mile from campus that Weld faculty tend to avoid, not wanting to advertise their thirsts to parents who take their children there on weekends. During the second round there, I caught a few forty-something females stealing glances our way from a corner table.

"They're not mothers of any of *my* students." Dave was indifferent.

"You know all your kids' mothers by *sight?*" I asked.

"No," he twisted over his shoulder for another look, "but parents are always anxious to say 'hi,' wherever you are." This is quite true. Such spontaneous encounters are usually quite pleasant, but Dave has a subtle way of conveying a *weltschmerz* to any impromptu social overture which is not his own. What is it about a bar on a Friday night that makes unremarkable women suddenly feel bold? One of the gossiping gaggle in the corner rose and began to glide our way, drink in hand. At that moment I felt like a character in a John Updike book or as though I was at a school reunion, until she came closer. It was Claire Sears, Barclay's wife.

Her sleeveless blouse, Lilly Pulitzer skirt and tennis tan were flawless. Even with the careful gait suggesting that the Manhattan in her hand was not her first, she had that effortless appeal about her, in a frosted lipstick - boutique owner trophy-wife-just-down-for the summer sort of way.

"Are you old enough to be in here?" She narrowed her eyes as she asked it, sitting down and touching her glass to mine. "Chin chin." This helped me to recall that she'd done a term in Italy while in college. Introductions were made, but she offered no hint of why she was there. It took Dave's casual candor to broach the matter, and Claire didn't miss a beat responding.

"I might be working in the Development Office here come the summer. It's..." she tipped a palm-down hand this way and that to indicate uncertainty, "maybe eighty percent a done deal."

"Really?" Meeks' eyebrows rose. "The Development Office?"

"Or External Affairs. July 1st, and...I guess they're still deciding which." She was running a finger around the rim of her glass, not looking up as she spoke. Then she toasted her words with a swig.

"Bit of a commute from...Griswold..." I was trying to tread carefully.

"Good, old sensible Peter." She clinked our glasses again, and had another sip. "Part of the deal would be me living in..." she turned to Dave for clarification, "Bosworthy? Bowditch?"

"Bogglesworth?" Meeks raised his eyebrows. "A girls' dorm. Nice."

"That's it."

"Well," he tipped his bottleneck her way. "Welcome."

"Hmmm." She forced a thin grin. "Back to a dorm." She seemed ambivalent, and tough as ever to read. "My first dorm was...at Miss Hall's, the year *Challenger* blew up. Had a girl on my floor from New Hampshire who had the teacher who was on the shuttle. She had to go home for a month afterwards, f'Chrissake."

"So..." Why I started to speak I don't know, for I certainly had no idea what I was going to say. It was as if I had six pieces to a puzzle that required ten to be complete, but asking for the missing ones seemed out of the question, at least on only one and a half Beck's. "From herding trustees at receptions to herding cats at 10:30," was all I could manage. She looked up and at nothing in particular, and then at me.

"I'd say it's a step up, in terms of the quality of people, don't you think?" Dave smiled.

"Well," I reasoned, "least you won't be worrying if some big donor is lactose-intolerant or only eats kale before those Capital Campaign Dinners." An alum with unusual dietary needs became a nuisance at Griswold's trustee functions the previous year.

"Nice thing about kids," she said to no one in particular as she craned for the waitress. "is they can change...adults...can't. Or won't." Catching the waitress' eye, she hoisted her glass and twirled a finger in the air. "More to the point," she steered her better-have-a-designated-driver eyes my way, "it's the last thing Barclay Crowninshield Sears *will* do." She held her glare on me, waiting for a reaction that I refused to offer.

"Well..." Meeks made an effort raising his glass without eye contact, "hope it's...everything you want here." Claire forced a perfunctory grin, the kind one sees after congratulating someone for coming in runner up in a squash tournament. Suddenly I felt emboldened enough to press on.

"So, is this all...known at Griswold?"

"Well," her fresh Manhattan arrived, "it will be. Chin chin." David met her toast and asked what kind of projects she'd be involved with. I heard them speaking but wasn't listening. It reminded me of one of those hospital waiting room conversations that you could tune out in spite of it happening right before you.

"So Peter Burnham," she turned and patted my hand, "gonna move into Elliott Cottage and babysit Barclay for me?"

"Hmm..." I felt a sudden license to be direct. "Long as I get a room with a view. What kind of hours am I looking at?" She took my measure, then offered carefully chosen words.

"I dare say he'd prefer…none, in terms of…monitoring his…use of *undedicated time…*"

"Is he writing a book and needs privacy?" Dave asked. Never clear whether Meeks is playing dumb or just as socially daft as Mike Huckabee at a rave.

"*I* could write the book, f'Chrissake." She sipped some and looked at no one, leaving in the air nothing short of venom with her tone. Dave looked at me for a translation, but I shrugged as slightly as possible. "Let's just say," she patted my hand, "let's just say there are some very hard working people at Griswold. Some work…all hours. Some say it can be…physically exhausting." This was *so* much better than the traffic on I-95 I was avoiding.

"Are you ready to order?" *Jesus.* Whenever you actually *want* a waitress…

"Well," Claire rose and struck a thin-lipped I'm-okay-to-drive grin, "*bon a petit,* boys. Nice to meet you David. Peter." She raised her glass. "Small world." Turning back towards her table, she was followed by the waitress who uttered something to her about her salmon taking longer than expected, but it was not clear that Claire had heard her.

"Fall term," Meeks raised his eyebrows, "should be interesting."

"Here, or at Griswold?"

"Both!" he chuckled. "I mean…you couldn't write this stuff." He shook his head in approving disbelief. "So what's the story?"

"News to me. I mean, there's talk and all, but, you know what Twain said about a rumor and truth…"

"What's the talk?" Meeks leaned in, elbows on the table.

"Actually, it's not talk, but…Bags, a guy there, old guard, he thinks that not everything's on the up and up with Barclay and his secretary, but then, when people get bored, they just talk about other people, right?"

Just then, one of Claire's gaggle let out a laugh that turned heads at a few other tables. "Should we ask them to join us?" I'd never seen Dave so animated by gossip. An alto howl was let out by someone seemingly oblivious to the one-too-many tone of it. Meeks and I exchanged looks and spoke no more of the idea.

April 30

THE JOB SEARCH IS officially depressing. The earlier interviews via STEAG went nowhere, I haven't heard from Blodgett-Ohlmstead, and while the firm has sent my papers to a few schools that have been in touch, none of them inspire me to follow up with calls. One is a day school in Texas, and the idea of spending a few weeks in Houston in August looking for an apartment has no appeal. A Friends school – Quaker – in the Midwest would be an interesting change, but its website is so steeped in Quaker philosophies and theology that I doubt anyone without a background at another such school would get a serious look. I pursued one lead at a school in Lexington, but during a walk-through over the weekend under the cover of watching sports, it seemed pretty clear that the place is keeping its lights on by filling the beds courtesy of the Beijing phone book. You can have so many international students that domestic kids stay away; hearing only Chinese or Korean in the dorms or on the playing fields does not a community make. Hopefully some peer at a good school between here and the Appalachian Trail will get a winning Powerball ticket this month and cash out, creating a late spring job opening.

May 1

SATURDAY MORNINGS ARE pretty quiet on campus, most students preferring to rise one hour before their athletic contest or at the crack of noon. With no kids in site, I strolled over to school mailroom for one of those *Hold / Forward* forms to fill out for the summer in case I headed for...who knows. While sifting through the catalogs and credit card offers I found an invitation to a summer memorial service for Kirk Mayhew on the island in a few weeks. On the face of it, this could seem like running it out, but no doubt there are lots of summer people who had ties to him who weren't at the Beverly Farms remembrance in March. It would probably tie in with some fundraiser for a noble cause as well, or simply end with a lawn party, at which the grass is trod on by sockless loafers and tasteful espadrilles.

Stepping into the morning sun, I noticed a long, black car rolling out of the shadows, over the bridge, around the quad and creeping to a stop in front of Hayden, the administration building The place is usually dead on weekends, so this was intriguing. After the longest minute, a driver emerged to walk around and hold a rear passenger door for someone. A lean, dark fellow in a crisp, khaki suit stepped out and turned around as he buttoned his jacket. He went around to the other side of the limo, opened another door and out stepped Faisal, unmistakable in his ill-fitting Paul Stuart sweater and ornery resignation. Heads down they plodded up the marble steps and disappeared between the pillars and inside. The morning sun showed the car to be as clean as the day was clear, and I couldn't help myself. I screwed up the nerve and strolled over to the driver, a quite fit fellow in an impeccably fitting suit and repp tie, who may have been one of the Kuwaiti security fellows in my flat in November. He straightened up from leaning against that car as I approached. We made some small talk, but as I broached the reason for the visit, he was politely not forthcoming.

"Mr. Aboody has an appointment with Mr. Sears. That is all I can say."

I acknowledged his position and chatted him up about Kuwait. He remembered the 1990 invasion and said that he believed that there was something to the stories of Iraqi soldiers unplugging incubators in baby wards of hospitals at the time. "It was a very bad time. We are grateful for what your President Bush did. He was very strong for us."

I asked about any common sentiment about the second Bush. He thought for a few seconds and offered the hint of a smile. "We have a saying in my country. The tree of greatness---" but the clicking of a latch interrupted him.

The wooden door to Hayden opened just then and out strolled Mr. Aboody and Faisal with Barclay a step behind them. If central casting could come up with an embodiment of a debonair, Middle Eastern man of the world, the result would mirror him. As his bronze forehead and slicked black mane picked up the morning sun, his chiseled features and tailored suit all combined to suggest a full-page ad in *Esquire* for an overpriced men's fragrance, *Oasis* perhaps. Faisal seemed a bit unnerved to see me at first, but behind them was Barclay, who patted the boy's shoulder in an *all will be well* manner.

"Oh, Peter," Barclay looked up. "Didn't know you were...here. I'm sure you know Peter Burnham, Mr. Aboody. Certainly Faisal does." His voice was businesslike, and had a grudgingly cool tone about it, saying *I didn't invite him, but can't ignore that he's here.* With him, if you know the story to a situation, you can read between the lines of his comments, but nevertheless, he is a master of social niceties. One should be when in that position, but my last Head of School was clueless. When a four-year senior's mother died mid-year, he blew off the funeral for his kid's soccer game, after the mom had arranged that in lieu of flowers, people should give to that school. How some folks charm or sucker their way into the big offices at some places is a testament to how useless some trustees at some schools are.

"Nice to see you Faisal," he returned my handshake with a sad excuse for one. "Sir," I turned to his father, "a pleasure. What brings you here before...today I mean?" Whenever parents show up before the end of the school year, it's seldom good.

"We have met with Mr. Sears regarding Faisal's future, and he has been most gracious in seeing that it is...on a wise course." The smooth elocution Mr. Aboody affected suggested years of offering the same on the heels of high-level meetings that yielded little, but satiated the press while the Middle East rolled along in chaos and violence.

"I...am glad to hear that," I forced a smile. "Sounds like...good things coming your way, Faisal, eh?" He studied me for a moment, then shot a glance at our dorm.

"I want to thank you for the support you provided my son during his time here." Mr. Aboody extended a hand to me and offered a warm, genuine smile. "Please, if you ever come to Kuwait, I insist that you contact my office." At this I caught Barclay's face out of the corner of my eye, and think I detected the pursuing of his lips, just a hint of sour grapes as a result of this offer to me.

There seemed a universal understanding of Sydney Greenstreet's maxim at the end of "The Maltese Falcon" that the shortest good-byes are the best, for in a matter of seconds, doors were held and closed, and the black car glided around the circle, over the stone bridge and disappeared beyond the imposing weeping willows which line the drive down to the gate.

Scott Paone suddenly stepped out of Hayden and came alongside Barclay. "Sometimes," Barclay said without turning to him, "some nasty lemons can make for some pretty good lemonade." As he spoke, I noted his madras tie instead of his standard weekend garb of a cotton tennis sweater, suggesting this was more than just a meeting finalizing a student's withdrawal.

Scott nodded and smiled, so I directed my question to him. "Lemonade in the form of…"

"Well, there'll be an official announcement later, but Mr. Aboody is quite pleased with how this whole matter concluded," Scott offered. "At least at our end. Not at his, I dare say. But, given his position, he's grateful, as you'll see."

Turning onto the school circle at that moment was a red Security truck that fixed all our stares. It wound the bend by Devine, and headed for the steps where we were standing, grinding to a halt in the space where a moment ago Mr. Aboody's limo had been.

"Morning folks!" Bill Murphy was grinning ear to ear. "Had breakfast?" He held up a bottle of Korbel champagne, prompting Barclay to rock back on his heels with laughter.

"That's not open I hope!" Barclay cocked his head. "Are you serious?"

"You're the boss," Murph shrugged, "but, if there was ever a day for it…"

"Let's get that inside," Barclay scanned the still quiet campus and waved Murph in.

"Peter, you should be in on this," Scott piped up as they were turning. "You knew the whole story." Barclay paused at that, he and I literally not having spoken since our chat the afternoon the hockey rink roof gave way. He tossed up a hand and shrugged, as if to say *whatever* without turning around. In his office he produced some goblets from a shelf as Scott, Murph and I sat before his desk.

"So what are we...apparently toasting?" I couldn't imagine.

"Barclay," Scott offered a gracious tip of the head. "It's all yours."

"Pop it Murph." Barclay set the goblets on his blotter and Murph sent the cork across the room, then poured. Barclay thought for a moment, then raised his glass and we followed suit.

"To the sovereign nation of Kuwait, to the first President Bush for keeping it free, to Gamel Abdul Aboody, for fathering Faisal, for his wisdom and grace...and to the folks at McLean; may their work serve a young man well."

It may be that this was not the first time I have drunk champagne before 9:30 in the morning, but an actual memory of doing so escapes me. We sat, and Barclay fiddled with his phone to see that it didn't ring. I had no idea how McLean, a hospital in nearby Belmont, figured in this whole thing.

"Unbelievable." Scott was beside himself, studying his glass in the light as if he knew what he was looking for. "Nice vintage, Murph"

"Yeah. April." Barclay sat back and folded his arms behind his head as we chuckled.

"Hey!" Murph offered mock umbrage. "Go make a pot o' that sewage Liz calls coffee – I'll finish your glass."

"Honestly, you couldn't write this stuff." Barclay took a sip, noticed my puzzlement, but remained mum. I don't think he liked that I was there, which made it all worth it.

"Turns out Peter," Scott turned to me, "that we are not in a terrorist group's crosshairs after all. The whole "Patriots of Kuwait" scare was a ruse. And from it all, Griswold will actually benefit."

"Holy crap." Murph topped up his glass and shook his head, "Never saw this coming."

"Remember where all those threats and demands came from? Never emailed, but postmarked, remember?" Scott continued. "Any ideas?"

"One or two were from Boston," I ticked off what I knew, "New York also, 'cuz someone knew Faisal was there over a break. Some from, inside Kuwait, right?"

"Exactly." Scott pounced. "All very…global, and scary. *Did they have cells, or spies or what?* Hell, I'll admit it: I was *spooked.* This isn't some "MI-5" episode; we're a school."

"Good show." Murph nodded and sipped. Scott gave a hint of surprise that a retired cop was familiar with a BBC TV series. When Murph caught the look, he was on him.

"What? You think I only know ESPN and "Family Guy" you freaking snob?"

"Boys, boys!" Barclay wanted his moment, waving down the matter. "So: any thoughts on who would have access to all these places during the course of the year?"

"Not a one." I shrugged. "A pilot, or probably anyone with some of the oil money flying out of the ground in Kuwait."

"*Exactly. Yes.*" Scott pounced. "It's so…*obvious. Now,* anyway, I can't believe we didn't see it. Someone who knew Faisal was in New York, yet could also send messages from inside Kuwait during the breaks and from around here otherwise. Someone who didn't want him here. Any school in the west, really, but mentioned us in particular. Any guesses?"

Three sets of eyes bore in, grinning and wondering if I'd get it. Somehow, the hints of geography sent it across my lips.

"Not, Faisal…himself…was it?" I ventured.

They eyed each other with happy surprise and two of them raised their glasses to me.

"Maybe you *did* go to Harvard after all." Murph clinked with me.

"Are you…" After a few seconds of shock, it began to fit together, but was still a knuckleball.

"Think about it." Barclay used his fingers to tick the pieces of puzzle off. "How happy was he here? Not very, but sort of under the radar, yeah? A letter sent from Boston. Someone spying on him? Un-uh. Mailed during, when you actually check the postmark, a Saturday school trip there. The one from New York? Sent while he was there with Toby. Tapped it out here, just had to walk past a mailbox in the city. A few more from inside Kuwait? Never occurred to anyone, *not even the feds*, that they coincided with his vacations home. Our guys and theirs chalked it up to some network of zealots."

"Death to America!" Scott raised his glass and poured himself a top up.

"Y'gotta love how it all came out." Murph was shaking his head in too-good-to-be-true form and turned to me. "Know how you folks always have to get the international kids to bus their trays after meals? They just have it too easy at home. *The help does it.* This kid was no different. He's back in Kuwait, banging out another threatening letter from the Patriots of Kuwait, and tosses his crumpled drafts on the floor of his room. *The help will get it,* right? Turns out the help is no fan of this kid they've been picking up after his whole life."

"Wait a minute, Murph," Barclay held up a cautionary palm. "We don't know that. Let's not get some…palace intrigue rumors going."

"Fine," Murph continued, "Point is, he, the help, takes the balled up drafts to daddy. Boy – woulda liked to been a fly on *that* wall."

"So, did Faisal admit to all?" I asked. "The whole thing?"

"We obviously don't know how it went down back there, but he came clean here." Barclay was drumming fingers on his blotter. "Here, he was…more embarrassed than contrite, but damn contrite still. Sat there scratching his palms with his father telling him to look me in the eye every ten seconds. Just didn't want to be here. At school, *any* school, away from home. Simple as that. But with some brother making the dean's list and tearing up the soccer fields at…Williams or Amherst, I can't remember, he couldn't bring himself to tell his dad directly: *he did not want to go to boarding school.*"

"So invents his own personal *jihad,*" Scott picked it up there. "And Barclay, you were masterful." Scott raised his glass towards the boss. "Should have heard him. Forgiving but no-nonsense with the boy, sage with the dad, lots of *when children seem least lovable is when they need our love the most* stuff. Some Ed school b.s. thrown in too…*there are many roads to success,* even mentioned the school in Amman that Abdulah built. It was like…John Dewey and Dr. Phil right behind that desk. I was impressed."

"Well, hell, it ended better than we thought it would a few months ago." Barclay gave an *aw, shucks* shrug that didn't suit him. "What was I gonna do? Call Logan and get him on a no-fly list?"

"So, this lemonade…" I couldn't imagine.

"Mr. Aboody was, as you might expect, embarrassed, chagrinned…poised, but damn apologetic. And, concerned. Faisal isn't headed home right away. But the father wants the whole thing behind him, and offered his...largesse in whatever form it would be most useful to us to help the matter recede."

"So, that form is…"

"Well, I noted how important language is to helping us understand one another, especially when people are from different cultures, and how...no one knows exactly why some people do what they do impulsively, after years of being a model citizen, or a good son, but that studying science is a good way to direct students to study human actions and interaction, in college and beyond. He agreed, and also agreed to endow a teaching position in the Foreign Languages Department, and to update the science labs in the Cutler Wing. The construction can start once we have plans – probably next summer."

"You got that out of *him? Here? Today. Before ten AM?*" I was floored.

"Well...as things became clear, there were a few conversations over the past week that helped this...take shape. Remember, this whole matter was his son's creation." Barclay leaned back, tapping the eraser end of a pencil on his desk. "He had us shitting bricks, and put Homeland Security and his own staff on alert. Dad was afraid to start his car or taste his food. He doesn't want this in the *Globe* tomorrow, and who'd be served if it were? This is his way of making sure that what's done is done. And, it *is* done. No leaks on this ship." He eyed each of us for unspoken nods of silence.

"And Faisal... as a student here…" I wondered.

"Yes." Scott sat up with a less-pleased, thin-lipped wince. "It's thought that he needs to...think through some things. And dad, I'm guessing, wants him back in a school here, the US, someday. Maybe not until college. But dad's done his homework, and wants to understand his son in western terms, so Faisal's going to...discuss things with some folks at McLean for a few weeks."

315

Outside Boston on grounds nicer than some universities, McLean Hospital is where Boston Brahmins, rock stars and poets have elegantly regained their mental health for generations. The odd student migrates there when it's clear that an affinity for vodka or carving one's name into forearms seem to be more than passing phases. In response to a child simply not wanting to be thousands of miles from home at the age of fourteen, the step seemed a bit drastic. The same could, however, be said about terrorist threats.

I left the meeting with a newfound respect for Barclay, albeit still hating his guts. He could have taken some different tacks with this thing, but took the one that left the family at hand with the matter still confidential and benefited Griswold in a practical sense using some nice circular reasoning. Heading on to Dunkin Donuts, it occurred to me that while I don't know how much the trustees pay him as a salary, it suddenly seemed that he is perhaps worth every penny of it.

Wonder if any schools in Kuwait are hiring.

May 3

LOTS OF VILLAGES ARE missing their idiots, as a number of seniors seem to be working hard to get kicked out these days. On weekends, a few always become oblivious to the noise generated by their drinking or smoking in a dorm room late at night. Last month, a slightly more malicious streak ran through some seniors who are particularly short in the gray cell department. A fellow at Buildings & Grounds reported a load of lumber missing from a school truck. Thoughts turned to 'townies,' since none of our own charges seemed the Home Depot - DIY type, and what would they do with it anyway? A few weeks ago a faculty wife returned from her dawn walk to announce that she'd come upon 'the most Bauhaus tree house' she'd ever seen a few hundred feet behind the chapel. As she went into its design and newness, Scott Paone slowly set his coffee down on the breakfast table. Once classes were underway, he trudged into the woods with a B & G man. By lunch, word was out among faculty that the missing lumber had been found, and a rotation of six teachers was arranged to lurk in a thicket near the structure and see who showed up. After sports and before dinner, they got their men. Not content to form a secret society on their floor with a blood oath and a name such as

Hubba Hubba Wow or I Phelta Thi, four lads ventured into larceny. A DC was held the following day, and as two of the offenders were four-year seniors, their fate seemed to consume the attention of the entire student body. Nicking dining hall trays in winter to go sledding is one thing, but stealing a truckload of pre-cut Balsam Fir is another. Expulsions across the board were recommended. A day later, in a development that surely prompted a 'no way' from most corners, all four were gone.

"Wow. Guess Barclay grew a pair." Remy nodded approval in his gym office when I shared the news. A few days later, the footnotes – unsourced but chewy – began. One was that the students would be mailed diplomas if they finished the year elsewhere in good standing. A rumor making the rounds was that if each family pledged the cash equivalent of the materials and labor costs of undoing the whole woodsy business to the Senior Class Fund, the matter would not appear on the boys' records. A most salacious upshot was that two sets of parents offered five-figure gifts to the Parents' Fund in return for their sons' departures being noted as 'withdrew' rather than expulsions. Students voluntarily withdraw from schools during spring term senior year as often as congressmen resign their seats "to spend more time with their families," and colleges know this, but college is a business, just as an independent school is. The actual disposition of things is not clear, and while a variety of outcomes are making the gossip rounds, the blur of spring term has made it impossible to care for more than five minutes what had happened to the boys. Even when there isn't a five-digit gift at stake, Barclay's got this notion in his head: discipline with dignity. Great idea if you're running a rehab center, but honestly, the one of the most unfair things you can do to young people is to draw a line somewhere, and then move it, for then they don't know where the line is.

May 5

THE SENIOR PRANK THIS month had a hint of panache for the first time in a number of years. Typical stunts in the past have included removing tires from all the deans' cars and leaving them on cinder blocks as dawn breaks over campus. Another year the school awoke to find the pond as close to brown and yellow as dyes would allow. This brought a few folks from the Boston office of the EPA to campus by mid-morning, and eclipsed the previous year's notion of raising of nautical flags up the school pole to signal distress and peril to all who saw it and knew their meaning - which is to say, as there are only a few others on campus who sail, perhaps four of us.

This year the jesters co-opted a recent alum with a real estate background. After snapping photos of some of the nicer faculty houses and concocting the name of a real estate agency, ads for a number of campus properties appeared in some local papers, noting open houses. Specifically offered were several Victorians on Faculty Row that were quite occupied, and emphatically not for sale. Weather for the advertised date could not have been better, and the school switchboard insists that it fended off calls from prospective buyers until early afternoon.

"Look," a faculty wife gritted her teeth at the door of her three-bedroom cape, bouncing a toddler on one hip, "this is a *school*. Look around. How could you *think* this house is…for *sale?*" Such wild goose chases and exchanges became quite common by mid-afternoon, with bewildered interlopers jabbing fingers at real estate ads in classified sections as they endeavored to have a look inside homes the school has owned since the American flag had forty-six stars. Eventually a B & G truck rumbled down to the gate where a maintenance worker found an 'open house' sign stuck in the verdant turf by the school entrance, a fictitious realtor's number also noted on it. He tossed it atop some mulch in his truck's bed and remained there for a while, steering prospective buyers away.

May 6

To: purnham@griswold.org
From: pmccarthy2@b-ohlm.org
Re: Position & Search

Dear Peter,

    Thank you for visiting Blodgett-Ohmsted recently. I know I speak for all of us when I say that it was a pleasure to meet you and hear your ideas on teaching. The year ahead has taken on a different shape than was the plan a few weeks ago, for a colleague here has deferred law school for another year and will be remaining with us. Although this means that we will not be pursuing your candidacy here, I am confident that students will continue to benefit from your efforts wherever you are. Best of luck with your search.

Sincerely,

Pat Mulcahy, Dean of Faculty
Blodgett-Ohmsted School
500 Moody Road South
Woodstock, CT 06267

I hope her little Max brings a stray rabid skunk home someday. The prospect of being jobless *and* homeless in another month over an email and a thin-skinned administrator is truly insane.

May 7

THE MAY MOON BALL – Griswold's prom – came and went without incident, and thankfully without me chaperoning it. Victoria's Secret and Tyra Banks have helped sixteen year-old girls perfect the art of looking ten years older for such occasions. It is difficult to write a genuine college rec for a girl once you've seen her grinding on a dance floor in slightly more material than a pocket square. Remy got off such duty years ago after hoping out loud at a faculty meeting that there were no trustees on hand to see the 'vertical dry humping' at the dance the previous year, referring to the females engaged in the act as 'debutramps.' Note to self: call things what they are and avoid work.

This morning I received an email suggesting that my summer address might be a landlocked city halfway between Seoul and Busan. Given the state of my search, the proposal from Sonny, Dr. Tang's…relative by marriage, was welcomed.

> *To: purnham@griswold.org*
> *From: stk.shakespeareenglissh.ko*
> *Re: Summer!*

Dear Peter,

I have a plan for you to come to Korea to stay for summer and teach eager students here.

Taegu is a city with many culture places you can experience and enjoy history. It is exciting to hear that you are thinking about staying in Korea after the summer, and I would enjoy talking with you about this once you are here. Here is your plan for the summer:

Time: June 10 – August 16

Work: Teaching- 1 English class, 1 US History Class, 2 Private Tutor Classes. These are US students who are back home for summer but must stay fresh for school. Jun Min Bae is a very famous person in Korea. We call her Kiki. She was an Actress on a popular KBS show for two years, she now studies at Harvard after one year of studies at Korean university. She is excited to have you help her to be ready for next year. You can teach morning and afternoon all week. Not on weekends. Then you can tour Korea.

Live - I have an apartment building next to school and a one-bedroom apartment - is okay? You can stay close to school easy.

Pay - $700 a week and I will buy a KTX pass for you to travel Korea as you like. I will reimburse you for your Korean Air tickets as well.

Visa-   You can get at Korean Consulate in Boston. Get tourist visa, not work visa so you can see Korea. If you like this plan, please sign and fax it to me at number here. I look forward to hearing.

Sonny
Sun Tae Kim, Director
Shakespeare English Academy
2F Yongnam Building
309-24 Cho Min Mon
Taegu, Korea

I'd already scheduled to take Friday off, hoping that I'd have an interview on the day, so without one, I headed for Nantucket

Thursday night. Friday broke a lot clearer than the previous night's ferry crossing, so I headed down for a sail mid-morning. A cousin I haven't seen for a decade was actually down in late April and hauled the Rhodes 19' out to the mooring a month earlier. Rowing the dingy out to it, I found a note from him going on and on about how it was time to either get the sails mended or get a new set, and that he'd taken them into town. This cousin drives a Jag and his wife made partner at her law firm last I heard, so I was pretty sure he had the sail maker cut new ones rather than patch the old ones. The four or five of us who use the boat would split the cost, which didn't annoy me half as much as not being able to sail then and there. Rather than stop by the sail maker's for the final total, I headed into the Athenaeum, which is Nantucket for library, to email Mr. Kim back and ask about paying for my airfare, recalling what my pal at dinner at the affair at Kirk's house said. I had some final papers to read and grades to do, but accounting for the time difference, I didn't plan on hearing back for a day. I guess Mr. Kim is an early riser, as I stopped back at the Athenaeum before dinner and found a new email from him. Mr. Kim noted that it had been his practice in the past to reimburse summer teachers for round-trip tickets as part of their final paychecks, and that having been operating a language school *since 1989*, he had found this to work best. I came back with how I'd had my ticket-purchase condition suggested by a "colleague whose judgment I trust" and that being in Korea and knowing when he wanted me there, he was in the best position to handle the arrangements. I sent it and gave the rest of the weekend over to grading papers on the deck, occasionally recalling how annoyed I was at the sails on the Rhodes being in the shop. I rose early Sunday to beat the traffic with the first ferry.

May 11

MEANDERING THROUGH A DORM room after a student leaves always affords some cryptic glimpses into the year that was for a certain individual. Dog-eared copies of *Gatsby* and *Things Fall Apart* are perennially left here, yet the odd $400 blazer strewn over a dorm chair and forgotten never ceases to amaze me. Faisal's room was barren except for a long-necked desk lamp on a dresser and a first year French book on a windowsill. I stopped by the Security Office, which doubles as a Lost & Found at year's end, figuring that some first year French student could use a cheap text next year.

Email from Korea today.

> *Dear Peter,*
>
> *We are excited to have you live in Taegu this summer and do your best teaching for students. In free time, you can enjoy many places and culture in our area as you will see. I will purchase and send you a one-way ticket to Seoul – to arrive here on June 19th. I am excited that you have expressed an interest to stay in Korea longer than the summer. I hope that $700 a week is satisfactory for you, and this will include a*

free one-bedroom apartment near the school. While this
salary can continue into the autumn, it will be necessary to
find you another apartment for after the summer for when
you want to stay and enjoy Korea after teaching. I can help
you find one, but cannot include it in your compensation.
Please call me Sonny and let me know and go to the Korean
consulate in Newton for a tourist visa. It is best if you say you
are coming for tourist reasons and not work. This will help it
be faster. Please e-mail when you have your visa. This will be
a good summer and a good year!
Sonny

Getting a job there and moving to Japan eight years ago was
like clockwork, as were honestly all of my three years there.
Travel, setting up a bank account…piece of cake. Every day I got
on the Sobu Line at Ichikawa Station just east of Tokyo at 8:28.
When I lost my watch, I set the new one when I stepped onto the
train. I'd get to a stop at 8:47 to change to the Yamanote Line
where an 8:49 train took me to Shibuya, and as long as I got my
first train, I never missed the following ones. Three years and
never late for work once; try doing that on the Green and Red
Lines in Boston. If Korea worked like Japan, this would be good,
but this reason I'm supposed to give for my visa – *tourism* - isn't
exactly accurate, and the *must find a new apartment after summer* bit
could make for one bitchy Mr. Burnham come September.
Hmmm…The consulate website says that a passport dropped off
by 10 AM can have a visa by 3 PM. Newton has a nice library, so
killing five hours there the day after tomorrow shouldn't be hard.
I'll email Sonny back once I get the visa.

May 13

RECEIVED AN EMAIL THIS morning from a school in Virginia, saying that its Dean of Academics would like to meet me, and asking if I could visit on May 27th. Woodberry Forest is all-boys' and ninety minutes south of Washington with lots more kids from that region than the North and a charge to make them all Southern Gentlemen; squash players who know to refer to that 1861-65 business as 'the war of northern aggression.' A few on-line searches painted the picture of a school that hasn't changed much over time: it's whiter than lots of other schools, has a dress code, a zero-tolerance policy for drugs and booze and has no gluten-free or vegan offerings in the dining hall. In short, some things to like, some things less so, but at least they know themselves; *here's who we are, so if you like it, come here, but if Saturday classes and seated dinners aren't for you, go elsewhere.* As a history teacher with an ancestor who fought under Chamberlain at Gettysburg, I almost feel compelled to toil in the former Confederacy a bit; maybe my New England prejudices are unfounded, maybe they're justified, but at least I could find out first hand, so I said yes. The curve ball is that the 27th is the island memorial service for Kirk, and perhaps the last chance I'll have to get there for a while.

May 15

UNLIKE THE TOWNHOUSE THE French government owns in Boston, the Korean consulate is on the third floor of an office building that spans the Mass. Turnpike in Newton. The website said a tourist visa can be issued the same day one applies for it, but the blazered bureaucrat behind the glass would not appear to have read her own web site. The fiftyish clerk with a Beatle haircut also seemed to have been weaned on a grapefruit.

"You want visa?" she spat. "Have funds?"

"Forty dollars, right?"

"Forty dollars. Fill out form. Pick up tomorrow." She foisted a sheet of information under the glass partition. Apparently eye contact is considered rude in Korean society. Never looking up, she went back to her paper shuffling with all the joy of a toll booth operator breaking a hundred Euro bill.

"Look," I began, "is there any way I can get it today? I'm a teacher and have to take time off to---"

"No help. Sick today. Tomorrow." I pitied the forms she was pounding with a rubber stamp.

A sobering wave washed over me as I considered what kind of bureaucracy I could look forward to until just before Labor Day in Korea. I fished out a debit card and slid it back under the glass.

"No card. Cash or bank check."

"No card?" No smile from me this time. "Are you *serious?* This is two thousa--"

"Cash or bank check. Visa after ten in morning."

In the kind of fleeting epiphany I can't recall having experienced earlier, I suddenly decided that sticking around for a visit to Virginia wasn't a bad idea, even if it meant passing on Nantucket and Kirk's service. My interaction with this charm school drop out at the consulate flipped a switch, quashing any excitement about meeting more such folks in a place where I'll need help with the language and...everything. But the calendar is unforgiving: it's late spring, Barclay hasn't suggested he's changed his mind about me staying on, no offer has come my way from a school I've applied to or interviewed at, and I'm running out of plank on the ship of Griswold. My position isn't posted on the school's website, probably because Barclay and whoever else knows of his capriciousness don't want to deal with questions a la *what's happening with Mr. Burnham?* They may be conducting a quiet search, letting a few firms know what they're looking for, and might post the position on the website after graduation. With nothing else definite, I jumped through the bureaucrat's hoops and picked up my tourist visa the next day. When I get there, I'll let Sonny figure out how I can stay on with just a tourist slip in my passport; if he wants me there, he can work it out.

Back on campus, I didn't feel the kind of elation one might when a visa for an intended destination is in hand. The second to last week of classes is a bit of a farce as kids are already checked-out mentally, and to be honest, I'm not all here either. Mother and a number of relatives will be at the house for the weekend of

Kirk's service, my current mental pastime being the task of figuring out how to beat traffic to the island a week from Friday.

May 18

BUILDING AND GROUNDS ARE starting to spruce up the campus for commencement. The dew on the freshly-mowed lawns gives some of the grounds a golf course look about them, and a few of the white clapboard buildings around the campus circle have been touched up with fresh paint. It being Saturday and sports having wound down except for a few teams in league playoffs, nothing stirs much before brunch, so I started out for the Dunkin' Donuts on foot when gradually I noted a persistent metallic ping popping through the morning calm. Given the day and hour, this demanded a look. At the cage in the gym, Remy was pitching overhand to his daughter Chrissie, an eighth-grader at the local middle school.

"C'mon. Open up the hips." Ping. "More." *Ping.* "That's it." *Ping.* "Better!" Chrissie is a fair haired version of her father; built for power and good at every sport she plays. Each swing mirrored the previous one - the follow through, the ponytail flip. A machine. *Ping. Ping.* She sent a rope into the screen right in front of me.

"Nice rip." I offered.

"Tis, inn't?" The proud father.

"I'm out Chrissie," Remy tipped an empty ball bucket. "We're good for t'day. Nice job, kitten."

"Not bad." I ducked into the mesh batting tunnel and helped him pick up the spent softballs. "She playing summer ball?"

"No - but you're looking at Chiswick's starting catcher next year."

"Chiswick? Chrissie?" This was out of nowhere. Chrissie has grown up at Griswold, has thirty or forty quasi-aunts and uncles, here. Half of them say at lunch how it'd be fun to actually have her in class someday.

"Heard right." Remy was dropping the yellow practice balls into the bucket with a bit of pluck, reveling in his news. "Coach from there saw her play against Newton last month. Two doubles and threw out four runners at second. We chatted after the game. I thought it was a lark, him talking her up, I mean he knew about me working here, but...long story short, when I mentioned that...her coming *here* wasn't definite, they came up with a nice package for her. Gonna do field hockey and b-ball too. Orientation is August 29th."

"Judas Priest. This is---"

"A pisser, yeah?" He smiled up from under his worn Middlebury cap. It was one of those grins people give when they know they're ahead of the game.

"Hmm..," I wondered, "wasn't her first choi---"

"Hell, her first choice changed weekly; she's a kid, right? But this was just too good to pass up. Nice financial aid package."

"S-s-s-o-o-o-o-o..." I waved towards the Admissions Building. "I gather the waiting list here never got too short either?" Remy was fit to be tied when she was put on the waiting list months ago.

"Hah!" He was now picking up balls and bouncing them off his biceps into the bucket. "Told 'em to pound sand. Said she wasn't interested in being here. Damn that felt great."

"Wow. But..." here I needed to be careful. Didn't want to reduce his daughter to a jock that her new school wanted just to beat Miss Porter's. "I didn't think Chiswick gave out ..."

"Aid for sports? Only for post – grads, right? Nice to think that, isn't it? I mean, truthfully, she's got great grades, and as a freshman, I think they're what got her in, but they know that from growing up here, she's no stranger to such a place, and she could probably start on some varsity teams next year. It's not a ride, I mean, we have to pay part of the tuition actually. It's not like a D-1 college, but just to have all she's got get recognized, especially after getting the finger from this place..." A very-satisfied grin was nearly reaching his ears. "I bet they kinda like the idea of a fac brat from here wanting to go there. If Chiswick sees what Chrissie has to offer and this place can't, hey - why be a fool and say 'no' then wait around here for another slap in the face next year?"

He turned away for a minute for a father-daughter conference, patted her on the head and waved her off. We lugged a few bats and helmets back to the cage, and all the way Remy was going on about how great the facilities and programs at Chiswick were, forgetting I've been there yearly for squash. When the gear was all stowed, he leaned back against the equipment room door and scanned the banners that ringed the old building, then pointed to the fading team photos on the wall to his right.

"See these guys? 1940 lacrosse...1941 squash...know where they are? Or were? Most of 'em, they did things that mattered. Not necessarily because they came here. But, the point is, this place once attracted kids whose families...had something, or could be something, and they entrusted their kids to us. Hell..." he wiped his brow with the front of his Patriots t-shirt, briefly revealing a spare tire courtesy of Bud Light. "That concourse overhead? Gift of the Dow family, the chemical ones." He eyed the walkway thirty feet overhead that ran the length of the building, allowing one to take in several basketball and volleyball games or squash matches with one comfortable, indoor stroll on the coldest of winter days. "Dows, Peter. *They* came here. Now what? "He offered his arms up from his sides in resignation. "She's going places. But not this place. She'd give more than she'd get out of it. And who'd she be lumped with? You should see some of the twits Admissions trotted through this year. Either post grads who should've gone into the service two years earlier – probably nineteen years old if a day - or some real gems. Some, admittedly, are great kids. Christ, who wants a school full of grade grubbing cheats, like that facebook geek? I'll take some of our kids over robo-kids any day. But it's the bottom third, these…" he turned his palms up and winced, searching for a word, "intellectual and moral waifs. Christ. What kind of kid plays a prank on a cabinet secretary who's visiting his old school? We got parents who call me asking for waivers so their kids can play a sport in spite of Ds in three classes, and whenever you point out the policy or suggest they get their kid to buckle down…Remember school, Peter? Y'show up, sit down, shut up, raise y'hand when y'know something. If y'don't know something, y'study, or ask for help…if you persist in carrying on with y'head up yer ass, eventually you got a D, or an F, and when y'got home, the folks were pissed that you were so stupid, or lazy, and…hell, reflecting poorly on them and blowing an education. Now, there's none of that. They need *trigger warnings* in case a sentence in a book is gonna give them PTSD. If a kid doesn't like to read, we get him an audiobook, rather than make him do something that thirty years ago, everybody could do by third grade. How's he ever gonna *learn* to read if we don't *make him*? If the kid wants to play with a ball or doodle in class, we let him, 'cuz he's got ADHD, but his mother says he doesn't like the side effects of his medication, so he doesn't take it. Instead, he asks to go to the bathroom twice every period and there's a big academic team meeting to explain how he shouldn't be expected to have his homework every day, because of his 'organizational skills' or 'executive functioning'." He made quotation marks with fingers from both hands, conveying bottomless contempt for the concepts.

"I may be a snob, but y'know what? When it comes to your own kid? It's okay to be one. So I gotta chance to get Chrissie to a place where kids are asked to own their learning, not make excuses for why they didn't do it. You should see their college list. And I'm not saying' she's headed to some ivy, but..," His hands descended to his hips, and he looked left and right, perhaps checking our privacy, and grimacing, as if wishing that his next words did not have to be spoken.

"Well..," I jumped in, "there's a right school for every kid. We're good for some kids."

"Oh, sure. God love 'em, and their over entitled parents with their hedge funds for what they provide, but I want...different for Chrissie. I'll nurse these kids through JV volleyball and intramural Ultimate Frisbee, but ain't my girl gonna be one 'o em.'

"Either of you seen Scott Paone?" Remy and I locked eyes as a familiar voice cut the silence in the wake of his rant. We tipped our heads skyward to see Liz Michaels on the Dow Concourse walkway, gazing down at us, yellow legal pad clutched to her blouse, her face betraying nothing.

"Not in here." I managed.

"How...long you been looking for him here?" Remy asked, hands on hips like a coach.

"A while," she pulled the pad away from her for a minute and appeared to read something on it. "A while, here, anyway..." and she turned on her flats, picking up a determined gait back towards the squash viewing gallery. However long she'd been within earshot, a feeling of dread washed over me. I was weighted with that awful feeling in my stomach that occurs upon realizing that some terrible toothpaste has been loosed and will never return to the tube, then realized that as it was Remy who'd actually been ranting about things, not me, I didn't need to sweat it…then recalling how, in my case, so what anyway? Shifting his jaw a bit, Remy gave a cat's-out-of-the-bag shrug.

"It's..," Remy nodded slowly, "a good thing I already signed my letter for next year."

May 22

"PETER! PETER! WAIT UP!" Kat was at a brisk gait as I was headed to lunch today, and nodded me to a veranda outside the dining hall before we went in.

"What's up?"

"Oh, you'll love this," she was actually giddy, and who the hell is giddy anymore? "Got my roster for Frosh English in the fall. Guess who's in it."

"Guess who's in your class? At Weld. You are joking."

"No, really Peter: guess."

"Kat..." I was tempted to let her know that as of now, I had no prospects for any class rosters of my own for next year, at least not in this hemisphere, but the urge passed.

"Fine," she sighed in resignation. "You're no fun. Chantal Matthews." Her words just hung there, and I drew a blank. "As in sister of Dickens."

"What? No way."

"Way."

"You're serious."

"Got it in an email last night." Chantal's older brother Dickens Matthews is third generation Griswold.

Three G! has been the cheer now and again when Dickens has made a stellar play on the court or athletic field. Three generations of an African-American family at a school is rare. Some bigger schools cast a wider net for kids of color before it was fashionable to do so, but St. Paul's didn't even know how to integrate itself in the 1950s, so started with a chaplain, Johnnie Walker, who obviously became 'Johnnie Walker Black' to all there. In a history of Choate written by an alum, the author lauds his school for having two blacks in the class of 1959. Griswold often seemed intent on swimming against the tide in terms of school trends, which explains why the yearbooks of the 1930s and 40s look like those of other schools thirty years later. To be sure, the Matthews' have done well; Grandpa became a federal judge and gave a memorable commencement address twenty years ago that is still talked of in alumni notes columns. Dickens' father went into medicine and married a record company exec. Natalie Cole, her pal from Northfield, sang at her wedding. Along with what The New Yorker once called the black aristocracy, the family summers on the Vineyard and has been good to Griswold's Annual Fund, supposedly carrying a scholarship student anonymously each year. With an older brother here even now, Griswold has been a home away from home for the family since the 1940s. So…Weld? I do envy David and Kat the resources the place offers them, but the Matthews brood has done well outside that gothic playground. This is like a Clinton voting Republican or Bill Buckley refusing to meet with the pope. Griswold, we have a problem.

"Holy..," I couldn't imagine how this would play in Admissions, "and you know this because…"

"Weld sent me rosters so I could welcome the incoming frosh with a message…and let them know I'd be following up with the summer reading titles. I remember she was here Parents' Weekend," Kat was nearly breathless. "I thought, yeah, she'll probably be in my class next year…here, I figured, right? I mean, this is like, a major defection, right?"

"Yeah," I agreed, "but, who knows? Maybe she didn't want to be in her brother's shadow here? I mean, there are kids in families who go to different schools. The younger Kennedys went to Milton after JFK went elsewhere, and ---"

"Yeah, yeah," she gave a weary nod, "but he's graduating – she'd be here alone. And we're a way more diverse school than the one I'm going to."

"You're right," I nodded. "Probably gonna be an interesting meeting in Admissions when this comes out.

"I know, right? They should sell tickets to it. Be a good fund raiser."

As we headed into the lunch, a grin crept across my face, and a small sense of schadenfreude made the wait in the food line quite bearable.

May 27

I GAVE MY SENIORS Friday off to edit their presentations for Monday – and because doing so allowed me to get a head start beating traffic to the Cape, or try to beat as much of it as one can on Memorial Day Weekend. Word of a second service for Kirk reached me weeks earlier, and no doubt there would be people here who hadn't made it to the March affair in Beverly Farms.

Mother had officially opened the house for summer, and was sorting old editions of The New Yorker on the coffee table, a glass-covered map of the island, and took a break to find me at the kitchen sink.

"You're not wearing that?" she glared at me hands on hips as I was trying to get a spot out of a seersucker blazer.

"Why not?"

"It's…a funeral."

"Actually it's a celebration of his life, Mother. He's been gone over four months, and I don't think it's a time to strike a maudlin tone."

"Still. Really, Peter. You can never go wrong in a blue blazer."

"You can if it's not here." Mother. Dear, sweet mother. Christmas 'thank you' notes by New Year's, no alcohol before five, sends two place settings as a wedding gift if she can't attend the ceremony. She raised her palms in surrender, dropped them in silent disgust and left.

Since before the United States was a nation, the First Congregational Church on Centre Street has been welcoming islanders to do what New Englanders loved to do long before political figures and TV figures talked about doing it: pray. If it weren't here, and Hollywood wanted to film a movie that included a New England church, they'd build this one. Under a white steeple visible for miles from the sea, weathered shingles and white clapboards combine to house rows of simple pews, each one with a latching gate to provide Puritan security from the dreaded center aisle. I was surprised that the service wasn't at St. Paul's on Fair Street, and as the stone of St. Paul's makes it cool indoors even in summer, a bit disappointed.

Cutting it close time-wise, I failed at finding a seat that would spare me the late afternoon sun through the windows, but could indeed tell Mother later that the garb of the day was something less solemn than what you'd see at a funeral in a Coppola movie. Here in late spring, the only people to be found wearing black might be handing you a wine list downtown. The day even prompted some male guests to forgo blazers and ties – so there, Mother. The service was almost like a retirement affair with more testimonials than laments. A few of Kirk's favorite hymns offered a nice touch, muttered out by bureaucrats, some state and national pols, a few media folks who summer here and beneficiaries of programs Kirk worked to make better. A sampling of each offered remembrances of his goodness and tireless commitment to leaving things better than he found them. His brother went last, sprinkling his thoughts with just the right amount of humor and quotes from Lincoln, Melville and Dave Barry. Younger than his brother and portly with thinning hair, he has that same winning smile and public speaking voice. His sailing motif tie bordered on goofy, which Mother will be sure to hear about. When he stepped down and returned to his pew, a hand reached out to offer a congratulatory pat on the shoulder. He turned and exchanged an unspoken nicety with the fellow behind him: Barclay Sears.

As the service concluded, and a reception at the Athenaeum downtown was mentioned, we filed out of the sanctuary, but a few of Kirk's former aides discretely handed small envelopes to certain guests now and again, and to my surprise, to me, whispering a plea that we please read it but refrain from discussing its contents with anyone. The logic of being targeted by this mysterious lottery eluded me until I read the note off to one side.

> *Dear Friend,*
>
> *You are invited to a small ceremony off Tom Nevers involving Kirk's expressed wishes. Please refrain from discussing this matter with anyone else, and if you can join us, proceed to Straight Wharf and board the Coast Guard cutter you will find there. Following a brief excursion there will be a reception at the family home to which the cutter will deliver you.*
>
> *Thank you for helping us to remember Kirk today and always.*
>
> *The Mayhew Family*

The essence of this interlude clearly involved some planning, and I was not about to miss the fruits of it. Stepping into the mid-afternoon sun, I saw Barclay at the end of the church walk. In an olive poplin suit, Griswold tie and already some summer color, he was a man in full. If, instead of an uneven brick sidewalk here, he had been standing in the middle of Paul Stuart or Barneys, people would be asking him where they sell cuff links. Spotting him before we locked eyes, I thought better of a conversation just then, so found my way back inside and ducked out through the kitchen.

To stroll down to Nantucket's docks in town on a May afternoon is to be flanked by a scene that reflects none of the ills of this world. The Land Rovers and Jeeps lumber over the uneven cobblestones on Main Street, well-scrubbed tourists in pinks and yellows walk without purpose up and down the sidewalks, shopping bags by their sides, heads turned towards the galleries and shop windows offering more of what they do not need. At the wharf, past the fishing charters and a few mega-yachts, was a sparkling white Coast Guard cutter with its unmistakable orange and narrower blue piping towards the bow. At the top of a metal gangplank, a young woman of some rank I couldn't begin to guess at nodded at the cards that we presented upon boarding. A few rows of folding chairs had been placed on deck facing the stern. As folks became knotted in small groups, it remained unclear to me how it was determined who was invited. A few I recognized as past or present government officials from D.C. and one or two others were local big wheels, or, more accurately, philanthropists who seem especially charitable at events at which there are cameras. The shiny faces, club ties and silk blouses all spoke in hushed tones while some older folks in pinstripes suggested more of a Washington connection. A lull in the chatter of one group afforded me a chance to step in, and the small talk that resumed explained how some came to be on this vessel, CG 257.

"Hell, I learned to sail with Kirk. Must be forty years ago. Once during race week…"

"I had an internship with him when he was at HUD. We went to see John Lewis, the civil rights guy once, and Kirk took my picture with him. It's on my wall in New York. Someone in my office asked me about it last week and said…"

The ship's gentle rolling with the tide was barely perceptible, and after half an hour, as if choreographed, all the heads turned towards the dock as Sally made her way up the gangplank. No big mourning sunglasses here; her head was high with a short bob cut, a single strand of pearls over a scooped neck powder blue dress with a Forget-Me-Not below her left shoulder. Her two sons and a daughter also sported the flower. The boys – ages 12 and 6 – were right out of Hickey Freeman and seemed pensive with their steps while the teenage daughter was on her mother's arm, a long, blond ponytail resting on the back of a sundress which was still tasteful enough for the occasion. Their purposeful gaits recalled the firefighters' families after 9/11. Apparently they'd made an appearance at the Athenaeum, but hadn't lingered. They gathered as a sort of phalanx by the cutter's stern, creating a photo op that nobody took advantage of. The slowly spinning radar overhead and some kayaks paddling off the bow made for some incongruity as we all looked on and then gathered in. Dinghies and larger boats bobbed in the inner harbor and the distant blast of a horn announced a ferry passing Brant Point.

"Thank you all for being here," Sally's voice honestly seemed to silence the seagulls and all the other sound clutter at once. "And of course, thank you to Captain Morris and your crew for making this remembrance of Kirk possible in a way that would please him." There was a clear lilt to her voice, suggesting a vulnerability. Her tone was softer than a school principal's, but she knew what needed to be said. "All of you here touched Kirk's life, or, I think, he touched yours." A few nods and 'here, here's' were offered. "I like to think that…actually I know that he improved many lives, and many of them were here, on his beloved Nantucket. Because of this…because of him…" she stopped short, and raised a clenched fist before a tightened jaw, willing herself to not give way. The daughter reached behind to stroke her back. Her shoulders fell and rose with a deep breath, and she found the strength she needed. "We'd like to help Kirk be where he was always happiest. We will motor out to the south shore, where we – Tad, Stuart, Sandy and I – will board Kirk's boat, which, under sail, will take us to just off Tom Nevers, where his ashes will become part of a place he always cherished." She let it all soak in, and took another deep breath. "In spite of Kirk's leaving us in winter, this sendoff is still…" she closed her eyes for a second, and with a polite curtness, waved off another patting from Sandy. "Still tender…for us. So thank you for helping us with it." She looked up and nodded to someone, and a few seconds later, under our feet, the cutter's engines rumbled to life. Heads turned in all directions as various hands started casting us off, and without so much as a jostle, we were edging, then gliding through the inner harbor. Behind us in tow was Kirk's boat, a considerable single-mast craft that was still modest by summer island standards.

"What does…" a pudgy, sunburned, 60-something fellow pointed to the vessel at the end of the tow line off the stern, "did, he have there?"

"That," someone perhaps ten years younger in a Marine Corps tie stepped in, "is a Westsail 32' – 36' with the bowsprit. Can run a main, a stay sail, a genie and a spinnaker." He looked around in a don't-you-know way, "but, 'course, not the genie and the spinnaker at the same time."

" 'Course," I offered, as if it didn't need to be said. We locked eyes a moment, then he turned back to the subject in tow fifty yards behind us. "Sleeps five, got a galley with a gas stove, and can take most things the North Atlantic can throw at it…unless you're truly stupid out there." He went on about how he and Kirk sailed it to Bermuda, at times 'in shit that would swamp New Orleans again.' "Last sailed with him out of Casco Bay. He wanted to see some gold star father on Peaks Island. Moored right off his beach. And we swam in. No…no…Cushing Island.

346

Always mix them up." The pudgy fellow could not escape the retired marine's gravitational pull, but off to the side a bit, I managed to step away without much notice.

The towline stretched to below the bowsprit, the oblong extension off the bow with a railing, from which to raise the genie up the forestay. From the cabin roof rose the mast, off of which the boom came, resting in a crutch over the cockpit at the stern. The decks were empty, and the image of this unmanned craft behind us gave it the distinct air of a ghost ship. Someone else had the same thought, and perhaps as a diversion from the task at hand, talk in a nearby cluster turned that way.

"Wasn't there a ship one time..." an internesque brunette in a navy shirtdress was squinting to recall some fact for a pair of blazered jocks not long out of school. "They found it, but, like, nobody was on it..."

"When?" Jock #1.

"Recently?" Jock #2

"No, like a hundred years ago. Maybe more."

"Yeaaah," Jock #2 scratched his chin.

"Celestial...something. And they never found----."

"The *Mary Celeste*," came gruffly from a nearby lifeline rail. A diminutive octogenarian with a snow-white handlebar mustache and madras blazer regarded us. "Name was the *Mary Celeste*." The younger ones shuffled his way, asking whether he was a history teacher. He closed his eyes and shook his head slowly, affecting a hint that he was only mildly annoyed at the suggestion. Apparently he was a retired judge who had sworn Kirk into some office at one point. Folks on the arriving ferry waved as we rounded Brant Point. Some sea lions lounging on the jetties off of Coatue couldn't be bothered to notice us going by. As if an invisible fog, a surreal quality touched everything about the moment; a flawless late spring afternoon on which the sky came down to meet the sea. We shuffled about, some looking like clichés on the deck of a United States Coast Guard Cutter for the final disposition of the ashes of a Cabinet Secretary who died because I invited him to my school.

A hale fellow with CEO hair who looked like he'd rowed in his school's varsity eight in during The New Frontier struck up a conversation, and worked in how, out of gratitude, he'd established a scholarship in Kirk's name at his college, which was the reason he was there. I offered the Cliff Notes version of my path there, still feeling a bit odd about having made the short list for the cutter.

"Ha." He nodded. "Gotta know Sally." He shifted his jaw, hinting at a story. "Sally has a keen sense of what's right. Never forgets a deed. It's like Acheson and Truman." He was correct, albeit presumptuous, that I knew who he was talking about. "Acheson was from a very different piece of cloth than his boss. Acheson with his detachable collars, pedigree and go-to-hell-if-you-didn't-go-to-Groton manner, and Truman, a failed haberdasher who didn't go to college. The senator from Prendergast. But when Acheson's kid was in the hospital while he was abroad, Truman visited her every day. Acheson never forgot it. If I know that story, you can bet Sally does, so you're visiting the hospital while Kirk was…lingering, especially being from Griswold, when you'd maybe want to crawl under a rock, that counts with her…"

Rounding Smith's Point, the North Atlantic spread out before us off starboard, and Madaket appeared off to port, with waves bigger than Surfside and sunsets at 9:30 in July. The engines downshifted as we came upon Cisco. To starboard, the sea stretched out to meet the failing afternoon in a mix of blues and yellows. Heads turned to the Westsail off our stern as three coast guardsmen appeared on her deck. Clearly they'd been waiting for this moment, and they set about clipping a spinnaker to the forestay and undoing the lazy jacks on the mainsail. No more than twelve feet at its widest point, the craft fell and rose gently in our wake, the nodding bowsprit suggesting impatience at being towed.

"Almost like a horse being led, isn't, it?" Sally spoke over my right shoulder. I turned, and in spite of the sun to our stern, she gazed at the bustle on deck behind us without squinting. "Kirk had the motor removed. Said it was a sailboat, and sailboats don't have a choke." There was ambivalence in her face – dignified melancholy. Her chin lifted a bit, as if doing so conferred more respect for the work at hand. "I'm so glad you could be here Peter. Kirk was a big believer in symmetry, and you being from his school, and with him...us...in the hospital...he'd like that." She now faced me, with a genuine smile, which may have been simply a kind of *enchante* for political wives.

"Wouldn't miss it," a hand on her shoulder didn't seem out of order, "for anything."

"Well..," she put two forefingers to her lips as if they would help her frame a thought. "perhaps it will have a cathartic effect...for all of us. Sure hope so. The Coast Guard has just been super. I can't tell you how...princes. Every one."

On the Westsail, one fellow was pulling on a halyard while another was uncleating two lines from both sides of the bowsprit.

"They'll get it close to the right spot, close as they can...and..," she thinned her lips the way people do when words don't come easily, "...we'll take it from there."

"Looks...like something he'd like." This new terrain left me less than eloquent. It was as if comets from different constellations of life – childhood summers, teaching, death – were all circling, rendering me pretty inarticulate. "Even Mother Nature cooperated."

"He went so 'green' towards, the end, she damn well better!" she forced a laugh.

"Really, Mrs. Mayhew, it's so---"

"Sally. One more 'Mrs. Mayhew' and I'll have our crew *keel* haul you." Her self-mocking schoolmarm tone forced a smile from me.

"Sorry. Sally. It's...grand of you." *Grand* of you. Christ, was I channeling Louis Auchincloss? She still made me nervous. "Most of these folks, they really knew Kirk. More than---"

"Peter, I'm sure you know this." This is in fact a rather disingenuous albeit very gracious preface. Whenever someone says, 'I'm sure you know this,' what they mean is, 'It seems that you *don't* know this, so allow me to explain.' It is a way of instructing an interlocutor in the politest of ways, a tack that is no doubt innate to her by now. "It is the things you do in life that are not asked of you that matter. I know that you were at Kirk's room at times that I wasn't. You went to see him, and never told anyone. You did something that mattered without looking for... anything. I know too that with all the press camped out at the school, a school Kirk loved, this must not be forgotten. For you to---"

Just then the voices off the stern became louder. Some short-long-short whistles sliced through the breezes and the engines gurgled into silence as a uniformed guardsman made his way to the cutter's transom at the stern. Sally waved the three children over and patted my shoulder as they arrived and took off *en famile* to meet the officer by the port side of the stern. We slowed in the water.

Squinting out at the horizon I actually had time to think about Sally's words, and then about everything I experienced in the academic year that was about to end. The whole Faisal affair, helping Aaron settle in, herding kids out of a collapsed hockey rink, inviting Kirk...for all the angst and misery the last nine months had ginned up, I wondered if it would all somehow be strangely useful to me. This came to mind as we were tossed gently on the swells beneath the cutter. I'd experienced the largesse of a generous parent from Korea and have even had a job offered to me, albeit twelve time zones away. My email inbox was a desert of hope this spring, but for all I knew, Dave Meeks was currently cloistered in an office in southern Connecticut making sure that no classes exceeded a certain number of students, and I was on a Coast Guard cutting cruiser in the North Atlantic.

On the bowsprit, a crewman was still working some clips on the forestay, something I usually do while on a mooring, but these folks were well-oiled machines who rescue fools from capsized day sailors in the middle of nor'easters. Trying what he was doing while sailing alone on my family's Rhodes 19' would be akin to taking a sunfish to the Flemish Cap in September. To the Coast Guard, however, this was like chewing gum. The Mayhews were nowhere to be seen until a motorboat scurried away from our port side and towards the sailboat in tow, which was now as idle as it could be under the circumstances. The guardsman manning the outboard on the launch slid it up alongside the Westsail, and over the side came some rubber fenders and an aluminum ladder, allowing the family to board. They shook hands with the crew on deck, and turned their attention to the bow. We were all headed downwind, so it took no time for the spinnaker to explode in our direction, prompting gasps and oooos!! from our deck. The huge red triangle bloomed towards us off the bow, like an inflated wad of bubble gum obscuring the person chewing it. Under its own power, the Westsail moved with a smoother poise than had I been handling it, but then the reason seemed clear: the guardsmen were at the wheel and manning the main sail so as to afford as tranquil a tack possible. We slowed again, the towline slacked a bit more and was then unclipped from the bowsprit. The family sat on the cabin's roof, seemingly sharing tales and jokes, brushing their blond manes out of their eyes. Even at this hour, the beach at Surfside was pretty full, and some in the water were still flirting with the incoming breakers. Farther to the east, the crowd on the sand thinned, and off to port, Tom Nevers appeared, a near-deserted beach with mere ripples lapping it.

The name "Tom Nevers" is said to hail from the name of a Native American figure in the area several centuries earlier whose name was Anglicized, perhaps more accurately bastardized, and whose legacy seems a bit vague except maybe to his descendants or their cousins, who might be counting the daily take from Foxwoods these days. For years, this area of the island was a bit of a well-kept secret, other areas being more coveted by those who have felt the need to bring a little bit of Greenwich with them here.

As we headed east, people on the beach became scarcer, and a bluff rose from the high tide mark. The day was failing now, promising the kind of sunset that real estate brokers pushing property in Madaket rave about. Here our engines were cut, and the Westsail came up on our starboard side. Checking the wind's direction, the crew dropped the spinnaker and brought it about so that it was straight into the wind, 'in irons' it's called, such that it lolled to a nodding idle. The family gathered close as if warming hands over a fire, then separated and made their way to the stern. It is impossible to know what was said, but clearly some words were spoken, and then, slightly out of time, which made it more sincere, mugs of a sort were raised and ashes were shaken into the wind and seas. Kisses were blown, and some audible sniffles broke the silence on the cutter, but no one spoke until the engines started up a moment later.

Either by family or government design, things proceeded like clockwork. The launch motored back alongside the Westsail, and once the family climbed down into it, it roared towards the shore with the American flag rippling on its stern. Extending from above the high tide mark and a hundred feet onto the water was a portable dock where the family was let off. In time the launch shuttled us all from the cutter to the same spot, and we trudged up to the bluff and into the Mayhew backyard.

I was one of the last off of CG 257, so by the time I landed and hiked up to a lawn that greens keepers at Augusta would envy, well-scrubbed guests were already sipping away in subdued cheer. Cocktails, Ray Bans, impeccable and effortless summer garb were the norm, and an upbeat tone in the chatter seemed to border on distasteful. It gave the moment a surreal feeling, as if I was walking into a Vanity Fair spread. They were the faces and lines of people to whom life has been good, whether it be via bloodline, investment choices or Botox. A few were familiar from the Sunday talk shows, others from the Times "On the Town" pages or the witness list of the Astor trial. It floored me that I was still here, secretly with my nose pressed against the glass, but by virtue of my presence, somehow inside it.

Barclay was there, and spotted me as a tray of refreshments arrived. I recalled Bags' tack at such times – helping himself to two glasses, 'in case you get stuck in a conversation not to your liking and want an exit: just raise the second glass and mention that you have to get it to someone.' I grabbed two goblets.

"S'pose I shouldn't be surprised to see you here, Peter." Barclay managed a shoulder pat.

"Likewise." Feeling off the clock and just off the cutter, words failed me. If I'm honestly supposed to vacate my flat in another month, I owed him nothing. But he actually went somewhere I hadn't expected.

"So," he dropped his head a bit, "any plans for next year?"

"Yes, actually." I refused to look at him.

"Oh..," he looked up with a hint of surprise, "that's good for you. What will you be...doing?"

"Teaching."

"And where will you be doing that?

"Actually, I think I'll leave it at that." I was happy to look him in the eye now.

"Peter," he slouched so as to suggest it pained him to explain something, "understand. I don't wish you ill in your...professional pursuits. It was just pretty clear from your email that you...didn't have much respect for administrators."

"No, no, no," I held up a not-quite finger without spilling a drop. "I had some issues with some stuff that went on last fall: my apartment getting shaved, Scott questioning my teaching...It just seemed that things were being decided, not discussed; no communication, or if there was some, just dictates. I've got a friend who's now an administrator at Weld, and I can't see him just cutting rooms out of someone's apartment like how my place got---"

"Weld?" Instantly Barclay went white. It was as if I suggested that in addition to his car being repossessed, his PSA test came back and the count was off the charts. "Weld?" He looked away and swallowed some merlot. "What about Weld?"

"Well, I just...knowing someone there, I'd be surprised if he dealt with Kat the way I was handled in the fall." Then I cracked the door a bit. "Obviously she's not the only person who thinks it's a good place to be next year."

He considered me for a minute, then checked the tips of his black loafers, and scanned the lawn in search of someone with a tray of glasses.

"Think I see an alum Peter." He gave me the six-shooter gesture with his wine glass hand. "Can we continue this in a bit?"

I nodded and he was gone.

As the shadows on the lawn lengthened, the mood lightened even more, and by six PM, there was little evidence of our maudlin task of an hour ago. I mentioned being over on Monomoy in one conversation and a gaggle of twenty-something girls offered me a ride there when it came time to leave. Apparently there was a party on a road there they didn't know and none of them had charged their phones, so with no GPS, I would be useful. I wasn't sure whether I should take them seriously. A generation earlier, they'd have been debutantes, but now, just a group of field hockey teammates with really good skin and closets full of J. Crew. I found Sally and said my piece. She offered something profound about a door closing and a window opening, and how meeting me had been a window. Nowhere near as practiced as she at partings, I managed a hug and lauded her dignity. I mentioned sailing sometime, but really just for something to say. This is a woman who knows her forks.

The post-modern debs signaled that they were leaving, and wondered if I indeed knew the island.

"Do you really know where Cathcart Road is?" one of them flipped her hair and squinted into the sun while asking.

"Sure, it's---"

"You do? Get *out!* Really?" It was as if she'd been told I had free samples from the Cisco Brewery with me.

"If you help us get there, we'll get you in," another offered.

I began to accompany four visions in sundresses on the crushed shell walk towards a Jeep. DNA, field hockey and SPF 10 can combine for good results.

"Peter! Peter!" Barclay was striding up from the lower lawn as if he were climbing the steps of the Lincoln Memorial and taking two stairs at a time. Seconds from a clean getaway.

"Who's that?" one of my companions asked.

"He's...my boss. Head of School."

"Glad I caught up with you." He slowed and eyed my situation. "Can I...we, finish our chat?"

"Actually, I'm off t---"

"I'd consider it a real favor." He then looked down for a second, and made a decision. "and I'd...be happy to write you a strong letter for...your use after Griswold." He turned to the girls and their thinly veiled impatience. "Would you mind terribly if I borrowed Peter for a bit?" This is what one asks of a person who does not know the inquirer well enough to object. By co-opting a third party into the request, the subject, in this case me, becomes a minority opposition. Owing to the impeccable graciousness of the inquiry, it becomes a fait accompli.

"So Peter: is this Carthcart Road, like, hard to find?" one of the girls asked. "We were sort of hoping..."

"Go right at the rotary," I used my hands to help with directions, "Monomoy Road, then right on Boston Road, and that becomes Brewster...and eventually Cathcart. It's not hard really."

"Hmmmm," one of them was writing this in ink on her forearm. "Ok-a-a-a-y-y-y. If you can make it, it's...oh, don't worry, you'll see the cars...and there's a tent."

"Ciao for now!" Another one affected a regal wave. They piled into the Jeep and were off.

Barclay and I strolled along the undefined roadside, crunching shells underfoot. He slowed to a contemplative gait, hands in pockets and head down, affecting the mode of a burdened executive trying to decide what to do about those missiles in Cuba.

Just them a Saab slowed up and came along side, and a tennis-worn matron lowered her passenger window for a final word with Barclay. I couldn't hear their conversation, but this hiccup afforded a moment to assess things. The Saab pulled away, and he flipped the switch, from glad hander to interviewer, turning back to me.

"So," he looked down the road, not at me as he spoke, "you know...someone else at Weld? Small world, right?"

"Yes, I was there a few weeks ago. That professional conference for history teachers."

He gave an ambivalent murmur, nothing more.

"That shrimp cocktail didn't quite hit the spot." He rubbed his stomach.

"No?" I tried to appear fascinated with some crushed shells underfoot just then, "You could probably head back for more..." I really didn't feel beholden to niceties with him. He seemed to let my suggestion pass, and wondered whether a dinner would loosen me up. He mentioned a few restaurants he'd heard good things about, and we turned to walk back to the thinning line of cars, finding a Ford Explorer he'd either rented or borrowed for the day.

We headed back towards town and he negotiated the roads smoothly while continuing to press his curiosity. I steered things back to people at the reception – an alum fresh out of Trinity angling for a squash coaching job, wondering how the Mayhew kids would fare after today. As we came to the rotary, I was curious as to which turnoff he'd take. The Sea Grille and 21 Federal would require reservations at this hour. I wasn't about to try to wedge us into the yacht club on mother's membership. For all I know, I couldn't anyway.

The rotary at the dinner hour has people in cars looking, not looking, negotiating the circle on bicycles and dashing to make a dinner table or a ferry, mindful that as one reaches town, everything grinds to a snail's pace. On one corner of the traffic circle is "The Roundabout," a good place to grab a sandwich when heading to the beach. For years I never knew what it was called until I backed into a delivery truck in the parking lot with the family car.

"Here we are." Barclay swung into the same lot that witnessed my fender bender a decade earlier.

"You...are joking, right?" I offered in a deadpan voice. "Burgers? Those girls mentioned a party..."

His few seconds of bafflement turned to a look of being wounded.

"What can I say? I didn't call ahead. Can you imagine the wait in town for a table?" In trying to demonstrate some familiarity with the island, he mentioned a restaurant that closed years ago.

"Barclay, I'm happy to chat, but I blew off an invitation to---"

"Yes you did. And don't think I'm not grateful. But are you really above eating with your boss? You've had quite a day Peter: Coast Guard cruise, lawn party..."

We eyed each other over the car's between-the-seats cupholders, and it occurred to me that there was perhaps some merit in not fussing over this point. He wanted something from me, and it was the dinner hour.

We sat at a table out front below a raised deck and ordered drinks.

"So: are you headed to Weld Peter?" he held an unblinking gaze.

"Well, Kat's there, and...I guess someone else too," I didn't mention Chantal Matthews by name, wanting the news of her going there instead of Griswold to reach him later in the summer, after it's too late to reach out to the family. "Nice place."

He sat up and appeared to take in a deep breath, as if expecting a punch. Just then a bee bothered my vision, and as I waved it away, he pursed his lips and gave forth.

"Life, Peter," he sat up even straighter and started peeling apart his napkin. "It doesn't come with operating instructions. There's no master plan that...everyone follows. I had an uncle who---" His Aaron Copland ring tone stopped him, and a slow motion blink betrayed that at that very moment, with every fiber in him, he loathed his cell phone. Checking the screen, he winced.

"Sorry – have to."

I was enjoying knowledge of Kat and a Matthews child migrating elsewhere as he put the phone to his ear, and it was then that the light came on for me and the jumbled letters fell into place. Barclay was convinced that the unnamed defector to Weld to which I was referring was not the sister of a current student, but could only be his wife, Claire, and he sensed that news of her being there would ripple through the world of New England schools, and no doubt result in some conversations at Griswold. *What the hell is our headmaster's wife doing at another school a hundred miles away?* He had no idea about Dickens' sister headed there, but was now on tenterhooks in his confusion. I couldn't have cared less about where his wife is or isn't, but such a spouse is always the *de facto* hostess of the school, for Senior Teas after Chapel, Trustee Weekends and the like. If he was worried about me spraying her move all around school, well, more of that. Questions would be asked, and while it might come out eventually, he may have thought I had an axe to grind and would really push the story out on social media, verbally, anyway I could. In theory, he was correct, assuming I had the time to do so between hail Mary job applications. He was imagining that the matter at hand was far more personal than an admissions' loss; his wife had abandoned him and taken up residence in the gothic cloisters of The Weld School.

"Lemme call y'back," he sputtered, and pocketed his phone. "Peter," he swung around to face me, "I'd really appreciate it if..," he wanted to get this just right, "if you're headed to Weld, or you are in touch with people there, that you not jump to conclusions about anything that...that maybe you don't fully understand. I'd be grateful." He affected the look of someone owed a favor.

He slumped a bit, and shifted his jaw, mulling over whether his words would work on me.

"Grateful. Hmmm…" I sat back, and noticed the stubborn spot on my blazer's sleeve, a spot I got from coffee while waiting for my Korean visa. The distastefulness of that whole episode now colored my excitement about going there at all. "How's the search for my replacement coming"?" I asked.

He winced a bit, like his bluff in a card game had been called. "Frankly, we're behind with it. It's been such a spring: the whole Faisal business. That was pretty time-consuming."

We sat in silence for a minute, eyeing our none-too-exciting-but-island-priced beers. Then he looked up.

"I may have been too impulsive last fall, about that email and all," he nodded in admission. "it seemed…quite an affront, if you will. But I can see how you..," then he sat up straighter and steeled himself. "if you're not on hundred percent committed to somewhere else for the fall, and…all things Weld can be wiped from the table, I'd prefer it if you remain at Griswold. Heading the History Department." He let it sink in, and then had to inquire. "Are you committed? Elsewhere?"

I savored the pause briefly, but wanted to be done with this. "I don't have to be…I could, make my apologies elsewhere."

Slowly, a cautious smile grew on his face, and he extended a hand over the table.

Over $11 burgers our conversation of the year that was winding down was almost as if nothing had transpired back in October; if not warm, at least cordial. I wondered where he was staying on island, but figuring it was on the school's dime and thus probably at a ridiculously pricey place, I didn't want to know. We parted and I walked up Monomoy Road to the house, forgetting about the party on Cathcart until after I'd picked at a lobster that my cousin couldn't finish. I caught a mid-Sunday ferry back to Hyannis as school loomed Monday. Just as Baptists don't acknowledge each other in the liquor store, private schools don't recognize Memorial Day.

Back at school Sunday night, I emailed Sonny Kim, letting him know that the summer alone would be the extent of my stay in Korea, adding that my school had not found a replacement for me – true - and that I couldn't leave them in such a state. On Monday, he wrote me back, disappointed, but still happy that I would at least be there this summer. The mood in classes that day was light yet the lessons seemed productive, and I felt a buoyancy as each class filed into my room.

June 3

FOR A COMMENCEMENT SPEAKER, THE school found a CNN correspondent from the class of '95 who only two or three of the older teachers could remember, suggesting she'd exceeded expectations of her former mentors. She was funnier than some, less original than others, and made an impassioned plea for us to educate ourselves about the ugly prevalence of human trafficking, coloring her point with anecdotes which, judging from facial reactions, a few grandparents had not bargained for when they sat down.

For student speakers, the salutatorian chastised her classmates for, "throwing away dining hall food and half eaten pizzas and taking twenty-minute hot showers while one fifth of the world's children are hungry and have no access to clean water daily," suggesting that the solutions to such problems are, "not in the words of the Thoreaus, Hawthornes and Fitzgeralds we were forced to read," while here; where they could be found was never actually explained. Next, the valedictory address was what you'd expect from a humorless, two-year senior heading off to bury herself in Womens' Studies at Oberlin. Hopefully, these two graduates can team up someday and ameliorate all this misery, obviously beginning by purging us of good dining and white males.

Dirty Little Secret: teachers do not get sentimental bidding absolutely every graduate *adieu* in commencement receiving lines. *Nice job. Glad you liked my class. Good luck.* Since it's often ninety degrees in the shade at commencement, getting out of the gown which affords all the comfort of a Hefty bag is all most folks want to do. After a few days of school awards, book prizes, yearbook signings and verbal wisdom which at times rivals fortune cookies, it is hard to get choked up over any pretense of a last parting, especially since social media makes the concept of truly parting a thing of the past. Thirty years ago when graduates wondered about ever seeing each other again, it was perhaps a valid question. Plaques on campus noting graduates who never came back for reunions owing to the Vietnam and Korean Wars and both global conflicts remind one of the true meaning of finality. Last year a day after commencement, two lads produced a 'best and worst' list review of commencement week from poolside in White Plains and posted it on YouTube. So much for missing you forever.

EPILOGUE

SEPTEMBER

ANEW SCHOOL YEAR means going from zero to fifty in a few days, so two weeks have passed without me jotting any of it down.

Claire Sears is on campus, but is said to be a 'consultant' to a school consortium in Connecticut, duties which she'll perform by commuting there when it is warranted. We've exchanged some nods at school since her return, and the odd glance of hers lingers just a few seconds longer than used to be the case. I sense she is wondering what I know, what I think, and wondering whether I recall all that was said courtesy of some Manhattans in Connecticut last May. I should probably consider these matters myself in the event that she ever asks.

Kat is loving Weld. "You won't believe what they have here: sabbaticals!" I could hear her OMG tone even in the email. Dorm duty sounds less of a chore there, and for her, the farther from MIT the better.

Schy is Schy, and will be twenty years from now. I can take him in small doses, and he may well say the same of me.

Remy had the varsities back early for two-a-day practices before school started and has fall sports off and running. It's hard to tell if the slightly perceptible spring in his step is due to the arrival of some genuine hulks for the football team, two Kenyan girls who are running cross country or that his daughter is said to be loving her new school where she is a field hockey co-captain. He's taken to wearing a Chiswick sweatshirt every other day or so. It will be fun to see whether or how Scott Paone, to whom the AD reports, addresses this. For a new teacher to wear a shirt of an alma mater is one thing; for the Athletic Director to be sporting, ne' living in, another school's jersey, and then perhaps be responding to queries as to why by mentioning that his daughter goes there is another matter. He could easily refer all follow up questions to the Admissions Office, who for all intents and purposes brought the whole business about with its foolish decision to offer a space to a student other than Chrissie. *Caveat emptor.*

Liz Michaels is gone from North Farmhouse, but with a new title and different digs. As Director of Special Projects, her office is now a glorified walk–in closet in Development, right next to the recycling room and about as far from Barclay's office as can be. Never underestimate a school's willingness to create a new administrative position at the drop of a hat. The Great Dane was lured out of retirement somehow and these changes will no doubt be rationalized in the first Head's Letter of the term. For all I know, the reasoning may in fact be chock full of rational logic.

Will Blumberg is said to be at some therapeutic school in upstate New York, that helps emotional amoebas reach their full potential. No formal charges were pressed, but he is banned from the Griswold campus for life.

For his part, Barclay has been cloistered in his office these first few days of the year, oblivious to the contents of the syllabi we've handed out, perhaps fine-tuning the details of Mr. Aboody's largesse. We nod at each other while engrossed in conversations neither of us can pull away from at the time. The sources of most angst among teachers is not the youth in our care nor issues surrounding textbooks, but the capricious tinkerings of administrators, who have abandoned teaching for the banal world of mission statements and scheduling. When I applied to grad school to become a teacher, I noted in my essay that I would rather spend the day sorting through ideas with forty 15 year-olds than haggling over administrative matters with fifteen 40 year-olds. I still believe firmly in the soundness of my preference.

With the advent of a new year, there are always those tiresome reminders of years past. In the copying room yesterday, Schy was wrestling with the toner drum of one of the older machines, trying to emerge from the struggle with a minimum of black soot on his white Golden Fleece polo. Colorful language from behind the machine suggested that the battle was not going his way. He segued into a rant directed at nobody in particular about how where he'd taught at over the summer, the copiers were all state of the art and how each classroom building had a Keurig machine. At a table in the corner, Wil O'Leary, the environmental conscience of Griswold, was whiting out an error on some copies rather than commit another ream of pulp to its death.

"No. We don't have that here, and no, we also don't have that, either" he muttered, never looking up, but with more conviction than was his custom, "but take a breath; you could do worse." For all his gray-pony tailed, conspiracy theory-loving, organic lunacy, O'Leary had a point. Whether it was lost on Schy, I don't know, but as it did last year with often-disagreeable Allison Manville, Father's favorite adage of even a stopped clock being right twice a day came to mind.

Stepping out into the late summer day, I took in the trees across the green: huge Weeping Willows were gently bothered by the September breeze. They rose to shade a dorm built when Woodrow Wilson was president. It all looked just as it had a year ago, and probably twenty years before that.

Around the corner, with an armful of old books came Bags. His corduroy blazer is perhaps older than I am, but the hint of a spring in his step of late suggests a newness about him, or perhaps it had just been a good week. He nodded and imitated the tipping of a cap to me.

"Donations for the library?" I eyed the bundle under his arms.

"Hell no!" He held up a cautionary finger. "First editions. Six. Five of them in great condition. Money well spent." When he showed me the titles, from what I know about such rare finds and those ads in the *Sunday Times Book Review*, it was clear that he'd possibly forked over the equivalent of a day student's tuition at Griswold for some old reading. Then he looked out to where I had been gazing a moment earlier. In pairs and a few groups of threes, the boys' and girls' cross-country teams were now skirting the far edge of the green. Some of the younger ones leapt up in attempts to grab some of the lower hanging willows. After they passed, a new faculty wife I have yet to meet emerged from the dorm behind the trees with a baby stroller and a Golden Retriever, and headed in the other direction. World without end.

"Congratulations," I patted the books, "Chapeau!" I knew he'd like that, but it begged the question, so I asked. "So, why then, if I may, if you can do that," I pointed to the five-figure pulp under his arm and turned up a palm in puzzlement, "why stay here and do this?"

His gaze remained unbroken. Slowly, a thin-lipped grin spread to the corners of his mouth. His chest heaved a bit, and he let out a big sigh.

"Keep a secret?"

I affected crossing my heart and leaned in. He turned to my ear, and spoke in more than a whisper.

"It beats work."

Of all his musings, to be sure, this is one with which I couldn't agree more.

Acknowledgments

BETWEEN SOME POINT IN the sixth grade when the notion of going to boarding school was floated and earlier this year when some meticulous editors scrutinized the manuscript, a cavalcade of selfless and wonderful people collectively made this work possible. Sally Cook, Mary Sharry and Maggie VanHaften were beyond generous with their input, proofreading and kindness. Doug Cook is the reason these words are actually on a page – his wisdom, expertise and time not only brought this book to fruition but also spared my neighbors streams of profanity had I tried to negotiate the path to publishing alone.

Arthur and Miriam Bernau put Northfield Mount Hermon School in Massachusetts on the family radar and more than anyone there, Charlie and Pat Tranfield and their family helped to make it a special experience; I doubt I would be a teacher today were it not for that place and people like them. Phyllis and Bill Macomber, my aunt and uncle, created a home on Nantucket where much of this was written, and from which Wendy McCrae mailed a manuscript to the mainland after I forgot it at the house more than once. My parents Edna and Richard Allen were always there with support and a compass to make the way easier and clear. Richard and Page Allen patiently abided my making editing changes amidst at least one Sunday brunch. "Uncle Lew" is the daysailer I'm on when the weather is too fine to stay inside and write – he has taught me a great deal, but is also a reason why this work was not completed sooner.

Finally, Holly my wife did her share of squinting as she typed away at some longhand passages, and has certainly put up with much more, making me very grateful and quite lucky indeed. In one way or another, the tale between these covers is the fruit of the blessings I have named here, and many more.

About the Author

DAVID STORY ALLEN GRADUATED from and has served as a department chair, dorm parent and coach at a number of the actual boarding schools which appear in this work. He has taught in Japan and South Korea, and holds degrees from Syracuse, the University of New Hampshire and Harvard. He teaches and sails in Michigan at Interlochen Arts Academy.

Off Tom Nevers

ARLY INTO THE ACADEMIC year at a boarding school outside of Boston, Department Chair Peter Burnham makes a simple misstep on-line that looks to render him jobless and homeless. Amidst differing teaching priorities and perpetual discipline issues, an alum working at the White House returns to campus with unexpected consequences and a terrorist threat involving an international student emerges. Issues of race and class simmer, and some actual and venerable independent schools appear here. As a vacuous future looms, these matters follow Peter to the family place on Nantucket and come to a head Memorial Day weekend.

Made in the USA
Las Vegas, NV
05 January 2022